WARRICK

Also by Marilyn Harris

Marilyn Harris

WARRICK

DOUBLEDAY & COMPANY, INC.
GARDEN CITY, NEW YORK
1985

LIBRARY OF CONGRESS CATALOGING IN PUBLICATION DATA

Harris, Marilyn.
Warrick.
I. Title.
PS3558.A648W3   1985   813'.54
ISBN 0-385-18815-3
Library of Congress Card Number 82-46012

FOR J.P.H.

"There are two types of oilmen, the infill driller weighted toward low-risk drilling in a proven field, and the elephant hunter, oriented to the search for large new discovery fields and willing to gamble all to find them."

—*Oil & Gas Journal*
July 1980

WARRICK

Prologue

(The following is an excerpt from the journal of Reverend Frederick Faxon on the Run of Oklahoma, April 1889, courtesy of the Gilden Historical Archives, Gilden, Oklahoma.)

"We was unique, don't you see, in that there was no aristocracy here, no old families with old names and older money and tradition and morality and philosophy, the sort of historical backbone that gives to a land, for better or worse, its identity and character.

"Here, you see, the land was virgin and we lined up on a cool, cloudy April day and ran for the land and whoever got there first and could stake out a hundred and sixty-five acres for himself and could defend it, then it was his, God willing, and he was the aristocracy.

"This awful randomness sometimes produced overrighteous and limited men who believed unduly in Fate and the stars and guns and all those illusions that have nothing to do with a man's true destiny.

"Oh, there was significant exceptions—elephant hunters we called 'em, Tyburn Warrick for one—who snuck in before midnight —illegal—with about fifty hired guns—also illegal—and by nightfall had staked out one hundred thousand of the richest acres God ever created on the face of His earth.

"If that same beneficent God was to grant me two wishes I'd wish first for the cleansing of vengeful jealousy from every man's heart and, second, to be granted the privilege of walking this earth again about a hundred years from now to see how that son-of-a-bitch Warrick's descendants are faring . . ."

11

Tulsa

MERETH REPLACED the phone receiver as though fearful of hurting it. Despite the broken connection, she still could hear Massie's voice trying to hold back her grief.

"He's not dead yet, but as good as . . . Stroke . . ."

From the opposite side of the bed came Hal's sleepy, ever-perceptive question, "Who died?"

"My grandfather had a stroke. Not dead yet. I have to go home."

"I understand."

Though his words were simple, she heard the shock and knew he understood all the ramifications. When she'd left Warrick six years ago on her twentieth birthday she'd told Hal with cold conviction that she would never, under any circumstances, return.

But there was no permanent escape from the past. One left nothing behind, but simply took it along in the form of heavy luggage. It probably was an unrecognized law of nature that we should always be drawn back inevitably to the place where we have suffered most.

"May I drive you?"

She looked up and tried to focus on his offer. Less than twenty minutes ago they had been making love, sleepy, predawn sex, good sex. Now one short phone call from Warrick and this man with whom she had shared a comfortable relationship for the past two years seemed literally to be fading before her.

"No," she replied. "I'll take my car. I don't know how long I'll be. Will you call the school for me?"

He nodded. "Done. What should I tell them?"

What to tell them? What to tell the headmistress of Oakhurst, that archaic and prestigious prep school on the outskirts of Tulsa which deluded itself into thinking it was preparing the daughters of the oil rich for life in the real world?

"Tell them . . ." But the thought faltered. She found herself staring across the bed at Hal, who returned her gaze with the circumflex eyebrows of the first person to arrive on the scene of a fatal accident.

"Is . . . he really dying?" he asked, well acquainted with Ty Warrick's theatrics.

"Massie said so."

"Then the newspapers will know by noon, and I won't have to tell the school anything. They can read it for themselves."

Of course. Why hadn't she thought of that? Again she took a good look at the man opposite her. What a comfortable relationship. No harmful passion, just compatibility and convenience.

"Who'll take your classes?"

"Dr. Fiske can cover for me."

"Shall I call him?"

"Please."

The quick exchange died for no reason other than their respective diversions, Mereth out of bed at last, forgoing the luxury of a shower, buttoning the beige slacks and pulling the sweater down over her waist.

Back to Warrick. It wasn't possible.

Hal stirred into action and drew on his bathrobe. "Look, why don't you let me come with you?"

"No," she said, though she did accept the offer of his open arms and enjoyed his embrace.

"It'll be a mess, won't it?" he asked softly, his voice tinged with redeeming humor.

"A mess."

"Everyone will come streaming back."

"Of course. There's a pie to divide."

Hal laughed. "One hell of a pie! A billion dollars plus . . ."

She heard the numbers, the rumored worth of Ty Warrick's wealth. She'd grown up hearing various figures, most exaggerated. They held no meaning for her.

"Will you be all right?"

"I don't know," she said. "I have to go," she added and drew free of his arms, her mind already running ahead to Warrick.

No time to think. Hurriedly she slipped on her shoes, grabbed her purse and stood at the door. Hal had yet to move from where they'd last embraced. She smiled at him and found it interesting how large a place a man could make in the human heart, without the name of love.

"I'll call you." His amused smile suggested that he knew he had just flunked a very important test.

"Yes, please," she agreed and threw him a kiss, then took the steps running.

Outside she found a dazzling early April morning, the well-kept grounds of Berkeley Place sparkling with the perfection of an Oklahoma spring.

As she unlocked the driver's side of her old Mercedes, she waved again and then headed the car toward the gate.

Home. Warrick. Was he dying? The world would have to be informed.

"Morning, Miss Warrick. You're up and about early . . ."

She nodded at the garrulous old security guard and angled into the slow-moving lane of early morning traffic heading into I-44 and the turnpike.

Home. Warrick. It was the old ranch house she had to avoid.

For the first time she felt dread. Despite the rapid flow of traffic on both sides, her foot faltered on the accelerator. Horns went off all around. She returned to this world long enough to dodge her way into the middle lane and there maintained a sensible 40 mph while, for the first time, she confronted all aspects of Massie's early morning phone call.

Tyburn Warrick dying?

"Is my mother and father dead, Grandpa?"

"Yes, Mereth."

"I love you so much, Grandpa. Will you die?"

"Never, Mereth, I promise. Never—"

Mereth clung to the steering wheel and felt a dangerous loss of control, felt furious with obscene grief. The bright morning through which she was moving became shrouded in shadow, as though the sun had flickered. A dark journey—or was it a purposeful flight? Pain. Pay the price. And loss. Keep them in check. The moment demanded cunning mental manipulation.

Massie said stroke. Not dead yet.

Mereth wasn't surprised. She could have predicted that. At seventy-six Ty Warrick would die like a Roman, superbly, without fear, without reluctance but without haste, as if starting off on an unexpected journey.

And, of course, everyone would come streaming back. Her two older brothers: Josh from Hollywood, his free spirit and sexual "life-style" intact and flourishing at thirty-eight; Brit from London, carrying all the guilt for the entire world and finding his only comfort in Socialist doctrine. How he resented the Warrick wealth and world into which he had been born!

A large Coca-Cola truck passed her by, and she felt the displacement of air and tightened her grip on the wheel and debated whether or not to stop for coffee. There was a Dunkin' Donuts up ahead, the last place before the turnpike. No, she didn't want to stop now. Maybe later.

"Can you come right away, Mereth, help me track down the others?"

"I'm on my way, Massie."

Suddenly she accelerated, pulled out and around the Coca-Cola truck, moved all the way over to the fast lane, her mind racing ahead. The turnpike for thirty-three miles, off at the Gilden exit, twelve miles to the north gate of Warrick, then about twenty minutes on the blacktop before she could even spot the red-tiled roof of the house.

House? Not a house. Mausoleum. Museum. Massive. Gray stone. Italianate. Immense.

Not dead yet.

Tyburn Warrick, Jr., the richest independent oilman in the Southwest.

For several moments her eyes glazed dangerously on the highspeed traffic around her.

16

WARRICK

"You see, Mereth, this guy named Bissell was the one who first asked if petroleum could be used for lamp fuel in the place of the standard whale oil. 1850, it was." ·

"Watch it, bitch! You're going to . . ."

The belligerent male voice faded along with the RV that sped past her, veering dangerously to accommodate her daydream.

She straightened up and vowed to be more vigilant and saw in the distance the toll plaza which led to the turnpike. Peace there. And monotony. At least one head-on crash every week. Thirty-three miles of monotonous peace in which to remember—everything.

In defense of the awesome threat, she turned on the radio, Kenny Rogers crooning in stereo about when to deal them and when to walk away.

She slowed for the toll booth. Heavy traffic for seven-fifteen. Inching forward, she saw nine cars ahead of her, all four lanes filled. To her right was a large Malone Chili truck belching black smoke. Unfortunately it was keeping pace with her.

Not dead yet. The three simple words made an unexpected assault on her consciousness. Dead? Not possible. Not the intractable, rocklike countenance of Tyburn Warrick.

Poor Massie. That repressed storm of grief that Mereth had heard in her voice this morning would have to break soon. Massie couldn't live with it. She'd try, but she would have to get rid of it.

"Ride?"

The sudden intrusion of a male voice, combined with a face peering in at her through the closed window, startled her. She drew reflexively back.

"I'm sorry," he called, his voice raised to penetrate the window. "Didn't mean to scare you. I'm hitching. You need company . . ."

Where had he come from? She saw specifics for the first time: a full head of dark though somewhat sun-bleached hair, dark beard, tanned features, incongruous blue eyes. Late twenties, early thirties. Not a bad face. She wished she could say the same for the rest of him. His clothes were filthy, a nondescript plaid shirt with two

17

buttons missing, dirt-stiffened, well-worn blue jeans and the inevitable backpack.

Throughout this brief inspection he stood still, displaying a degree of patience as though he knew he were undergoing inspection.

"Do I pass muster? You need company."

That was the second time he'd said that. Not a question, more a statement of fact, as though he knew the nature of her journey.

"N . . . no," she stammered, and heard an angry car horn behind her and realized she was holding up the line. "I'm not going far," she called out, still through the closed window, and stepped on the accelerator and saw him move back to the concrete island, to solicit someone else.

Yet what was he to do? Hitchhiking was not permitted on the turnpike. They had to catch a ride here or run the risk of paying a stiff fine. Josh had gotten caught several times hitching back from poker games in Tulsa, once when he had thrown in his car as part of the stakes and lost. The next day the newspapers had had a field day, and her grandfather had dealt out harsh punishment.

The memory did damage, and she idled the car and closed her eyes as she tried to deal with the new wave of emotion.

If her parents had lived, would it have been any different? Probably not. Events in her life had always had a touch of the inexorable.

Only four cars ahead now. There was the hitchhiker again, walking back down the concrete island. Apparently he'd struck out with all the cars behind her.

Tall, lean, strangely anonymous. Not a cowboy, though the "costume" was right. It was just that, a costume, not showing wear in the right places for a cowboy.

An oil-field roughneck? There were always plenty of those streaming into the state.

Certainly not an Eastern preppie on his classic rites-of-initiation journey. Too old for one thing. There was something about him that—

Suddenly, to her embarrassment, he sat on a concrete ledge, punched his backpack down between his legs and returned her stare with a deliberation which suggested that he'd known all along she'd been staring at him.

She continued to inch the car forward, averting her eyes, studying with undue concentration the Malone Chili truck. Peterbilt, or so it said on the tire flaps.

When she looked back at the man, he still was staring. As she eased past, heading toward the disembodied outstretched arm coming from the toll booth, she saw him deliver for her benefit a starched salute.

She smiled in spite of herself and secretly wished him well and briefly fantasized what it would be like to travel with him, perhaps all the way to California.

"Thank you." She smiled up at the humorless attendant and took the ticket. She placed it on the dash, shifted gears and felt the car move forward as though glad the idling period was over.

"See if you can't come back from town, Mereth, just once without getting a speeding ticket. I'm supporting the goddamned police department."

"Yes, Ty."

The Malone Chili truck sped past her, still issuing black diesel smoke.

She clung loosely to the wheel and helped the car find a good safe speed between fifty-five and sixty. Cars passed her continuously. Let them get the tickets. She really was in absolutely no hurry.

Thirty-three miles to the Gilden exit.

Not dead yet.

In the distance there were velvet foothills, red clay formations in the shapes of dinosaurs and lizards, grazing grass like breaking waves. She suffered a sense of speed, of gigantic transition, a sense of descent without having the least notion of what she was doing. She was on an impossible journey, entering forbidden territory. Stay away from the Ranch House.

"Ty, the branch broke. I fell. My arm hurts. Make it stop hurting."

"It's broken, Mereth, baby. Hold on. I'm going to take you to Doc

Buckner. Hold on, my little girl. We'll make that arm as good as new. Oh, my sweet Mereth. Don't hurt, my love—"

Suddenly and without warning there were tears, an unspeakable weight of grief descending upon her, causing her to pull over onto the shoulder, where she turned off the ignition, set the brake and clung to the steering wheel and pushed her forehead against it.

———

Chris knew who she was and thus had the advantage.

He hadn't recognized her at first. But on his return trip down the concrete island of the toll plaza, he'd recognized the Warrick self-possession, the resolute manner, an almost carelessly serene expression on her face.

What he didn't know and therefore wasn't prepared for was how beautiful she'd become. The last time he'd seen her—about ten years ago—she'd been a scant fifteen, still shedding baby fat, with a child's face, vacuous and unused, a slightly pampered and poutish angle to her features.

No more. The petulant, unused child was no place to be found in the intense blue level eyes that had stared back at him through the closed car window. The simply cut blond hair had not framed her face so much as it had pressed softly against it, and the features had been those of pure enchantment, graceful, flawless, light, though once or twice he'd seen the eyes just barely concealing something frightened.

Long after the Mercedes had pulled away from the plaza, Chris continued to stare into the distance, hands lightly shoved into his pockets, thinking what a difference the years had made.

Beautiful beyond description, beyond question, but it was that something else he was interested in, that expression of bewilderment and apprehension, like the look of an intelligent pet when it has done wrong.

Suddenly he had a feeling of despondency at his own isolation, his alienation from that Warrick world and the Warrick "advantage." He'd grown up bearing witness to it, first in Josh, then in Brit. Somehow he had hoped that Mereth would be denied it.

He looked over his shoulder for the blue Warrick pickup that was supposed to have come for him. It would have been fun to ride in with the enemy, with Mereth. But he'd known she wouldn't give him a ride. The Warrick kids gave nothing away. No matter. Emanuel would send someone. At Deeter's request. And as for Chris's alienation from the Warrick world, it wouldn't persist much longer. Old Ty couldn't go on forever. The first signs of faltering had already begun, and Chris was fully prepared to step in and claim what was rightfully his, what had belonged to his father before him and his father before him, an ancient act of thievery at last set right.

His eyes blurred on the distant and fast-moving traffic. Mereth Warrick had long since disappeared, but he continued to see her. A mystery there. Why was she going home? Deeter had told him that she had left suddenly, under mysterious circumstances, about six years ago and had never returned. Something had happened between the two of them, according to Deeter, who claimed further that Ty had never discussed it, became mad as hell, in fact, when anyone brought up the subject of Mereth.

The smartest of the lot, Mereth Warrick, or at least that's what everyone said, from the kitchen staff to Deeter himself to Red Pierson. The one to watch.

The one to defeat.

Chris abandoned the empty horizon and made his way back to the concrete shelf where he'd left his backpack. Where in the hell was the pickup, anyone who could get him to Warrick as fast as possible. The battle lines were already being drawn, and there was no doubt in Chris's mind it would be full-scale war before they were finished. And the only hope in the events of the morning, as far as he could see, were the small white hands that had gripped the steering wheel with such force that he'd noticed distended blue veins, a tension suggesting tremendous effort, as though the steering wheel was a lifeline and she had to exert maximum effort just to maintain her grip.

A comforting weakness, for no man would be a match for her beauty, for that built-in, blood-deep Warrick self-possession, for the intelligence visible in cobalt blue eyes, for the signs of willfulness and control.

But it was what existed beyond the control that interested Chris, and while he had no clear-cut idea, he intended to find out, to play with her for as long as he could, learn all about her, without letting her know anything of him, keeping her at a perpetual disadvantage. What had happened to cause her to grip the wheel in that fearful manner?

He had to know all this and more if he stood a chance. And he fully intended to defeat her and anyone else who stood in his way.

Curious, but the resolve evoked a strange peace in him. A discordant horn sounded at the end of the toll plaza. He looked up and saw a familiar blue Warrick pickup, the wide grin of one of the Mexican workers, leaning out of the window, waving.

"Señor Chris? You come?"

Chris waved back, grabbed his pack, slung it over his left shoulder and started off at a trot. He felt new excitement as though something momentous was about to happen, something of extraordinary importance. He was prepared to be patient and wait.

He'd already waited almost a hundred years . . .

Warrick

IN AN ATTEMPT to fight off what was taking place in the master bedroom across the hall, Jo Massie stood on the balcony in the early morning April light and fed on the beauty of the vast formal gardens and waterfalls which stretched out in dazzling symmetry before her, culminating in the reflecting pond which, come summer, would be filled with pink water lilies. There at the bottom of the garden the dazzling white gazebo with intricate Victorian ginger-bread stood like white lace against the pale green backdrop of hundreds of morning-still willows. Beyond the trees, she saw the top of the marble-domed family mausoleum.

Except for the mausoleum the sight pleased her enormously, as it had the first time she had seen it exactly thirty years ago. Then the Warrick gardens had been the brainchild and artistry of "Mrs. Ty," Tyburn's wife, who had died quickly, decently, eleven years before, of a heart attack. Since then this singularly beautiful world had belonged to Jo Massie.

Massie had hired the small army of gardeners and landscape art-ists, scheduled the seasonal plantings—now daffodils and tulips and lilacs and jonquils and hyacinths, next azaleas—so that always there would be color interspersed with evergreens and the white falling waters, which commenced from the marble fountains directly be-neath her and cascaded the length of the gardens, culminating in the reflecting pond.

"We really should open the gardens to the public, Ty. It's wrong to keep this to ourselves. Let young women have their weddings here."

"Over my dead body."

She turned as she heard a noise. The heavy oak doors leading to the master bedroom blurred, and she felt that Ty would walk out, rubbing his chin.

"Get me someone to knock off these whiskers."

She'd "knocked off" his whiskers for the last ten years, a loving chore that Mrs. Warrick had refused to perform.

Keep your mind on the beginning, not the end. Dr. Buckner's with him. He'll be all right.

She folded her arms against the chill and walked back to the edge of the balcony. Her life here, had it been miracle or illusion? If he died—

Then the moment and the question sped past. The wind played in the tulips, and the light of morning shone and faded. The vision was gone. Down below she saw three of the Mexican gardeners

23

working a large bed of jonquils. A few flowers had already shown yellow trumpets.

Abruptly she again turned her back on the gardens and confronted the closed doors across the corridor, across the oriental runner, across the entire expanse of her life.

How outraged Ty had been that morning thirty years ago at the Tulsa airport.

"What in the hell is this? A nigger? A black woman? What do you mean you're Jo Massie?"

"I am, sir."

"Bullshit!"

"You've seen my credentials, Mr. Warrick. B.A. and M.A. in business and accounting from Harvard. My father is professor of economics at Harvard. My mother sings with the Metropolitan Opera. I'm a certified public accountant and I can do the job you've hired me to do."

"I didn't hire no . . ."

"You hired me!"

Then she remembered, for she would never forget, what he said next.

"You're one of them coffee-colored niggers, aren't you? Which of your folks was white?"

She'd vowed before the plane had landed not to feel anything.

"My mother," she'd responded.

That had passed, along with everything else. Ty Warrick had fired her on the spot and walked away about twenty feet when he had succumbed to some perverse instinct, some stray sense of humor, and he had turned back and waved her forward in her prim little navy blue suit with white collar, had placed her in the front seat of his black Rolls next to his black driver and had said not a word directly to her for the next year.

Thirty years ago.

The master bedroom doors opened. She stepped forward and tried to read old Doc Buckner's expressionless face.

"He's sleeping," came the first blessed words, and Massie suf-

24

fered a small collapse. She felt an arm go around her shoulders and was amazed that Dr. Buckner could move so fast.

"Come on, Massie, let's have us some breakfast."

"You must tell . . ."

"I'll tell you everything, but I need coffee and so do you. Still got that little Mexican cook in this goddamned museum?"

Rough talk. That's what Ty demanded of all those closest to him. He distrusted proper grammar, distrusted a diphthong that hadn't been flattened, distrusted a sentence of more than twelve words that didn't include at least one "shit" or "goddamn."

"Come on." She smiled wearily and took Buckner's arm—partly a gesture of affection, partly for support—and led him down the broad second-floor corridor past a small gallery, part of Mrs. Warrick's art collection: two Turners, three Picassos, one Matisse. They had been hung on the second floor because there was no room for them in the large gallery downstairs.

"How is he?"

"Coffee first. And some eggs, over very easy, and cinnamon toast, that would be nice."

She nodded, despite her impatience.

"And no goddamn hot sauce, you hear?" Dr. Buckner scolded, drawing away from her as though to put distance between them.

She nodded again and walked slowly ahead by herself now and caught an unexpected glimpse of the future without Ty's protection. Despite everything, despite the years she'd spent at Warrick, despite the love, despite her own financial independence and growing worth, despite all this, to many of Ty's best friends she was and she would always be the Negro girl who had arrived under false pretenses thirty years ago and "caught old Ty at a weak moment." For many years she had feared that she had conquered Tyburn Warrick's affections out of spite and for revenge against such attitudes.

"This way, Dr. Buckner," she said with new formality, her thoughts doing damage to her already shaken emotions.

Halfway down the broad staircase, Dr. Buckner caught up with her.

"Look, I'm sorry, Massie, you hear?" he said gruffly. "You just stop right where you are. Right there." He stabbed comically at the step on which she stood. "I'll tell you what I know, which ain't much, 'cause it's never much with a stroke. Not without a scan, and I couldn't move him in to St. Mark's if I'd wanted to because the old bastard probably would rise up out of that big bed and get a stranglehold on me and not let go."

"How ill is he, Dr. Buckner?" she asked.

"That's what I'm trying to say, Massie. He's had a stroke. His left side seems . . . unresponsive. I can't assess the brain damage until I move him into the hospital, and I'm not sure I should move him."

The doctor was right. Ty would never agree. Before that happened he'd have the hospital moved out to Warrick. Massie took several steps backward until she felt the security of the carved oak banister behind her and leaned against it.

"Do you think . . . ?"

"I'm not thinking much of anything at this point," the old man broke in and proceeded down the stairs, rubbing the back of his neck. "I have a course of action, though. I want me some breakfast right now. Then I'll get on the phone and first I'll find the best R.N. in the area. She'll need security clearance. Can you get it?"

"Of course."

"Then she and me will watch the old bastard carefully for about twenty-four hours, see what he's up to, see if he can tell us his name, rank and serial number, and then we'll proceed from there."

As a medical prognosis it left a lot to be desired.

"Shouldn't you . . . ?"

"You want to call in someone else?"

The rapid-fire challenge was delivered angrily from the bottom of the steps, where he stood squinting up at her as though she were an inferior object on which he'd spent enough time.

"I've . . . called Mereth."

"Good. You should call the rest of them as well. If you know

26

where they are. Never could figure out why in the name of Hades Warrick kids couldn't stay at home. It hurt old Ty, I can tell you that."

Massie looked away. She didn't have many ready answers this morning, but she had an answer to that one. If anyone had the stomach to hear it.

"Come along, Dr. Buckner. I'll have your breakfast served in the terrace room. You always enjoy looking out over the gardens."

Without another word she led the way across the marble vestibule into the wood-paneled library. Beyond the library was the corridor which gave access to the rooms on the first-floor west wing. Among them at the far end was the terrace room—Ty's favorite, thus hers—a pleasant white and green room with a south wall of glass, giving a breathtaking view of the gardens.

Generally she and Ty had breakfast there. "Shouldn't I go back upstairs and be with him? I hate to . . ."

"He's sleeping, Massie, like a baby. I want him to keep on doing that for as long as he can."

For a moment they stood in open confrontation as though staking out their respective claims to Tyburn Warrick. Massie faltered first. Sweet God, had the battles already started?

Hurry, Mereth!

She turned away and closed her eyes and walked with a knowledgeable blindness to the intercom on the far wall. Even with her eyes closed she found the button and pressed and heard a young voice on the other end.

"Ramona, please," Massie said softly.

There was a pause, then she heard the good, firm voice of Ramona Evans, Ty's "plain" cook for the last fifteen years. A Mexican-American—more American than Mexican—Ramona had grown up on a southwestern Texas farm and was a master at the art of country-Mexican cooking that Ty preferred.

"Breakfast for Dr. Buckner please, Ramona," Massie said, keeping her voice low. "Eggs over easy and cinnamon toast. Be sure and check the book," she added, the "book" being a ledger with the dietary preferences and needs and habits of about twenty of Ty's oldest cronies. The "Warrick Posse," they were called in the kitchen.

"Sure," came the voice on the other end. "How is . . . ?"

"Sleeping. That's all I know."

There was another pause as though Ramona had detected the tension in Massie's voice.

"And what about you?"

"Just coffee."

"The boys delivered me some nice early melons this morning. I'll send one up, just in case you find an appetite."

Massie rested her head briefly on the wall near the intercom, fortified by a friendly voice. Ramona's "boys" would be the retail produce dealers from Tulsa, all of whom saved the best for Warrick, knowing they'd be paid a good price and a bonus as well.

"Thank you, Ramona. We'll be in the terrace room."

As she turned she was surprised to see Dr. Buckner sitting sprawled, legs akimbo, in one of the leather chairs beneath Mrs. Warrick's collection of original English cartoons from nineteenth-century *Punch*. As long as he was relaxed, Massie had another important question.

"Dr. Buckner, what is the difference between 'not yet dead' and 'still alive'?"

The confusion on his face had nothing to do with hearing. "I don't . . ."

"When you first arrived this morning after you had initially examined him, you told me he was not yet dead, implying that . . ."

"Implying the hell nothing!" the old man snorted and pushed laboriously up out of his chair. "What was I supposed to say?" He turned on her defensively. "For that matter, there are a few questions I'd like to fire at you, Missy."

Missy! Where had that come from?

"Ask anything you like, Dr. Buckner."

"All right." He assumed a lawyer's stance in front of the dead fireplace. "When and where did you first find him ill?"

"He awakened me about three this morning and asked if I could get him something for a headache."

"You mean he came to your room?"

She looked up, debating. It was such an old battle and she was so weary of it. "We share the same bed, Dr. Buckner. I'm sorry. I thought you knew."

His eyes leveled beneath bushy white eyebrows. The silence was going on too long. She'd better end it.

"So I fetched him two aspirins and a glass of water. He seemed to want to talk."

"About what?"

The irrelevant question surprised her. "Dallas," she said at last. "Yes, Dallas. He wanted to make a trip to Dallas."

Dr. Buckner reached in his upper vest pocket and withdrew a well-gnawed pipe. He made no attempt to light it but seemed content to clamp it between his teeth.

"Was he making sense?"

"Of course."

"Nothing slurred about his speech? No hazy memory?"

"No. Not that I . . ."

"Then what?"

She shrugged. "He went back to sleep. At least he seemed to be breathing easily. But when I checked on him later and . . ." She broke off, unable for the moment to continue.

". . . the side of his face was covered with blood. Nosebleed." She sat weakly on the arm of the sofa and wondered how long it would take to rid her memory of that image.

"Did he say anything?"

She shook her head.

"Was he conscious?"

"I don't think so. At least, he never opened his eyes."

For several moments the library, the house and even the world beyond seemed to echo with a resounding silence.

"Tyburn Warrick, if you ever lay a hand on me again, I'll . . ."

"Oh, come on now, Massie. You'll what? You aren't big enough to swat a healthy flea."

Sweet God, the oceanic years between that first physical contact and the passion they had come to enjoy! Ty made love like he made his deals, like he made money: with aggressive and confident authority. He had the imagination and vision of a dreamer, the mind and education of a scientist, the daring of a born gambler.

Over? It couldn't be.

Fear moved in and produced tears which she wiped away. Dr. Buckner tried to help and offered crude comfort.

"Come on, Massie. Everybody has to die of something sometime."

It seemed the most patently insensitive statement she'd ever heard anyone make. Coming from a doctor, it approached the insane and unforgivable. She needed to change the subject as well as the scenery.

"Come along, Doctor. I'm sure Ramona has coffee waiting for us now."

When she led the way into the terrace room a few minutes later, she saw Elaine, one of the local women from Gilden whom Ty had come to trust. Now her plain, good face was moist, her eyes red from crying.

"Good morning, Elaine," Massie said quietly and received only a brief nod from the woman, who moved about the circular glass garden table, smoothing a white linen cloth into place, then setting a dazzling bouquet of red carnations—Ty's favorites—fresh from the greenhouse in the center. That was followed by service for two and at last the silver coffeepot, a thin vapor of steam escaping its spout. At one place Elaine arranged a silver-domed platter—and at the other, a cantaloupe with fluted edge and a small scoop of lemon sherbet in the hollow.

"Breakfast," Elaine sniffed and pushed the tea cart toward the serving pantry and quickly closed the door behind her.

"You're joining me, aren't you?" Dr. Buckner asked gruffly. "I hate to eat alone."

But at that moment Massie was beyond response, for she had looked up to see the moss green velvet recliner chair which was positioned directly in front of the glass wall, Ty's chair, where he had sat only the night before, his empty scotch glass still on the table, his wadded handkerchief beside it—he'd been fighting a cold —the cushions indented by the weight of his body, a stack of *Oil & Gas Journals* on the floor beside his chair.

"God, I'm tired, Massie."

"You need a rest."

"From what? This is heaven! Look out there. Since when does a man need a goddamned rest from heaven?"

Massie pointed blindly toward the phone table by the pantry door. "Please call the nurse as soon as you can. I'll be in the gardens."

She drew open the glass door and stepped onto the flagstone porch and saw stretching out before her the stone path that led down to the reflecting pond.

"What do you call the yellow trumpets, Massie?"

"Jonquils, Ty."

"They're nice."

Dear God. It had not been her intention to fall in love with the man. She'd simply wanted to travel, to see the West, to see how she reacted to other minds, other points of view, philosophies other than those of the liberal academic communities of Boston and Cambridge in which she'd grown up. The salary had been good, the surroundings exotic: Indians, oil and Oklahoma.

"I'll take the job for a year, Father. That's all."

"Do be careful, Jo. There are men out there who, believe it or not, wear bedsheets."

The jonquil beds to her left blurred into a field of solid yellow, the tulip beds on her right a field of red.

What *was* the difference between "not yet dead" and "still alive"?

Oh, Mereth, hurry! For once I need you.

She increased her step on the downward path, trying to keep her heels out of the cracks, trying to deal with the illusion of escape, knowing better than anyone that hers was and always would be the flight of the alone to the alone.

───────────

When given a choice, Dr. Horace Buckner always chose the wide open, safe sea of impersonality. Such emptiness served a doctor well. Humanity was never victorious. Oh, we thought it was. That was our favorite delusion. But in the end, neither life nor death was known for the quality of mercy.

So, proud of his emotional distance, he peppered his eggs and watched the black woman making her way down the garden walk and felt the same surprising objection he'd first felt when old Ty had introduced her to him thirty years ago.

It wasn't that he was bigoted. He wasn't. He really wasn't. He'd swear to God he wasn't. It was just that—

The pepper shaker came to an abrupt halt in midair while Dr. Buckner fastened his gaze on the retreating and very attractive backside of Jo Massie. Still a damned good body for a middle-aged female, the firm rounded buttocks causing small ripples on the green silk. Ty dressed her like a queen, fancy fag designer clothes from Neiman's in Dallas.

Strange, he'd forgotten how tall she was, slender, her hair done up straight and silky about her face, not kinky like most of them. Well, after all her ma was white.

They'd come once several years ago, Jo Massie's ma and pa, after Mereth had moved out lock, stock and barrel without a word to Ty. Massie's dad was dignified, uppity, black as the ace of spades with white kinky hair. Professor emeritus in economics at Harvard. Obviously brains was color-blind. And her ma, a pretty woman, white as driven snow, who'd spent three days at Warrick looking nothing but uncomfortable.

Dr. Buckner shook his head and put down the pepper shaker and lifted his fork and ate nonstop for several minutes, enjoying Ramona's country cooking. God, but he was hungry! He'd been up since

4 A.M., since Massie's first phone call and the hectic trip to the airport and Warrick's private plane which had brought him out in less than fifteen minutes. Ty's friends in Tulsa called it the stock-market flight. "You're up; then you're down."

Speaking of Ty's friends, how many should he call and what in the hell should he tell them?

The sobering question caused the first interruption in the steady movement of his fork. Hell, Ty had had a serious cerebral accident, he was certain of that. He needed a specialist. Buckner glanced at the phone and thought of the smart-ass Dr. Siad, the hotshot neurologist from India via Johns Hopkins.

Then call him! Let the foreign hotshot take a look at old Ty. Let the treatment be on his head.

Decision made, the fork resumed its steady movement. Of course, if Ty up and died on them the shit would literally hit the fan. All three Warrick kids—a worthless bunch, if he'd ever seen one—insisting on the division of Ty's estate. About a billion at last reckoning. Some reckoning.

Buckner looked up in search of the black woman as though feeling a need to keep her in his sight. Of course *she* needn't worry. She was one rich bitch in her own right, so reliable rumor had it, a happy combination of her own business skills and old Ty's boundless generosity, giving her a little one-eighth override here, a little three-sixteenth there, a sliver of each new and rich oil pie.

Harry Beekman at the bank had once told Buckner—in strictest confidence—that Jo Massie had one of the goddamnedest portfolios he'd ever seen.

Harry Beekman. He should be called. No, not just yet.

As Buckner sopped up the excess butter with the last of his toast, his thoughts turned back to the Warrick grandkids. Truly a useless bunch, and he'd delivered every one of them up there in that big bed where Ty would be doing his dying. Only one of them could sit a horse and that was Mereth, the girl who was the spitting image of her grandmother, Mary Beth.

For the first time the steady motion of his jaws ceased and he

33

gazed at the egg-smeared platter, seeing not the remains of his breakfast but seeing Mary Beth Lacey Warrick, the most beautiful woman he'd ever laid eyes on.

Out of Kansas City she'd come, her father a banker looking for a good investment in cattle and finding himself in the early twenties on the Warrick ranch trying to wheel and deal with young Tyburn Warrick, Jr., already the master wheeler-dealer of them all, who in all respects was a mirror image reflection of Tyburn Warrick, Sr., the gentleman thief who had stolen these one hundred thousand acres.

Buckner chuckled at the nostalgic scene he'd re-created in the remains of eggs and toast. As the truth had come out later, Banker Lacey from K.C. in fact had wheeled and dealed Ty, Jr., out of fifteen hundred of his best white-faced cattle, the young Warrick apparently not hearing one word of the hard bargain, concentrating as he was on the vision sitting high atop that two-wheeled gig, that Mary Beth.

Ty later confessed to Buckner that he had to keep listening to Banker Lacey because he couldn't move away from the side of that gig on account he had a hard-on the size of a drilling pipe.

One year later Mary Beth Lacey became Mrs. Tyburn Warrick, Jr., and when she'd expressed dislike of the old rundown ranch house that Ty was living in, he gave her a blank check and her choice of sites, ranging over these one hundred thousand acres, and for the next fifteen years Mary Beth had amused herself with the creation of Warrick, this great gray mausoleum fashioned after an Italian villa she'd admired outside of Rome. And every week crates filled with paintings and Italian marble and Venetian crystal chandeliers and German wood carvings and Brussels tapestries had arrived, and the only time she took a breath from getting and spending was to bury her firstborn, a son, Tyburn Warrick the Third, who at age two had toddled down the hill that was now these formal gardens and had fallen into the brand-new reflecting pond—that one right down there—and had been found by one of the maids, lying peacefully beneath a foot and a half of crystal clear water.

The phone rang behind him with a suddenness that startled. His hand on the coffee cup jerked reflexively. The coffee spilled, spreading brown stain on white linen. He looked over his shoulder and felt his heart accelerate. What the hell? Should he answer it?

Third ring, then no more. Obviously someone had answered it in another part of the house, thank God.

"The child is dead, Ty. I'm so sorry."

Something had died in Ty and Mary Beth at the same time, because they took separate rooms in the big house after that and he got drunk one night and mounted her one more time and nine months later she gave birth to another son, Joshua, who somehow managed to grow up without love and marry the little Whitson girl from Tulsa, a good banking family, and they had produced the three Warrick grandkids: Josh, Jr., Brit and Mereth.

But Ty had argued endlessly with his son about everything, including all aspects of the Warrick empire.

"Trying to take over, the bastard is. I don't need him. I don't need anybody. He's in my way."

One day in the mid-fifties about a year after Mereth had been born, Joshua and his wife boarded the Warrick plane on the first leg of a European holiday and a much-needed breather to give the old man time to cool off. But the Warrick plane that was to take them to the Tulsa airport had crashed and burned on the runway, killing all aboard, leaving Mary Beth and Ty to raise the grandkids and leaving Ty complete control of his empire again, which it was maliciously rumored was exactly the way he'd wanted it all along.

Wearily Buckner closed his eyes on the smeared platter and equally smeared past. He belched pleasurably and tasted black pepper from his eggs.

He'd best get busy. If Dr. Siad could get his foreign ass to the airport by noon, a plane would be waiting for him. And Siad could bring along Ruby Kent, one of the best R.N.'s at St. Mark's, and, that done, Horace Buckner could rest easy, confident that he'd done his best and no one could fault him.

He paused a moment longer, facing for the first time the full and painful realization of precisely what had happened. His friend—possibly his best and oldest friend—was very likely dying upstairs, a relationship that stretched back further than Mary Beth, to the time as a young doctor he was called out to the Warrick ranch to fix the first of an endless string of broken fingers and arms that occurred on those old crude oil rigs, to look after the hundreds of cowhands required to run the Warrick herds.

God, he'd thought all this had been heaven then! And Ty Warrick god-in-chief. Right off they'd taken a shine to each other, the young doc and the young millionaire rancher/oilman. And now—

Buckner bowed his head and blew his nose noisily into his napkin and made a desperate grab for some of that invaluable impersonality that had seen him through a lifetime of doctoring and tragedy, and he wondered, as he was wiping his nose, who would inherit old Ty's V.I.P. season football tickets at the university.

Surely those good-for-nothing grandkids wouldn't want them. Well, then maybe, just maybe—

———

Gilden exit—two miles.

Mereth edged the car into the right lane and swallowed the last bitter drops of Howard Johnson coffee. For some reason she bit the edge of the Styrofoam cup and tossed it onto the floor on the passenger's side.

Carefully she slackened speed for the sharp curve that led around to the single toll booth at Gilden, a dead little farm town six miles north of the turnpike.

When she saw the booth ahead, she reached for her purse. "Good morning," she called out as she drew even with the booth and made fleeting eye contact with a large middle-aged woman in an undersized brown blouse with the green state seal on the breast pocket.

"Ticket," the woman demanded in a flat, rural voice.

Mereth detected a trace of hostility and wondered why and kept on counting nickels and dimes.

"You drive a car like that and you can't put four dimes and a nickel together? Where you headed?"

Beyond the fact that it was none of the woman's business, Mereth started to snap a response and then changed her mind.

"Warrick," she replied as the last penny in the coin purse made forty-five cents.

"Well, move it on, honey. You're blocking traffic."

She glanced in the rearview mirror and saw a pickup truck—blue, a Warrick truck—dusty and idling directly behind her. Who? she wondered and drove away, trying to see who was driving the truck. Once she'd known most of the Warrick roughnecks. But now—

In her desire to see, she pulled over to the side of the road and looked back and saw the logo on the side of the truck, a blue circle with the name Warrick connecting in two arcs top to bottom and in the center a white oil derrick. She stared out at the slowly passing truck but could see only the man on the passenger's side, who grinned at her and waved.

The hitchhiker? From the Tulsa toll plaza? It was him, she was certain. The same hair and beard, the same tan or olive complexion, the same bemused expression. A good face, natural and easy, a little on the arrogant side.

But what was he doing in a Warrick pickup? She'd been so busy noticing the passenger she'd forgotten to identify the driver and too late now, for the truck had disappeared at high speed over the first rise of land. No 55 mph enforced on Warrick roads. Ty had long ago chased off the Highway Patrol.

"We're capable of looking after our own."

As she pulled away from the shoulder and out onto the two-lane road, Mereth felt curiously old, as though at some point in her past she had flung the whole of her life into a solitary instant of time and now that she was returning to Warrick, age was catching up with her. There still was time to turn back.

Ty Warrick.

"You see, Mereth, this is all grazing land, can feed up to fifty thousand

head without so much as missing a blade of grass. God knew what He was doing here. And see over there where the tops of the oil wells show, where the edge of the earth meets the sky? It's all here."

Something hurt. Desperately. It was the wrong moment for cheap music, and almost in anger she switched off the radio and allowed the silence to wrap itself around her. At the first crest she saw the road stretching ahead like a discarded narrow gray ribbon and in the far distance the moving dot that was the Warrick pickup.

Had it been the hitchhiker? And if so, what—

Endless blue straight ahead. She had the peculiar sensation that the car might become airborne. To the right now she saw the never-used road that Ty called the roundabout. It had been created by the heavy vehicles used for the construction of Warrick. Now it was little more than a cow path, brown stubble on either side mixed with early spring green to form an impressionistic pattern. Where were the cattle, the big ones with white faces that "made the best eatin'?" They were grazing by the thousands, lost in the Warrick vastness.

"It's roundup time, Mereth. Get on your ridin' things. We'll go out and give the boys a hand."

Not dead yet.

Could six years have made any difference? She doubted it and, as the re-created image of Ty Warrick settled in the car with her, she slipped easily into the seduction of the road, of Warrick itself, and watched unconcerned as the speedometer crawled steadily up to ninety, then ninety-five.

Death would not defy Ty Warrick for the simple reason that the common pathological horror of death had never entered his consciousness.

It had entered Mereth's plenty of times. The main Warrick hang-up—Josh used to call it—a fear of death, probably the result of watching their parents' plane crash and burn.

A pleasant thought intersected the grim ones. Would Josh come home? Of course. They both would come. Josh was in Hollywood, she knew that, but where was Brit now? England still? Massie would know.

The dot that was the pickup was gone now. Probably taken the back road to the ranch house and the oil fields beyond, the place where the real work at Warrick went on. She looked in that direction and saw an image of the ranch house and in fear hurried past it. The great Italianate mansion, the showplace, sat well apart, separated by about twenty-five miles from the industry that made it all possible.

"What you're running here is worse than the old company towns. It's a feudal system."

"Get out with your goddamned Communist ideas, I don't want you here."

Two men's voices raised in anger cut into her memory, and the Warrick landscape in the April morning shattered. One belonged to her grandfather. The other? Brit, her self-proclaimed Socialist brother who wore the Warrick name like a weight of penance about his neck.

Why the hitchhiker in a Warrick pickup?

Who would be on the security gate this morning? Would they even know her? Had Massie called down and given her clearance?

As incoherence joined the chaos in her mind, she was at last aware of her ever-increasing speed, the Mercedes performing beautifully.

Break speed.

The dash clock flipped to 9:27. Her first class just over.

"Young ladies, attention, please! Turn to page 158. Now who can tell me what Miss Dickinson meant by 'I felt a funeral in my brain'?"

No response. But then why should she expect a response from these girls who carried plastic rounds of birth-control pills in their backpacks and Talking Heads tapes in their portable stereos? Not that they weren't capable of some kind of response. It was just that Mereth had not yet found it.

Turnoff straight ahead.

She angled the car into the turn and knew that within fifteen minutes she would spot that first slant of red tile roof. Seven minutes after that she would approach the front gate, and beyond the security check there would be no turning back.

Not dead yet.

Memories lifted in and out, faded and disappeared; the rainbow sherbet swan Ty had ordered from a New York restaurant and had shipped out in tons of ice for her tenth birthday party . . .

The Greek islands under flamingo-colored clouds. After her grandmother had died, Ty and Massie had taken her to Europe. She'd been fifteen and miserable, despite the poppies blooming amid the feathery grass by the Parthenon and the sunshine that flooded the white marble of the Acropolis . . .

Ty had wanted only to go home, had never wanted to leave in the first place, had spent all his time on the telephone, shouting long-distance to Junior Nagle.

Even Massie had lost patience with him finally and had ordered him home from Rome and had said, "Good riddance," as he headed for the plane which would take him home alone. But a wide, quiet place had developed in Massie shortly after Ty's departure and Mereth couldn't penetrate it and finally gave up trying. The first time Massie had laughed out loud after Ty's departure was in London at Heathrow six weeks later, waiting to depart for New York, where Ty had sent his private plane to meet them and "bring them home where they belong."

There!

She saw it, that first fleeting glimpse of glittering red tile, and knew what was beneath it: a long north corridor, an open colonnade along which visitors entered by the main entrance on the west front on their way to the art gallery.

It seemed so quiet, this early morning. If Tyburn Warrick did die, she foresaw heavy traffic on this road, for the reverberations would be felt all over the world. An empire the size of Warrick did not suffer transitions gladly or easily.

There again! Over the next rise she saw the gray security gate, the discreet, though high electric fence which stretched out in both directions.

She pulled the car over to the side of the road and allowed the motor to idle and rubbed the palms of her hands where they were numb from gripping the wheel.

This was far enough, Massie would have to handle things on her own. Mereth would be of absolutely no help in this condition. She felt as though the artificial composure was beginning to poison her. In the rearview mirror she saw her public face, every feature in order, holding steady. But a voice inside her head was uttering shrill and despairing shrieks, and she saw beyond the public face to the gloomy and triumphant face of a madwoman, thin, irregular, black agate-like pupils of her eyes moving restlessly, showing the saffron yellow whites above.

Despite this interior face, Mereth held her constant gaze on the reflected image.

No. She'd have to go on. For Massie's sake. Massie needed her, and Mereth loved her too much to abandon her.

Decision made. Now all she had to do was find the courage to see it through.

It seemed to her that something with heavy, rhythmical strokes was striking all about the car. It was the beating of her own heart, torn with dread and terror. And love.

A man was waving her forward now, a stern tight-jawed man she'd never seen before. Well, it *had* been six years. She looked more closely. My Lord, where did the uniform come from? Warrick security guards had never worn uniforms before. In the past they'd resembled ranch hands more than—

"Morning. I'll need your name."

"Mereth," she replied idiotically, then at the last moment added, "Warrick," and heard a distinct edge in her voice.

She was about to say something else when she saw him punch a series of buttons on a small electronic panel, then lift a black receiver to his ear and wait.

"I'm sorry, Miss Warrick. I have you now. You may proceed."
No apology. Simply less stiff.

Then, open sesame! And the high gates swung open, thus clearing the way for her, and she foolishly remembered the ease with which as a child she'd roller-skated down this long, smooth black driveway, past this very point where no gates or sentry boxes or guards had existed.

Easy on the curves, which with great melodrama obscured the house. What the first-time visitor desired most at this point was a long unobstructed view. It would come, but in her design Mary Beth had displayed the genius of a premier landscape architect. Give them only a glimpse here, a glimpse there, whet their appetites, the entire promised vista withheld until the very last possible moment.

And then there it was, Mary Beth's dream. Though Mereth had crested this last hill thousands of times, the vision never failed to move her, the sense that she was looking at a part of herself, perhaps the best part.

The poplars had grown. What a curious thing to notice first! She'd helped Ty plant them years ago. Now they lined the drive on both sides. The house faced south, turning its back on the commerce of the turnpike miles away, ignoring Tulsa in one direction and Oklahoma City in the other. It paid homage to no one. It was its own capitol.

Not dead yet.

Mereth brought the car to a halt about two hundred feet from the covered colonnade. She had the feeling that others knew she was here, but she could see the large carved oak front doors still closed. Somehow she wanted them to open, wanted Ty to appear and welcome her back. That's how the Prodigal had been received, wasn't it?

Still closed.

Large white urns of red geraniums were arranged in a semicircle about the overhang. The buds looked young, underdeveloped. Greenhouse born and bred.

There! The left panel of the massive doors had been drawn back only a foot, as though the weight of it had proved a problem for someone. Then Mereth caught sight of her, the lovely face that graced her earliest memory of life at Warrick, who had consistently soothed her with reassurances of love that did not have to be earned.

A mistress? For some reason it was very difficult for Mereth to think of Massie as a mistress. A mistress was one thing; Massie was quite another.

In her eagerness to greet the elegant woman who had just stepped out onto the marble arena, Mereth quickly switched off the ignition and abandoned the car and did not stop until she found herself tightly enclosed in familiar arms.

For several long moments the two women clung to each other amid fragile greenhouse red geraniums and said nothing.

"Carl called." Massie's first words were interspersed with telltale sniffles.

"Who's Carl?"

"On the gate."

"The Nazi?"

One surprised look and then a smile, then a renewed embrace, better this time, less fear, more gratitude that they were together again, regardless of the circumstances.

From Mereth's point of view the woman was more beautiful than ever, the face a cast bronze of high cheekbones, clean, strong jawline and black eyes, black hair shoulder length and smoothed into a classic curve about her face. The elegantly simple light green shirtwaist dress, matching heels, no jewelry save perfect pearls in each earlobe and the magnificent ruby solitaire—"radish size," Josh had called it—on her right hand, one of Ty's many gifts.

By contrast to this elegance and style, Mereth felt plain and nondescript.

On cue, Massie whispered "You're beautiful!" and gently caressed Mereth's cheek. For the first time Mereth saw a residue of tears in those dark eyes.

"How is he?" she asked.

Massie shrugged and took Mereth's arm for a slow walk back to the car and the still-open door. "I don't know," she confessed. "Buckner's been with him. He's not told me a great deal."

"You must call someone else, you know," Mereth said.

"Yes," Massie agreed. "Buckner's called a Dr. Siad, East Indian at St. Mark's. I've sent the plane. He should . . ."

As they walked, Mereth noticed that both of them were walking with heads down, arm in arm, the pace easy, belying the nature of their words.

At the car Mereth invited, "What happened, Massie?"

"Nothing to tell, really. He awakened about three with a headache. I got him aspirin. Couldn't sleep myself. I read, took a warm tub. I came back to bed around five. He was . . ." She broke off and walked away from Mereth.

The splintered silence demanded respect, and Mereth looked back at the front door to see a man in a white jacket she'd never seen before. New staff, of course. Life moved on here without her. The man seemed hesitant to approach and stood his ground directly in front of the door, clearly waiting to be signaled.

But Massie was in no condition, and Mereth took the initiative and called, "I'm afraid I didn't bring any luggage, so there's . . ." She smiled and shrugged and was pleased to see that she had interpreted his role correctly.

When the man stepped back through the open door, Mereth caught a glimpse of the large black and white entrance hall, the high-vaulted, delicately painted, pastel ceiling, fanciful scenes of Utopia and Paradise, landscapes of verdant greens and deep blues, lavenders and unearthly pinks.

As a child, Mereth used to stretch out flat on her back on the cool marble tile floor and stare straight up into the nonexistent Paradise. On the extreme left she'd discovered a path strewn with rose petals leading off into the curve of the ceiling itself. She used to try to imagine what was beyond that path and used to think that if she

44

stared hard enough at the ceiling scene she'd fall up into it and then could explore that path to find out whatever was at its end.

"May I see him, Massie?" she asked hesitantly.

Massie turned, and Mereth felt a strong compulsion to withdraw her request. Fortunately she saw Massie shake her head.

"Dr. Buckner won't even let me."

"Is he still here?"

Massie nodded. "I left him in the terrace room having breakfast. He was going to make some phone calls."

"Did he give you any prognosis at all?"

"Not much. He said it was difficult to tell anything without a scan and sometimes not even then."

"Come," Mereth urged, "I suggest first a brief professional chat with old Sawbones Buckner. Then, on his advice, we may or may not have our own calls to make."

Massie nodded, uncharacteristically meek.

Their heels gently clacked on the marble floor and Mereth clung to Massie's arm and spoke softly, aware of the museum atmosphere. More art gallery than home, this was the place where public receptions were held, the place where the family had never really lived, the place where the huge entrance hall gave way on either side to two long galleries filled with Mary Beth's major pieces: Matisse, Renoir, Picasso, van Gogh, two Vermeers, two Van Dycks, several tapestries woven after the celebrated cartoons of Raphael. Also in the west corridor were the Boulle cabinets containing antique china and crystal: a Sèvres service of rare design and coloring; several unique Meissen two-handle chocolate cups and Pinxton mugs, among other items.

The focal point of the entrance hall was the graceful staircase, broad enough for six to walk abreast, the white marble flanked on either side by gilt ironwork like lace, which was repeated in the balustrade. It had always seemed to Mereth more a stage setting than anything else. Oedipus could have reigned over these steps, or more likely Electra.

Halfway up the steps Mereth stopped Massie. "Have you called anyone?"

"Just you. And Dr. Buckner."

"Then no one else knows?"

"The house staff, of course."

"How many are there now?"

Massie appeared to have to think a moment and leaned back against the balustrade. "Ten."

"Are they trustworthy?"

Massie looked shocked. "Of course. What are you saying?"

Mereth proceeded on up the steps. What was she trying to say? If Ty got up out of his sickbed, moderately recovered yet capable of carrying on, why alert anyone? Let the complex Warrick business structures stand as they were.

"Come on," Mereth said, taking Massie's arm. "Let's see if we can get a direct answer out of Buckner."

As they were approaching the terrace room door, a young woman in a black uniform passed by coming from the opposite end of the corridor. In her arms she carried an immense stack of clean linen.

"The balcony room, third floor east," Massie said.

Her childhood suite. The idyllic pink and white ruffled cocoon in which she'd more or less grown up. The pink and white ruffles had disappeared in high school and had been replaced with Beatles and Donovan posters, and that decor had given way to tasteful blues and ivories and mauves with no revealing character.

"Your old rooms, Mereth. Will that be all right?"

Mereth nodded. As the girl drew near she said, "Just leave those on the bed. I can make it myself."

"Oh, no. I don't mind."

"I do."

"Come along, Mereth. I need you."

A little surprised by the edge in Massie's voice, Mereth watched the young girl hurry past and guessed her age as high school and wondered why she wasn't in school. At the door of the terrace room she rejoined a mildly bemused Massie.

"You're lousy with servants, you know, Mereth." She smiled. "Always were."

"Always will be," Mereth agreed. "They make me nervous."

"Why? I pay them enough."

"She should be in school."

"She *is* in school. At Tulsa Christian College. Classes in the afternoon. The money she's earning here pays her tuition at college. She's in pre-law."

Chastised, Mereth looked back in hopes of getting a glimpse of the future lawyer on her way to put clean linens on the bed. But the girl was gone.

"You're an antisnob snob, Mereth," Massie accused lovingly. "Something in your concept of the order of the world prohibits a girl from putting clean sheets on your bed while pondering all the historical and social ramifications of the Magna Charta."

"I said I was sorry," Mereth murmured and felt like an inferior child again, surrounded by superior giants.

Then Massie pushed open the door to the terrace room and stood back for Mereth, who heard the deep, hoarse voice of Dr. Buckner. He was shouting into the telephone at someone, and she suffered a rapid explosion of Proustian recall.

"Hold still, Mereth. Must take a look down your throat. Measles. Keep her quiet for a couple of weeks."

"That's a nasty break, Mereth. No more climbing in trees for a while, you hear?"

Every pain, major and minor, of her childhood had been attended to by that old man in the rumpled brown tweed jacket bending over the telephone, shouting into it as though he needed volume to carry his voice as well as the meaning of his message. As far as she could tell, he was unaware that they had entered the room.

"I don't know, Doctor," he shouted further. "That's why I called you. Now it would help immensely if you could clear the rest of your afternoon appointments and join me out here for . . ."

Apparently someone on the other end of the line was giving him a hard time.

"Warrick!" he bellowed. "The name may not mean much to you, but drop it in that hospital corridor and see what kind of reaction you get."

Another pause.

"It's not a matter of intimidation, Doctor. I don't mean to intimidate you, believe me."

Mereth and Massie exchanged a glance.

At the same time Horace Buckner rubbed the back of his neck and sat wearily in Ty's chair overlooking the garden. "Hey!" he shouted into the phone, anger increasing, "Is Dr. O'Rourke around?"

Chief of staff. Big guns. Mereth moved silently away from the door a step or two.

There was another pause.

"Then put him the hell on!"

Massie moved to the coffee service and was now extending a steaming cup of coffee to Mereth. The old doctor still did not know they were present.

"Jim, this is Horace," Buckner said and relaxed into the chair. "I've got big problems out here at Warrick. Ty's had a stroke. I don't know how bad. That's what I tried to tell that foreigner, who may be bright but he ain't too quick. Now look, can you say something that will get his ass into gear and out to the airport . . . ?"

Another pause.

"Now! I need him now, Jim! What the hell, we're talking stroke and we're talking Ty Warrick. Something wrong with you? Just get him out to the airport and Ty's plane will be waiting."

Jim O'Rourke knew. Between Ty and Mary Beth, they'd practically built St. Mark's brick by brick, gift by gift, endowment by endowment.

"God, I thank you, Jim," Dr. Buckner said. "Oh, and by the

way, Jim, I'll need a good R.N., the best you can get. See if that Kent woman is willing. Tell her, in case she's dense like Siad, that money ain't no object but I need someone with Ty more than the black woman, if you know what I mean."

Mereth did not look up at this. The battle was so ancient surely Massie could deal with it by now.

"No, I'm going to stay put, Jim. I owe it to Ty. Yeah, I'll call you. And, Jim, don't talk to the newspapers, you hear? Not yet. We need to find out how much of Ty's brain is left. You understand."

At that moment Mereth put her coffee cup noisily on the silver tray, no longer interested in concealment. She couldn't hold the old bastard responsible for what he was saying if he didn't know he was saying it in front of an audience. At the first clink of china she saw Buckner whirl about in the chair as though under attack. His lined face was a shock. Age had not dealt kindly with him. There seemed to be a jaundiced pallor to his skin, his nose an ominous red, loose skin hanging down, gobbler fashion, from his chin.

"I said I didn't know, Jim," Buckner bellowed, patience gone. "Just get your fancy doc on that plane and we'll let him tell us both."

With that he slammed the receiver down and managed to raise himself, all the while grinning.

"Mereth, as I live and breathe!" he gasped and made his way around the chair.

"Dr. Buckner." She nodded somewhat stiffly, still hearing in echo, ". . . how much of Ty's brain is left." As he approached full steam, she steeled herself for his embrace and recalled she'd never liked his embrace even as a child.

"I'll be goddamned, Mereth!" he exclaimed, his eyes up close buried behind large blue pouches. "Hell, we must have done something right. Look at you!"

She smiled and waited while the old man studied her. "Thank you," she at last replied. "My grandfather, Dr. Buckner, how is he?"

He looked up as though surprised by the question. "Don't know.

What I mean is . . . Well, a hotshot wog is on his way out. He'll tell us."

"Who would that be?" Mereth asked.

"Bakir Siad is one of the foremost neurologists in the country."

The efficient response did not come from Dr. Buckner but rather from the opposite direction, from the serving table and the woman carefully studying the surface of her coffee as though in search of clues to a very great mystery.

Now Massie looked up as though startled by the silence she had caused. "Well, isn't he, Dr. Buckner? Isn't that what you told me earlier?"

The old man cleared his throat and nodded. "Oh, he's an expert all right. At least he thinks he is. What he truly is is a colossal pain in the ass . . ." He broke off and gave a harumphing laugh. "Well, Jim O'Rourke cut through all that foreign bullshit. Now if you'll both excuse me, I'll get back up to Ty's room. Someone should . . ."

Massie caught up with him at the door. "Let me come with you," she begged. "If he's awake I can . . ."

"He ain't awake and ain't likely to be for a while."

From where Mereth stood she thought she detected a tinge of enjoyment in the old man's gruff rejection, as though at last he could separate Tyburn Warrick from this "embarrassment" of his flesh. For one brief moment she experienced an uncomfortable anger. When had Massie lost her backbone? Mereth could remember instances in the past when Massie had leveled her enemies using simply her superior wit and intelligence.

Now Massie turned away from the old man and his smug expression, avoiding eye contact with Mereth, walking slowly back to the serving table, where with maddening meekness she began to collect the breakfast silver.

Enough! Mereth had seen enough.

"Dr. Buckner, before you go we need to ask some questions."

Dr. Buckner started out into the corridor. "You can ask all the questions you want, Mereth, but I'm afraid I might not be able to answer them."

"Why not? You've seen him. You've examined him. You're a doctor."

"The expert's on his way out," he called back with weary condescension. "Save your questions for him."

"Then your opinion, Dr. Buckner. Give us your opinion. You're an old family friend, Ty's friend. Give us that much."

She'd not intended to appeal to his vanity but apparently she had, for he walked slowly back, his head bowed and shaking, an apology of sorts.

"Sorry, ladies. It's been a hell of a morning."

"I know." Mereth nodded sympathetically. "And while we're grateful you've sent for the specialist, still your opinion means a great deal to us."

Buckner seemed visibly to melt. He withdrew a crumpled handkerchief from the pocket of his coat and made a swipe at his face, the kind of gesture a man makes when in hot and uncomfortable weather. But the morning was cool.

"Bad," was the first word he said, and for several moments he studied the crumpled handkerchief. "Real bad," Buckner repeated with significant variation. "I . . ." He broke off.

"What?" Mereth prompted.

"He either couldn't or wouldn't talk to me. I don't know. I've never known Ty not to cuss at something, but I couldn't get even one good goddamn out of him."

As medical barometer it left a lot to be desired, but where Ty Warrick was concerned it was as good a test as any.

"Do you think we should call the others?" Mereth asked, sorry in a way she'd pushed for this "opinion."

"With a stroke it's damned hard to tell," Buckner elaborated, coming back into the room and snagging a wrapped peppermint from a candy bowl on a near table. "I've seen patients I wouldn't have given you a red hot damn for their chances at survival, let alone rehab . . ." For several seconds he played with the twisted end of the cellophane wrap. "Of course, it all depends on how much is left of his brain. If there's enough, then the will of the patient becomes everything, and Ty's got more will than he has greenbacks, so . . ."

"Then why do you call it 'bad'?" Mereth asked.

" 'Cause I just simply don't know. From the looks of the man I treated upstairs, I'd say go ahead and make your phone calls. You'd better get your brothers back here. Even if Ty don't oblige them and die, then they ought to be back here anyway, pay a visit to the man that sends them their checks. Out of courtesy, you know what I mean?"

Then he was gone, leaving the echo of his words in the pleasant sunny room like a bad odor.

Mereth stared at the open door, stunned by the depth of his resentment. Most certainly she too had been included in that scathing indictment.

She wasn't even aware that Massie had joined her until she felt the slight pressure of a familiar arm about her shoulders.

"Pay no attention," was Massie's quiet advice. "He's old, doesn't know what he's saying half the time."

"Oh, I think he does." Mereth smiled. "And what's more, he's probably right."

She wandered away from the door and down toward the large window which gave a perfect view of the gardens below.

"That pink water lily, Grandpa, you see it? I'm going to jump in and get it for you."

"You stay to hell away from that pond, Mereth!"

"Does he still have his breakfast here?" Mereth asked, easing down into the velvet chair that had served as Ty's "throne" for as long as she could remember.

"Always. He likes to watch the men working."

Mereth looked back for clarification.

"Out there." Massie pointed toward the gardens where Mereth saw, just now emerging along the lower flagstone paths, half a dozen men all carrying various pieces of garden equipment, two balancing loaded wheelbarrows filled with large white and green plastic bags.

"On more than one occasion," Massie murmured, "Ty would go yelling out that door at something he felt they were doing wrong or that he could do better."

Mereth remembered well the sight of Ty's ungovernable and impressive temper. Even when it was aimed at others, the rage was unbearable. And if it had been aimed at her—

The thought proved painful and Mereth moved away from it, refocusing her attention on the men at the bottom of the garden. Suddenly she peered more closely.

"Who's that?" she asked and reached back for Massie in an attempt to draw her attention down to the garden. "Down there, Massie, look!"

"Which one are you talking about?"

"Down there. That man."

"There are several."

"That one!" She pointed sharply at a tall, lean figure clad in blue jeans and jacket, taller than the others, bearded.

"Do you see?" Mereth asked as the man lifted two of the large white plastic bags onto his shoulders and carried them around the lily pond toward a large flowerbed. "That one," Mereth specified.

"Emanuel?" Massie asked, puzzled. "He's been with us for years. You remember. He started here as a boy. Ty finally got him his citizenship. He's head gardener now. Does a beautiful job."

"No." Mereth shook her head, recalling the number of wetbacks who always streamed into Warrick each year from Mexico.

"Come on, Mereth. We have phone calls to make. Shall we do it here or would you rather . . . ?"

"Yes," she said vaguely, still looking down on the man in the garden, who had emptied a bag of fertilizer and stood absolutely motionless, hands on hips, staring up toward the house.

"Massie, that one," Mereth whispered.

"I'm sorry, Mereth. Without my glasses I just don't know. Why?

Is it important? If it is I'll call Emanuel. As I said, he hires and fires. Do you think it's someone you know?"

"There was a man hitchhiking at the toll plaza outside Tulsa. He was most insistent."

Massie smiled. "And you think . . . ?"

"Forget it. Come on. Who's first? Josh? Don't forget the time difference in California. We'll wake him up. Good." She was talking fast in an attempt to cover her own embarrassment. From a distance the man did resemble the hitchhiker. At the door she stopped.

"Where is a quiet room? With a phone."

Massie shrugged and half-smiled. "The entire house. Quiet as a grave."

"Oh, Massie!" she whispered and drew the woman effortlessly into her arms and held her close as Massie had held her through all the hurts and trials of growing up. From the trembling in the slim shoulders, she knew there were tears.

"I'm sorry," she heard Massie splutter.

"Don't apologize."

"I've always told that old bastard if he dies first . . ."

More tears. Mereth tightened her grip.

"It's just that I have no life without him."

"Then if it happens, you'll have to find one."

"I . . . can't." Her voice broke.

Mereth grasped her closer and held on. It was, if nothing more, a moving testimony to the mysterious and bewildering power of love, two of the most mismatched bookends ever created, hurled together by God. The aging multimillionaire roustabout had broken every law on the books and staked out a large portion of Oklahoma paradise, rough-hewn, crude to the point of being offensive, selfish, self-centered, egocentric, bull-like in all respects from his sheer massive physical size to certain key ingredients of his character and personality. How had he attracted, captured and held the affections of Jo Massie, liberal daughter of two superb intellectuals,

54

a woman part black, part white, wholly elegant, wholly refined, wholly genteel, gifted, cultured, and selfless?

As the enigma grew, Mereth kissed Massie and gave up trying to understand it. Surely the liaison of almost thirty years was no longer a real scandal in any quarter.

"Come on," Mereth urged, "why don't you go lie down and let me make those phone calls?"

"Are you sure?"

"Of course! In fact, I think I'll stay right here. Ty's chair looks inviting. Between calls I can enjoy the gardens."

"The numbers are in the book there, all up-to-date. Would you like a fresh pot of coffee? Anything to eat?"

"No, I'm fine, believe me. You go ahead."

Massie still looked doubtful. "What are you going to tell them?"

Suddenly Mereth understood why Massie didn't want to be here during the phone calls. Difficult questions would be asked, and the air would be filled with terrible words.

"I'll tell them the truth." Mereth shrugged.

"Do you know the truth?"

"No, but I think they'd both better come home."

"When will the newspapers . . . ?"

"I don't know, Massie," Mereth said, suddenly feeling the weight of the task ahead of her. "You run along now," she urged gently, guiding her out of the door. "I'll come to your rooms when I'm . . ."

Massie shook her head. "I'm going up to Ty's room. If Buckner won't let me in, I'll at least be in the sitting room across the corridor." Her voice drifted off as she moved down the hall.

Mereth watched her and realized Massie was beginning to stoop. If Ty died—

Make the phone calls, spread the news. The patriarch may be dying.

Quietly she closed the door and leaned against it. The telephone was by Ty's chair in front of the glass wall.

"Don't ever bother your grandfather, Mereth, when he's on the phone."

"Junior, I want that lease, do you hear? I don't give a goddamn how you get it or what you pay for it. Just get it!"

Junior Nagle. Good Lord, had anyone thought to notify him? Ty's business partner for over fifty years? They'd brought in the first Warrick well together. As a child Mereth couldn't remember a day without Junior Nagle's enormous presence in the house, at table, writing down endless figures, barrels per day, drilling depths, cost overrides, inventories. Junior Nagle. She'd have to call him in Dallas. Later.

Slowly now she approached Ty's chair. She reached down for the address book, leafed through it and recognized Massie's neat, efficient handwriting. Every number was there. She could pass the rest of the day here and—with the help of this one little book—notify the entire world.

Suddenly, when she least expected it, she felt a curious tremor of excitement.

"Tell me, Mr. Warrick, what makes an oilman take the risks?"

"Goddamn, what a stupid question!"

"Ty!"

"No, it is a stupid question. Any jackass knows the greater the gamble the more it inflames the imagination and the more helpless a man is to resist it. The desire for gain is always a basic motive for all exploration, but something more hounds the oil gambler."

Mereth stared unseeing down at the phone, transfixed by the echoes in her memory. The hapless reporter had later fled.

"No more, Massie. They all look like queers."

Feeling weak-kneed, she sat in Ty's chair and was instantly swallowed by the velvet hollow he'd made for himself. No velvet at the ranch house. Just the essentials required for survival. *Where are you, Ty?*

Call Josh.

This disciplined voice spoke sternly to her and she turned through the book to the W's and found Joshua, Jr., a Malibu number listed as well as one in Beverly Hills. She decided on Malibu first and looked at the digits and remembered the endless games of hide-and-seek she'd played with Josh in the labyrinthine corridors and halls of Warrick. She'd always worshiped him, as little sisters are supposed to worship big brothers. He hadn't always returned the affection.

Here I come, Josh, ready or not.

Before she picked up the phone, she stole a quick look back down into the garden. Tall, bearded and lean was gone.

Beverly Hills

April 10, 1984

JOSH WARRICK stood poolside at Craig Evanston's estate and watched the party in full swing, and out of boredom started playing a mental game with himself. Look hard and find something, someone, some situation that was not a flaming cliché.

Hard to do. From the sweetish acrid smell of good pot which blended with the obscene overabundance of gardenias into a fragrance, Nausea Number Five, to the twelve ample tits belonging to the six ample starlets who were self-consciously skinny-dipping in the pool, to the four bars, one on each side of the pool, to the familiar faces from all the current television shows, a recognizable gallery of pap, pablum and fucking mediocrity, to the coke-sniffing behind the glass doors leading to the library, to the moves, sexual, professional that were being made on everyone by everyone, all of it, every last bloody bit of it, was a roaring, flaming monstrous cliché.

Suffering the self-disgust that he was here and so a part of it all, Josh shifted his dream, the new script, to the other hand, away from the splashing water babies, and looked toward Evanston's closed "office" door on the west wing of the rambling fieldstone house.

His turn next. Josh's turn. If and when Craig got through screwing Lola Patten.

"Hey, Josh, good to see you. How's Peter?"

He looked up at the close voice into a female face, overly made up, that he'd never seen before. Middle-aged and miserable among all this youth. Still important-looking. Agent, perhaps.

"Loved your last picture," she went on. "A little substance among the sex. You're going to be our new Orson Welles. Give the world *Citizen Kane Two—*"

Josh glared, puzzled, caught off guard by the compliment issuing from the too-red lips. He turned in a slow circle in an attempt to follow the female, who had never stopped moving through the crowd and who was handing out one-liners right and left. Finally she disappeared into someone's arms and both slipped through the glass doors into the library, heading for dreamland.

Who? Friend of Peter's, no doubt.

Josh continued to watch the zoo, spying now a well-known leading man from a hit police series, gay, putting gay moves on a local fag-hag, false sexual gestures designed to conceal what everyone knew.

He smiled at his own reluctance to take that last emotional step out of the closet. Oh, what the hell. Ninety-nine point nine percent of him was out, liberated, free. Who gave a damn that somewhere in the murkiest lower dungeon of his torture-chamber mind, Ty was still snapping the horse whip over the flesh of his bared back and screaming "Queer" at him.

Tyburn Warrick.

Where had that bastard come from? Like shit on a shoe, Ty Warrick was damned hard to get rid of. Citizen Kane was a Boy Scout leader compared to Josh's grandfather.

The water babies were splashing higher and higher. Several others had jumped into the pool to join them, or screw them, or whatever. In another attempt to safeguard the script, Josh moved away from the pool. Everything was a cliché, including Josh himself, a cliché created by hacks, designed for consumption by functional illiterates who occupied a world that, if it had ever known, had long since forgotten any definitions of beauty.

"Scotch, please—"

The young bartender looked up at his request. "Neat?"

Josh nodded.

A group of jackasses brayed noisily behind him. Apparently the bartender read the expression on his face.

"Try to have a good time." He grinned and extended the glass across the bar.

"You got a bathtub of this back there?"

"Just about, and more when that's gone. Mr. Evanston doesn't like to run short of anything . . ."

Josh drained the glass and refused to say what he was thinking and drew his teeth across the pleasant burning and wished that Peter had been able to come with him. He really *hated* these parties without Peter. Peter helped him to feel as though he belonged, even though he didn't.

Now he moved slowly across the lawn, keeping his eye on the still closed doors.

How long could it go on? If Evanston screwed as many women as he was reported to have screwed, his cock must damn near be worn down.

Cosmic-question time. Why did assholes like Craig Evanston hold all the power, all the authority? It had always been the case, starting with Ty Warrick—

With the noise of the party behind him, he felt a good delayed warmth from the scotch and thumbed through the already well-thumbed script. Just a masterpiece, a true original, flawed, brilliant, insistent. Josh's agent had brought it to his attention.

"Don't know if it will sell, but I still have a twinge of conscience that says someone had damn well better look at it. You've been chosen for some damn thing, Josh—"

And Josh had read it and had been frozen by it and hadn't been able to get it out of his mind and had seen Peter in the lead role, along with De Niro, a chance for all of them to make a contribution.

Four producers had turned it down. Craig Evanston was number five and to date Josh's best hope, a highly successful television producer who was busting his balls to get into full-length films.

Again he looked over his shoulder. Doors still closed. Josh turned about in search of a suitable diversion and found it in the new arrival, Span Sterling, the heartthrob from ABC's slick new soap.

Josh watched from a distance the muscle-bound eighteen-year-old clad in black leather, a young starlet no more than fourteen clinging to his arm, sullen, pouting, cleavage down to her toes.

So damned young, both of them, Josh brooded, and simultaneously old. Without warning he thought of his sister Mereth as he'd last seen her, about fourteen, fifteen, but so different from that pouty little bitch hanging on the black leather arm.

Josh smiled. At last he'd found something that was not a cliché. In his memory Mereth, alive, vibrant, running helter-skelter through the halls of Warrick, a summer sprite. Try not grinning at her. It was impossible—

"Josh, know what I found? A whole patch of four-leaf clovers. Is it fair if you find a whole patch?"

And later, the same day . . .

"Hurry, Josh, it's only half a rainbow, but—"

Suddenly Josh turned his back on the party. He missed Mereth, missed her vitality with a longing akin to pain. He heard a door open and saw Craig Evanston emerge, pulling the cord of a yellow silk robe tightly around his waist. Behind him a step or two was the woman in matching robe.

"Mr. Evanston?"

Josh called ahead, then hurried over to the sidewalk.

Evanston looked back at him and continued to draw the cord tighter and tighter about his waist. "I—don't—"

"Josh Warrick. We had an appointment—"

The woman looked annoyed.

"It's about this script, *The Brothers*. I sent it over a couple of weeks ago. You said—"

Evanston nodded slowly, leaned over and whispered something in the female's ear, patted her on the buttock and with a smile of apology sent her toward the party and the excitement of Span Sterling.

"Now, Mr.—"

"Warrick—"

"Of course. I remember—"

"The script. Have you—"

"I'm afraid, yes, of course. I vaguely—"

"Set in Wisconsin. Two brothers. Winter—"

"Oh yes. Cold feeling—"

"Yes—"

Evanston paced off the flagstone walk for a few moments, head down. His bare legs showed through with each step.

"It's—"

"Would you like more time?"

"No, interesting, no more," he conceded, and Josh started the downward spiral.

"Take another week or so," Josh offered. "No decision now—"

"You have a good track record, Warrick. Why did you come at me with something like this? Who in the hell wants to watch two brothers confront reality on a Wisconsin dairy farm? We need money-makers, don't we?"

Josh nodded and wondered how long it would take him to live down *Sweet Sexteen*.

"This one," Evanston went on and pointed distastefully toward the script in Josh's hand. "Well, I just don't hear bells. And I don't take on material that doesn't make me hear bells."

Josh gaped. "I—beg—your—"

"Sorry, Warrick. Now if you can think up some way to jazz it up, more ass, you know what I mean?"

"I—"

The female called from poolside.

"Got to go, Warrick. I'm hosting this do. Find me something with bells and broads. Then we'll do business together. Okay?"

"C-could we t-talk again?" Josh always stammered under the duress of rejection.

"No need. Find me a really class-A piece of material, then—"

Then he was gone. Josh started to say something crude and changed his mind. Part of him, the most important, the best part wasn't surprised.

As new frustration blended with old, he looked nervously about in search of one small place for himself. But there was none, never had been. He'd never been able to find an inch of unoccupied, hospitable earth on which to stand and pass his time in this world. Certainly not at Warrick, not at Princeton, not in New York, not even here in Never-Never Land.

He needed Peter, needed the ocean breeze, needed a place where he could release the tears that had been building for a lifetime. To that end he walked steadily through the laughter of the party, around the driveway, past the endless line of Rollses and Cads and felt worn-out and wavering, and tried to conceive of a place where he could go for comfort, for courage.

Malibu

WITH PETER still asleep beside him, Josh awakened in the predawn darkness, slipped quietly out of bed, snagged a pack of Marlboroughs and the lighter from his bedside table and moved silently out onto the balcony, where less than fifty yards away the Pacific surf was pounding with a rhythm that seemed to set the pace for his pulse.

Four tries later he lit the cigarette and felt slight discomfort as the smoke burned the raw tissue inside his nose. Too much coke—or not enough. Maybe he should give up smoking and limit his vices to snorting.

As the waves of the incoming tide crashed noisily beneath him, he looked down on the ghostly white foam, awed anew by his proximity to the ocean.

"If any more beach erodes we'll be in it," Peter had warned.

Peter. The hardest part of any affliction was the wasted nervous effort of trying to pretend it away. Was being gay an affliction? Some thought so. He thought not.

He took another long drag on the cigarette and looked down at his erection protruding from his pajamas and wondered if it was passion or simply a need to piss.

Might as well find out.

He drew aside his pajamas and relieved himself on the sand and belatedly glanced left to his neighbors, a house now leased to a psychiatrist and his family. In the golden days it was rumored to have been occupied by Errol Flynn. True or not, Josh enjoyed telling people he lived in the house next to Errol Flynn's.

Endless piss. Too much booze. Strong smelling.

"Josh, take care of yourself."

What would he do without Peter Taunton?

At last finished, he looked down. Limp now, his penis. Not passion. So be it.

Feeling better, he flicked his cigarette out over the balcony and wondered for the first time why he had awakened so early.

They were taking the day off, remember? The sewer that was Beverly Hills was beginning to get to him. The deal had fallen through.

"Who in the hell wants to watch two brothers confront reality on a Wisconsin dairy farm?" Deal. There had never been a deal.

He closed his eyes, feeling fresh humiliation. "Damn!" he said aloud, though it was lost in the surf.

Josh leaned heavily on the balcony railing and let his head hang loose and tried—as he had tried every day of his life—to deal with what he had become. Not what he was. At least he had that satisfaction. He knew what he was, what he was capable of doing. He knew what was buried deep inside him that no one had ever seen.

Nothing could be truly transfixed and known except through Art.

So melodramatic. Art? What was that? He was thirty-eight years old. Maybe he was too old to think about Art.

As he lifted his face to the surf in search of something cleansing, he smelled the good odor of fresh coffee and looked back to see Peter just emerging through the beige burlap drapes, carrying two large earthenware mugs.

"I'm sorry." Josh smiled, finding nourishment in a face he loved.

"What for?" Peter responded, admirably lucid at six in the morning. "As far as I'm concerned, this is the only hour of the day worth witnessing. Six A.M. to 7 A.M. After that God goes downhill."

Josh took the cup and the love that was offered with it. They'd met several years ago on the set of an NBC Movie-of-the-Week. Peter, a Canadian-born, New York–trained actor, had had a supporting role. Josh had directed. But it had been such a colossal piece of shit that even the retards at NBC had changed their minds, and that weekend Josh and Peter had gone to Baja to lick their wounds and spend some of their large and useless salaries.

They'd been together ever since.

Now Josh took a sip of the spiced coffee, grateful to Peter and grateful as well for his thoughtful inquiry.

"You okay? Early risers tend to be . . . well, you know, ill in one way or another."

Josh smiled and recognized the mild humor for what it was, Peter's way of inviting him to talk.

"You know," Peter began in that offhand manner that generally signaled he was about to say something of importance, "we don't *have* to go through a studio."

In defense against the frustration that was building inside, Josh said simply, "It's the best script I've ever read. If we don't make it, someone else will. It's only a matter of time."

"Then I suggest we make it."

There was such a simple, almost childlike innocence in the statement that Josh felt a flare of anger.

"How?" he demanded, and realized he'd had enough of breaking surf.

He was aware of Peter following, veering off to the kitchen bar where he refilled his mug and added a few drops of Kahlúa. As Josh stretched out on the oversized sofa, Peter fixed him with a stern expression.

"If I talk now, will you listen?"

Josh nodded. "I love you."

Peter caught the mood, kissed his forehead, smoothed back his hair and then drew a chair close and spoke earnestly.

"And I love you. And I know it and you know it. And in a way we owe it to that love to fight for this."

He held up the dog-eared script of *The Brothers*.

De Niro had expressed strong interest if they could get studio backing, and he had approved of the casting of Peter Taunton as the younger brother, claiming it would be a pleasure to work with him. Then why in the hell were they being blocked at every turn?

Josh's new frustration dragged him upward to a sitting position, shoulders rounded, his face buried in his hands.

"All right, you promised you'd listen," Peter reminded quietly. "You must learn how to tell the difference between a temporary setback and a permanent one. This is temporary."

Josh looked up. "You call the lack of a producer, the lack of a studio and the lack of fifteen million dollars temporary?"

"Yes."

"You're insane."

"Possibly. But you are too or you wouldn't be here."

"I'm listening," he said, knowing all too well the source of Peter's dogged determination. The role of the younger brother would, quite simply, make his reputation. How Josh would love to give him that!

"I said I was listening," he repeated, "though you'll have to say something that will drown out the stupidity of last night's meeting with Evanston, who doesn't hear bells, only his balls."

"Screw Craig Evanston, screw the bastard," Peter scolded. "Now listen. What we must do first is obtain full control of the material—and I mean full. No limited three-to-five-year option. Go around your agent if you have to."

Josh listened and knew that Manny would be no problem.

"So I think we need to go to Wisconsin, meet with the author, make him a reasonable offer. No time limit, as I said, but with a clause that gives both of us the right to renegotiate when we start production."

It made sense. But there was one problem.

"This . . . unlimited option, this fair offer, what are we talking about?"

"Fifteen thousand dollars."

Josh smiled. Did Peter have a secret bank account?

"How?" he asked.

"Borrow."

"I don't think our credit would . . ."

"We could try."

Their finances were simple. Peter lived on what he made in the profession, a commercial now and then, an acting part, modeling. Josh relied on less-frequent directing jobs and a five-thousand-dollar-per-month disbursement, a trust fund set up by his grandfather. Though it sounded like a hell of a lot, try to make it stretch with an office in Beverly Hills, a Malibu beach house, a fondness for good wine and food, coke and clothes.

"Fifteen thou," Josh repeated. "You must know something I don't."

"No. Except if you believe in this property as much as you say you do, we've got to find a way."

"Oh, for God's sake, Peter, don't put it like that! You know I believe . . ."

Halfway up from the sofa, destination not clear—anywhere to escape Peter's naive enthusiasm—the phone rang.

Both men looked at it in mutual surprise, then at each other. Who in the hell—

"Did you tell Gloria . . . ?"

"No. She knows not to call here unless it's an emergency."

Josh approached the phone on the third ring and looked at it. Gloria? Though he could ill afford one, it did sound good to be able to tell the studios and producers to "call my secretary."

On the fourth ring Peter suggested, "Well, answer it. Maybe it's Evanston with an apology and an offer."

On the sixth ring, Peter reached for the receiver and thrust it toward Josh. "Hell is a room filled with ringing telephones," he said quietly. "For God's sake, just say 'hello' and 'good-bye'!"

Josh had not wanted to answer. Whoever it was could get him at his office tomorrow. If Gloria had given out his private number, it would be her ass.

"Hello," he said, cradling the receiver close.

No response. Endless static.

"Hello? Who is it?" he demanded, suspecting long distance.

Then he heard something. A faint voice. Female.

"Josh, is that better? Can you hear me?"

"Yes, I can hear you," he nodded, "but I . . ."

"It's Mereth, Josh," the voice explained. "Your baby sister, remember?"

Then he did.

"Where are you calling from?" he asked, mystified by his feelings of pleasure and excitement. If she were in L.A. he and Peter would go immediately and fetch her, bring her here to Malibu.

"I'm . . . home, Josh. At Warrick."

Disappointed, his smile faded. Home. Oklahoma. Redneck capital of the world. He took the receiver and walked to the window, looking at but not seeing the ocean.

"Mereth, to what do I owe the pleasure of this call? I trust everything is . . ."

"No, Josh, everything isn't all right."

He peered off into the ocean toward the dot-sized hull of a distant freighter. "What's the trouble now? The old bastard acting up
again?" The last time Josh had been home—eight, ten years ago—
Tyburn Warrick's name had been plastered all over the newspapers,
peripherally involved in some banking scandal. Three had gone to
jail, if Josh recalled correctly. Tyburn not among them.

"Whatever it is, Mereth," Josh said, turning back into the room,
snagging a package of cigarettes from the coffee table and trying
with his right hand to shake one free, "I doubt if I can be of any
help. I suggest you call his attorneys. They know best how to keep
his name out of . . ."

"Ty's had a stroke."

Josh dropped the package. He was aware of Peter picking them
up.

"Did you hear me, Josh? I said that Ty has had a stroke."

"When?"

"Early this morning. I was in Tulsa. Massie called."

"How . . . bad?"

"We don't know yet. Buckner's with him. A specialist is on his
way."

Peter extended a lit cigarette to him, and Josh took it.

"Josh, are you there?"

"I'm here, Mereth." At last he took a drag and tried to think of
something sensible and suitable to say. Failing, he let Mereth take
over.

"Massie thinks all of us should return home. Buckner agrees. He
implied it wouldn't look good if Tyburn Warrick died alone."

Died.

"Then they don't think . . . ?"

"They don't know, Josh. You'd better come on home."

Josh snubbed out the cigarette. "I'll . . . have to make some
arrangements here first."

"Of course."

"But I should be able to get there by tomorrow."

"Good."

"Have you called anyone else?"

"Not yet. You're the first."

"Thanks, Mereth."

"You *will* come, then?"

"Of course. Will you meet me in Tulsa?"

A pause. "I'd better stay here, Josh. Massie needs . . . Eddie will be there with a car."

"How is Massie?"

"She worries me."

Josh was sorry to hear that. He loved Massie without qualification, though he'd never been able to understand her blind adoration of the bastard.

"Well, then . . . ." He heard her voice drift and felt he should try to sound like a big brother.

"Are you all right, Mereth?"

She didn't sound all right, sounded old and frozen and buttoned down, not a trace in her voice of the little girl who had brightened the lives of all the suffering prisoners of that dreary fortress. Tyburn Warrick had doted on her, and Mereth had shadowed him wherever he went. His death would be hard on her.

"Everything will be all right, Mereth. I'll be there tomorrow at the latest. Hold things together until I get there. Be a good girl."

Suddenly the connection was broken. It seemed an abrupt conclusion.

"What in the hell was that all about, and where are you going?"

The questions came from the sofa. Josh glanced in that direction and saw Peter flipping through the pages of the manuscript. For a moment Josh savored that feeling of a glorious secret, when a person knows something—like God—that no one else knows and yet which will transform every life within hearing distance.

"Ty has had a stroke."

The bull was not indestructible, was apparently susceptible to at least one law of nature, that when blood vessels explode deep inside the head—

He broke off the thought, finding it contemptible, and took his glorious secret back to the window, where he again peered out at the ocean. A thought intervened.

Had he ever fully discussed with Peter precisely what it meant to be Joshua Warrick? No.

"Are you going to tell me?"

"Would you like to fly home with me tomorrow, Peter?"

"Home?"

"Back to Oklahoma." Suddenly he saw a clear image of Warrick, that great, gray mansion-mortuary filled with art and beauty and taste and the meanest son of a bitch God ever created.

"I don't . . ."

"My grandfather's had a stroke," Josh explained. "That was my sister Mereth. She's calling everyone to come home."

"No. No, thank you," Peter demurred. "Warm family circles depress me."

"Then don't worry about depression," Josh laughed. "There's nothing about the Warricks that could even remotely be misconstrued as warmth."

He felt a chill from the window and abandoned it, trying to deal with the multiple images that were bombarding his senses.

"*Will* you come with me, Peter? I want you to see where I grew up."

"What's so unique about it?" Peter asked, placing the manuscript lovingly on the low table.

Josh looked down on him, finding him—as always—attractive and marvelously naive, at least on certain subjects.

"There's no possible way I can tell you," he replied simply. "You'll have to come and see for yourself."

"You're being mysterious."

"Everybody loves a mystery."

"What about that?" Peter nodded toward the manuscript.

Again Josh smiled and sat down beside him on the sofa and lifted Peter's hands to his lips and kissed them.

"That," he repeated, nodding toward the manuscript, "is a dream on the verge of becoming reality."

He saw the puzzled look on Peter's face and chose to ignore it and opened his mouth and tasted the flesh of Peter's fingers, drew lightly on the index finger and was pleased to discover that this time he did feel passion. Soon he felt the pressure of Peter's head in his lap and arched up to accommodate him, closed his eyes and thought with a wave of black humor—while thinking was still possible—that if he had tried, he could not have conceived of a more appropriate way in which to mourn Tyburn Warrick.

Warrick

"GOD, BUT I hate queers!" Buckner grumbled.

Mereth quickly closed the door and hoped that Dr. Siad had not heard the callous remark.

"Aren't you being judgmental, Dr. Buckner?" she scolded, feeling ill at ease scolding the man who had scolded her through childhood.

"Judgmental, hell! I can spot 'em a mile off. So can Ty. He'll have a fit if he comes to and sees that queer examining him."

The object of his condemnation was Dr. Bakir Siad, the neurologist who'd just arrived by limousine from the airstrip, his tall, lean, ascetic Indian appearance apparently signaling more than foreignness to Buckner. As far as Mereth could tell, the man had been merely polite, too formal, perhaps resentful that he'd been ordered to disrupt his normal routine for one old man who obviously was meaningless to him. Nonetheless, he'd come.

"Shouldn't you go with him, Dr. Buckner?" Mereth asked, remembering she had yet to call Brit in London.

"Why? The fancy doc don't want me. You saw how he looked at me, like a pile of shit to walk around."

Mereth averted her face and took refuge in a cup of coffee. No wonder Ty was so fond of Horace Buckner. They spoke the same language.

"I don't think that's true," she said. "And whether it's true or not, I want you there. You are my grandfather's oldest friend."

As she looked back from filling her coffee cup she was amazed to see the old man partially undone, leaning against the back of the chair. No tears, please, she begged silently and was grateful when she saw him withdraw a mussed handkerchief, blow his nose noisily and, without a word, leave the room.

She felt a small interior collapse and abandoned the coffee to sit in Ty's chair and think back on her conversation with Josh. He'd sounded much the same. She had detected that subtle condescension with which she'd grown up.

"You just hold things together until I get there tomorrow. Be a good girl."

Three world-class male chauvinists: Ty, Josh and even—to a lesser degree—Brit.

What precise function does the female serve except as a receptacle for the male?

No, don't do that. That kind of recollection she could do without.

Quickly she pushed out of Ty's chair as though the unproductive memories were embedded in the worn velvet. She stretched a moment before the window and gazed down on the working gardeners.

There he was again. She focused on the figure just standing upright, his cowboy hat in his hand, adjusting a sweatband around his forehead. The same one? The hitchhiker from the toll plaza. So what was the mystery: he obviously was an employee.

Suddenly he waved. At her.

She felt heat on her face climbing rapidly up into her hairline, and for one stupid moment she felt an overwhelming compulsion to wave back.

"Miss Warrick?"

The voice came from behind and startled her.

"I'm sorry, Miss Warrick. Didn't go to startle you."

She saw a pleasant, middle-aged face, Mexican, very familiar.

"Ramona, it's so good to see you!" she murmured and opened her arms to the woman and was pleased with the feeling of reciprocal warmth and slightly less pleased with the sound of breaking emotion.

"There, don't," Mereth comforted.

"They said you were here," Ramona said and sniffled and produced a handkerchief from the pocket of her black uniform. "Course our Lord tells us this day is coming for everyone but we don't always believe our Lord, do we?"

Mereth looked puzzled at the strange evangelical tone in Ramona's voice. When had that happened?

Ramona pocketed her handkerchief and held Mereth at arm's length with gentle instructions. "Now stand still. Let me look at you. Let me see if you've walked with Our Lord since you've been gone from Warrick."

There it was again, and Mereth felt self-conscious under the woman's scrutiny, her black eyes narrowed as though passing judgment on everything she saw.

"Ramona, I . . ."

"All right, I know. Well, what I come to find out is how do I cook today? For how many? Will the rest of the family be arriving, and what about Mr. Warrick's friends?"

Stymied, Mereth paced in front of the window. "I'm not sure. The rest of the family won't be here today. Maybe tomorrow. Dr. Buckner's here and the new doctor. And Massie, of course."

"She eats like a bird."

"Do the best you can, Ramona. Please."

Apparently the "please" came out tinged with desperation, and Ramona's ears were as sharp as her eyes.

"You can't shoulder it alone, Mereth," she said and stepped closer, that predatory expression on her face that Mereth had seen in local evangelists since she was a child. "You'd best ask for His power, His grace, and He may overlook your sins and give it to you. But you'll have to make a promise."

"Ramona, I . . . have some telephoning to do."

"That's right, pay no attention. But mark my words, when the night gets black enough you'll come to God."

What had happened to her? It was a wonder Ty hadn't fired her. He used to despise "Jesus bull," as he called it.

"Do you want me to pray with you, Mereth? I'll be happy to pray with you."

"Ramona, not now. I must call the others. I'm sure you understand."

The woman smiled. "Oh, sure, Ramona understands. The trouble is, our Lord and Savior Jesus Christ might not understand and, while Ramona has no power at all, our Lord and Savior has the power to turn trees into writhing serpents and the sun into a ball of fire. So that's the One you don't want to offend, Mereth, you hear? I will pray for you, Mereth, whether you want it or not because your granddaddy would want me to."

Then the door slammed and Mereth was left with a new mystery.

For several moments she stared at the closed door as though feeling the need to keep her eye on it at all times.

Place the call to Brit in London, at least start the process. She'd never get through the first time.

Drawing a deep breath, she lifted the phone from the table and into her lap, found Brit's number in Massie's book—a central London number, she noticed. Unlike Josh, who was capable of intimidating her, she thought with affection of Brit, whom she had adored from the beginning. Dear Brit, the most loving and perhaps the most troubled of them all.

As she dialed the overseas operator, she settled back into Ty's chair and thought of the "deals" that had been consummated here involving millions of dollars.

"Yes, Operator. I want to place a call to London. The number is . . ."

As she read out the numbers she tried to solve two problems simultaneously. What was the time difference and would Brit be asleep or out politicking? And the second problem: why couldn't she find Junior Nagle's phone number here?

"Yes, Operator, I'm here. Will there be a delay?"

The answer was "Yes, approximately two hours."

"Then will you call me back?" Quickly Mereth gave her the terrace room number and extension, thanked her and hung up. Disappointed? A little. She'd been in the mood for Brit.

Then take a break. Thirty minutes, how would it hurt?

She glanced up at the ceiling as though she were capable of seeing through it to the second-floor corridor, to Ty's room where Dr. Siad was conducting his examination.

Suddenly she leaned forward and stared fixedly down at the carpet, worn where Ty's feet had moved back and forth. Indentations and shadows and impressions of the man everywhere.

But at least she was here, had made it this far and was still relatively intact. These were the most difficult moments, when she was alone, when the seams of memory strained to hold back the past. Most of the ghost faces appeared briefly, then darted swiftly away. But one remained constant and was capable of scattering her composure like a flock of scared birds.

The paralyzing fear left her in a state of mind akin to the delirium of fever. The lighted rooms of Warrick held no real threat. And there was absolutely no reason why she should have to return to the old ranch house. That she could not endure, and now she leaned over as though under the weight of new fatigue, new panic.

What if he did die? Who could replace him? What group of men could create a mind, a personality, a force as powerful as Tyburn Warrick's?

She continued to stare down at the carpet and knew the answer to her foolish question even before she thought it. No one could replace him. Which meant one simple and terrifying alternative.

They all were facing a vacuum of awesome proportions and the only valid question remaining was:

Who or what would rush in to fill it?

───────

No answer. For the third time no answer, and quietly Massie put down the receiver and paced the limited area of her sitting room in a familiar pattern, tracing the rectangular moss green border of the oriental carpet which was the exact width of her foot and which in the past she'd walked around as much as five hundred times in an afternoon. It relaxed her to follow this moss green border like some cosmic sobriety test, around and around and around, solving the basically insoluble problems of being a black woman in a white world, of being a black mistress to a white man, of being a rich and well-educated black woman in a landscape of rednecks and too much poverty and too much wealth, of being a black woman who had inherited three white children from a dead woman, of being—

She turned in an aimless circle and glanced back toward the phone as though it were the offender. Where was he, Junior Nagle? His secretary in Dallas had given her one of his Dallas numbers—a familiar one, the Woodleigh Hotel, a luxurious apartment hotel on the fringes of downtown Dallas where the rich, powerful and discreet kept their mistresses.

"God, you're lucky, Ty. You've just got yours bedded down right here under the same roof."

Massie smiled at the remembered envy in Junior's voice. She liked Junior Nagle. She hadn't liked him at first. He'd been the biggest bastard of all when she'd first arrived.

For a moment she stood, transfixed by those early and ugly memories, still amazed that she'd stayed and survived, though on more than one occasion she'd left, vowing never to return.

She thought she heard something and hurried toward her door

and peered down the corridor in the direction of Ty's suite. What was taking the doctor so long?

She looked again down toward Ty's suite, the entire distance of the long corridor, his at one end, hers at the opposite, the original living arrangement which had never been altered, though he'd asked her several times to explain the logic behind such an arrangement when every night he was either in her bed or she in his.

Slowly she closed the door and leaned her forehead against it. *Ty, please don't die!*

The thought, not quite a prayer, was more than a thought. "Why do I love you so?" she whispered, and in her deep grief realized that after thirty years she still couldn't answer that question.

Without warning she remembered Valentine's Day about two months ago. They'd taken the horses out at noon and it had started to rain and they'd made for the ranch house, empty now. The rain had ceased and the clouds were parting. It was chill and damp, especially in their wet clothes. As they had explored the high-ceilinged rooms, she'd spotted a red envelope propped askew on one of the mantles.

"*Ty, what's this?*"

"*Open it.*"

"*How did—*"

"*Open it.*"

And she'd opened it to find a lovely old-fashioned sentimental dime store valentine complete with white lace and the simple declarative statement, "I love you, Ty," written on the bottom of the card.

Later she'd learned from Eddie that Ty had made a special trip into Tulsa the day before, just to buy the card. He'd picked it out, had placed it in the ranch house on that morning so that it would be waiting for her to find.

They had sat on the front porch and watched the purplish blue clouds, flushed red by sunset and scudding before the wind. The drooping branches of the giant elms had dripped bright raindrops upon the steps.

Tears made her eyes sting.

The phone rang on the desk. She looked up and knew who it was —Junior Nagle—and hurried to answer it. Enough thinking. As Ty says, it never does anything but get a man into deep trouble.

"The intellect should follow faith, Massie, never precede it and never disrupt it."

Dallas

ALMA, Junior Nagle's secretary for twenty-three years, thrust the telephone number at him the minute he came into the office. Though he was out of breath from the short walk, he knew that it meant trouble.

"Are you all right, Mr. Nagle?" Alma asked.

"Hell, no, I'm not all right," he mumbled and turned away in an effort to conceal the shortness of breath and thought, what the hell, he wasn't doing so bad for seventy-eight. Just spent a pretty active night in the sack with Inez—though it took him longer now than it used to.

"When did she call? Massie, I mean," he demanded of Alma.

"She called the hotel about . . . oh, twenty minutes ago. You'd just left. They sent the call on here."

"Get her on the line right away. I'll be in the office."

"Yes, sir."

Breath restored, he tested the system with one deep inhalation and felt only a nagging ache in his chest. Good. Nothing wrong with him. A quick glance in the gilt-framed oval mirror outside his office confirmed it. A bit bald, of course, but what the hell? And overweight, but he could work it off at the club.

He closed the door and surveyed his office with a curious sense of discovery, as though he was seeing it for the first time. One hell of an improvement over the corrugated metal shack that he and Ty had used on the first Warrick field years ago.

Even though a fag decorator had done this office, Junior still liked it—smoky grays and silvers and lots of glass and metal. The west wall was covered with panels of gray glass, a good background for the bar—one of the best damned bars in Dallas—three glittering pyramids of crystal highball glasses fronting the smoky glass, which always reminded Junior of the windshield of the old Jeep he and Ty had used to go quail hunting on cold November mornings at Warrick.

One drink. How could it hurt? Junior stared for a moment like a small boy trying his damnedest to resist temptation. The scotch decanter was filled to the brim. Alma was efficient.

He considered checking his watch but decided to hell with the time, snagged a glass from the pyramid, filled it with a generous shot of scotch, eyed it, then tipped the decanter again until the glass was over half full. He lifted it, took two swallows.

What was Massie calling him for this early in the morning, and why was she calling him at all? He was going up to Warrick this weekend. He had some drilling figures to show Ty, and he wanted to deliver a message personally on the new geology of the Warrick Basin.

Junior emptied his glass in one satisfying swallow and leaned heavily on the bar.

The Warrick Basin.

God, the potential was there! They both had known it since the early seventies when, despite all the naysayers and the growing line of creditors and creditors' liens, they had brought in the No. 1 Mary Beth. The well became the deepest in the world when completed, at 26,437 feet to be exact, and Junior loved to be exact.

Two years later in seventy-three, using the Warrick Drilling Company, they brought in the No. 1 Blue, setting a new world record at 31,440 feet. Then in seventy-five Warrick Drilling drilled the No. 1 Massie to 32,345 and with it Warrick Drilling had recovered methane, ethane H-25 and sulfur, proving for the first time porosity, permeability and reservoir capability, meaning that the basin might be every bit as good as it looked.

Eyes glazed with the activity of his mind, Junior grasped the empty highball glass with undue strength as though it were his support. God, but he and Ty had dreamt big on the basin! And Ty knew his history. He had that kind of mind, could look at the mistakes of others, study them and avoid them or learn from them.

"This ain't gonna be no Spindletop, Junior."

He'd said it repeatedly, shouted it, whispered it like they were lovers' words he was whispering to a woman. No Spindletop, the Beaumont boom of the 1890s.

"The cow was milked too hard, don't you see, and moreover she was not milked intelligently. If we treat her good, she's gonna treat us good."

Junior smiled recalling this "conversation," one of their favorites. And they had favorite conversations, kind of like private theatricals where they would agree without words that now for a while they were going to talk about land values, or the past, or the time they brought in their first gusher, or the time Ty hid Mary Beth in the ranch house so that her dad couldn't find her, or—and this of late had been their favorite "conversation"—the Warrick Basin.

"What's your estimate, your conservative estimate on the reservoir, Ty?"

"Oh, you know, Junior."

"I know, but say it out loud."

"One hundred and forty trillion cubic feet of natural gas, give or take . . ."

He always added "give or take."

As if the recall were draining him, Junior climbed stiffly up onto the bar stool. He lifted his head and looked beyond the drapes to the Dallas skyline. Growing, ever growing, as many cranes visible as buildings, something pulsing in the city, something tangible and aggressive, ambitious, optimistic, capitalistic and good, lots of jobs, decent livings on all levels, people thinking about the future without knowing they're thinking about the future, just assuming it's going to be there and it's going to be good, better than the past.

God, but Junior loved this country, loved Dallas which had always struck him as being the best of this country, the very best the old U.S. of A. had to offer, where a man could reach for the sky and, with just a little effort, grasp it. It was, of course, where oilmen had to be—at least part of the time. But he liked the wide open country of Warrick as well.

"Hell, you know what we're sitting on, Junior? It's going to pay off like none of the Warrick fields ever paid off before because, one, we know it's there and, two, we know it can be produced economically and, three, it's the best market in the world because of the pipelines already in place."

"How much, Ty? What are we talking about, just in round figures?"

"Seventy-five billion dollars."

Junior spoke the figure aloud, his eyes still fixed on the spectacular Dallas skyline. When they'd do their "Warrick Basin conversation" they'd always conclude with:

"We're talking seventy-five billion dollars, Junior. I said billion with a 'b,' as in son of a bitch."

Suddenly the phone rang on his desk and he jumped a foot, damned near lost his balance on the bar stool. It rang again while he was waiting for the thumps inside his chest to settle down. He limped his way over to his desk, never taking his eyes off the ringing telephone.

Why would Massie call him this early in the morning, particularly at the hotel? She knew what went on at the hotel.

Third ring. You gotta pick up the goddamned thing, you know. Then he did and demanded gruffly, "What?"

"Miss Jo Massie from Warrick, sir. You asked me to . . ."

"Well, put her through. What are you waiting for?"

He lifted the phone and slid up on the desk and allowed his feet to swing in midair.

"Hello, Junior? Junior, are you there?"

It was Jo Massie.

"What are you doing up and about so early, Massie? Ty needs his beauty sleep, don't you know?"

There was a pause. He eyed the empty highball glass and wished he'd taken time to refill it.

"It's . . . about Ty, Junior."

"What's the bastard gone and done now? I told the old . . ."

"He's had a stroke."

There was a solitary man in a bucket hanging from one of the high cranes outside his office window. He wore a red bandana around his head and clung to the sides of the bucket.

"Junior, did you . . . ?"

"Who's with him?"

"Dr. Buckner . . ."

"Shit!"

". . . and a Dr. Siad. O'Rourke sent him out from St. Mark's. They're both with him now."

"I'm coming, Massie. Leaving immediately. You all right?"

Another pause. "I've been better."

"Well, get on down to the kitchen and whip me up some of your jalapeño salsa. I want it waiting for me when I get there."

"Hurry, Junior."

The connection was broken and he was left holding a dead receiver. What had he said? What goddamned nonsense was that about salsa? Why had he said that? Give her something to do.

Get organized.

Quickly he pushed the button on the intercom. "Alma, call Love. Get Tony out of bed. Have my plane ready in one hour."

"Sir?"

"You heard me. I have to go to Warrick."

"You have two board meetings this . . ."

"Fuck the board meetings! Just do as I say."

He slammed down the receiver and stood up too suddenly and felt shooting pains in both legs. The pain seemed to calm him, and for that he was grateful.

Everything was going to be all right. He'd stake his life on it. Ty wasn't going to die. He wouldn't dare. God, but they'd had themselves some times in this world.

Those trips to Mexico during the sixties. "Going native," Ty called it.

"You can't be grown-up all the time, Junior. Come on, let's go find us some tequila, some high green mountains and dark Mexican ladies—"

And that was about the order in which the treats had come. They'd picked up a Jeep in one of the border towns, no luggage, no need for a change of clothes. Junior remembered wearing the same khakis for three weeks. They'd always grown beards, and they'd driven miles over high mountain back roads to avoid all of the well-known watering holes. If you could pronounce it and knew where it was on the map, forget it.

Consequently they'd found some hells for themselves as well as some heavens. In one small village, Ty had taken a real fancy to the female population—thirteen in all, not counting the ones too old or too young or too married. And they'd stayed a week and Ty had screwed them all, then left enough pesos for the men to dig a new water well, which they sorely needed.

"Drilling's my business, Junior." He'd grinned as they'd gunned out of the village in the dusty, road-weary Jeep.

In an unnatural calm Junior walked slowly back to the bar, stopped a few feet from it and stared at the glittering surface of mirrored smoky glass. Nothing was moving, inside or outside. It was like someone had cut off all the power of his mind. Maybe if he could get there in time, he could talk Ty out of doing something stupid, like dying.

Suddenly the energy started down deep in his legs, a building crescendo of agonizing grief. He could feel it like a torrent raging unchecked, rushing up through his groin, the pit of his stomach, still coming, a tidal wave, until it reached his shoulder where, without warning, he drew back the hand that held the empty highball glass and hurled it with murderous strength at the gray mirrors and the glittering pyramids of stacked glasses.

The resulting crash was like a resounding explosion as each breakable object fell onto other breakable objects, a cascading shower of mirror and glass, which he watched with boy-like fascination, amazed that he was the cause of such effective destruction.

When it was over he lifted his head straight up and let tears come and whispered two words and somehow knew that this would be the extent of his grieving, that quite possibly it was all he could afford.

"Ah, Ty!" was what he wept to the ceiling and did his best to deny any comprehension of life or death.

Warrick

SUCCUMBING to a blend of frustration and fatigue, Mereth slammed down the receiver and thought irrationally, "It's a conspiracy!" Though she'd reached Josh effortlessly on the first try, Brit was proving more elusive. The transatlantic operator had informed her there was no response at the London number.

She stood indecisively before Ty's chair, staring down on the gardens, free of gardeners now. A quick glance at her watch told her why. Eleven-thirty, lunchtime.

Fresh air would be nice. She should call Hal. He would be concerned. Later— She looked about the empty room as if to see if there was anyone present with new demands on her. No one, though at that moment there was a soft knock and a young girl appeared, politely asking if they could set up the luncheon buffet here.

"Of course." Mereth smiled and quickly vacated the room and walked with false purpose down the corridor which led to the entrance hall.

Once there she dropped the pose and pushed open the front

door and felt the warmth of the day on her face and walked to the top of the gardens.

Her hands laced behind her back, she sauntered down the path which she knew by heart, having raced up and down it as a child.

Suddenly she felt something brush against her leg and glanced down to see an enormous gray cat, clearly a tom. Quite dusty as though he'd just had a morning "bath" in one of the turned flower-beds.

"Hello," she murmured and bent to pet him. The kitchen cat, no doubt. They always turned up, stayed for a while, got fat and left again.

"You know what Mr. Warrick calls him?"

She looked up at the near voice, and grew startled when she couldn't find a face and a body to go with it. Then she saw two blue-jeaned legs, well-worn cowboy boots, the rest of him obscured behind the lilac bushes, burgeoning with buds.

"No, I don't . . ."

"Gary Cooper. That's what Mr. Warrick calls him."

For a moment she was torn between focusing on the gray cat, who continued to rub against her leg, and the disembodied voice speaking to her from behind the lilac bushes.

"I'm . . . afraid . . ."

"Aren't we all? Of one thing or another."

"I can't see you."

Suddenly, comically, the lilac bushes parted and a face appeared, the face she'd seen several times before. He was grinning.

"Our karmas must be hopelessly entangled," he said.

"I didn't know you were coming here."

"I always come here."

"How did you . . . ?"

"Emanuel was supposed to have picked me up. He was late."

He pushed his cowboy hat farther back on his head, revealing smudges of dirt and perspiration on his forehead.

The cat at her feet was growing more aggressive, rolling over on

85

his back on the warm flagstones, kittenish despite his size, and cuffing at the hem of her slacks.

"He wants you to pick him up," the man said from the bushes. "Mr. Warrick used to sit down there in the gazebo and hold him for hours and tell him of his oil deals."

"What are you doing in there?"

"Having lunch." He grinned and held up a sandwich and a Coors. "I'd ask you to join me but . . ."

"No, thanks."

"No, I thought not."

For some reason she felt embarrassed and stepped around the cat and walked on down the flagstones for a few steps.

"You're Mereth," he called out.

She looked back and started to reply, then changed her mind, increased her pace and crossed over the second bridge. As she reached the middle level of the gardens, she glanced back up to see if he'd emerged from the bushes.

Nothing. Even the cat was gone as though, given a choice between her company and his, he'd chosen the latter. Forget it. She had other things to do.

Brit. She vowed to place the transatlantic call again after she'd inspected the gazebo, that white and serene vision at the bottom of the gardens, sitting like a jewel on a flawless expanse of green lawn. She'd always considered the gazebo to be special, the magic place where they celebrated birthday parties, where clowns and jugglers performed, where mountains of presents were always stacked. Mereth probably had shared some of the most important secrets of her life with the white gingerbread of the gazebo. She'd certainly shed enough tears there. Some of the memories were safe, others not so safe.

She increased her speed and crisscrossed another rose rock bridge. As though to make certain she was still alone, she glanced over her shoulder and saw—nothing.

A gardener? He looked more like a roughneck. Mereth knew the breed. She used to ride with Ty in the Jeep over to the Warrick fields where the new rigs were drilling, the road lined with mud-encrusted Chevy pickup trucks, license plates from Michigan, Texas, Ohio, Indiana, men coming from all over for the thirteen-dollar-an-hour jobs.

Mereth stopped at the edge of the green lawn which led to the gazebo. She could smell it. Oil. An unmistakable odor, slightly acrid, slightly earth-smelling, wholly pleasing.

She mustn't stay too long in the gazebo. The doctors might be finished, and Massie would need her. Still, a few moments wouldn't hurt.

Thus resolved, she picked her way carefully across the damp grass, her eyes now fixed on the small structure itself, as lovely and as pristine as she'd remembered it from childhood.

On the first step she stopped, running head-on into a safe memory of one of her birthday parties—her eleventh or twelfth; Mereth couldn't be certain—surely the most beautiful party she'd ever seen, baskets of pink roses lining these steps while in the gazebo itself stood an enormous five-tiered pink birthday cake on a pedestal. Massie had hired a calliope out of Dallas and clowns and puppets, and there must have been a hundred kids playing in the gardens and Ty was right in the middle of it, wearing his ten-gallon white Stetson that he was so proud of, the one that Laurel and Hardy had autographed for him. Later Ty had stood on this step—right where Mereth was standing—and every time a child had come near, he'd pulled a silver dollar out of his pocket and pretended like he'd found it on top of the child's head. Everyone went home with at least one silver dollar that day.

Slowly the sounds of the calliope faded, along with the shouts of excited children, and the air no longer smelled of hotdogs and chili, just a good oil smell on a quiet April day in the empty gazebo.

At that moment she heard voices approaching and looked out over the edge of the gazebo to see the gardeners returning from lunch. Mexicans—all of them, as far as she could tell—toothpicks dancing out of the corners of their mouths.

All right, where was he, the other? The one who didn't match. Then there he was, bringing up the rear.

And there was Emanuel. She recognized him in the lead, short, squat and probably the largest conduit for Mexican aliens in the Southwest.

"Good morning, Emanuel. Your gardens are as beautiful as ever."

At the sound of her voice she saw the man look up, a hint of accusation in his expression.

"I'm Mereth," she smiled, starting down the steps. "Mereth Warrick. You used to scold me for picking your loveliest flowers."

"Miss Warrick! How good . . . how nice you look, how grown up!"

She felt embarrassed as all six men—seven counting the tall one bringing up the rear—now focused on her, toothpicks stilled.

"I have to get back now, Emanuel. Good to see you."

"How is he?" the old man asked. He made a quick sign of the cross. "You know, just last week I thought, 'Death will be here soon.' I thought it all day. I could not *not* think it."

Mereth sensed deep consternation. "Don't, Emanuel. Luckily we can't make death happen by thinking about it. Besides, my grandfather isn't dead."

"Will you let us know, Miss Warrick?"

"Of course I will."

"And we *can* make death happen. You're wrong. But maybe Mr. Warrick stronger than Emanuel's thoughts. I hope so. I pray so."

"I'm sure he is," Mereth said, feeling not at all uncomfortable to be speaking in such an irrational way. Funny, she'd felt terribly uncomfortable with Ramona's irrational fundamentalism. Why not Emanuel's?

As she walked past the men, she was aware of them drawing back in an act of deference which she disliked. The deference was short-lived, for the odd man out, the tanned face with the unkempt hair and equally unkempt eyes stood his ground on the path. Suddenly there seemed not to be enough room.

"Excuse me," she murmured.

"Did you enjoy the gazebo?"

"Yes, thank you."

"Where's the cat?"

"Asleep somewhere, I suppose."

"Smart creature."

As she adjusted to the climb, she adjusted as well to the certainty that she was being watched.

Near the top of the gardens, breathless from the speed with which she'd covered the last steep rise, she felt herself back on track.

Call Brit.

Renewed with purpose, she pulled open the heavy door and saw a grim company consisting of Dr. Siad, who stood ramrod straight near the far wall, his eyes pinning her instantly.

Hovering over the buffet table was Horace Buckner, fork raised in midair, his plate heaped. But most alarming of all was Massie. She must have watched Mereth the full length of the gardens. From where Mereth stood she saw a handkerchief in Massie's hand, saw it pressed tightly against her lips.

Standing behind the buffet were two young women in black uniforms with white aprons. Mereth had never seen them before. Sitting on the love seat was a thin, middle-aged woman in a nurse's uniform.

At the moment Mereth pushed open the door, all the faces looked up at her save one.

Had death come while she was revisiting the gazebo, remembering pink roses and calliopes and silver dollars?

Then, even though she knew that if there had been a shipwreck, the castaways must have courage and each try to save themselves, she spoke the name of the one person who had seen her through most of the nightmares of her life, and who had not looked up: "Massie?"

Massie followed Mereth's progress all the way up the path, thinking how beautiful she had become, how remarkably intact considering the scar tissue, most of which she'd successfully concealed behind a serene personality and a character as strong, in some ways stronger, than Ty's. Oh, now and then it showed, a hardness, something in her eyes which looked cold and part dead.

It was an ancient mystery and doubly tragic because it was still unsolved. Massie would never forget the morning she'd found Mereth in the gazebo, sobbing. Repeatedly Massie had tried to pull her wet hands from her face and question her and comfort her. But Mereth had continued to cry, trembling, as though something had beaten her to ground.

Finally she'd fled the gardens and locked herself in her rooms and that night she'd left Warrick, without a word, and it had been seven months before Massie had even heard from her.

Ty had been of no help, for that very same day he'd taken the plane to Dallas and had not returned until week's end and for too many days only a sorrowing silence and a sense of death had filled Warrick.

Now, as she heard her name being called, she answered, "Here, Mereth." When she turned toward the young woman, she saw nothing serene or hard. Where had that child come from? It was Mereth, age seven, terrified.

"It's all right, Mereth," Massie soothed. "Dr. Siad confirmed a cerebral hemorrhage, does not know at this time how serious it is, advises we leave Ty where he is for a while and watch, and Dr. Buckner concurs. This is Miss Kent."

She gestured back toward the nurse, whose face seemed to be tightly laced into a permanent vacancy.

Mereth murmured, "I . . . don't understand." Her words were aimed at all three medical professionals. "Surely something more definite is possible. I have phone calls to make. Questions will be asked. I don't know what to tell them."

Dr. Buckner placed his heaped platter on the buffet table.

"We've done everything we can do, Mereth," he said. "Now why don't you come have a little bite of lunch with me?"

Mereth pulled angrily away from Buckner's hand and headed directly toward Dr. Siad, who seemed to be in the room and yet not in it. A Far Eastern trick of consciousness, no doubt.

Now, as he saw Mereth heading his way, Siad lifted his head from private meditation and appeared to straighten to meet the onslaught head-on.

In truth there was no onslaught. Mereth—more than any of the grandchildren—had Ty's impetus, his vast capacity, indeed his need for honesty and his almost dictatorial insistence on it. But whereas in better days, when Ty was in his prime, Massie had literally seen him beat a man senseless for telling less than the truth, certain influences had tempered Mereth and she stopped short of Dr. Siad and bowed her head and from this position of classic female subservience asked:

"Surely, Dr. Siad, you can tell me more. We must know more."

"I wish I could, Miss Warrick," he said, his voice as cold as January, his gaunt face reflecting nothing that remotely could be called compassion.

"I . . . don't understand," Mereth confessed.

"If Mr. Warrick could be moved to hospital," Dr. Siad added, "the scan could tell us what we need to know."

"Then move him."

"No, I don't think that would be wise. Not now. Not yet. His system is behaving with a degree of irritability. We must be patient and wait and see."

The silence in the room was as taut as though everyone was trying to adjust to this chill god, who in a way had passed judgment on them all.

Massie looked out of the window, recalling her recent conversation with Junior Nagle. On his way. Hurry, Junior! Ty wouldn't open his eyes for this cold Easterner, but he might for one of his beloved cronies.

Deeter Big Cow. My God, yes.

She must call Deeter, the old Osage, Ty's adored friend. The two were still like the boys they'd been growing up together.

"May I see my grandfather, Dr. Siad?" This voice was the old Mereth, strong, aggressive, but controlled.

It was Massie's question, the same one she'd asked repeatedly since the doctor had first come down from Ty's room. Now she listened to see if the answer would be the same.

"No. He's resting as comfortably as possible, Miss Warrick, which is precisely what his system requires. In twenty-four hours I'll be able to assess the damage and make the decision whether or not to move him."

Mereth glanced up at the man as though searching hard for something to rail against. Help came from an unexpected source— the prim Miss Kent, who suddenly stood, straightening the belt of her white uniform and talking quietly to no one in particular.

"I think what Dr. Siad means is that we mustn't disturb Mr. Warrick at this time. So I'll get right up to my patient, and when he . . . wakes up and looks as if he wants to talk, I'll certainly call you." With one glance she took in both Mereth and Massie.

Massie was grateful. All she could think of now was what was she to do with the stern Dr. Siad? Would he be staying on? Would he require a plane back to Tulsa? Eddie was waiting with the limo at the garage.

"Dr. Siad, will you be returning to Tulsa or shall I . . . ?"

"Yes, of course," the man replied, somewhat snappishly. "I do have other patients."

"I'll call for the car," she announced with matching curtness. Massie lifted the receiver, punched Eddie's extension and heard the phone answered with the first ring.

"Car, Eddie. Airstrip," she said, lacking the energy to form a complete sentence.

"Any change?" The voice was husky, in need of an answer.

"None."

"I'll be right there." The line went dead.

"The car is on its way, Dr. Siad."

Horace Buckner, Massie noticed, had gone back to the buffet, concentrating on Ramona's various treats. Leave him alone. He would stay because he belonged. This slim, cold pencil of a man did not.

Momentarily stunned by her own bigotry, she foundered. Then, as though to apologize for her thoughts, she offered to walk with him to the door.

"We . . . thank you for coming, Dr. Siad," she murmured.

"Mr. Warrick is paying the price for a life of self-indulgence and greed."

"I . . . beg your . . ."

"God was generous with Mr. Warrick. If he'd only practiced a degree of self-discipline, he could be in the middle of his life now instead of at the end of it."

Massie tried to avert her eyes from the pious face before her.

"The . . . end of his life?"

"I said so, didn't I?" Dr. Siad pronounced, and all that Massie wanted was the smugness in the face before her removed.

She would have to leave him. She couldn't stay another moment in his presence. God help his patients! He should never be allowed to come within a country mile of a truly ill person. Now the thought that those fastidious fingers had probed Ty's once magnificent physique outraged her, and she was on the verge of walking away when she heard Eddie guiding the black limousine through the arches which led to the portico.

Massie greeted him wordlessly and watched as he stepped out and opened the rear door for Dr. Siad. Just as Eddie was on the verge of pulling away, Massie bent close to the driver's window.

"Check with the office at the airstrip. See if Junior Nagle has filed an ETA. He's due sometime today."

As the limousine left, Massie took a final look at the erect head of the man just visible in the rear oval window. She closed her eyes and for one brutal instant forgot everything and found herself thinking that Ty was waiting luncheon for her and she mustn't keep him waiting.

93

"Massie, do you ever get lonely?"

"Occasionally, Ty. Why?"

"I don't know. Sometimes the quiet hurts your ears, don't it? I remember the grandkids used to use the halls like they was racetracks, yellin', you never heard such yellin'— Liked to drive me crazy—"

"They're grown up now, Ty, and—"

"—and gone. Good riddance. Is Reverend Jobe coming out tonight? Jobe's always good for some noise—"

For a moment she had absolutely no choice but to sit on the top step in the cool shade and hug her knees and rest her forehead and try with all the discipline at her command to make her mind a safe, uninhabitable blank.

"Ty, stay. Please!" she whispered and pressed the palms of her hands hard against her burning eyes as though to plug the holes in the dike before the dam broke.

Notting Hill, London

April 11, 1984

THE STREET FESTIVAL was in full swing. Two reggae bands beat out their simple rhythmic repetition from the flatbeds of trucks at opposite ends of the block. The sounds met midstreet in a friendly collision and somehow blended. The street itself was jammed, all held joyous prisoners by the colliding music. There were Jamaicans, West Indians, Pakistanis, smoky-colored sons and daughters of the Empire, not quite at home here but making an effort, patinas of sweat highlighting their bronze beauty.

Brit stood to one side with Sophie in his customary observer's stance, moving in gentle rhythm with the music, trying to take in that sea of unrepressed, exultant, free faces. Somehow it helped to soften the major disappointment of the morning. The lesson here seemed to be: never set dreams so high they cannot be accomplished.

Sophie kept inching forward as though drawn to the sights and sounds.

"Brit, look!" She pointed across the way to where an old woman was leading a group of kids in a dance, a highly erotic dance, her hips moving in sensuous rhythm with the music, the others laughing and urging her on as though she were a beauty of twenty. Ageless—

Behind him he heard a disturbance and turned to see a young woman sitting on the high stone steps of the disreputable tenement, no more than twenty-five, her black eyes dancing with the music and beat of the street, though in her arms she cradled a child about three. Quite fretful he was, as though feverish.

Sophie noticed and smiled knowingly. "The sacrifices of motherhood," she mourned. Then she turned to the more pleasurable direction of the street and once again urged, "Look!"

She had redirected Brit's attention to a small bonfire across the way. An ineffective light now, lost in early evening sun, but when night fell the bonfire would undoubtedly grow and become a beacon.

"Come on, Brit. What do you want to do? Just watch? Come on, let's . . ."

He laughed. "Let me watch for a minute," he begged. The witness could see it all while the participant could only savor one small sensation at a time. And Brit had been an observer all his life, though seldom had he seen anything so free and fine and unfettered. In that respect these Notting Hill street festivals were unique, an amalgamation of second-class citizens, socially and economically deprived, all laughing and celebrating life with the abandon of a chosen elite.

Beginning to relax, Brit leaned back against the stone columns, hands in pockets. Behind him he heard the child fretting, without looking heard the young mother's soothing tone. Lucky child. To have such a mother.

"Are you all right?"

He nodded and put his arm around Sophie and drew her close and knew he loved her.

The spicy smell of curry wafted over them, as insistent as the reggae beat itself, and he saw a two-wheeled cart, the vendor pushing his wares through the crowds, sometimes surrounded, the next minute alone. There were other odors as seductive: the heavy smell of Turkish honey blending with garlic everywhere, spun Jamaican sugar, the unique and inviting sharpness of good hash and chickens roasting. Encompassing them all and in a way conquering them was the ubiquitous and greasy pungence of fish and chips.

Brit closed his eyes to give his olfactory senses pleasant supremacy. Even with his eyes closed he still could see the packed street, humanity displaced, lost, the beat of the music sustaining them, a mixed people celebrating life with perhaps little reason to celebrate but celebrating anyway, because it was the natural thing to do.

So different from Warrick and that pudgy, overfed, spoiled rotten and sullen little kid who—

Behind him the child cried out, then was instantly quiet. Such a contrast warranted a look, and he saw the woman's bared breast, the child suckling, his eyes closed, his left hand a tight fist upon her breast. Brit doubted if there was still much milk, suspected that it was simply a soothing sensation. He continued to stare for a few minutes, aware of what he was doing but finding the tableau compellingly beautiful.

At the same time the reggae band reached the end of the music and the musicians relaxed.

For the first time Brit noticed something he'd not seen before. Arranged at intervals about the flatbed of the truck he saw half a dozen or so bobbies, unarmed, looking nervous and out of place in their heavy blue uniforms. They appeared to be trying to see everything at once, an impossible task considering the mobs of pushing, dancing people confined within the limited area.

If there was trouble—

But Brit canceled the thought. Why trouble? The recent strain of racism seemed to have exhausted itself—as irrationality and incoherence frequently do—dying from its own excessive passion more than anything else. Most Britons at least were able now to live and let live. There were other, more pressing problems for the average Englishman. Of far greater danger than these people who inhabited the slums of London were the white-robed Arab sheikhs who were buying London itself. Still-radical organizations—like the National Front—now seemed merely quaint, a trifle embarrassing, like a bad photograph—

That's the way we looked once, but we weren't at our best—

So there would be no trouble, and the unarmed bobbies were merely a token show of British law and order amid all this happily unharnessed life, designed to reassure everyone that the umbrella of British justice was broad enough to cover all.

Again the sound of the fretful child. Brit saw an older woman pass a brown bottle of something up to the young mother.

To his surprise, he felt a degree of peace after the difficult morning and felt content to let the sights and sounds wash over him like a cleansing wave, washing free all the clinging and repressive things from his childhood. For some reason he felt compelled to take childhood memories with him everywhere, like a penance, either trying to understand them or to shake them off.

Tyburn Warrick.

The name swept through his mind unexpectedly like a sudden wind, forceful, disruptive, destroying all semblance of order. Brit had tried to please the man, he really had. But such differences of character and perception could not be bridged.

Not that those distant days were all bad. There was Massie, beloved Massie, and funny Josh, and best of all, that small source of warmth and joy and life that had sustained them all, little Mereth. It was Mereth who had kept Warrick from becoming a hell.

Warrick—

—was supposed to have been a paradise of plenty. This raucous and undisciplined London street scene was supposed to be hell. Why was he having trouble separating the two?

"Brit, look!"

The soft command came from Sophie, who pulled ahead in her eagerness and pointed toward the opposite side of the street where a contingent had newly arrived, a dozen or so of mixed ages, mixed sexes, and all cut from a very different cloth than the rest of the crowd. These few were not skanking or moving or dancing in any way, no movement at all.

There was something about them that Brit recognized. He'd seen those same taut, puritanical expressions at political rallies near the university, seen them demonstrating outside certain theaters and art galleries where artistic visions were being expressed that they did not understand and so felt threatened. The National Front? Perhaps, though what did it matter? Their capacity to inflict sorrow and grief was monumental, the witch-hunts, Mencken's words:

"... the puritan who lives in fear that someone somewhere may be happy ..."

"Do you suppose they're lost?" Sophie joked, sensing with her finely honed instincts the possibility of trouble.

They weren't lost. Brit knew that, as did Sophie. They had found a target, had moved on it with unerring instinct, finding displeasure in pleasure, hate in love, finding in the colorful anarchy of this Notting Hill street everything that was most repugnant to them.

For several long minutes the grim little group simply stood on the opposite pavement, a negative presence, as though waiting for someone to recognize them. If the bobbies encircling the flatbed of the truck even saw them, they gave no indication.

As the colors and lights and sounds swirled around them, as both reggae groups launched themselves into new music, the group across the way seemed literally to be absorbed into the heart of the festival itself.

Brit felt Sophie's hand relax inside his. Perhaps they were just sightseers, though for a few minutes more Brit felt compelled to keep them in sight until they were devoured by the crowds.

Enough observing. Sophie was pulling on his hand, the reggae rhythm was more insistent than ever, the beat hypnotic, both combined into an intoxicant such as Brit had never known before, one great inarticulate hymn of thanksgiving to life.

Then Sophie darted pell-mell into the street. Laughing openly at himself, and at everyone caught in this colorful web of a world, Brit threw up his hands and launched into a spirited and loving chase, half-dance, half-pursuit.

As he did so, he heard something not of the reggae beat, a sharp sound, followed immediately by a single scream. He heard the noise again, isolated though now less foreign, the clear report of a gun, then several guns firing simultaneously, new screams, others beginning to realize something was wrong and scattering for protection from whatever they couldn't see or identify.

"Sophie!"

He cried out her name and tried to see where the gunfire was coming from and tried at the same time to protect himself against the rising panic of the street, the music still playing as though the musicians, lost in their own beat, were impervious to the new mood and movements of the crowd, joy now being replaced by fear.

As Brit turned frantically and pushed back to the sidewalk he saw a curious absence around the flatbed of the truck: the bobbies were gone. Those passive guards had disappeared from the scene, leaving only the still sporadic crackling of gunfire. Concealed snipers obviously, for he could see nothing.

"Sophie!"

As he shouted her name a second time, he scrambled back to the curb and from this limited elevation was about to call again when someone fallen caught his eye, the young mother whom he'd seen nursing her child.

Now she lay sprawled at the bottom of the tenement steps, a single bullet hole spreading red across the left side of her still-bared breast, while beneath her the child lay, caught by the press of her body, shrieking.

Brit closed his eyes, hoping the nightmare would vanish. But as additional gunfire peppered the crowd, he crawled on his knees to the woman's side and grasped her face and felt her neck in search of a pulse.

At his touch, her head turned toward him. Her eyes were closed, blood already seeping in a limited stream from her mouth. Though her breathing was labored, she opened her eyes.

"Take . . . him . . ."

"What is your—"

Brit wasn't certain what he was going to ask her. It made no difference. Still crouched on his knees, he looked over his shoulder at the street, emptied except for half a dozen bodies, all of whom bore a resemblance to the dead woman beside him, all sprawled at distorted angles. The living pressed into every available alcove of safety, and still the gunfire came like staccato fireworks. The music had stopped, leaving a second of silence that was instantly filled with new cries.

"Sophie . . ."

As he pulled the little boy out from beneath the dead mother, he shouted her name again. For one incoherent moment he perceived an image of dead quail lined up on the long racks behind the garages of Warrick after one of Ty's massive hunts, hundreds of small birds, neatly arranged, with shattered wings and glassy eyes.

"Brit, are you . . . ?"

The voice was familiar and frightened. Sophie dropped to her knees at his side like an answered prayer.

"Are you . . . ?"

"Yes. What . . . ?"

"Come on."

Brit grabbed her hand and took a final look at the sobbing child. Surely the dead woman hadn't meant what she had said. There might be relatives close by, those who would—

"Take . . . him . . ."

Brit looked down at the child. "Come on," he ordered again and this time scooped up the child and felt the little boy's feverish forehead rest bonelessly against the side of his face and heard the nightmare sounds of new gunfire coming from behind, new screams, new death, new fear.

He heard Sophie keeping pace behind him, sensed her need for questions and was grateful that she refrained from asking them. He looked back once.

"Are you . . . ?"

"I'm all right."

"Let's go . . ."

"Run . . ."

"I have the child."

"This way. I know a shortcut."

He let Sophie take the lead and clasped the child closer, felt him go strangely limp in his arms and heard the fearful street's sounds diminish behind them as they cut down alleys and through empty buildings, all the while moving farther and farther away from the death, though as he ran Brit tried repeatedly to rid himself of that foolish and macabre image of men armed with expensive and high-powered shotguns standing triumphantly, arrogantly over long rows of small, dead brown birds, none larger than the hands that had killed them.

Bloomsbury, London

BRIT HELD the nameless child in one arm and with his free hand dipped the cloth into the bowl of cool water and carefully reapplied it to the boy's forehead. If he could break the fever here and keep him out of hospital, it would be better. For the child, at any rate.

Children had a way of getting lost in the endless red tape that was British Socialism.

Now he heard the late night cacophony of a London emergency vehicle, that awful, discordant, two-tonal alarm designed to raise the dead if not bury them. At that same instant he thought of Warrick and saw his rooms hidden away near the top of the house, isolated as one would isolate a contagion.

The child whimpered. No more than three. Though they'd left the Notting Hill riots far behind, Brit could still hear gunfire, could see the dying woman.

Sophie leaned close, her good, plain English face a patterned web of concern. "Let me take him, Brit," she said, her hands outstretched.

"In a minute," he whispered and continued to rock the sick child. He still couldn't believe it.

"A cup of tea?" Sophie whispered, and without waiting for an answer she disappeared into the small kitchen.

As Brit heard the clatter of the teapot, he rearranged the damp cloth on the little boy's head, heard him whimper and stood with him effortlessly—so light, so thin—and walked with him to the narrow window where he drew back the curtain and stared down at the silent Bloomsbury street, no one moving at four in the morning except an occasional taxi, sign lit like a predatory rectangular eye in the black night.

He looked across the street directly into the silent brooding hulk of the British Museum, scrubbed and polished now after years of neglect. One of the reasons he'd taken this inadequate, overpriced flat was for this view alone. Below him was a dusty lithograph shop; to the right a noisy, smelly pub; to the left a joke shop; humanity piled atop humanity in a way human beings were never intended to live.

On the reading table near the window he saw the blue volume of Saint Exupéry and with his free hand opened it to:

Old Bureaucrat, my comrade, no one has helped you
escape and you are not responsible for it. You have con-
structed your peace by piling up cement, as the termites
do in closing all lighted openings . . .

Brit rocked the child gently and enjoyed reading the words that,
as a young student, he had read with such zeal.

A school. Of his own. Unique. All that was needed was for the
old order, the old thoughts, the old way of perceiving things to die
off. Peaceful revolution. But Marx said it would never happen.

Then he was reading again, still cradling the fitful child.

. . . You have raised up a modest rampart against the
winds and the tides and the stars. You do not want to
concern yourself with great problems. You've had enough
trouble in forgetting your human condition. You are not
the inhabitant of a wandering planet. You do not ask yourself unanswerable questions. You are a petit bourgeois
from Toulouse . . ."

Brit looked up from his reading. He was a petit bourgeois from
Oklahoma. But he was trying to learn something. He found his
place on the page again.

. . . While there was yet time, no one grabbed you by
the shoulders. Now, the clay of which you are made has
dried, and has hardened, and no one will ever know how
to awaken in you the sleeping musician, or poet, or astron-
omer, who perhaps still live within you.

The words made a special music inside his head and when he
ceased to read, the music ceased and the ensuing silence and the
child in his arms worked a peculiar effect.

"Tea's ready," Sophie murmured as she placed a brown mug
within reach on the table and took hers and sat on the edge of the
bed.

"We didn't do very well today, did we?" she asked softly, looking up.

Brit gently placed the child on the far side of the bed, hearing in echo the futile early-morning meeting, the criticisms which had been leveled—at him as well as his project—by the Socialist union at London University. They had gone to the Notting Hill festival this afternoon to soften the failure of the morning.

Incongruously he smiled, realizing for the first time the oceanic distance between what he'd thought would happen today and what in fact happened. Generally he wasn't so far off the mark on his dreams.

The students had been mildly supportive, but he needed more than student support. He needed the kind of funds and grants available to faculty members for city projects. Of course their hostility had sprung from a myriad of sources. One—perhaps the most significant—he was an American.

"And what do you know, Mr. Warrick, of the tradition of Robert Owen and Lord Shaftesbury?"

Unfortunately, he'd proceeded to tell them, which hadn't helped matters.

"I take it, then, Mr. Warrick, that everything is in shipshape condition in your own country, every child fed and accounted for?"

It had seemed irrelevant. Still he'd answered.

"No . . ."

"Then why are you here?"

Sophie stretched out on the bed and cuddled the child. What were they to do with him? How many had died in the early evening riots? Who was responsible?

"I made the appointment for ten o'clock," she said. "I really think that they'll help us."

Brit looked down and tried to recall what appointment at ten. He took the cup of steaming tea and sipped at it, then remembered. Philosophically he would have felt more at home with financial aid from the Socialist union at the university, but Sophie had set up an appointment with the Salvation Army.

She continued to nuzzle the child, rearranging the damp cloth and drawing the small comforter up around him.

"Don't be discouraged, Brit," she said and kissed the little boy. "You mustn't be, you know."

He stretched out beside her and closed his eyes, not seeing anything too clearly. His dream. The school. Why was it so difficult? For every positive reaction, he'd received ten negative ones, condemnations ranging from "illegal, meddlesome, intruding in government affairs" to "robbing the system, Communistic, immoral." And yet what was he doing that was so illegal, so immoral?

Six months ago he'd gone down to the dock area and leased for a song a front flat in an abandoned warehouse, had put a broom to it, arranged apple crates and lettuce cartons, a few pictures and one world globe. Then he'd gone out on the streets and that very day he had rounded up eight youngsters, ranging in age from seven to ten, a mixed bag, male and female, all of whom had in some way slipped through the cracks of the numerous government agencies. All of them had one parent or the other, though still they were alone, more or less on their own. They survived doing pub work, petty street thievery, true descendants of Fagin's brood.

Brit had corralled this motley crew and led them back to the makeshift flat and by the end of the first day they had accomplished twin miracles: they all had washed their faces and hands, had invented names and exchanged them.

From that tentative beginning a sort of an institution had evolved. Not a school—because there were days when they never opened their secondhand primers, days when Brit would simply lead them out to the edge of the river where they would watch the foraging habits of seagulls; other days when they would troop en masse to Covent Garden for end-of-the-day bargains in produce, day-old bread, all the bounty going back to the flat for cleansing, preparation and eating. They were always hungry.

About three months ago they had met Sophie, a prostitute from Soho, and he still wasn't certain whether she'd adopted them or they her, but she'd been unofficial den mother ever since and had proved invaluable in obtaining certain sorely needed items. Their numbers had grown to fifteen—more of a family than Brit had ever known—and he loved each of them with passionate intensity and had frequently thought at last he was whole and reconciled, his actions with his words, his dream with his reality, his faith with his deeds.

Then two weeks ago, the first threat. The building that had housed them was being torn down. They would be out on the street within a month. Of course there were other flats in the area, but they cost money and not too many landlords wanted Brit's disreputable crew.

Then what? Where could the kids go? There was no government aid because he was an alien and his "family" was neither a school nor a home nor a social agency.

"We could bring them here, you know," he said.

Sleepily, Sophie turned. "You can't do that," she said sadly. "This here is zoned. The coppers would be on you. Besides, the kids would never trot up here. This ain't their London Town; they wouldn't feel right."

Her protests were fast and accurate beyond dispute.

"Look," she soothed, "let's go talk to the General tomorrow. He's a good man, and the Salvation Army has property all over. You're doing their work for them. The least they can do is put a roof over your head."

He didn't want to argue with her, but privately he knew the Salvation Army would not help them either.

"Get some sleep now," she soothed. "Tomorrow we'll make something work. I promise." With that she turned on her side, though he still could feel the warmth of her hand on his chest.

"Tomorrow we'll make something work . . ."

For a few minutes he stared up at the ceiling. Cracks and water spots formed monster faces like the clouds at Warrick on a high, blue July day.

"Do you see that one, Josh? The Wolf Man."

Warrick. He'd spent all his life trying to get away from it. Now why was it occupying his mind? He hadn't belonged there—a small but important fact he'd learned at about age eight.

"Massie, where do you think I should go? What should I do?"

"Go where you want to, Brit. You're among the blessed. You can do anything."

How many times he'd been prepared to debate that point.

"Brit, wherever you go, can I come with you?"

"You're too little, Mereth—"

"I'll grow up if you want me to—"

"And you giggle too much—"

"And I'll stop giggling, I promise—"

"I hope not. Come on, I'll give you a head start and race you to the gazebo—"

"You're thinking about something, aren't you, Brit?" Sophie whispered. "I can always tell when you're thinking something."

The vivid memory of Mereth faded. "Yes . . ."

"You shouldn't be. It's late."

". . . thinking how indebted I am to you, how important you are to me, to the children."

"You're the one. You get the ideas. We just . . ." Her voice drifted.

Was he truly fresh out of ideas now? He needed permanent quarters and—perhaps more important than anything else—he needed definition.

"What exactly is it you're attempting, Mr. Warrick? A school? A home? A shelter? A counseling service?"

"Yes to all four. And more. Or maybe less. Maybe just an open door, someplace where they can come to get out of the rain, have a cup of tea, talk to someone. What would you call that?"

He opened his eyes. Idiocy most likely is what you'd call it. Then why, of all the varied and misled and misconstructed and dubious activities of his thirty-five years, did he feel most at home here in this place, in this city, with these abandoned kids, his insignificant existence at last justified?

"The earth teaches us much more about ourselves than all the books because it resists us."

The recall was good and prompted another recall.

Warrick.

He had to admit he'd learned that at Warrick from Ty himself.

"Plant seeds, boy, and watch them grow. In the growing are all the secrets."

Outside the window in that vast London world, nothing moved. There would be milk trucks soon, bottles clattering; and silent headlines screaming the latest Notting Hill riots, the dead woman's name lost in the column of the dead; and there would be an occasional siren of alarm, cabbies chugging by, black derby hats, slim stick umbrellas and drab feathered birds, lorries rumbling down narrow, ancient streets. The greatest city in the world was on the brink of waking and here he was sitting in the middle of it and all he could clearly see was the long, vast, empty approach to Warrick, a twisting road which reappeared as a ribbon miles ahead, the first distant glimpse of red-tiled roof, the woods behind a black-green backdrop of giant native trees, and in the deeper distance the symmetrical black fingers of oil wells, hundreds of them.

Suddenly he turned on his side as though to turn his back on the scene which had appeared unwanted in his consciousness.

He closed his eyes and the phone rang, that uniquely English ring of two sharp bells, then silence, then two more.

As he crawled out of bed he saw Sophie raise up over the still sleeping child, apparently concerned that the ringing had disturbed him. But it hadn't. Brit scooped up the receiver.

"Hello?" Even before he spoke he heard a flurry of static. "I can't hear you. Please, could you speak . . . ?"

He cupped the receiver in his hand and hunched his shoulders as though if he made a cocoon of himself it would work better. Then the voice spoke his name, and he blinked out at the mammoth columns of the British Museum, wondering if he'd heard it correctly, that sweet voice from his childhood, from his past, the same past that had plagued him this evening.

The voice called his name again and he was fairly certain, yet he

needed confirmation and recalled the armed camps of his youth—
Josh on one side in all matters, and on the other side he and—

"Mereth, is it you?"

Warrick

"BRIT? OH, it's good to hear your voice!"

She pressed back into Ty's chair, not quite prepared for the emotional jolt that the mere sound of Brit's voice gave her.

"Brit, make Josh stop!"

"I want Brit to get the splinter out."

How long had it been since she'd seen him? Years. He'd left Warrick long before she had. He'd gone to Princeton and never bothered to come home.

"Brit, how are you? I hope I didn't . . ."

"I can't believe it!" he marveled.

She heard his voice—the same as ever—the deep, calm voice to go with equally deep, calm eyes and sandy-colored hair and a sense of compassion large enough to embrace the whole world.

"Mereth, are you still there?"

She nodded foolishly, and felt some mysterious deep emotion that she couldn't identify and therefore couldn't deal with.

"Mereth, is everything . . . ?"

"You, Brit. How are you? What are you doing in London? Overthrowing the monarchy?"

She heard a good laugh and remembered Brit's laugh.

"No. It doesn't need overthrowing," he countered. "It will crumble all by itself in time."

"Then what? School?"

"Not formally, though I manage to receive instruction of some sort every day."

She nodded, understanding, then decided, Enough. Get him home and then they could talk endlessly as they used to on every subject imaginable. "Brit, I'm afraid there's a purpose to this call."

"I suspected that there was."

"It's . . . Ty."

There was a pause. "Is he dead?"

The voice that posed this question bore absolutely no resemblance to the same warm voice that just a few seconds earlier had been talking about lessons and monarchies.

"No, not dead, Brit. A stroke early this morning. Massie . . ."

"How is Massie?"

"She's been better, of course."

"I'm sure."

"Will you come home, Brit? Dr. Buckner has suggested that . . ."

"Old Sawbones?"

"The same."

"I thought he was dead."

"He is. But he's still walking around."

There was that laugh again. It belonged in special places. In a houseboat on the Seine. In the shadow of Notre Dame. On Torcello. Champagne, warm sun, cool October breezes.

She smiled and shook her head at her persistent ability to remember.

"Will you come, Brit?" she repeated, canceling the lovely memories.

There was another pause, too long to be good. Then—

"Why?"

The direct and basically unanswerable question caught her off guard. Of course she understood. The estrangement between Ty and Brit had been the harshest, more damage done, more vicious accusations, more irreconcilable differences. To the man who'd built one of the largest capitalist empires in the United States, such words as "unions," "workers" and "share the wealth" were anathema, if not criminal.

When precisely Brit had developed his Socialist philosophy no one knew. As Massie had once pointed out, they couldn't blame Princeton because he was reading Marx before he was out of high school. Then if blame was due, blame it on Marx and his dialectical materialism.

But she wasn't interested in placing blame—on anyone—wasn't certain if it was a matter for blame.

"Because I want you," she said simply. "Because I need you."

"I have no money, Mereth, to come home."

She could have predicted that. Brit never had money.

"I'll call Red Pierson," she offered. "Give me an address. He'll wire."

"Have him send it to me in care of the American Express on Haymarket."

"Then you promise you'll come?" she asked.

"Is Ty really dying?"

"We don't know. A specialist was just here from St. Mark's, but he seemed to know less than Buckner."

"Poor Mereth. When did you arrive?"

"Massie called me early this morning."

"Where are you living now?"

"Tulsa."

He laughed. "You didn't make it very far, did you? Tulsa. So close!"

She heard again Brit's special charm combined with Brit's special cynicism, which together seemed to flame up into a vital warmth when one least expected it.

"Let me know your flight," she added, sensing the end to their conversation.

"I'd say tomorrow. The day after at the latest. Where can I fly in to now?"

"Dallas. I can have our plane meet you there. Is that . . . ? Well, I mean . . ."

She faltered, belatedly realizing that the Lear jet with the Warrick logo painted on the sides might offend him.

"Would that be all right, Brit?"

"No. I'll get a flight from Dallas to Tulsa. I'll call you from there." His voice had become toneless. The vital warmth had been turned off.

"Soon, Brit. Make it soon."

"Soon."

"I miss you."

Then the connection was broken, and she was left with the buzzing of the dead line.

Broke. Not surprising.

Why had she offered to call Red Pierson? Why couldn't she just wire the money herself? Why involve Red Pierson—although it was inevitable the man be involved sooner or later.

Round-trip transatlantic fare— Damn Brit!

This sudden burst of anger startled her. Still she meant it. Brit's disbursement was the same as everyone else's. Why couldn't he manage?

All right, then. Call Pierson.

Behind her she heard the door open a crack and looked over her shoulder, hoping it was Massie. It wasn't. Just one of the girls to clear the buffet.

"Give me five minutes." Mereth smiled apologetically.

The girl withdrew and Mereth flipped through the address book to the P's, found Pierson and an Oklahoma City number. She muttered the number aloud, commenced to punch the panel and in that brief interim tried to decide why precisely she disliked Red Pierson so.

He'd been Ty's personal lawyer for as long as she could remember, working independently of the legal firm in Dallas. Red was different. True he was—like Horace Buckner and Junior Nagle—a lifetime member of the inner circle and yet in another way he was different from these men. Not rough cut. In fact, rather fastidious.

As the phone rang for the third time, Mereth perched on the arm of Ty's chair and closed her eyes and decided that she was bone tired.

"Ty, Miss Caldwell told the sixth grade that you helped to build this state. Is that true?"

"Mereth, baby, come and sit with me. There's room enough in this big chair—"

"Is it true, Ty? What Miss Caldwell said?"

"I reckon. It's good to give yourself to something big, Mereth, something you love more than you love yourself. Don't ever waste yourself on little dreams, you hear?"

She remembered how she'd nestled in his arms and he'd nodded off and she'd wanted to draw a deep breath but did not dare to, and breathed with careful self-restraint for fear of disturbing him.

Then she heard a voice on the other end of the line, a slightly haughty female voice announcing:

"Mr. Pierson's office. May I help you?"

Oklahoma City

RED PIERSON hung up the phone and stared at the memo in his hand, a message conveyed to him only moments earlier by the youngest Warrick girl. What was her name?

"Miss Campbell, please check with American on the precise cost of a round-trip ticket from Heathrow to Dallas–Fort Worth to Tulsa. Then wire that amount to Mr. Britton Warrick, care of American Express, Haymarket Street, London WC-1. Is that clear?"

Of course it would be clear. Campbell could run the world if she put her mind to it.

Duty executed, he crushed the memo into a ball and dropped it into the wastebasket on his left, then looked out at his perfect view of the imperfect, ever-changing Oklahoma City skyline, momentarily postponing the need to think about Ty Warrick and all the vultures—including Ty's grandchildren—who shortly would be circling over Warrick.

Consciously he stood erect, aware of his seventy-five years and denying all of them. Why not? He was trim, slim, almost a full head of hair, his own teeth, reading glasses. He'd done something right, hadn't he, the results of a conservative life. His philosophy? "When it isn't necessary to change, it is necessary not to change."

That said it all.

Feeling a good surge of rightness that always gave him a lift, he moved from the perfect arena of himself to the imperfect arena of his native city. He looked down on the destruction, whole blocks dynamited for nonsense called urban renewal. Urban destruction, more like it. Every morning he had to pick his way through chaos which resembled a war zone. He was getting tired of it. The city would never be anything more than it was now: an overgrown cow town run by inept, corrupt men of small vision. No foresight. Tasteless.

"There's more profit in Puccini than in pigs."

Red shuddered, recalling that obscenity uttered several years ago by the president of the Chamber of Commerce on behalf of a fund-raising drive for a new fine-arts complex. Blessedly, the funds had never been raised, and Art still was safe in Oklahoma.

Oh, not that Oklahoma wasn't notable for something—oil, gas, wheat, nationally ranked football teams and corruption. The most corrupt state in the Union, according to *Newsweek*. Well, it was good to be best at something.

Indeed, the stench of political corruption predated statehood and it was smelling worse all the time with indictments and convictions of house speakers, majority floor leaders, county district judges, contractors, county commissioners, state supreme court justices and three governors. What this foul chronology suggested was even worse: that it probably was only the tip of the iceberg.

Suddenly Red reached to pull the cord and drew meticulously pleated ivory antique satin to blot out the scene. Time to work.

Ty was ill, perhaps dying. A stroke. Regrettable but not surprising. How many times Red had told him to slow down, take care of himself, for no one else would.

Tyburn Warrick dead?

The question occurred a second time with awesome clarity. The ramifications! Particularly for Red as executor of the will. There'd been recent changes. Ridiculous ones. But then Ty was always changing his will. Someone was always displeasing him, disappointing him, challenging him.

"Red, bring out that tin box of yours."

Red settled comfortably behind his polished mahogany desk and reached into his vest pocket for the single key he kept there, withdrew it and unlocked the bottom left-hand drawer.

The youngest Warrick girl had sounded vague, distracted. Well, nothing to do but go out to Warrick and see for himself. Nothing important going on in Red's life except his close proximity to Tyburn Warrick and the Warrick wealth. The annual fee Ty paid him enabled him to live well. Now, though, things might be different.

If Ty died—

The thought continued to occur with exciting regularity. It was one hell of a rich tree, the Warrick tree. Shake it but once and a man could be buried in its fruits.

Again he felt a need to look at the will. Ty had been altering it—with great regularity—every two, three months. There were more codicils than he could recall.

Check it. The predators were coming. He'd better be informed, because an informed man is a prepared one.

Why hadn't Massie called him? He'd never done anything to her, felt he had her trust. Massie needn't worry. Ty had taken good care of her a long time ago. She was a wealthy woman in her own right.

No, it was those worthless kids who'd come streaming back. But that was the way it was, wasn't it? He'd seen it happen time and again. There was the progenitor, rare stock, good genes, all the gifts God could ever want to bestow on a man, but it always seemed somehow to become watered down with each successive generation until the end result was a pallid, inept imitation of the original force. And what an original force it was. Red remembered the time during the thirties when Ty had taken him to dinner at some little two-bit diner over near Pawhuska after one of the big oil auctions. There were about twenty-five people in the place, part Indian, part white, a few blacks. Ty left a five-hundred-dollar bill with the lady at the cashbox and said no one in there was to pay for a meal or to leave hungry, and if the various men had hungry kids at home, they were to take food to them. When Red asked him why he'd done that for people he didn't even know, Ty said, "He who obtains has little; he who scatters has much."

The intercom buzzer sounded.

"Yes, Miss Campbell."

There was a pause. "Sorry, sir. There was a call from a man who said he was an AP reporter. He didn't want to talk to you. He just wanted to know if we had heard of Mr. Tyburn Warrick's . . . death."

There was another pause, Campbell reacting like the female she was.

"Why would anyone make such a cruel call, Mr. Pierson?" She sounded weepy.

Red held the receiver out as though it might be contaminated. "No need to spread alarm, Campbell. Just a joke, that's all. I have an appointment with Mr. Warrick tomorrow, and I generally don't make appointments with dead men."

"No, sir."

"No calls from now on, Campbell. And don't respond to any reporters. On any subject. Is that clear?"

"Yes, sir. I wired four thousand dollars to the American Express, the Haymarket Street address in London, first-class round-trip ticket."

"First-class!" Had he told her first-class? Bum class is what it should have been. "All right, Campbell. Remember, no calls for an hour. Is that clear?"

"Yes, sir."

He released the intercom and without hesitation opened the bottom drawer, lifted up the strongbox and withdrew a blue leather folder. The Warrick will. Heavier than most wills, but then why not?

Carefully, as though he were handling a religious document, he placed it on his desk. He flipped quickly to the last codicil—the only valid one, bent over and read.

About twenty minutes later he looked up from reading, swiveled about in his chair, reached over and pulled the drapes and stared out at the Oklahoma City skyline that had offended him a few moments earlier. Now he was smiling.

No need to take the codicil seriously. Obviously it was a joke. One of Ty's best. It could be broken. Like that! And Red Pierson fully intended to break it.

Warrick

MASSIE FOUND Mereth in the terrace room sitting in Ty's chair, three empty Bloody Mary glasses on the table, apparently relaxed but not asleep. It was five-thirty. Dinner at eight. If anyone wanted it.

Massie watched her, worry increasing, and started to call to her. But at that moment she heard a familiar rattle, one she heard every afternoon at this same time, a vehicle of ancient vintage coming too fast. In about fifteen seconds the horn would sound, a tinny rendition of a fake alarm—standard equipment on all World War II Jeeps, especially those that had been abused.

117

Right on cue. There was the horn, a continuous and decrepit siren, like a comic horn in a circus.

At the noise, Mereth looked up.

In answer to the question taking shape on Mereth's face, Massie said, "Deeter Big Cow. My God, I forgot to call him!" and was appalled by her own callous oversight.

As boys, Ty and Deeter had scouted every inch of Warrick, knew where the best quail were, where the deer watered, where the fattest rabbits burrowed, a deep bond developing until they were closer than brothers.

Deeter's father had been a popular Osage chief, full blood, his mother the daughter of a white missionary. In the land rush of '89 Tyburn Warrick, Sr., had confiscated the southwest corner of Osage tribal land. It would have been a simple matter to say, "Sorry, I'll pull back my fences," but apparently Ty Warrick, Sr., wasn't known for his ability to apologize.

In the beginning it had been open warfare between the Osage Indians and Ty's small army of cowhands and hired guns. Then, after a few years and too many deaths, everyone—to their credit—lost interest except for the two major protagonists. They met in the woods that flanked Warrick on the west and, under the pretense of trying to determine a boundary dispute, they beat each other senseless.

It became a kind of "favorite entertainment" in the area. No weapons were allowed, bare fists only. Families would bring picnic lunches on hot Sunday afternoons. The wagering was hot and heavy, and generally the two men inflicted matching damage and their wives would cart them away to nurse their wounds and six weeks later word would spread of a "rematch."

It was in this fashion that Deeter and Ty, Jr., met, and if there was cosmic and fateful animosity between the fathers, there appeared to be, from the beginning, only the rarest kind of mutual respect and dependence and love between the sons.

Deeter had married a tribal woman and they had produced one son, a brilliant man, a Rhodes scholar who had studied at Cambridge and now taught there, a highly respected anthropologist who suffered extreme ambivalence about his own heritage.

Deeter had visited his son in England only once, had been impressed with Buckingham Palace and had commenced to build a reproduction on his land. Childlike, he had hoped to lure his son home and regain his affection. Partially completed, Deeter's castle rose from the Oklahoma prairie like a bizarre hallucination. But the ploy had failed. The son was still in England and likely to remain so, and Deeter had lost interest and now seemed content to live in a small apartment tucked inside the huge shell and let the bats have the rest.

Deeter Big Cow, eighty—more nearly resembling a man of fifty —immense, steel-gray hair, copper-penny profile, enormous beer gut, a force of nature, like Ty.

Watching the two men together, Massie had decided long ago, was like watching two gods at play, making up their own games, hence their own rules, drinking too much, eating too much, bouncing roughshod over Warrick in that dilapidated Jeep, laughing, telling raunchy stories or sometimes just sitting quietly together for hours, saying nothing. But Massie was not so insensitive as to believe there was no communication going on.

"Guess who!" Massie whispered.

"You mean Deeter knows . . . nothing?" Mereth said.

Massie nodded, momentarily lacking the energy to talk above the ever-increasing blare of the horn which, according to the volume of noise, was just making the last turn before reaching the covered portico.

"Why is he here now?" Mereth asked, following Massie down the hall to the front door.

"They always have a drink. Several," Massie replied. "And Deeter's been driving Ty out to the new wells. Generally he stays for dinner. Ty worries about him." Her voice drifted, unable to rise above the horn.

As Deeter caught sight of the two women he executed a syncopated rhythm on the horn. At the same time he lifted his once white ten-gallon Stetson and waved it in the air above his head, white teeth cutting a swath in his full, fleshy bronze face. Even from that distance Massie could see the three gold teeth glittering in the last ray of sun before the ancient Jeep entered the shadows of the portico.

He grinned at them on the first pass and feigned that the Jeep was out of control or brakeless. Massie had seen the same performance countless times for Ty's benefit, an adolescent trick but one which seemed to bring both men enormous pleasure. In fact, after thirty years of witnessing this relationship Massie was still bewildered by how a mind as multifaceted as Ty Warrick's was consistently amused and captivated by Deeter's simple slapstick humor.

Then the squeal of brakes brought her back to the impending confrontation and she looked up to see Deeter forcing the Jeep into a sharp left turn and heading back at reduced speed.

She saw Mereth's face alive with anticipation. Massie remembered the special friendship that had existed between Ty's youngest grandchild and the old Indian. As a little girl, Mereth used to ride her horse over to the castle and take to Deeter bread she'd freshly baked or a bouquet of wildflowers.

Massie heard a bellowed demand. "Who's that standing over there?"

She saw Deeter crawling, stiff-legged, out of the Jeep, the heavy plastic on one window hanging torn and loose, the Jeep itself almost obscured between coated layers of red mud. The game was on.

With Deeter it was always a game. He stood stock still by his Jeep now, hat in hand, his eyes squinting across the shaded drive, a look of bewilderment on his face.

"Massie, I know you. I've seen you often enough and, no offense, but who's that pretty thing standing next to you? That ain't Lana Turner, is it?" he asked, still playing his game, dating himself, as he began to creep slowly forward, looking like a great swollen bronze beetle.

"Hell, no, I was wrong!" he groaned, slapping the tattered cowboy hat against his leg as though doing an imitation of Gary Cooper or John Wayne. "Why that's Marilyn Monroe! I swear that's the likes of her. What's she doing here at Warrick, Massie? Ty's newest, I suppose. God, but ain't she a pretty thing!"

Throughout this charade Massie's attention was torn between Deeter's foolish, crouched approach and Mereth's broad grin. Just when Massie thought she could endure no more, Deeter dropped the pose, stopped in the middle of the drive, clamped his hat on the back of his head and opened his arms wide, an expression not unlike pain on his face.

"Mereth mine . . ." he whispered.

Mereth took the stairs in one step and was in his arms, into a monstrous bear hug, the force of which literally lifted her off her feet as the two turned twice, three times in an awkward circle, no words spoken, a degree of intimacy that pleased Massie.

For several moments she found herself grinning foolishly at the old man and the young girl and soon selfishly began thinking to let Mereth break the news. Obviously any news coming from her would be more palatable than—

Then Deeter lowered Mereth, though he kept his arms about her, his black eyes seeming to search out and record every feature as though committing it to memory.

"You're Mary Beth come to life, you know," he muttered.

Massie recalled his adoration of Ty's wife.

"Ain't she, Massie? Ain't she Mary Beth come to life?"

The question sounded plaintive, as though he ached for confirmation. Massie said, thinking, anything to postpone the mention of Ty, "There is a good resemblance."

"Resemblance, hell! You put that pink lace thing on this girl and center her atop a two-wheeled gig and you got Mary Beth!"

Massie saw the joy of the reunion fade, Deeter's fleshy smile replaced by something more serious.

"Hey, where you been?" he demanded, holding Mereth at arm's length. "You know how worried Ty's been? Hell, of course you don't. Kids never do. They don't give a damn."

Deeter scowled. "Why did you just walk out on him like that, Mereth? Why did you just walk out on all of us? Liked to killed old Ty, didn't it, Massie. Never seen a man brood so, and we was left to pick up the pieces—"

The reunion was over. Mereth turned away and Massie saw a grim expression on her face, one of inhuman self-restraint. Yet there was a look of soft longing in that rigid control, and that was what made it peculiarly sad. "Well, no matter. You're here now and old Ty must be about to explode. Where in hell is the bastard? We was going to take a spin, if that's all right, Massie." Suddenly he raised his voice. "Ty, where in hell are you hidin'? Mereth, go fetch him, will you?"

Massie saw Mereth glance her way as though for help, but at the moment she had none to give. In her confusion she looked behind her as though she'd heard a disturbance at the door, when in truth she'd heard nothing.

But Deeter saw her and wrongly interpreted it, thinking she'd heard Ty coming. Now he started like a freight train toward the door, still shouting at the top of his voice, "Ty, you buzzard, you bastard, why didn't you tell me Mereth was comin'? Selfish bastard. Always were, always will be!"

Massie saw his destination and sought to block it. "Deeter . . . wait!" she commanded.

"Wait, hell! I don't like Ty holding out on me like that. I could have at least run a sharp edge over this." Roughly he grasped his chin, which was covered with the stubble of several days' gray growth of beard. "Ty ain't never . . ."

"Deeter!"

This voice came from behind and was surprising in its strength.

At the sound of Mereth's voice, Deeter obeyed. He turned away from his assault on the door and Massie caught a whiff of his garments—his "uniform" as Ty called it—faded stiffened Levis literally molded to fit his mammoth frame, the jeans defying gravity, belted about four inches below the bulge where his waistline had been, an equally decrepit flannel shirt which Deeter wore summer and winter, the fabric absorbing all sweat. The boots likewise were molded with years of wear to fit his feet. The Stetson completed a picture which had remained unchanged for the last thirty years.

"Deeter, please come back for a moment," Mereth invited with compelling and fascinating calm.

Apparently the tone of voice was completely foreign to Deeter for, though his instinct was still to charge the door, he retraced his steps. "He ain't gone and started drinking without me, has he, Mereth? I mean, Ty don't drink well alone, you know that. He needs someone. He needs me to set a pace for him, you know what I mean?"

"No, he hasn't started drinking."

Mereth broke off as though suddenly aware of the stupidity of prolonging the message. Still, Massie felt compelled to warn her. Deeter was not like everybody else. His relationship with Ty was unique as well.

Don't just blurt it out. Please, Mereth!

She realized why she hadn't called him. Cowardice, pure and simple.

Massie noticed a rip in the sleeve of the flannel shirt and felt a wave of pity for the old Indian. Alone—except for a son who had denied his own heritage and a grandson who turned up now and then.

"Deeter, please listen," Mereth soothed, a soft smile on her face belying the message lurking behind the words. "Ty's sick, Deeter. We should have called you, but it happened suddenly early this morning. Only Massie was here."

Massie saw Deeter look back at her, his face a blank as though he'd not understood a word.

"She's right, Deeter," Massie said. "Ty took ill early this morning. Dr. Buckner's with him now. I'm afraid we don't know a great deal . . . yet but . . ."

She'd thought she was doing very well, thought Deeter was doing well too. He appeared to be listening quietly, rationally. But the laugh that now cut through the silence was not rational.

She saw Mereth move back, startled by the suddenness with which Deeter threw back his head and started to make a sound not unlike that of a pig call, a single, shrill, high-pitched note which climbed even higher and which he held forever, or so it seemed.

"You two sisters!" he shouted on the first sustained breath of air he could manage. "Ain't you awful, and Ty, that bastard, too! In fact, he's worser than you. All right, enough fun at old Deeter's expense. Go get the bastard for me, will ya?"

In her innocence Mereth tried again. "Deeter, Ty's ill."

"Don't . . . say . . . that . . . to . . . my . . . face . . . again!"

This was a threat in every sense of the word, a cold sober threat with a knife edge which was all the worse for coming so fast on the heels of his mad humor.

Massie thought she probably should phone the garage complex and alert Eddie O'Keefe. Not that Eddie was a match for Deeter physically, but Deeter liked Eddie, was fascinated by his red hair and his talent for tall tales. On more than one occasion Massie had seen Eddie talk Deeter out of a drunken madness and drive him back to the castle, when even Ty's efforts had failed.

But there was no way she could contact Eddie now, and Deeter stormed inside. Mereth reached for him but Massie said, "Let him go. He must see for himself. He'll never take our word."

Now from inside the entrance hall came a booming voice. "Hey, ain't you comin'? You must think old Deeter's one crazy Indian to fall for this bullshit!"

They heard his boots on the steps moving upward, the quiet air punctuated every third step with, "Ty, you bastard, what the hell's going on?"

"I'm going to call Eddie," Massie announced.

"Shall I go on up?" Mereth asked. "Does he know where to go? What will be . . . ?"

In answer to the first two questions Massie nodded yes. Mereth's third question was unanswerable. "Let me call Eddie just in case. You go on."

124

Massie watched as Mereth started up the stairs, taking the first few steps quickly, but halfway up, her energy apparently flagged. Massie saw her reach out for the banister and hold on as though to wait out the reverberating voice which echoed throughout the second-floor corridor, mindlessly repeating, "Ty, you ol' bastard, where in the hell are you? Do you know what they tried to tell me down there?"

Massie hurried toward the phone room.

Quickly she dialed.

Come on, Eddie! Pick up the phone!

Then a man's voice on the other end of the line demanded, "Who's there? This is Eddie."

Before she could respond she heard a scream, followed by a man's wail. Accompanying these unholy sounds was a resounding crash—glass, and following this a woman's continuous scream, a shouted warning, echoing threats.

Massie closed her eyes and turned back into the phone room and felt the hair on her arms stand up, felt a chill on her face.

She grasped the receiver and begged, "Eddie, come quick! It's Deeter . . ."

———

Mereth had just reached the top of the steps when she heard Deeter's cry and thought: we should have stopped him downstairs. But he'd been like a runaway freight train. Age had made him cumbersome but had done nothing to diminish his strength, which she remembered as both awesome and reassuring.

She glanced down the corridor and saw movement, a flash of white darting out, then disappearing again. It was Miss Kent, the nurse in charge of Ty.

Where was Buckner? She'd thought Dr. Buckner was in Ty's room as well.

Then she heard the nurse pleading for someone to "Put it away! Please don't. I'm sure he'll . . ."

As Mereth approached the door she was stopped by a curious

sight: Deeter backing stiffly out of the room, his arms partially raised, his shirttail pulled loose, his movement almost sedate, as though he'd at last met a threat worthy of consideration.

Edging out of the double doors with him was Miss Kent. She looked up and saw Mereth.

"Please, Miss Warrick, help us. He has a gun."

Mereth blinked at the bizarre, slightly melodramatic announcement. Who had a gun? Ty? Ty had an arsenal of guns, all downstairs, locked in the basement club room. What would he be doing with—

Then she saw the overfed features of Dr. Buckner, his tie off, shirt unbuttoned, sleeves rolled up and in his hand a shiny blueblack snub-nosed Saturday night special which he held firmly in his right hand, index finger on the trigger, thumb on the hammer.

Mereth stopped, suffered the distorted image of grown men playing a game like those staged reenactments of gun fights at amusement parks.

"Keep moving, you dumb Indian. You're going in the right direction, on back where you come from. Ty ain't up to talkin' or drinkin' or ridin' today."

Suddenly, as though impervious to the presence of the gun, Deeter started forward, saying nothing intelligible, making only a guttural sound of raw fury.

"*Stop.* I mean it!" Buckner shouted and lifted the gun higher and held it with both hands now, the barrel aimed at Deeter's broad chest.

Mereth saw Miss Kent scurry back into Ty's room. Once inside she quickly closed the doors, leaving the corridor filled with the confrontation between Buckner and Deeter.

"Who let this crazy bastard in here?" Buckner demanded as he spied Mereth, who had taken refuge on one side of the corridor.

Suddenly Deeter stirred out of his silence and stood his ground. "Mereth," he called out, "answer me a question, will ya? Who is it they've got tied up in that room there? Do you know? I sure don't. I come up here looking for my old friend Ty Warrick, but some other poor bastard's in his room. In his bed even! I don't have the goddamnedest notion who it is or where Ty is. You tell me what happened. Tell me where I can find him."

"Get him out of here," Buckner muttered to Mereth. "Good thing I was packing this in my case. Docs need 'em now, you know. Protection against junkies." He looked directly at Deeter. "And crazy Indians."

Suddenly the same wail exploded from Deeter, a kind of tribal war cry. At the same time Deeter made a giant leap forward, hands outstretched, aimed for Buckner's throat.

The attack caught Buckner off guard, though in the split second before Deeter reached his throat Mereth saw the flash of the gun barrel as it flew instinctively upward, heard the thunderous report of a single shot and in terror she turned away and pressed against the wall.

With her eyes closed she heard running and looked up to see Eddie O'Keefe. While she was still trying to deal with her fear, she heard Massie's voice.

"Are you all right?"

Mereth nodded, then both women looked back as Eddie O'Keefe's angry voice filled the corridor. "Are you out of your mind?" he shouted at Buckner. With remarkable efficiency he relieved the old man of the gun and held it at arm's length and continued to shout out his rage, all of it aimed at Buckner while Deeter stood mid-corridor and looked smug.

"You're an idiot! You know that, don't you? Where did you get this thing anyway?" he demanded, holding the gun up gingerly. "And what in the hell gave you the right to fire it in this house?"

All of a sudden Horace Buckner found the energy to meet Eddie's rage.

"I used *my* weapon only when Mr. Warrick was threatened by that drunken idiot there!"

He pointed one accusing finger at Deeter, who—with all the self-consciousness of a schoolboy—commenced awkwardly to restore his flannel shirt inside his sagging belt.

"He's the one," Buckner accused, stabbing at the air. "He came roaring up here, busted right in those doors there and proceeded to tell me and my nurse to clear out, that he was taking Ty for a drink and a spin in his Jeep."

As the account spilled out, Deeter turned slowly about, caught sight of Mereth and Massie and winked at them as though to say they weren't to believe a word they were hearing. He seemed now to be searching the wall for something.

Buckner glanced back at the closed doors which led into Ty's room. "And when I told him to get the hell out, he started smashing things up, all the equipment. You ought to see the place in there. I.V. broken. Oxygen setup. Everything! I've got to call the hospital, get all new stuff sent out. It's a mess! All because . . ."

As he looked toward Deeter, his rage seemed to build anew and quickly Eddie stepped between them.

"Still you oughtn't to have . . ."

"What in the hell was I supposed to do?"

Mereth looked up and concentrated on the huge expanse of Deeter's back. Apparently he'd taken this opportunity to study Mary Beth's art collection. Puzzled, Mereth watched as he leaned close to a delicate Monet, then moved on to a Seurat. A Turner—a watercolor, one of the early seascapes, seemed to hold Deeter's attention.

"Here 'tis!"

The musical, childlike voice belonged to Deeter, who continued to lean close to the Turner watercolor, one grimy finger pointing at something near the lower half of the painting.

"The bullet hole." He grinned. "I thought it went in this direction. Old Bucky there never could hit the broad side of a barn. You know, Ty and me used to take him quail huntin' and shoot every goddamned one of them for him. And then let him think he'd done it . . ."

"That ain't true, you goofy goddamned Indian!"

As Eddie had just returned the gun to Buckner, now he literally herded him toward Ty's doors. "I think you're needed in there, Doc."

A short distance away, Massie studied the bullet hole in Turner's ocean.

"We could put some Scotch tape over it, Massie," Deeter offered. "The bullet's probably not an inch in the wall. You want me to dig it out?"

Massie shook her head and looked desolate.

Mereth indulged in an amusing projection: a hundred years from now, Warrick descendants assessing the art collection and discovering the bullet hole in the J. M. W. Turner, the result of the Wild and Woolly West period. Of 1984.

"Anyway, Massie, there's something I want to tell you. That ain't Ty in there. Did you know that?"

Mereth looked up.

"No, it ain't, Massie. I thought it was at first, but I looked close and I'll swear it ain't. What we all got to do is fan out and find old Ty. You know sometimes he makes a beeline for the old ranch house. He might be there."

As he talked, he followed Massie down the corridor. A small voice instructed Mereth to get him out of here. Circumstances were difficult enough without dealing with Deeter's unique love for Ty.

So she'd give him a drink and then take him back to his castle. She would get a chance to escape from here for a while and, by taking him in her car, his old Jeep would stay put, parked below, and he couldn't come chugging over so quickly tomorrow.

Tomorrow—

Josh, Red Pierson, possibly Junior Nagle. And call Hal. Must call Hal.

She hurried after Deeter, heard his voice echoing up from the downstairs entrance hall, his voice bouncing off every marble surface, still reassuring a distraught Massie.

"That ain't our old Ty up there, Massie, so don't you worry. I don't know who it is but it ain't Ty, and we got to find him 'cause he may need us. Did I ever tell you about the time that his daddy and my daddy beat each other senseless?"

Ramona had no sooner cleared away the uneaten lunch than it was time to prepare what surely would be the uneaten dinner as well. Now she stood in the white and stainless steel kitchen, peeling potatoes with a vengeance. To make matters worse, Massie had requested the dining room. Extra work.

Ramona didn't really mean that. She liked Massie. It was just that she was overworked and misused and she'd been prepared to draw the line at the dining room but she'd let Massie talk her into it. She had more important things to do than polish crystal and silver all afternoon and set the big table. God's work, that was her true calling. In fact, she was waiting for a phone call this very minute.

"Carrying the Word," as Reverend Jobe put it, was what she did best. According to him, God had performed a "master stroke" when He'd put her down in close proximity to Mr. Tyburn Warrick. A Holy Partnership, that's what they had formed with Mr. Warrick, to the greater glory and good of Jesus Christ, His only Son, our Lord and Savior, Amen.

Ramona could do nothing for a moment but stare down on the unwinding potato skin, seeing neither potato nor skin nor the copper bowl nor the marble counter nor the shaded pool of late afternoon sun which filtered down over her work area.

All she was capable of seeing at the moment was the face of the miraculous man who possessed the equally miraculous voice, the Reverend Gerald Jobe, spiritual leader to hundreds of thousands of lost souls, spokesman for the Righteous everywhere, President of Tulsa Christian College—the place where young people could gain a Christian education, cleansed of Satan and his influences.

Flooded with spiritual grace, Ramona closed her eyes and prayed out loud:

"Lord Jesus Christ, help him with his numerous crosses and make us good disciples for You to use through him. Amen."

Prayer over, the knife picked up speed, moving skillfully over the potato, the long curlicue unbroken. Ramona glanced toward the far side of the kitchen, where Elaine and Lois were washing up the luncheon service. Good girls, both, Reverend Jobe's girls attending his College, working part-time out here. Ramona got all her girls now through Tulsa Christian College. That way she was guaranteed young people with good Christian characters.

All right, now what to do with these spuds once they were peeled? Old Doctor Buckner would eat anything. Massie would eat nothing. And Mereth—

Ramona shook her head. Sad, that one. She'd taken her eyes off God and she'd fallen.

What an evil transformation. Ramona had never seen Satan move with such unholy speed. One day Mereth Warrick had been whole and healthy and open, the very next sick and enclosed and despairing. Ramona, along with Massie, had stood outside her door on the awful day six years ago and listened to her cry and had tried to plead with her to open the door and had received no response.

Clearly she had abandoned God.

Such a horrible thought, to abandon God. And that very night, under cover of darkness, like a thief, Mereth had crept out of Warrick in the company of Satan and Satan alone knew what had happened for the last six years.

Well, she was back now—

Maybe Ramona and surely Reverend Jobe could reach her while she was here. God's forgiveness was rich. No one in her right mind could afford to turn her back on such a gift.

Though now, unexpectedly, Ramona remembered the time when she'd almost turned her back on that same forgiveness and would have fallen straight into the pit of everlasting and fiery Hell if it hadn't been for—

Reverend Gerald Jobe.

"You okay, Mrs. Evans?" This inquiry came from Elaine, who apparently had looked up to witness Ramona's weakness.

"Just a passing whisper from Jesus." Ramona smiled.

"Praise the Lord!"

"The Lord be praised."

The two girls turned back to their work. Ramona settled more comfortably upon the stool, dropped the peeled potato into the copper bowl and reached for another. She cut out the eyes with the tip of her knife and wondered if Mr. Warrick would be up to eating dinner this evening. If so, she'd fix him a batch of cottage fries. She had a few good purple Bermudas in the basement bin. Slice 'em thick, the way Mr. Warrick liked them, fry them in bacon grease with the spuds and a dollop of chili sauce to "give them character."

She smiled nostalgically down on the peeled spuds. She adored Mr. Warrick. He'd seen her through some rough patches, paid the whole hospital bill for her cancer scare, had even come up to see her once in that big, black limo of his, hand-carrying every long-stemmed rose in the state of Oklahoma, and before he left he'd kissed her on the forehead and had whispered that a woman's tits had nothing to do with her heart and soul, and those they had not cut off.

Suddenly, to her embarrassment, her eyes went watery.

It was God's will, according to Reverend Jobe, all of it, the disease taking her breasts, the infection that kept her in the hospital and even her husband leaving her were all part of God's will.

That hurt, though. Still did. Always would, even though the Reverend had tried to help her along the path to salvation and forgiveness where her husband was concerned.

Her hands were shaking so hard that wisely she laid down the sharp knife, bowed her head and closed her eyes.

At that moment the phone rang.

Before Elaine picked up the receiver, Ramona smiled, bowed her head and concluded her heartfelt prayer. She knew who it was on the phone.

"Thank you, Jesus Christ," she murmured and looked up as Elaine announced with unmistakable awe in her voice:

"It's him, Mrs. Evans. It's Reverend Jobe . . ."

After forty-five minutes of listening to Deeter's persistent claim that that wasn't Ty upstairs in that bed, of watching him grow progressively drunker, of Massie's growing sense of mourning, of Eddie O'Keefe's silent watching out of the window, of Ramona's announcement that Reverend Gerald Jobe was on his way out and she was setting another place for dinner—after all of this, Mereth found she was having difficulty drawing enough air into her lungs.

Now she stood and delivered both an announcement and command in a tone of voice which she hoped left no margin for debate.

"Come on, Deeter. I'll drive you home. Bring the bottle if you wish, but let's go."

She added, "We'll need several cars tomorrow, Eddie. Josh is coming in from California, Red Pierson from the city—I don't know if he's flying or driving—Junior Nagle from Dallas. Just stand by and be available, will you?"

"I always am."

"Why don't you stay for dinner? Ty always enjoyed your company."

"My pleasure."

"Come on, Deeter," she repeated, grabbing the big man and leading him toward the door. "I'd invite you to stay for dinner, but I don't think you're in an eating mood . . ."

To her relief, Deeter came peacefully, lovingly cradling the almost empty bottle of bourbon in his arms like a baby.

Eddie asked, "Are you sure you can handle him?"

Mereth nodded. "We've been handling each other for years. Besides, I want to see the castle," she added, seeing in her mind's eye that bizarre half-completed replica rising less than majestically from the prairie floor.

"Please don't be too late," Massie requested softly. "Dinner around eight-thirty."

Mereth nodded and started out of the door after Deeter. Then, on a delayed reaction, she stepped back to the terrace room and peered in at Massie.

"Reverend Gerald Jobe?"

Massie looked up. "Yes."

"What's the . . . connection?" Mereth asked. What possible reason could Gerald Jobe have to come to Warrick?

"Ramona," Massie said simply. "And Ty. Reverend Jobe saved Ramona's soul after her surgery several years ago, and of late they both had started on Ty."

It had to rank as the most ludicrous announcement of this day. In her wildest imaginings Mereth could not envision Ty Warrick sitting still to listen to the melodramatic unintelligible fundamentalist hocus-pocus which was Jobe's stock-in-trade.

"Has he—Reverend Jobe—been here before?"

Eddie answered this one. "Reverend Jobe comes almost every week, sometimes twice a week. Mr. Warrick told me he really enjoys his company."

Mereth was aware of the stunned expression on her face but could do nothing to alter it. Eddie's reverent tone told her which side he was on and that perhaps she'd better watch what she said about the multimillionaire Jobe, whose "Christian ministry" was making him one of the richest men in Oklahoma—in the United States—a super-slick media-oriented Elmer Gantry who pitched more than he preached and gave new dimension to the phrase "the tyranny of righteousness."

"Massie, how do you feel about all this? About Reverend Jobe, I mean."

Massie shrugged. "Ty liked him. Anyone is welcome here who brings Ty pleasure. Ty made a donation to Tulsa Christian College about three years ago, wasn't it, Eddie? A million dollars for a new student prayer center."

Feeling like Alice down the rabbit hole, Mereth pulled the door closed behind her, calling out, "Be back soon."

She found herself alone, Deeter nowhere in sight. She hurried down the corridor and glanced up the staircase, hoping he had not gone back up to Ty's room.

"Miss Warrick."

This voice came from the top of the stairs, and she looked in that direction and saw a flushed Miss Kent, a white sweater drawn over her nurse's uniform, an apology in her voice.

"If you're looking for the big man, I think he went outside. He started up here, but I just suggested that he go on outside and get some fresh air."

Mereth smiled, grateful for the woman's quiet authority. Deeter never could resist a woman. "Thank you, Miss Kent. I'm sorry for . . ."

"No, I'm the one. I think I could have handled it, but Dr. Buckner . . ." She broke off and shrugged, apparently not wanting to make a direct accusation.

Mereth liked her for her honesty, if nothing else.

"Miss Kent, may I ask you? How is my grandfather? Dr. Buckner has told us nothing."

The two women searched each other's faces. Miss Kent glanced down the hall. "He's doing well, considering. Strokes are difficult to predict."

"Be specific, please."

"One, the cerebral damage may be such that no recovery is possible. Two, he may regain partial cerebral efficiency in which case physical therapy could commence. And three—"

"Which is—?"

"He's doing well, Miss Warrick. I must go now. Please don't worry. It's in God's hands." Then she was gone.

This day had to end soon.

"Deeter?" Mereth called his name as she pushed open the front door. Glancing toward her car, she saw a lump slouched in the front seat, a huge, unmistakable head. Old Deeter had obviously not been so drunk that he'd failed to hear her offer to drive him home.

Having found him, she relaxed, the relief of a worried mother

who locates an unruly child. Well, then, to the castle, see him settled and safely drunk for the evening, and then back here to prepare herself for dinner and the Reverend Gerald Jobe.

She'd never met the man personally but felt as if she knew him.
His organization boasted a high-powered and highly paid public
relations staff. Few days went by when one did not see his face or
hear his voice, either on television or in the newspapers, frequently
both. She believed in God, believed in turning to Him, and therefore resented these self-appointed spokesmen who made God seem
so unholy.

"I lost you, Deeter," she called out to the man who'd carried her
on his massive shoulders before she could walk.

"I've been right here, Mereth, waiting for you. I had to get out
of that place."

"I know." She nodded and crawled wearily behind the wheel,
saw the keys in the ignition, her purse on the floor.

As she executed the turnaround, she saw Deeter tilt the bottle of
Jack Daniel's and drain it. One down, but there was a full one in
the seat beside him. He glared at the empty bottle as though unable
to decide what to do with it. Just as Mereth cleared the covered
portico, he tossed it into the lilac bushes.

They drove in silence until she passed the security guard, his
right hand resting on the holstered gun on his hip. She stepped on
the accelerator and increased her speed, taking delight in his quick
maneuver backward in order to avoid being run down.

A curve in the road blotted him from view and she settled more
comfortably behind the wheel and was aware of Deeter breaking
the seal on the virgin bottle of Jack Daniel's and wished in a way
he'd not drink any more. She wanted to talk with him, knew that—
next to Junior Nagle—Ty told Deeter things he told no one else,
not even Massie.

"Deeter, why don't you put that down and listen to me for just a
moment, will you?"

"All ears," he muttered, making a face at the bottle from which he'd just taken a long swallow. "But don't try to tell me that old man back there's Ty, 'cause he ain't."

They were now on the flat expanse of blacktop that led to the intersection—left to the turnpike, right to the Warrick oil fields and drilling company and straight ahead to Deeter's castle. Mereth floored the accelerator and watched the slim needle climb effortlessly to ninety.

Deeter slid down in the narrow seat and tried to get comfortable, but his protruding stomach spilled out in all directions, his long, heavy legs raised at an awkward angle. Despite this, his head rolled back on the cushioned headrest, eyes closed, too drunk to care how uncomfortable he was.

"Things have changed around here, Mereth," he muttered. "I don't know half the time what to expect from anyone. When everybody just leaves Ty alone he's okay, you know? But . . ."

"How have things changed?"

"I don't know," he slurred. "Ty has secret dealings all over now. Foreigners. They come and go a lot. They're all phony as three-dollar bills, you know? Ty don't always know and that worries me, Mereth. He don't always know it or want to believe it, like something's fucked up his thinking." Deeter opened his eyes and looked directly at Mereth. His eyes were bloodshot.

"The worst thing, Mereth, is he's got a real bad case of God. Never thought I'd see the day. Talkin' shit about rich men entering the Kingdom of Heaven. Goin' through the eye of a needle, I don't know. I can't understand him half the time. Mumbo-jumbo crap."

For several moments the only sound was the shrill whistling of the wind the car made under duress of speed. Abruptly Mereth slowed and watched the needle slide down to a safe seventy.

"Go on, Deeter. Tell me about Ty and this sickness."

"Why did you slow down?" he whined, looking like a disappointed child.

"Intersection up ahead."

"Ain't no car coming. Deeter likes speed, likes to listen to the wind talk."

Mereth smiled. With Deeter there was always that sense of a painful straddling of two worlds. Despite the approaching intersection, she stepped on the accelerator and felt the car shoot forward and watched Deeter out of the corner of her eye, saw him settle back against the headrest, a look of relaxed pleasure on his face.

"That's good, Mereth. That's good."

"Now turn about. Tell me about Ty and God," she requested softly.

Suddenly a slow smile cracked the old Indian's face. "Damnedest thing I ever saw," he said.

"How do you mean?"

"Well, the more God he got the meaner the bastard got."

"I don't . . . ."

"He got all . . . I don't know . . . stuck up, you know? Kind of prissy, like a reformed whore. I used to tell him, 'It ain't God that's got ahold of you; it's Satan. You done let Satan win the day.' "

Mereth listened, impressed by the perception of this "drunken Indian." "What did Ty say to that?"

"He called me a stupid heathen. I had to look the goddamned word up, but he was right. Heathen, that's me. Trouble is, I haven't always known the word but I've always known what I am. But he don't have one idea in hell who he is now."

Intersection straight ahead. Clear vision on the left, blind side on the right. What the hell! Take it flying.

And she did, peering around the tall obscuring weeds just in time to see a dusty pickup traveling at an equally high rate of speed coming toward the intersection.

Jesus—

The squeal of brakes came from the pickup while she veered and accelerated even more and, with less than a coat of paint to spare, the sports car shot ahead while the pickup swerved behind.

"Whoopee-ee-ee!" Deeter cried, sitting up in the seat, looking alert for the first time, his arm on the back of the seat holding on as Mereth struggled to bring the car under control. "Goddamned roughnecks, that's who it was." He grinned, craning his neck to follow the pickup. "Hell bent for Tulsi Town and whores!"

"Are they . . . all right?" Mereth asked, bringing the car down to a safe fifty, then forty, the needle still dropping.

"All right!" Deeter mimicked. "Ain't nothin' can kill them bastards."

She drew a deep breath and felt a curious exhilaration. If she'd crossed the intersection five seconds later there was a good chance she and Deeter and the pickup filled with roughnecks would be splattered about in the nearby ditches.

Stupid. But fun.

"You're pretty much like him, you know?" Deeter said reflectively. "As long as I've known Ty he'd take the goddamnedest chances that nobody else would take. And he didn't always get away with it, either. Once when we was boys, when our daddies was beatin' each other black and blue every Sunday afternoon, Ty and me, we'd head for the woods back there behind Warrick and we'd shoot us a rabbit or two and light a jet and roast the critters and eat like we was kings. Well, there was this old mountain lion in those parts that smelled our cooking and come running to dinner even before we could angle our guns and old Ty just up and started wrestling him. Damnedest thing I ever seen, dust and fur and bare flesh, and finally the old lion ran off and Ty was left with a shredded back that looked like hamburger. Oh, he hurt like the devil for days but did all his chores 'cause he didn't want his daddy to know he'd lost a fight."

For several moments they drove in silence. She'd seen scars on Ty's back, had not known what had caused them, knew now only that the pain of longing was moving through her again, dragging her down, and felt even more strongly at that minute the sense that some sort of control was killing her, robbing her of life, of all, annihilating her.

Ahead in the diminished light of early dusk she saw the topography changing again. There was something for everyone on Warrick, flat west-Texas-like, sand and sagebrush, appearing deceptively barren, for beneath it hid some of the richest oil reserves in the Southwest. The central section was verdant and green, the best grazing land in the Southwest, some claimed. Then the extreme northwest and northeast corners were rolling in timber, dotted here and there with high-producing wells, untapped riches and unknown treasures—as Ty was fond of saying.

"All a man's got to do is talk Nature out of a portion of her treasure."

"You know, startin' right there," and Deeter pointed with the bottle out of the window, "Ty's daddy stole all that," he gestured broadly through the windshield, "from my daddy."

Yes, Mereth had heard the story—countless times—and said nothing. The expression on Deeter's face spoke of memories, of two boys riding Indian ponies bareback across the disputed land, mutual attraction, mutual respect and love growing in spite of everything.

"You know, Mereth, I wanted so bad I could taste it to be Ty Warrick. I didn't just want to look like him. I wanted to crawl inside his skin and *be* him. There weren't nothing he couldn't or wouldn't do, even then."

Mereth waited out the silence, almost preferring the man drunk and blustery and obscene.

He drew a wheezing breath and made a broad pronouncement, as though a splendid idea had just occurred.

"Wouldn't it be funny as hell if he was sitting over at the castle waiting for us? He did that sometimes, you know? He'd sneak away from Massie and all his chains back there at Warrick and come over here to the castle looking for my freedom."

Mereth glanced his way. Deeter might be one of those men who made more sense drunk than sober.

"That isn't possible now, I'm afraid," she murmured. Mereth rubbed the back of her neck, feeling a residue of tension from the near collision with the pickup back at the intersection.

Josh would get in tomorrow. And then Brit. A gathering of the oddest clan in the history of families. Would it have made any difference if their mother and father had lived, had survived the plane crash?

"You ain't forgotten the way, have you?" Deeter asked and tipped the bottle of Jack Daniel's to his mouth and wiped the excess off his chin with the back of his hand.

"No."

She looked ahead and saw in the distance the first jagged, incomplete crenelated roofline of Deeter's never-to-be-completed castle rising from the prairie floor, the same yellow masonry as Buckingham, the scale enlarged but the lines basically the same.

The last time she'd been here the high walls had been in place but the interior empty, a massive hollow shell like one of the old English church ruins, gutted center reclaimed by grass and weeds and wildflowers, surrounded by a perfect facade. Deeter had built a small apartment inside the east wing, had moved his cot and sleeping bag and blankets and television and the accumulated junk of an eighty-year-old pack rat into this small apartment and called it home.

Occasionally the Osage Indians held tribal meetings inside the castle's empty interior, and now and then a wandering tourist would depart the turnpike and come investigating. Generally Deeter would receive him warmly and put on his black top hat which he'd bought in London and would take great pride in showing him around.

"Big changes." Deeter grinned and sat up, clutching the bottle between his legs and searching the road ahead. "You just wait and see."

As she topped the slight incline and looked down, she saw it in the distance, the aberration, a castle's facade looking remarkably dignified with the blessing of distance. There *was* something new. She squinted through the windshield, trying to see around the shadows of dusk.

"Well, what do you think?" Deeter asked proudly.

"What is it?"

"A gate! You gone blind? Two of them little guard boxes and a frilly gate just like that one they got over there, 'cause I took a snapshot, that my boy took of me in front of the one over there, down to a foundry guy in Oklahoma City and I said to him, 'I want this; can you do it?' And lookee there, he did it!''

Despite the incoherence Mereth understood what he'd said, and she slowed the better to see the "new addition": sentry boxes resembling the ones at Buckingham and, stretching between them, an elaborate piece of black forged wrought iron complete with mounted gilt insignias of the lion and the unicorn, impressive from a distance and growing more so. Someone had done a good job of reproduction. The filigree etched against the horizon resembled black lace in whorls and spirals, giving the impression of Victorian seclusion and elegance.

"It's marvelous, Deeter!" She smiled, bringing the car to a halt about thirty feet from the closed gates. "Has your son seen it?" she asked, curious about the tall, black-haired man she'd seen only once, in the early sixties. She must have been about six, seven. Deeter's wife had just died, and the son was on his way to Cambridge in England. She remembered nothing about him except his name and that he had never smiled.

"Robert, that's his name, isn't it?" She was instantly regretful that she'd asked.

"He don't come home no more. He's ashamed of me."

Mereth thought how much Deeter and Ty really did have in common, wandering offspring who never deigned to come home unless they wanted something.

"Well, get going," he ordered. "This bottle is dead. Deeter needs another."

She could have debated his need for bourbon but refrained from doing so and guided the car forward, wondering if he or she should jump out and open the gate.

"Just go around it," Deeter muttered, slumping back into the seat. "The goddamned thing don't open, so just go around it."

She looked out and saw twin forked roads beaten into the prairie grass like a wishbone, one leg going around the right sentry box, the other going around the left. Through the black filigree she saw the dirt roads rejoined on the other side and leading in a straight line to the castle about a quarter of a mile away.

They were less than five hundred yards from the castle when she looked ahead and saw a dusty, slightly battered blue pickup truck parked at the end of the road. She stared at it, some element of recollection dawning.

"You're coming in, ain't you, Mereth? I want you to see my place. I've done some fixin' up. Massie give me some things she don't need from the big place and . . ."

"Whose truck is that?"

"Hell if I know. Looks like a Warrick truck. Oil-field crew. Hell, I don't know."

"Why is it parked over here?" she asked, certain now that it was the same truck that had come barreling through the intersection.

"It's probably just Chris. Comes over when he's in these parts and brings me some beer."

She listened to the vague explanation and pulled alongside the truck.

"Come on. Deeter's castle!" He crawled out of the car and started toward the open door and the warm light coming from beyond the threshold.

The sizable living area was cluttered with mismatched furniture —a few pieces she recognized from her childhood. That desk there had once been in Ty's old office, and the table had come from the kitchen.

The walls were decorated with posters, one of Russell Means, the Indian leader of the sixties; one of Pike's Peak; and one nondescript mountain scene—probably the Grand Tetons.

On the cracked linoleum floor was a good Navajo rug done in shades of brown and rust and cream. She noticed a small fire glowing in the black beehive fireplace, then saw a pair of long, blue-jeaned legs, sock feet raised on a cracked brown leather hassock, the owner of the legs obscured behind the wings of the chair which once had been in Massie's sitting room.

Whether Deeter had seen the legs or not she didn't know, for he disappeared immediately into the kitchen. Embarrassed by the presence of another person, she held her position and noticed now an arm clad in a blue jean jacket, a can of Coors clutched in the hand. Then a voice, male, slightly sleepy, came from the recesses of the chair.

"Deeter? You?"

Mereth kept quiet.

"Deeter, you old bastard, I asked if it was you!"

"Now who do you think it would be?" came a muffled reply from the kitchen.

She heard the refrigerator door open, heard a pleasant curse.

"Son of a bitch! You bring the beer?"

"Sure did. Though it came close to ending up splattered all over the crossroads back there."

Deeter reappeared in the kitchen door. He'd taken off his shirt and stood revealing a good physique for a man his age, marred only by the protruding stomach. In his right hand he held a can of beer from which he tore the fliptop, dropped it onto the floor and went to meet the voice coming from the recesses of the chair.

"Chris, it is you! How in the hell do you know when Deeter needs you?"

"Generally it's when I need Deeter."

Deeter slumped onto a low stool, looking like an accordion folding up. "When did you get here?" he asked.

"This morning. Emanuel picked me up. I understand there's trouble in paradise."

Deeter nodded. "Ty's gone. Flown the coop. You haven't seen him, have you?"

Mereth closed her eyes. Which was worse? Facing it or running from it?

When she looked back she saw the long legs slowly lifting from their relaxed position on the hassock and planting themselves on the floor. A second later a strong profile appeared and she started forward, stunned.

The same. It was he, the man from the toll plaza and the gardens, the one having lunch in the lilac bushes.

"Ty's ill, Deeter," the man said gently.

"Ty ain't sick!" Deeter exploded. "He's just done flown the coop, that's all."

"No, he's ill, Deeter. Perhaps dying."

"Bullshit!"

"A stroke, Deeter. The doctor's come and gone."

"Fucking bullshit!"

Suddenly Deeter looked up as though he'd forgotten something. "Mereth? Where in the hell are you?"

Mereth drew a deep breath and stepped out of the shadows. "Here I am."

She saw the tall man, on his feet now, his face flushed.

"It's a four-way stop back there at the intersection," Mereth said. "One of us probably should have obeyed the rules."

"There is no four-way stop at that intersection. For north-south traffic. It's a two-way stop for east-west."

"I'm sorry, but you're wrong."

"Would you like to bet?"

She stared up at the face which had appeared before her at unexpected intervals throughout most of this long and unhappy day. "Deeter, I have to go now," she concluded, stepping toward the door.

"Don't, Mereth," the big man begged and reached out for her hand, missed it and in the process almost fell off the low, three-legged stool.

Within the instant the younger man was there, assisting Deeter until he could relocate a center of balance.

"You know Chris?" Deeter asked.

"We've . . . more or less met."

As she walked to the door she took the plunge. "Chris, have you been to Warrick before?"

The question prompted a laugh. "Yes, I've been here before. Many times."

"Do you live around here?"

"No. I live on the East Coast. Sometimes the West. Once on Majorca. Twice on Mykonos. Once on Capri. Once on Corfu. I like islands, which is of course why I like Warrick."

From this distance she couldn't tell if he was making fun of her or not.

"How dull we must seem after those places." She smiled.

"Yes," he agreed.

At the door she looked back, baffled by her feelings of anger. "Are you all right, Deeter?"

"I'll look after him." The younger man smiled. "I always do. Have for as long as I can remember. No need to worry."

She started to respond, then changed her mind. How and why he'd taken up at Warrick in general and with Deeter in particular, she didn't know and was forced to admit was none of her business. She didn't have the time to take a census of every roughneck and cowhand and odd man and gardener employed at Warrick. Ty used to call his burgeoning employees his only true family, making every member of the true family within hearing distance feel like hell.

Suddenly she remembered that she'd not yet called Hal. Good Lord. He'd be worried sick. And she wondered what the school had said about her absence. And what was the reaction of the "outside world" to Ty's illness? At Warrick there was always a feeling of extreme isolation.

He was right at least on one point: it was an island.

"Good night, Deeter," she called out with studied effort, overlooking the tall man.

As she reached her car, she heard, "Miss Warrick! A word, if I may. Thanks for bringing Deeter home," he said.

Mereth slipped behind the wheel and was on the verge of turning the key in the ignition when the man leaned close to her open window.

"I wanted to ask you about Red Pierson," he said. "Have you . . . called him yet with the news?"

The blunt question took her by surprise.

146

"He certainly should be notified, don't you think? When I tried to call his office a while ago, I was told he would be out of town for a few days and beyond reach."

Mereth was bewildered. "I'm afraid I don't see what business that is of yours, Mr. . . ."

"Chris. Just Chris." He smiled. "And it is, at least in part, my business. I'm surprised Red Pierson didn't say anything about . . ." He raised up and backed away from the car as though aware he'd said too much. "Just tell me if he's on his way to Warrick."

"As I said, I don't see . . ."

"What you see isn't that important." Despite the nature of his words, his voice was polite. "I'm sorry. I shouldn't have said that. Ty Warrick and Deeter worked out an . . . arrangement some time ago on the disposition of certain lands. Red Pierson was handling the negotiations for them. With your grandfather ill, Deeter would like to . . ."

"What is your interest in all this?" she interrupted, beginning to envision the chaos to come, people making claims on the Warrick estate.

Still, he'd not answered her question, and she turned on the ignition. "You'd better see to Deeter. He's had too much to drink and he refuses to accept the fact that my grandfather may be dying."

"Do you accept it?"

"I don't make the rules of nature. I do try to abide by them."

"Awkward, waiting for someone to die."

"I'm not waiting for my grandfather to die. I'm waiting for him to get well."

"Have you called Mr. Pierson?"

Weary of his questions, she jerked the gears into place, stepped on the accelerator too hard and shot backward, belatedly thinking to look in her rearview mirror. Fortunately there was no obstacle, only the night vastness of the prairie itself.

She switched on her lights and saw him standing at the end of the washed-out path, hands in pockets, a smile on his face as though he were well aware of the disturbing nature of what he had said and left unsaid.

She stared at him for a second, caught in the direct spill of her headlights. Since childhood she'd been warned to be wary of people. The man who had driven her to school had been both chauffeur and bodyguard, and there was always a gun in the glove compartment of every limo. Kidnapping had been explained in nightmarish details to all the Warrick kids and impressed upon them as something to take very seriously. In adolescent years she'd been warned about the "friendly stranger," the "persistent new friend." Now who was this man, and what did he want?

Under the urgency of these unanswered questions, she stepped on the accelerator and shot forward down the narrow, rutted dirt road which led away from Deeter's castle.

Looking up, she saw looming before her a great black barrier and remembered Deeter's newest toy, the reproduction of the massive gate flanked on either side by the sentry boxes and no fence. She slammed on her brakes and felt the car slide to the left.

She came to a stop and for several moments gripped the steering wheel and vibrated along with the car and rested her head on the wheel.

For one bleak moment she considered not going back. It mattered little to her what happened. She'd like nothing more than to return to her apartment in Tulsa, fix a vodka and tonic, soak in a hot tub and crawl into bed with her notes for tomorrow's lecture on Emily Dickinson, the Middle Years.

Then do it. Some might interpret it as an act of cowardice and thoughtlessness. But there were things she had to do. She *did* have a life beyond Warrick, had worked hard to create one. There was Hal. She owed him the courtesy of a few hours and, well, there were other responsibilities that she had neglected long enough.

Then leave. Now. And she did. With remarkable ease she guided the car around the useless gate and instantly felt a sense of release, as though a prison sentence had been suspended. Freedom ahead. The turnpike. Tulsa. Warrick behind her. She'd tried. She'd really tried. It had been a mistake to return. She was a stranger now, the staff foreign to her, two brothers coming home that she didn't know, Massie changed, Ty's associates, Chris—whoever he was.

She rolled down the window and felt a pleasing April evening breeze, part fragrant chill, part promise of warmth. At last she'd made a right decision.

She made it as far as the intersection when, without warning, the breeze became a freezing wind and a punishing guilt simultaneously cut off her resolve, and she knew there would be neither retreat nor escape. Not now. She couldn't. Massie needed her. Then, too, Mereth felt a powerful curiosity. There was a good chance that the most fascinating three-ring circus in the world would be gathering at Warrick over the next few days. The blood part of her, the Warrick part, wanted nothing to do with it. But the detached witness knew that to miss it would be like missing a great sporting event.

No, she must stay and arm herself with her most awesome weapon—objectivity. For she wanted nothing, expected nothing from Ty Warrick. He'd already done everything to her he possibly could do, and she had survived. For the others, their ordeals were just beginning.

Then Warrick it would be. She reminded herself to ask Massie again about this Chris, who apparently knew Ty's personal attorney on a first-name basis. Then she would go to her girlhood rooms and search through her old wardrobe for something suitable for dinner and dress and go down to meet God's man in Tulsa, father of Tulsa Christian College, shepherd to millions of lost souls, the man whose fertile mind had conceived and built Tulsa's newest embarrassment on State and Commerce streets, a modern drive-in with parking slots like a bank or restaurant, the Faith-O-Mat, where on each "menu" was listed the various trials and tribulations that might befall a human being struggling in the course of a day or a lifetime. "Adultery"—"Alcoholism"—"Drug Abuse"—"Terminal Illness" —"Bearing False Witness"—The penitent would then make his or her proper selection, drop half a dollar jukebox fashion and, through headphones, receive a "personalized, pretaped counseling" from Reverend Jobe himself.

Mereth shook her head, amused, seeing clearly the absurdity as it stood in actuality at one of Tulsa's busiest commercial intersections. Less funny was the fact that at almost any hour of the day cars bearing "sinners" were lined up well into the street, forcing traffic policemen to be on duty almost around the clock.

Faith-O-Mat.

What kind of a mind could conceive of such a thing, and what was his connection to Ty? Where had all these strangers come from? For a man who always had preached wariness of strangers, Ty clearly had broken his own rules.

Nothing new there. Her foot pressed down, the car picked up speed. She opened her window and breathed evening air again and wondered when she would give up trying to solve or resolve certain mysteries.

Warrick

MASSIE THOUGHT she heard a car on the drive outside the window and left the terrace room and an uneasy company consisting of Eddie O'Keefe, Dr. Horace Buckner, Ramona Evans out of her cook's uniform and wearing a navy blue dress and circumflex eyebrows and, of course, the Reverend, who'd just arrived in his chauffeur-driven Continental Mark IV with the equally simple license plate of JOBE.

Everyone seemed at cross-purposes. Reverend Jobe was in the process of explaining the proper pronunciation of his name to Dr. Buckner, who turned his back on the man and his explanation: Jobie, the affectionate diminutive of Job, God's Little Job—for

150

while God had sent him many a trial and stumbling block, he could not and would not begin to compare his trivial travail to that of the noble biblical Job.

Massie had heard it before, countless times, and had been grateful for the sound of the approaching car. She heard footsteps coming across the marble hall and hoped it was Mereth but knew better, and saw Miss Kent walking toward the front door in what seemed to be a great urgency.

Had something happened?

Her fear increasing, she followed after Miss Kent. Through the front door she saw the nurse standing at the bottom of the steps, peering around Reverend Jobe's black Mark IV.

"Miss Kent, may I . . . be of assistance?"

"I'm sorry, Miss Massie. I didn't mean to . . . They called from the security gate. The new equipment is coming in. Also another nurse. Round-the-clock, you know. We do need relief. We all do."

Massie moved slowly down the steps during this incoherency and wondered if it was just her or if the woman was unduly nervous or a combination of both.

"Here she is!" Miss Kent exclaimed.

Massie looked up to see a white panel truck, ST. MARK'S HOSPITAL painted on the side, a white-coated man driving and a large, broad-faced, middle-aged nurse filling the front seat beside him. As the driver of the truck tried to pull up in front of the steps, he confronted Reverend Jobe's Continental, which blocked the entrance to the portico.

"Who owns that?" the nurse shouted out the window. "Get it out of here. Immediately! We need that space. This is an emergency vehicle." She hit the pavement on a run, gesturing with both hands, a mountain of a woman. Over six feet was Massie's guess, well over two hundred pounds, mostly muscle. Short, cropped brown hair and a flat, no-nonsense face.

She was on the verge of shouting again when Reverend Jobe's driver appeared in the doorway of the small brick building at the end of the driveway, the place where chauffeurs met for beer and sandwiches while they were waiting.

"I'm sorry," Jobe's chauffeur called out. "I'll move it."

A college student, Massie thought, though his polite cooperation was lost on the huge nurse standing center driveway with her hands on her hips and a withering glare on her face.

As the Lincoln glided forward, Miss Kent hurried across the driveway to greet the new arrival, and Massie saw a warm smile pass between the two women and saw something else as well, a premeditated purpose in the arrival of this specific nurse. Dr. Buckner's doing. No one else would burst willy-nilly into Ty's room, not even Deeter Big Cow.

For a few moments, as the hospital truck jockeyed close to the steps, Massie felt a new and bleak loneliness. Ty was moving farther and farther away from her, more people coming between them.

After the hospital truck rattled to a stop, Massie moved back up the steps to get out of the way and watched with a sense of foreboding as three large pieces of equipment were unloaded by the man in the white coat. Miss Kent took the lead and called out, "This way. Follow me."

Shivering from the night chill, Massie felt a slight resentment. *She* should be leading the way. Maybe she could steal a moment with Ty while the equipment was being set up, just to touch his hand. Glancing back, she saw the large nurse reach inside the truck, withdraw a piece of Samsonite luggage and tilt her body away from its weight as she slammed the doors.

Go to her. Introduce yourself.

Massie was on the verge of doing this when suddenly the woman spied her. A look of relief covered the flat, blank face.

"Oh, good. I don't have to carry this now. Here, take it up to my room, and I'd like a pot of coffee and sandwiches in an hour."

She thrust the heavy Samsonite luggage at Massie who, stunned, took it with both hands.

"And tell the family," the nurse called back as she started up the steps after the other two, "that Miss Nellie has arrived and I'll not

152

answer any of their questions until morning, so they needn't bother."

Then she pushed through the front door and was gone, leaving Massie alone on the steps holding the heavy, blue, battered Samsonite luggage with both hands.

Her first impulse was to laugh, which she did, a single, short expulsion of air. But it was an instinct not to be trusted. Slowly she put down the luggage at her feet and, as long as she was bent over, she stayed there and gave in to the breaking dam of grief and cried as she had not cried since that first lonely night she'd spent at Warrick over thirty years ago, cut off from all that was familiar to her.

Now again she suffered those same despairing feelings of aloneness. The force that had held her world together for so long and given it a richness of life had been wrenched out, and all seemed to have collapsed into a heap of meaningless refuse.

As soon as she shut her eyes she saw Ty's face, so moving especially in the strong simplicity of his love. She tried again to console herself for what had happened but could not. Unable to rise, she bowed her head lower and wept fresh tears and knew she would have to go on, but could not for the moment figure out how.

The only thought that brought a particle of comfort was the realization that she had known Ty for thirty years and that should be enough for any woman.

But it wasn't.

Eddie O'Keefe sat at the end of the table in the family dining room and tried not to let too many of his rough edges show and thought how lucky he was to be sitting here at the Warrick dining table. Who would believe it back home?

Home was the south side of Oklahoma City, where everything inferior resided. There had been a brief claim to fame in high school, an amateur middleweight Golden Gloves championship, his photograph in the paper. But all it got him was a paternity suit from some little whore who claimed he'd knocked her up. A lawyer got him off, took all of his prize money and suggested he leave the state for a while.

So he did what every Okie in trouble does, headed out to California, went to mechanic's school, joined the Army, served three years in 'Nam—no big deal—got out and came back to OKC. He'd opened a little garage and had just settled down to tedium when one day this huge, big black Rolls came smoking into his garage and he fixed it just like that. This guy gets out—old but like a bull, sixties maybe, traveling with a real classy-looking black chick—and hands him a card and says he needs a full-time driver and mechanic and if he's interested—

Interested! Everybody in this part of the woods knew the name Tyburn Warrick. That was fourteen years ago, and Eddie now had a snazzy apartment over the Warrick garage and baby-sat four Rollses, five Mercedes, two Lincolns, three Cads, and when their ashtrays filled up he had the authority to turn them in to the Tulsa dealers for new models.

Click, clack. Click, clack. Silver on china, too much silence, not good, everybody eating like they was being paid to do it. Eddie speared the final bite of his prime rib and placed his fork on the edge of the plate and looked up toward Massie and thought her eyes looked red and wished he could help her.

Truth was, Eddie O'Keefe worshiped Jo Massie, had from the beginning, which was strange because he'd grown up thinking niggers were all alike. But Massie was different. She'd treated him like a human being from the beginning. In the old days when she and Mr. Warrick took car trips to Dallas or Santa Fe, Eddie ate every meal with them on the road in the best places. She'd taught him more in the last ten years than he'd learned the rest of his life put together. And she'd done some teaching on Mr. Warrick, too. Eddie remembered that time at the Compound in Santa Fe, when they'd been eating dinner after the opera and a big blond opera singer had come over to the table to say hello to Massie—the singer knew Massie's mother, who also sang opera—and they'd chatted for a while, dropping all these French and Italian and fancy names.

And old Tyburn Warrick had just sat there and listened and was as polite as though he was at Sunday school.

After the opera singer had left, Mr. Warrick had leaned over and, just like a kid, asked Massie if she'd teach him all she knew about opera, said he was just a dumb Okie with oil under his fingernails and he wanted to know who Verdi was and why he'd had to write music instead of being a doctor or lawyer.

Massie had started teaching him that very night about the Italian whose wife and children had died and who had written out his grief in music.

"More roast, Eddie?" The soft question came from Massie, who somehow could keep an eye on everyone's plate as well as on her own.

He shook his head. "No, I'm fine, Massie." He felt a flush creep into his hairline as he sensed the combined weight of all those other eyes—the most piercing of all the Reverend Gerald Jobe's, who sat on the opposite side of the table between Massie and Mereth.

Also at the table in the large, wood-paneled dining room was his good friend Ramona Evans, who would see to it that he got the rest of that beautiful hunk of meat in sandwiches for the next couple of days.

And Doc Buckner was there, still eating, never looking up, apparently not bothered by the silence as long as there was plenty of food.

Why the Reverend was being so quiet, Eddie didn't know. Generally the man talked all the time, but beyond the prayer he'd delivered at the beginning of the meal about "the tragedy that has descended on this great house today" and exhorting Jesus Christ to sit with them at table and give them the strength to face the difficult days ahead, the man had sat between the two women and said nothing.

Then, when Eddie least expected it and had about given up—

"You teach in Tulsa, I believe, Miss Warrick?"

The question shattered the stiff silence and all looked up at Jobe who, having finished eating, pushed back his chair, arranged his napkin in his lap and appeared to wait patiently for Mereth to respond.

"Yes," Mereth replied, dabbing at her lips with her napkin. "I teach at Oakhurst."

"A fine school," the Reverend said, nodding. "We always have a few Oakhurst girls at our college. Not many, though, I'm afraid. For some reason they think that our poor little college isn't quite good enough for them."

"I disagree," Mereth said politely. "Most of the girls were born in Tulsa, have grown up there and want to go away to school, a need to spread their wings. I'm sure you can understand that."

For a moment Eddie wasn't certain if Reverend Jobe understood or not. He continued to gaze at Mereth as though he was puzzled by something, and while these two held their curious nonconversation, everyone else at table kept their heads down and ate nervously.

"What is it that you teach to these special young ladies?" Reverend Jobe asked, still interested in Mereth.

Abruptly Mereth placed her fork to one side, pushed the plate back and replaced it with a glass of water. "American Literature," she said to the glass. "Primarily poets."

Reverend Jobe nodded. "God's messengers, good Christian authors. Of course, a few of them work for Satan, but there's your classic division."

For the first time Mereth looked at Reverend Jobe, and Eddie thought he saw a smile on her face.

"I never thought of them as God's messengers or Satan's."

"You *what?* I can't believe what I just heard!"

"I teach literature, not morality or ethics or theology, and certainly not religion."

"But how in the world can you separate them?"

"Simple. Certain critical criteria are relevant; certain others are not."

"But an artist's morality, his concept of Jesus Christ . . ."

"In a large proportion of the world's great literature, Reverend

Jobe, there are no concepts of Jesus Christ." The girl put a clean edge on her voice and didn't do a damned thing to soften it.

Massie stirred herself out of her silence as though sensing the evening might need a referee. Eddie had seen her perform this service countless times when Mr. Warrick would be in a feisty mood and there would be some hapless and boring guests at Warrick.

"Dr. Buckner." Massie smiled. "I forgot to tell you: your new nurse arrived. She's upstairs, also the equipment."

Dr. Buckner wiped the beef gravy from his plate with the business end of a biscuit, pushed the whole dripping thing into his mouth, swallowed once, looked over his specs at Massie and grinned.

"Dainty little thing, ain't she?"

Massie smiled. "You know the one, then?"

"Hell, yes. Nellie. Next time that drunken Indian goes bustin' into Ty's room he'll meet up face-to-face with Miss Nellie and think twice if he knows what's good for him." He made a swipe at his mouth with his napkin and eyed the near basket of biscuits.

Massie pushed the basket toward him.

"Oh, no. Enough. Got to watch the figure. How do you manage so well, Preacher?"

Reverend Jobe laughed and self-consciously smoothed his hands over the expensive dark suit. "Well, I can't say I do manage so well," he said. "Unfortunately, my large flock boasts of numerous excellent cooks, like Ramona, so the waistline pays the piper. What a delicious price it is."

Polite laughter, followed by silence, followed by a tinkling of Ramona's silver bell.

As Elaine and Lois appeared to clear the table, Mereth stood up and without a word walked around the table to the mahogany bar which ran the length of the west wall and which now had been discreetly disguised by the lowering of mahogany louvered panels. She pushed a button which simultaneously caused the panels to lift like a stage curtain and caused a brilliant flooding of blue-white fluorescent lighting to accent every bottle, every crystal glass—only one of the many well-stocked bars at Warrick. Mr. Warrick's friends talked better business with a drink in their hands.

Eddie knew why the bar had been closed for tonight. Reverend Jobe was a staunch abstainer. Alcoholism was one of his major crusades, and he'd built a small private hospital in the blackjacks north of Tulsa where those with the bucks to pay could come and dry out and find God.

Now there was a sense of collective shock as Mereth, unperturbed, went behind the bar, carefully selected a bottle of Russian vodka, reached for a highball glass, filled it a couple of fingers full, sipped once pleasurably and then, without so much as a missed beat, leaned across the bar and asked Reverend Jobe:

"How did you meet my grandfather, and how long have you known him?"

For several moments there was a sense of confusion about the table, as though they hadn't recovered from Mereth's first indiscretion of pouring herself a drink when here came the second, the impudent questions themselves.

She'd ask with a nice smile on her face. Mereth Warrick had grown into a good-looker. Funny how no guy had grabbed her and made off with her. Mr. Warrick used to call her the smartest of the bunch.

Despite the unspoken confusion, Reverend Jobe rose admirably to the occasion. He left his chair, and Eddie was impressed with something unseen about the man. Not his face, because his face was ordinary. Not his physique, because that too was ordinary—like most middle-aged men's. So it was nothing visible but still there was something, a power source, a weird magnetism. When he moved, you watched no one else and when he spoke, you listened to no one else.

"Two very good questions, Miss Warrick," he said smiling, coming up on the other side of the bar and straddling one of the round barstools with the agility of a twenty-year-old accustomed to straddling barstools. "What's that you're drinking?"

She held up the glass and took another sip. "Vodka."

"Is it good?"

"Yes. Would you like some?"

"What does it make you feel?"

"It helps me to relax."

"Why are you tense?"

"Because it's been a difficult day."

"In what way?"

"I should think that would be apparent."

"And that makes you feel better?"

"How did you meet my grandfather, and how long have you known him?"

A pause. Eddie felt curiously breathless at the rapid exchange.

As Mereth posed her questions a second time, Reverend Jobe raised both hands in a gesture of surrender and lightened the moment with a laugh. "All right! I've seen that persistence before. You are your grandfather's granddaughter."

Old Buckner coughed. "In more ways than one," he muttered and then in a raised voice asked, "Mereth, would you scare me up a Coors as long as you're over there? Help settle my stomach."

So the floodgates had been opened, and as Mereth placed a chilled can of Coors on the bar Eddie considered going over and helping himself. A little bourbon would suit him fine. But try as he might, he couldn't quite muster the courage. Reverend Jobe wouldn't be pleased. Eddie had just joined the flock about a year ago, and it felt good to be on the side of right for a change.

The next sound was a burp of pleasure coming from Buckner, who'd just consumed half a can of beer in one swallow.

Then Reverend Jobe took the floor in front of the bar as only Reverend Jobe could take any floor.

"In answer to your questions, Miss Warrick, I first had the inestimable pleasure of meeting the great Mr. Tyburn Warrick about six years ago outside that dear lady's hospital room." He pointed a finger at Ramona, who stopped clearing the table. Reverend Jobe's voice softened. "It was six years ago, wasn't it Ramona, that God asked you to walk through fire for Him?"

Ramona bowed her head, gave one short nod and sank slowly down as though mysteriously weakened by the unexpected mention of God's fire.

"I don't believe you were in residence at Warrick at that time," Jobe said, smiling at Mereth. "Of course not, or you would remember everything and not have to ask."

As center stage was now the area fronting the bar, Eddie adjusted his chair in an attempt to get a better view. Massie sat across the table, giving an impression of calm.

"And so one day as I was leaving Ramona's hospital room after a prayer session, I saw Mr. Warrick coming down the hospital corridor. There were others following behind but he was the one I was interested in, for in his face was such an expression of compassion and human understanding. You see, Ramona had served him loyally for many years and he had made the mistake of believing her doctors, who had told him the prognosis was not good, her illness terminal."

All the attention in the room now belonged to the Reverend. Eddie leaned back, enjoying himself.

"So we talked that night," Jobe went on, "and I told him God would spare Ramona for all of us but He would expect something in return, a new commitment to Christ's teachings and to those of us who conduct His ministry here on earth . . ."

Massie leaned forward, a sharp movement.

". . . you see, your grandfather was a very lost man at that time as well."

Doc Buckner made a harrumphing sound. "Ty Warrick ain't been lost a day in his life!" he said and drained the Coors.

Reverend Jobe laughed. "I don't mean literally, Dr. Buckner. Ty was a very rich man and a very lonely one. I think it's meaningful how often the two go together, don't you? He had everything he wanted and he had nothing he wanted. He was alone. His wife was dead, his son was dead, all three grandchildren had deserted him."

Dr. Buckner stood up from his chair. "So you went to work on him, didn't you, Jobe? And before you were done you relieved him of a million smackeroos!" He walked the length of the table, endlessly adjusting his belt and shirt, trying to accommodate the bulk of his stomach after the heavy meal. "And now you've got yourself a brand-new . . . what in the hell was it you were trying to build? I can't even remember." He stopped at the door and looked back, genuinely puzzled as though he'd forgotten something important.

Throughout this attack, Reverend Jobe simply stood erect, hands laced in front, head bowed as though in prayer.

"Student prayer center, Dr. Buckner, a place where students can go and meditate and ask for guidance for their problems."

"Yeah, that's it," Dr. Buckner responded flatly. "Frankly I don't remember having the need to pray all that much when I was a kid, but then I guess times have changed, haven't they? You'll excuse me now? I'll go see my new nurse and be sure the equipment is set up. Thanks, Massie. Dinner dee-licious, as always."

With that he closed the door and left an uncomfortable silence in the room, broken at last by Massie's quiet request.

"Ramona, coffee for all, please."

Mereth examined the bottle of vodka as though she'd discovered something wrong with it. "Where is this . . . student prayer center, Reverend Jobe?" she asked. "I don't recall reading anything about it in the paper."

"Ah, it wasn't in the paper, Miss Warrick. At your grandfather's request. It's a room, a large room inside the west wing of the Student Union."

Mereth looked up. "A million-dollar . . . room?"

"Quite complete, it is. A new organ . . . pipe organ, and mahogany pews, private booths for meditation."

"Is all this necessary for simple prayer, Reverend Jobe?"

"Prayer is never simple, Miss Warrick."

"Still, I didn't realize it required so many trappings."

"We try to create an atmosphere."

"Obviously you do."

As Mereth's moods were always reflected in her voice, Eddie caught clearly a pissed-as-hell mood and watched as she left the bar and circled the table.

She passed behind Massie and said full-voiced, "May I see you for a few moments, Massie?" and not waiting for an answer, proceeded on to the door and was about out of it when Reverend Jobe stirred himself.

"Miss Warrick, if I've said anything to . . ."

"Oh, no, not at all."

"I would be very honored if you'd inspect the room. We've named it the Tyburn Warrick Student Prayer Center. There's a gold plaque . . ."

Watching the conversation was like watching a fast-moving Ping-Pong game as Reverend Jobe held his position at the far end of the bar and Mereth stood poised at the opposite end of the room.

"No," she said by way of reply to his invitation. "I only hope my grandfather was pleased."

"Oh, he was. Indeed he was. I can assure you of that. In fact, he even used it himself on occasion. He told me once the last time he could remember praying, his mother was holding him on her lap. Can you imagine a lifetime without the healing balm of God's mercy and forgiveness?"

"Massie, could I . . . ?"

Reverend Jobe interrupted her with a request of his own.

"Miss Warrick, would you pray with me now? Pray with all of us, for this is a house in grief, facing difficult times, and Jesus Christ is here to help us. All we have to do is ask."

From where Eddie stood he saw a look of helpless shock on Mereth's face, saw her on the verge of a response when suddenly Massie interceded as only Massie could intercede, gently, graciously.

"Yes, lead us in prayer, Reverend Jobe. I think we all have a mutual need . . ."

Between the extreme pleasure coming from Reverend Jobe at

one end of the table and the rather pathetic sense of defeat coming from Mereth at the opposite end, Eddie felt divided.

"Our dearest Heavenly Father, Who looks after us all and never sends us a heavier cross than we can bear . . ."

Eddie bowed his head. He liked listening to Reverend Jobe's prayers. He didn't always understand his words, but somehow just listening made him feel good. It wasn't until he heard the door slam that he realized someone didn't like to hear Reverend Jobe pray.

He glanced sideward toward the door where Mereth had been standing. Gone. The door was closed, though the silence was filled by Reverend Jobe's soaring voice as he talked on to God in an intimate fashion, asking Him to forgive all those who had sinned against Him and to make of all those who disbelieved a fertile place on which the seeds of belief might be planted.

Why Mereth had stomped off in a huff, Eddie had no idea. And he closed his eyes and gave himself entirely to the soaring voice which seemed capable of wrapping itself around each individual heart, enclosing it in a cocoon of divine strength.

How could anyone resist? Why would anyone want to?

The trouble was there was nothing she could do with her outrage, and thus she was stopped by the need to make a decision in the entrance hall. Outdoors? No; chilly. Up to her room? No; the past was there. Then where?

Confused, Mereth looked back in the direction of the dining room. Massie. She had to talk to Massie. But how in the hell could she get her out from under the influence of that man?

Reverend Gerald Jobe. How she loathed him and his kind!

"Satan wins the day when he provides us with reasons for self-approval."

She heard a distant door close somewhere at the far end of the second-floor corridor.

Ty's room.

A one-million-dollar prayer *room!* Had Ty lost his mind?

Dr. Buckner. There was an ally. Maybe he knew more. It would be worth a try. Decision made, she started up the stairs, peering around the banister, hoping to catch sight of Dr. Buckner. At the top of the staircase she stood alone, staring down the length of the corridor.

"Allee-allee out's in free! Come on in, Josh, Brit! No fair!"

"Go find 'em, little girl. You can do it."

It was Ty whispering in her ear as he'd done when the others made her the seeker while they ran and hid in impossible places.

"Go on, little girl. Smell 'em out. If I can smell out oil, you can smell out those two worthless brothers of yours. Go on. I'll be watchin'."

The memory was too real, the power of the man like a force of nature still inhabiting her. Without warning, a combination of fatigue and grief and confusion joined forces and in the silence of the immense house she sat slowly on the top step.

"Go and find 'em, little girl."

Somewhere, visible only inside the fever of her mind, she saw a house, saw someone standing outside the window, watching for a long time the daily life of the house. The father was there near the lamp, the mother sewing. The chair where a child usually sat was empty and the window-peeker ached with desire to take the empty chair that usually belonged to the child and sit in the presence of a loving father and mother.

In protection against the vividness of the image, Mereth closed her eyes and leaned her head against the banister and waited out the confusion and the pain as one would wait out a flooding summer storm.

Tulsa

JUNIOR NAGLE resented Eddie's question. Yes, he'd arrived in Tulsa last night. Yes, he'd not called Warrick until this morning.

"I had to see a man about a horse," Junior snapped, hoping to put an end to the questions that were none of Eddie's goddamned business.

"Just asking, Mr. Nagle." Eddie grinned and lifted the luggage into the trunk.

Junior Nagle thought, What in the hell business was it of Eddie O'Keefe's what he'd done between last night and early this morning? Business, that's what he'd done. His and Ty's. He'd gone to the Tulsa Petroleum Exchange Bank and the disturbing meeting with Harry Beekman. My God, he hoped that old Harry was just approaching senility, that's all!

As Eddie placed Junior's luggage in the trunk, Junior spied another piece, brand-new, one of those fag designer bags. Brown with a red and green stripe down the side.

"Who belongs to that?" Junior demanded suspiciously. He knew when he woke up this morning he should have just dialed Doug Knowles over at the Cadillac agency and leased a car and a driver for himself. One thing he hated about Warrick was its isolation, like getting stuck on the far side of the moon.

"Josh," Eddie whispered succinctly, gesturing toward the back seat. "Flew in this morning from L.A. on the red-eye special."

Junior shoved his hands into his pockets and looked morosely down at the near gutter and its contents. "Shit!" he muttered. "Wait. I think I'll call . . ."

Eddie kept the trunk lid raised, waiting for Junior to make up his mind.

But to call Doug Knowles now would take another hour, maybe two, before he could get a driver and a car over here. He looked behind at the Parke Suite. He'd already checked out; no place to wait. Hell, but he hated riding with other people! And that one in particular, Ty's primary embarrassment, a queer grandson and everybody on God's green earth knew it.

Well, nothing to do but grin and bear it, though he sure as hell would have a talk with Massie later. No more shared rides with anyone—but Ty.

"Close it up." Junior sighed, indicating the trunk. "Eddie, how is he?" he asked, suddenly scared, that godawful cold feeling constricting his gut. He'd suffered the sensation all the way up from Dallas yesterday. First he thought it was something he'd eaten, but he'd eaten sensibly all day and he remembered feeling like this before, a long time ago—1924, to be exact—when he and Ty had sunk every red cent they had into their first well. Fifty thousand dollars begged, borrowed and stolen, and they'd hit rock formations, breaking drill bits, the crew discouraged and laughing at them behind their backs. Junior had had this same feeling then.

On that last day, when they were out of bucks and spirit and courage, Ty had crawled up on the rig, so dirty he looked more like a nigger than a white man. He had shouted the god-awfullest things at the crew. A madman, that's what he'd been. But he'd made it pretty clear: wasn't no one walking off that rig that day because if they did it would be the last time they walked off anything, because Ty was standing right there with his best quail-hunting shotgun aimed right at their kneecaps.

Just one more day, that's all he'd wanted, and they'd started drilling at 9 A.M. and at 11:20 A.M.—and only one hundred and thirty feet deeper—the well had gushed. Damn, what a gusher! Everything covered with oil for miles around, and Ty Warrick and Junior Nagle were sitting on the granddaddy giant of all oil fields, the biggest since Spindletop! The first Warrick field—

"Hey, Mr. Nagle. You okay?"

At the sound of the near voice, Junior came back from the past and brought the smell of oil with him.

"F . . . fine," he stammered, finding it harder and harder to make that transition back from the past. Hell, both he and Ty were getting too old. "So how's the old bastard, Eddie?"

"I told you, Mr. Nagle. Doctors say no change."

"What in the hell is that supposed to mean?"

"No . . . change," Eddie repeated.

"Is he up and about?"

Now it was Eddie's turn to gape. "No. No, of course not. Doc Buckner said this morning he has never regained consciousness from . . ."

"Shit! That pile of sawbones? Can't Massie spring for a specialist? I wouldn't trust Horace Buckner to read a thermometer."

"A specialist has been out. Yesterday."

"Who?"

"Some foreigner from St. Mark's."

Junior listened, then: "I'm going to take Ty back to Dallas."

"Can't be moved."

"Who's out there now?"

"Massie. Mereth. Family's coming," and Eddie pointed toward the back of the limo. "Deeter Big Cow was over yesterday and busted up the place pretty good. Drunk, you know. Doc Buckner took a shot at him."

Junior was looking forward to seeing Deeter. "Shit!" he muttered, thinking of who was sitting comfortably in the back seat.

"Look, sir, if you wish I can take him on out and then come back in."

Suddenly, coming from the front door of the Parke Suite, he heard a man call his name and instantly recognized, not the man's face, but his manner and the notebook in his hand, three others trailing behind him—one female, two male, though nowadays sometimes it was difficult to tell. He looked over his shoulder. Goddamned, bloodsucking reporters!

"Come on, Eddie, let's get out of here." He reached up and slammed the trunk down himself and beat Eddie to the far side of the limo and was just opening the rear door for himself when he heard the voices behind him.

"Mr. Nagle! Just a few questions . . ."

"What are you doing in Tulsa? Is it about Mr. Warrick?"

Eddie was right beside him, and simultaneously they took refuge in the black limo. As soon as the door shut, Junior heard the automatic locks click.

He sat on the edge of the seat and stared furiously out of the smoked one-way windows. The newspaper reporters were still bent over, tapping at the windows, their faces new and bland and unused. What right did such human vacuums have even to inquire about a man like Ty?

What really pissed Junior Nagle was his god-awful suspicion that somewhere in the cosmic universe they weren't making Tyburn Warricks anymore. The model was too expensive to construct, too full of character and vision and courage. Oh, they were making a lot of the shitheads outside the car windows, nonproducing, mediocre, small-minded, self-righteous sons of bitches, and all this meant was that when Ty died the world would never see his likes again. And then what would the world do?

"Fags, get away! Go on!" Junior shouted. "Let's move it, Eddie."

As the car pulled away from the curb, Junior settled back in the seat. And remembered. For the first time. Josh seated in the far corner.

Oh, shit!

"Josh," he said gruffly, looking sideward, seeing the face he still saw as a meticulous little boy, more Mary Beth's kid than Ty's. All the grandkids had been spoiled by Mary Beth, with the exception of the baby, Mereth, who had more balls than all of them put together.

"Good to see you, Josh," he said, trying to cover his embarrassment.

But Josh Warrick had yet to acknowledge him in any way and

continued to sit over on his side, a *New Yorker* magazine opened and partially obscuring his face, a discarded *Tulsa World* on the seat beside him.

Finally the man managed a polite, "Good-morning, Mr. Nagle."

As they approached the toll plaza, Eddie flipped on the TV mounted before them. There was Reverend Gerald Jobe, standing in front of the security gate at Warrick.

Junior Nagle sat up straight, the better to see the son of a bitch. Jesus, what was he doing out there?

". . . and so, we all are praying for Mr. Warrick's speedy recovery, and I would like to entreat those within hearing distance of my voice to bow your heads and pray with me that God spare the life of this great and remarkable man . . ."

"Where'd he come from?" Junior muttered and thumped the glass behind Eddie's head.

"I beg your pardon, sir?"

"Jobe. Where did he come from?"

"Reverend Jobe was at Warrick late last evening. Massie asked him to speak to the reporters for the family."

As Reverend Jobe prayed on—endlessly—Junior again muttered, "Fag preacher!"

"I beg your pardon, Mr. Nagle," Josh said quietly. "What precisely do you have reference to when you call a man a 'fag'? Do you have a clear definition? For instance, someone who engages in different sexual practices?"

Junior looked at Josh sideways.

They weren't making any more Tyburn Warricks.

"Different sexual practices?" Junior repeated, hearing something mincing and overprecise in the voice. "Naw. A 'fag' is just someone who sucks for sex. A world-class fag like that one," he said and pointed toward the television image of Reverend Gerald Jobe, "is just someone who sucks, period. You know what I mean?"

And those were the last words spoken during the entire trip out to Warrick, except when Junior warned Eddie not to stop at the gate for any "fag reporters or fag preachers" and "just plow straight ahead into Warrick itself, no matter who he ran down."

Warrick

AFTER MERETH convinced Massie that Donovan, Beatles, and Woodstock T-shirts wouldn't do as a wardrobe for the next few difficult days and that a quick trip in to her apartment was a necessity, she decided to ask a pertinent question.

"Do you know anyone named Chris?"

Massie looked up from the coffee service, the pot steaming with the delicious odor of blended coffee.

"Chris who?" Massie asked and handed Mereth a cup and saucer, her face revealing the telltale fatigue of an unsatisfactory night.

"I don't know. Wish I did," Mereth murmured and took the cup to the window seat and thought how beautiful Massie's private suite was. Redone in shades of mauve and pink, it was like being on the inside of an early-blooming summer rose.

The phone rang in the other room.

"Shall I get it?" Mereth offered, taking note of the fear on Massie's face.

"No."

On the third ring Massie put down her coffee cup and disappeared into the bedroom. A few moments later Mereth heard the ringing stop, heard nothing else and waited out the silence. She looked back at the bedroom door and saw a strangely diminished Massie clinging to the door, her simple, white peignoir accenting her dark beauty.

"What is it?"

"Dr. Buckner said . . . I could see him . . ."

This simple announcement seemed to echo endlessly back and forth between the two women. It was what Massie had wanted more than anything yesterday. Now she looked stricken.

"Come with me, Mereth! What does it mean? What do you think it means?"

Mereth felt Massie's terror and wondered in an objective way if it was wise to succumb to an affection that deep—for anyone. Not to love had long seemed to Mereth the safest course of action.

"No," she answered with conviction. "You go on. I'll run in to Tulsa to get what I need and be back by noon. I promise."

"Josh . . ."

"I know. Eddie has gone to pick him up."

". . . and Junior Nagle."

"They're coming together."

"Brit . . . ?"

"Not certain. I haven't heard yet."

There was a salvation in annihilating nit-picking detail.

"Go on, Massie," Mereth urged gently. "Get dressed. Ty's favorite. He's waiting." She felt like a mother soothing a frightened child and as Massie's paralysis continued, Mereth made an awkward offer. "Shall I help you? Dress, I mean."

"Of course not," Massie snapped, the old Massie back on track. As she slid open her wardrobe doors, she looked about with a second tentative plea. "Will you . . . walk with me to his room?"

Everything in Mereth suggested a firm no, and yet if the end was near, wouldn't it be better to hear it now than in an hour on the radio driving into Tulsa?

"All right." Mereth smiled. "I'll go dress and meet you at the top of the steps."

A look of relief flooded Massie's face. "Thank you, Mereth. I've never been so • . . scared."

This honest statement moved Mereth and again she felt very much the adult, Massie the child. Bonds do weaken.

"Twenty minutes?" she asked from the door and closed it on the rose room and hurried down the corridor back toward the central hall that would lead her to that made-over childhood room. Where had that ingenuous little girl gone?

Dead. Hurry.

Massie was frightened. Deeter was frightened. Only Reverend Jobe seemed confident and secure.

Voices then. Coming from—where?

As she approached the second-floor landing, the voices grew louder, more recognizable. Just this side of the staircase Mereth stopped, taking refuge behind the wall, leaning out only far enough to look down into the entrance hall.

Reverend Jobe was speaking to about a dozen young people. Ramona stood to one side in her dress-black uniform and white apron. Job assignments were being made. Reinforcements had arrived from Jobe's Tulsa Christian College. Or spies? Was he taking over entirely? And by what right?

As her anger vaulted, Mereth made a conscious effort to rein it in. It would serve no purpose. Quietly and keeping well back to the wall, she moved past the hazardous landing and hurried on down toward her room.

Spies? Watch the paranoia. Gerald Jobe's spies, those fresh-scrubbed and wide-eyed expressions?

Through the broad, leaded-glass windows which broke the monotony of the west wing she caught passing glimpses of the dazzling morning, the sun bathing everything in that special spring radiance. Although the windows were sealed closed for security purposes, she could smell the fragrance, for she'd grown up with it, that green, fertile April smell of thawed and warmed earth and burgeoning buds and freshly plowed fields and oil somewhere near.

She paused by one window. What was there about this house that made one want—more than anything else in the world—to get out of it?

As she started to turn away from the windows she caught sight of the dusty, blue pickup truck just pulling into the covered drive.

Bad pennies.

And there he was. Deeter Big Cow, just crawling down from the high seat. Once out, he wobbled a bit as though suffering a hangover. Then she saw the driver. No worn jeans jacket this time. Now he was wearing a white dress shirt open at the neck, the cuffs rolled up around his wrists. Blue jeans, of course, the uniform of mankind.

He stretched as though he hadn't been awake too long and lifted his arms straight up into the air and said something to Deeter, an amusing something, for Deeter looked back at him and laughed. Then someone called to them from the porch. Mereth couldn't see who. There was a pleasant expression on Deeter's face as he lifted a hand in a curiously "Indian" greeting and led the way back beneath the porch beyond Mereth's range of vision.

For several moments she stared as though transfixed down on the shimmering morning sunlight, which cast a patina on the highly polished red brick pattern of the drive itself.

Chris who?

"Miss Warrick, Miss Massie has gone ahead to Mr. Warrick's room. She said she would meet you there."

Mereth turned on the voice and found herself staring into a young female face she'd never seen before. Self-consciously, she drew her bathrobe more closely about her.

"And you are . . . ?" she faltered.

"Peggy Sue," came the bright, young chirping reply.

"Peggy Sue," Mereth repeated witlessly. "Are you one of Reverend Jobe's . . . ?"

"I'm a student at Tulsa Christian College," came the relentlessly bright voice. Then, "God is love." She smiled further, apparently unaware of the non sequitur.

Mereth had heard enough. How could any of them survive surrounded by this army of Christian youth? As though fleeing, Mereth stepped quickly into her room, closed the door and bolted it.

Get dressed. Same old wrinkled slacks, sweater. Massie waiting. Ty not dead yet.

"Go find 'em, little girl. Sense 'em out."

173

Another April day, cold, Ty pacing before the fire.

"I want to talk private, Mereth."

"Then let's ride."

"It's raining."

"That's never stopped us before. What is it, Ty?"

"The ranch house. We'll go there after lunch."

"Are you feeling all right?"

"Fine. I just want—"

"Don't get sick, Ty. I need you."

Go and dress. Massie waiting—

Although she recognized the imperative commands such as "Go and dress," she found herself for the moment incapable of movement, as though something had short-circuited inside her. She was receiving the message but for the moment was totally unable to carry it out.

Turnpike

JOSH STARED out of his side of the limo window and felt more tension in every muscle of his body than he'd felt for years, since the last time he'd come home to Warrick. It was tension unlike any he'd felt anyplace else, the closest thing he'd ever experienced to primeval survival tension, all muscles, nerves, bones, blood saying, Be on guard or you may die.

He smiled at his reflected image in the smoky tinted window. Cut the crap, Warrick. That wheezy, aging, senile old crony of your grandfather's is scarcely life-threatening.

Toll plaza up ahead. If Josh had a dime for every time he'd passed through that toll plaza, he'd be able to give his dream the full treatment—a lavish production budget and pay De Niro's salary to boot.

He wished now that Peter had come with him. But perhaps instinctively Peter had made the right decision. Josh was fairly certain that, despite Peter's vast experience, he probably had never met anyone quite like Junior Nagle.

Josh had always thought that what this state needed more than anything else was a whole string of pioneer funerals. Too much old blood. People lived too long out here. New blood, creative blood —though not his, thank you. He hated the place, hated the small minds, the smaller imaginations, hated the ignorance and superstition that automatically bestowed upon an asshole like Gerald Jobe unlimited power, hated it all as thoroughly and deeply as he'd ever hated anything in his life. And of course, since he'd come from all this, he hated a large portion of himself as well. But he could handle that as long as he understood it. And he did understand it and viewed it as a kind of cosmic handicap to make the game more interesting.

He felt a warming relaxation of the tension that had commenced with Junior's wholesale indictment of fags and queers. Now he relaxed his grip on the *New Yorker* and examined his left hand and saw smudged blues and greens from where the dye on the back-page ad had smeared. And saw his hand trembling.

Fuck off, old man, Josh thought and studied the back of Eddie O'Keefe's head and decided it would be pleasant to chat with Eddie.

"Eddie, how are things going for you?" he asked, full voice, shattering the silence inside the car. Josh could feel Junior's eyes upon him. "You're not married yet, are you?" he persisted, recalling that in his off-hours, Eddie had acquired quite a reputation as a ladies' man, those still firm boxing muscles apparently a turn-on for most women.

"Oh, no." Eddie laughed. "No time for marriage, not working for Mr. Warrick," he added and slid the limo right through the toll plaza, not stopping to pay or get change or a ticket or anything mere mortals were compelled to do.

Josh looked back through the rear window to see if a patrol car was in pursuit, but through the gray-tinted glass he saw only a tumbling concrete mixer pulling away from the far lane, jockeying with a battered VW, both ultimately falling far behind the slick, black, Warrick limo.

Josh straightened himself in the seat and recalled the built-in privilege of being a Warrick, for no other reason than that the name always seemed to have a profound effect on people wherever one dropped it. And he was the first to admit he'd taken full advantage of it, hundreds of times, and would undoubtedly do so again. Such privilege was not the source of all evil, as Brit had found it to be.

Poor Brit. Silent, sleek limos like this one had pushed Brit right out of the country and into the welcoming, suspect arms of British Socialism.

Well, Josh wasn't that stupid. The only thing "evil" about inherited wealth was that it tended to make one soft, slack, unrealized. Why bother posing questions when all the answers to everything were in your bank account.

Brit. The thought of his younger brother stopped him for a moment. Brit fascinated him, always had. Poor Brit had selected for himself a tough role: conscience for the entire Warrick family. Christ, what a thankless job!

"Eddie, do you know if my brother is coming?"

Again Eddie's head bobbed upward toward the rearview mirror. "I think . . . Well, I'm not sure. I believe Mereth contacted him but, like I said, I wouldn't swear."

As his confusion filled the vacuum, Josh withdrew the question and all further questions. No need to make Eddie suffer. Junior's negative presence had succeeded in casting a pall over the entire car, the son of a bitch!

Where the rebellion had come from, Josh had no idea—but it erupted full-blown, made manifest behind a mask of almost unctuous politeness.

"Hey, Junior, how in the hell is the oil business?"

Not until he heard himself in echo did he hear—also in echo—his grandfather. It had never occurred to him how similar the voice tone and pattern. He might have been doing an imitation of Tyburn Warrick.

Apparently he'd taken Junior by surprise. For several moments the old man's heavily lidded eyes blinked rapidly at him like a frog's.

Josh, rather enjoying himself, added, "It's all those fag Arabs, if you ask me, playing with oil prices like prices were their private toys. Don't you agree, Junior?"

Without waiting for an answer, fairly certain he wasn't going to receive one anyway, Josh spied the small portable bar concealed in the cabinet in front of him.

"Got any Chivas back here, Eddie?"

"Sure thing, Josh. Full tanks all around. Help yourself."

Beginning to enjoy himself, Josh lifted the cushioned lid and saw a marvel of compartmentalization, crystal highball glasses tucked neatly into their own fitted white velvet coffins on one side, a deep airtight ice chest—filled—in the center, and to the right—like virgins—new bottles of Stolichnaya vodka, Chivas Regal, Jack Daniel's and Beefeater gin.

"Junior?" he invited.

"No, nothing," the old man muttered and stared out of his window, and Josh noticed a diamond on the third finger of the man's right hand roughly the size of a large olive.

"Well, hell, there's my answer," Josh grinned, pointing to the ring, "to the question how's the oil business. Eddie, you seen this?"

Josh looked up to see poor Eddie trying to bring into simultaneous focus the road ahead and the back seat behind.

"Out in Hollywood, do you know what we'd call a rock like that?" Josh persisted, aware that he was making everyone uncomfortable and not giving a damn. "We call a stone like that life insurance. A man just wears his policy on his pinkie. Sure you don't want that drink, Junior?"

Even though Junior had yet to shake his head, Josh interpreted his silence as a negative answer, lifted the highball glass to his lips, swigged almost half of its contents and closed his eyes against the good burning sensation, which wouldn't burn for long and would ultimately numb.

Despite his awareness of Junior's relentless stare, Josh settled back in the seat, crossed his legs and looked out of the window at the passing landscape. Nondescript in every way, lacking color, lacking variation, lacking drama, lacking imagination, lacking everything.

The list proved almost too much, and he drained the glass in a second swallow and wondered if it would be physically possible within the next thirty or forty minutes, which was their approximate distance from this spot to Warrick, to get totally, completely, consummately bombed out of his everlasting fag head.

No answer, but it sure as hell wouldn't hurt to try.

Warrick

MERETH PACED the corridor, studying the paintings on the wall, her eye moving to the new alteration in the Turner, that small singed hole in the lower left-hand corner of the Thames estuary, anything to keep her mind off the bedroom down the hall.

Poor Turner. She remembered reading of his conversations with Munro of Novar in 1836 on the Aosta tour, complaining of his difficulties in managing oils in the open air. She'd studied at length one small oil on linen over millboard in the Tate.

Oils do not correspond with my vision—
She wondered if bullet holes did.

Then she heard it. The door opening. Though for the last half

178

hour she'd been eager for it to open, now she refused even to look in that direction, though she knew that several had joined her in the hall and one was weeping.

Dead?

"Massie?" She saw her bent over, a handkerchief pressed against her face, Dr. Buckner's arm protectively about her while the two nurses stood at attention before the closed doors.

"Massie, is he . . . ?"

Unable to answer, Massie shook her head and at last Horace Buckner deigned to give all the benefit of his medical wisdom.

"Not dead yet," he grumped. "And knowing Ty, he could stretch this thing out forever."

Mereth put her arms around Massie and assumed that by "this thing" Buckner meant the act of dying.

Massie pulled away from Mereth's arms and moved into the safety of the bay window, where she sat on one of the cushioned seats and hid her face with her hands.

"Goddamn him," Buckner said like a small boy shouting an obscenity. "Don't know when to quit! Never did. Nothing and no one could talk the stubborn bastard off a rig if he smelled oil and nothing, I suspect, will talk him out of life except a goddamned blow from God Almighty Himself!"

Mereth listened carefully. "Then . . . are you saying . . . ?"

"I'm saying machines are doing everything for him."

The next question was inevitable and she asked it.

"Are you suggesting . . . ?"

"No!" The protest was strong and came from Massie. "I forbid it! I absolutely forbid it!"

Her voice, despite the debilitating grief, rose and perhaps carried down to the first floor and all those young, scrubbed Christians. Mereth moved to Massie's side in an attempt to quiet her.

"Is it . . . necessary, Dr. Buckner, to discuss this now?"

"Hell, no. Don't ever have to discuss it, if you don't want to. Medical technology could keep him alive for . . . years."

Massie was weeping. The rock was gone, leaving only a woman.

"Come on," Mereth whispered. Her first task was to pull Massie back into some sort of coherence. People would be arriving today.

For a few steps Massie seemed in need of physical support, but halfway down the corridor she drew away from Mereth.

"No," she said with conviction, "absolutely not," and there was nothing in her tone that even vaguely suggested she wanted approval. A decision had been made and nothing or no one would alter it.

As they approached the top of the staircase, Mereth heard voices coming from the entrance hall below, someone shouting, other voices trying to talk, a drunken one, and Eddie O'Keefe's blending in.

Then Mereth saw Josh wavering in the center of the entrance hall, tie undone, his sports coat trailing behind, wobbling on spaghetti legs as he searched each face around him for a familiar one.

For a few moments Mereth and Massie stood like minor gods in a Greek tragedy looking down upon the chaotic human comedy. There were half a dozen of Jobe's kids jockeying around the new arrivals. Ramona stood to one side with a clipboard scribbling something, and she sent two boys scurrying toward the man who just now appeared in the doorway.

Junior Nagle.

Massie started down the steps.

Mereth tried to concentrate on the three-ring circus below which was growing more chaotic by the minute. Josh continued to stand at the exact center of the entrance hall, looking closely at every passing face. Mereth found him older, and thinner, while Junior Nagle looked miraculously younger.

Massie was at the bottom of the steps now and Mereth watched her, grateful at least for one thing: she appeared to be fully restored from the nightmare image she'd found in Ty's room.

"Josh, here!" Massie called out, her voice cheerful.

Mereth continued to watch her with a mixture of amazement and just a tinge of envy. She walked straight into the chaos, as much at home there as she was anyplace in the world.

About thirty minutes later, after everyone had been shown to their rooms, Mereth didn't care how she got out of Warrick. She would happily walk if need be, anything to put distance between her and this place which was reassembling all its victims for a dead man to pass judgment on.

"How about breakfast?" Massie whispered as though she were proposing an intimate private meal, the sort they used to have before Mereth left Warrick, when Ty would be gone on business or staying at the ranch house.

Remembering the good times helped, and she reached the terrace room with spirits lifted and saw the tall, bearded man named Chris who had run along her same track for the last twenty-four hours. He was standing at the far end of the room, looking down on Ty's chair as though talking to someone.

As Mereth and Massie, followed by Eddie, appeared in the door, Deeter turned and the young man looked up. And there was a third surprise. A head, balding except for a fringe of red, and then an immaculate figure rose slowly from Ty's chair and stood upright, straightening his tie, smoothing his vest over his trim belly, a limited though characteristic smile on his face.

Massie spoke first. "Red," she said and smiled warmly.

"Massie!"

That was all he said as she went effortlessly into his open arms. The embrace was simple and private.

"And Mereth's here . . ."

At the sound of her name, she looked back to see Massie extending a hand in her direction.

Red Pierson, the keeper of the Warrick purse. Not a man to cozy up to like Deeter or make fun of behind his back like Doctor Buckner or laugh with like Junior Nagle. Pierson was all business, had been for as long as Mereth could remember. Cold, passionless, efficient, though as Ty said, one did not have to love one's lawyer or one's banker, just trust them.

"Mr. Pierson." She smiled and received a polite kiss in the general vicinity of her left cheek. The remote closeness left a lingering fragrance of expensive after-shave. Red Pierson did dress well and smell good.

"It's good to see you," she murmured at the end of the chilly greeting. "I hope I didn't bother you yesterday when I called about . . ."

"Oh, no, of course not," the man reassured quickly, his arm dropping from around Massie's waist as though to say that was enough of that. "My secretary wired first-class fare to the American Express, Haymarket address. I assume that was correct?"

There was an accusation in his voice. For a moment the condemnation hung like a bad odor on the air. Mereth was aware of tension building. Maybe the trick was to keep talking.

"Deeter, how are you this morning?" she asked and turned away from Red Pierson.

"I'm good," the big man muttered. "We left my wheels over here last night."

"I thought it best."

"Probably right. Anybody found Ty yet?"

The question created a deeper silence in the room which Mereth doubted seriously could be altered. When no one seemed inclined to respond, Deeter went on, undaunted.

"I went out late last night. Chris there, he come with me, and we went to all his haunts. Isn't that right, Chris?"

Mereth was tempted to look back and see if he was supplying Deeter with an insane confirmation.

"We went everwhere. All over. Down to the old ranch house. He goes down there a lot, and Massie knows it. He says he don't always feel comfortable here. And we even went all the way down to the oil fields. He likes to sit on them workin' rigs sometimes at night, don't he, Massie? 'Course he does. Don't do it much anymore, though. I'm going to go look for him in Tulsa. He has Tulsa hideouts that nobody in this room knows about but me." A curious tone had crept into his splintered monologue.

The next sound she heard was the clink of silver. She glanced toward the buffet and saw Chris join Eddie, their heads bent close in conversation. Behind she heard Red and Massie in an equally close huddle. Only Deeter remained unengaged.

Mereth walked the short distance to his side and saw a gray stubble on his chin and the effects of the night's boozing in his eyes.

"Are you really going into Tulsa?"

He nodded, and she hoped he would hear her next question and answer it as quietly as possible.

"Deeter, who is he?" she asked, taking his arm and looking toward the buffet.

"Chris?" Deeter asked, full voice, automatically silencing every conversation in the room and at the same time summoning the man himself, who appeared at Deeter's side bearing a platter heaped with enough food for four people. "You know old Chris," Deeter insisted idiotically, then slowly amended the statement. "Well, maybe not. Maybe you was too young at first and then you flew the coop. Well, what the hell? This here is Chris Faxon."

As an introduction it left a lot to be desired. Chris smiled down on her. "I thought we'd met, more or less."

She nodded.

"I'm . . . sorry for all those questions last night."

"No need," she replied.

"We'd not been able to reach Red Pierson. Of course, we know why now. He was en route."

For the first time she noticed something different about his manner of speaking, not altogether an Oklahoma accent, just occasionally an edge on certain words.

As she approached the buffet, she overheard Red Pierson talking to Massie.

"Was that Junior Nagle I heard a minute ago?"

Eddie spoke up, talking around the last few bites of sausage. "It was, sir. Picked him up this morning at the Parke Suite."

"Who else?"

Massie filled her coffee cup. "Josh."

"I believe we all need to sit down and talk," Red said. "Reporters are already outside the gate. Before I left, I received three phone calls from Houston. It will be only a matter of time before we have to make an official statement. Massie, what I must do immediately," Red continued from the opposite side of the buffet, "is see Ty. I must speak with him, determine precisely what his condition is. We may not want . . ."

Mereth, along with everyone else, took refuge in silence. Unfortunately, Deeter heard at the far end of the room.

"Pierson!" he shouted. "Didn't you hear? Ty ain't around. How can you talk to a man who ain't here?"

The question was posed with such sincerity that even Red seemed momentarily stunned. Mereth looked to Massie. She was the only one who could answer Red's questions. She was the only one besides Deeter who had seen Ty, though that one glimpse had apparently almost been her undoing. But when Massie showed no indication that she was going to clarify anything, Mereth was forced to volunteer.

"Red, why don't you talk with Dr. Buckner? I'm certain that he can tell you everything. Eddie, I must go now. Would you . . . ?"

"I'd really rather you didn't," Massie spoke up. "In fact, I wish you didn't have to go at all."

"But I do. I promise I won't be long."

Eddie spoke up from the door. "Don't worry, Massie. Chris will drive her and have her back in no time."

Mereth started to object, then changed her mind. She didn't want to make the day even more difficult. Eddie was needed here and she needed to get into Tulsa. Hal. She must call Hal. She'd kept him waiting long enough. How pleasant it would be to sit in his easy, uncomplicated presence and listen while he effortlessly put everything into perspective, tempering all with reason and good judgment.

Since Massie would never allow her to leave alone in her own car, then Chris was the obvious solution.

Not until she was well down the corridor was she aware of footsteps following behind her and looked back to see Chris Faxon and Eddie close to his elbow, apparently giving him instructions.

"Mereth, how long do you think you'll be?" Eddie called out.

"I have to make a stop at my apartment for some clothes, a few phone calls. An hour.

"Will they be all right?" she asked then, indicating the terrace room. "Will you be here all the time?"

"Unless I have to go someplace."

"Josh . . ."

"He's fine. He's sleeping. Hey, they're not all your responsibility, you know."

She smiled. Funny, but at some point she'd begun to think that they were. "Stay close if you can, Eddie. At least until I get back." Then she looked ahead to see Chris holding the door open for her.

"Which car, Eddie?" Chris called out as Mereth went out into the April morning that was beginning to turn warm.

"Why don't you take mine?" she suggested, pointing toward her trusty Mercedes, looking like an old friend. "You can drive."

As she approached the car she looked back to see Eddie and Chris still in conversation. How strange to have outsiders orchestrating life at Warrick. But maybe that was always the case in emergencies. Strangers were often the best ones to take over.

Eddie waved. "You're in good hands!"

She waved back and watched the man approach the car with a relaxed gait, his tall frame moving easily inside his clothes.

"Got everything?" he asked.

"That's the point," she replied. "I'm going in to get everything."

For one last moment she questioned the wisdom of leaving.

"Ty, where are you? I can't find you."

"Don't leave me, Mereth. I need you."

"I can't stay here."

"You belong here. You'll never find what you're looking for except here."

"I'm not looking for anything."

"Yes—"

She saw him so clearly, as though he were standing before her, full of dignity, pensively shaking his head. She felt a sudden rush of tenderness, which was instantly followed by something less pleasant . . .

Voices jarred her back, and she looked up to see Chris Faxon speaking to the security guard. Beyond the gate she saw several cars, two mobile units from local television stations and a scattering of people standing about, fighting boredom in whatever way they could.

"I'm thinking about calling the Highway Patrol," the security guard said.

"I'd notify the house first," she heard Chris say.

"Oh, I would. But more of the buzzards are coming out every minute. Word's spread that Mr. Warrick's a pretty sick man."

"Don't leave me, Mereth. I need you. Please stay—"

She tried to clear her mind of voices blending—past and present —and stared straight ahead and saw a dozen or so reporters spot the car and start toward the gate.

"As you can see," the guard muttered, squinting at the oncoming group.

"Do you want to speak with them?"

The question came from Chris and was unthinkable. "What would I . . . say?" Mereth faltered.

"They just want news. It's their job."

"I . . . I don't know what I'd . . ."

"Shall I?"

Before she could comment, he put the car in park and slipped out of the driver's seat and was striding toward the gate and the eager reporters, more of whom came forward at the sight of someone approaching. Mereth rolled down her window, wondering not only what he was going to tell them but how he would identify himself. Then she heard, for he lifted his voice, and again she tried to recognize that curious speech pattern. Not this part of the country, she was certain.

"My name is Chris Faxon; I am a friend of the Warrick family," he began in a clear, simple manner. "I wish I had news for you, but

I'm afraid there's nothing to tell. It's true, as you know, that Mr. Warrick has suffered a stroke. Early yesterday morning. Specialists have been here but there's no change. These things take time, so you must bear with us, please."

His courtesy seemed to work a strange effect on the group, and they stood silent and watched as he turned back to the car. Someone from the front of the group asked a single question.

"Is all the family coming?"

The "spokesman" nodded. There was a confusion of several additional questions, but this time he did not stop to answer them. Chris proceeded on back to the car and advised the security guard before he got in.

"Remember, I wouldn't call the Highway Patrol, not without getting permission."

She heard the guard agree as though he'd just received an order from someone in authority. What was going on? The hitchhiker she'd passed by yesterday was now speaking for the entire family?

She saw the guard open the gate. Chris guided the car slowly through the reporters, who moved back to make way. A camera snapped, but she kept her eyes straight ahead. Not until they reached the end of the drive did she glance in his direction.

"What did you tell them?" she asked, pretending not to have heard.

He smiled. "Basically that there was nothing to tell them."

"In what capacity did you speak?"

"As a family friend."

"Are you?"

"What?"

"A family friend."

"I hope so. I've spent a portion of every year here for as long as I can remember." He honked the horn and waved at a large florist truck. Apparently word was spreading.

"What baffles me," he said, drawing himself up on the seat, "is how they know these things. Reporters, I mean. How did they know to come out here? There has been no official word from anyone."

She looked out the window. "All Junior Nagle had to do yesterday was cancel two board meetings in Dallas."

"But he didn't cancel them."

She looked at him.

He smiled. "Both boards of the Warrick Corporation met as scheduled at the Adolphus. Would you like some music?" Before she could respond, he flipped the dial and a din of country and western filled the car.

With equal facility she reached forward and turned it off. "How did you know? About the board meetings."

He didn't seem surprised by her sudden gesture or her question. "Pierson," he said simply.

"What is your connection with Red Pierson?"

"I have no connection with Red Pierson."

"You were inquiring about him last night."

"For Deeter, yes."

"What is Deeter's connection with Red Pierson then?"

He laughed as though at her suspicious questions. "They're both old friends of Ty's."

"And you? Who are you?"

The bluntness of her question seemed to sober him. "I'm sorry," he apologized. "You see, I remember you. I just assumed that you remembered me."

She gaped at him. "Would it be possible to start at the beginning?"

"Of what?"

"Of you!" she exclaimed. "Why and how am I supposed to remember you?"

As he glanced at her, she saw that partial smile on his face, as though he were aware of her confusion and thoroughly enjoyed it. "Well, let's see. I first visited Deeter when I was a kid. You were real little. Chubby. Wore braces. Into everything."

For several moments, she couldn't quite bring herself to prod further. Not that she was finished, just an interval of civil silence before she started again.

He seemed content with the silence and whistled softly.

She looked out at the undulating green land stretching, unbroken, on all sides. So vast and open. There were times, certain moods when she would look out at the flatlands or at the jagged canyons and the high skies and monstrously beautiful sunsets and feel an affinity, a belonging. At other times she felt little or nothing. The entire state was strangely devoid of the sort of chauvinistic fanaticism that marked, say, a Texan. They wore their identities like a brand on their faces. No one could mistake them nor would anyone want to mistake them.

But Oklahomans, not so. In the course of a week she heard more apology than boasting, people, friends, colleagues, flying out for reasons that ranged from the Met in New York to horseracing in New Mexico, to shopping in Dallas. No one stayed at home for much of anything. Look at Brit. Look at Josh.

"You okay?"

The thoughtful inquiry came from the left and brought her back to the car. A glance out of the window informed her that they had already turned onto the intersection which would take them to the turnpike and Tulsa. For some reason she glanced behind to see if she could see Warrick, though she knew she couldn't. Warrick was like that, a presence that clung, that tended to follow.

"Do you know Ty Warrick well?" she asked.

"I guess. Eddie let me drive for him once."

"Did he trust you? My grandfather, I mean."

For the first time he looked at her. "You'll have to ask him that," he concluded, and his voice had a new edge to it.

She was sorry but hadn't the least idea how to go about apologizing. Her childhood had been one in which the central lesson was *Trust No One.* It was impossible to grow up with security guards and chauffeur-bodyguards without developing a distorted view of the world and everyone in it. Still it seemed a weak excuse, so she kept quiet and tried to send her mind ahead, not behind.

First off, when she reached her apartment she would call the school. It was impossible to tell them precisely how much time she would need. A week? Two, maybe three. They'd better make a firm arrangement.

Then call Harry Beekman, president of Ty's bank, the Tulsa Petroleum Exchange. She was certain that no one had thought to notify Beekman.

And then call Hal. A twinge of guilt there. But he wouldn't be angry with her. She was certain of that. Hal never got angry with her. About anything. Sometimes she wished that he would. But on the other hand, his calm, reasoning, objective, dispassionate face had always struck her as being almost beautiful, particularly after her twenty years at Warrick, exposed constantly to the various theatrics and melodramas of the inmates there.

Hal. His office was only a few minutes from the apartment. Perhaps he could drive over. She would like that.

"Turnpike ahead." His tone was conciliatory.

"You were hitchhiking here yesterday." She smiled.

He nodded.

"Where were you coming from?"

"Tulsa, where else? My God, what is it with you?" For the first time anger shattered his easy manner.

She looked away and knew she should apologize.

"Why are you so suspicious of me?"

"I don't know who you are."

"I've told you."

"You've told me nothing."

He gave the center of the steering wheel a slap with the palm of his right hand and looked out of his window. He might have said more, but the Gilden toll booth was ahead. The driveway was empty, and as he drew close to the booth Mereth saw a woman, not the same one as before. This one was younger, prettier.

"Hey, old Chris!" she called out as the car came to a halt before the high window. "You're moving in style this mornin', ain't ya? I usually see you comin' down that pike there with your thumb out."

"And you'll see it again, Millie, I promise."

She handed over the turnpike ticket, along with a smile. "How are things up at Warrick?" she asked. "Is the old man dead?"

"No."

"Had an uncle once, stroked, lived two years. Jesus, it was awful! They had him in diapers."

"See you, Millie."

Without waiting, Chris gunned the motor and put an incredible amount of distance between them and the toll booth in a short time.

"You hungry?" he asked after he'd managed to find his way into the fast lane and had settled the car at about seventy miles per hour. "It's noon. How about Mexican? I know a great place."

She wanted to say yes. She said, "No, I'd better not. I have to get back. Massie looked . . ."

He accepted her refusal with good grace, as though he had understood everything.

She shifted in the seat. "Where is *your* good place? Everyone in Oklahoma has a good Mexican place."

"I don't think you'd know it."

She laughed. "Try me. I grew up here, remember?"

"Tio's."

She frowned at the name and searched her memory and couldn't find it. "It's not in Tulsa?"

He nodded. "The best. Want to reconsider?"

And she did, though there still were qualifications. "Let me go to the apartment first. Then maybe on the way back . . ."

It seemed to suit him, qualifications and all. "You like hot?" he smiled.

"I've never tasted any that's too hot." She leaned back against the cushion and closed her eyes, giving the impression of sleep.

"Do you have any idea how I can get hold of Harry Beekman?" His voice shattered the new ease between them.

"Harry Beekman," she repeated.

"Deeter asked me to call him. I've met the man only once. Can't

even remember where his office is. I was hoping that you could
. . ."

"Why Harry Beekman?" Mereth interrupted.

"I told you," he replied. "Deeter asked me."

"But why would Deeter want Ty's banker?"

"What the hell. They're old friends!"

"I still don't understand. First Red Pierson. Now Harry Beekman."

He stared straight ahead for too long, a visible tightness in his
jaw. "Why don't you ask Deeter?" he muttered.

She would. And Massie as well. Obviously some relationship had
developed in her six-year absence about which she knew nothing.
Maybe it wasn't important that she know. Still—

"Which way to your place?"

"Follow I-44 after the toll plaza. It's around by the Hilton."

"How long do you think you'll be?"

The question was chilly, as was her answer. "I don't know. An
hour. Maybe an hour and a half."

"May I drop you off and run a few errands, then come back?"

It was a reasonable request. Then why did it make her so angry?

"Of course," she said and kept a vigil on the turnpike.

As they approached the Tulsa toll plaza, she glanced over into the
oncoming lanes. About four cars from the toll booth she saw a
black Lincoln Continental Mark IV, a small gold cross on the driver's door.

"Hell!" she muttered and attracted Chris's attention, who followed her line of vision to the car.

"Guess where he's going," Chris said.

Mereth shook her head. "I don't understand. I can't believe that
Ty . . ."

"Oh, it wasn't Ty who let Jobe get his foot in the door," Chris
said with that same maddening confidence that was beginning to
drive her crazy. "It was Massie. She was the one."

Mereth listened, not wholly believing everything she was hearing but listening without response.

At that moment the toll lane ahead was empty and as Chris was forced to pull forward, both lost sight of the Mark IV.

"Do you know him? Reverend Jobe, I mean," she asked, straightening around in the seat.

"I know him."

"And you don't like him?"

"I don't like any threat to well-being. Mine or anyone else's. Jobe is a hypocrite." He was speaking calmly, his eyes leveled on the heavy traffic, all headed toward the Tulsa skyline.

Mereth felt a comforting relief in his answer. At least the subject of the Reverend Jobe would not be a sore point between them. Apparently everything else was.

She studied the passing clutter of I-44, endless motels and restaurants, mostly franchised, the traffic fast-moving and growing thicker, bumper to bumper, requiring constant vigilance.

"Where is this Tio's of yours?" she asked.

"In a part of Tulsa you probably are not familiar with."

"I know all of Tulsa."

"Not Tio's part."

This sparring was harmless. He never looked at her, couldn't afford to take his eyes off the chaos on the highway.

"Turn right at the Hilton exit," she instructed and began to think of the tasks facing her when she reached the apartment.

As the car took the off ramp he gradually reduced speed.

"Left here." She guided him toward the block of condos. "There," she said, pointing toward No. 18.

"Do you live alone?"

The question was his, the surprise hers. "Yes. Why?"

He shrugged. "Some people have roommates."

"I don't. It's never been successful."

"Why did you leave Warrick?"

Caught off guard, Mereth literally was incapable of a response. Her departure from Warrick six years ago was not a fit subject for a bright morning. It belonged in that shadowed musty trunk where everyone stored failures.

"He wants to see you, Mereth. Now. He's in his room. Go to him."
"See you later," she murmured without answering his question.
"Hey, sorry."

As he called out to her she waved again without looking back, trying to convey the illusion that everything was all right.

Warrick

JOSH COULDN'T remember the last time he'd indulged in daytime sleep. He hated sleeping in the daytime. It made him feel sluggish, lethargic, childlike. But here he was, in his childhood room in the children's wing of Warrick, gazing out of the window at a 4 P.M. sun, feeling sluggish and lethargic and childlike.

Encircling the arch which led to his sitting room, he saw an embarrassment of framed certificates, once so important, local speech contests, debate teams, National Forensic honors.

He lay on his back on the mussed double bed and was grateful that he couldn't read specifics from this distance, and wondered if his glasses were still inside his coat pocket. Without them he was blind, though now he was grateful for his failing eyesight, for it enabled him to see nothing of what he once had been.

In fact, the whole suite took on the comfortable blurred appearance of an impressionistic painting. Of course, part of his disability might be directly traceable to the successful state of inebriation he'd been able to accomplish between the Tulsa toll plaza and Warrick.

Congratulations. He'd set himself a goal and had accomplished it. For once. Old Ty, that world-class goal-setter, would be proud of him.

That stark thought, if nothing else, was sobering. He managed a tentative move upward on propped elbows and held still a moment and waited until the bedroom ceased to spin.

He needed—something. Quite possibly another drink. More probably a cup—no, a pot—of black, strong coffee, the kind that was Peter's specialty, with just a hint of Amaretto.

He peered to one side and saw the phone on the bedstand. Kitchen extension. Growing up, they were forbidden to ask the servants to bring food up to their rooms. They were permitted to phone down an order, but they had to go down to the family dining room or the kitchen to fetch and eat it. Massie's orders.

My God, he couldn't even remember greeting Massie! He did vaguely remember Mereth. Dear little Mereth. How she'd grown up. And changed. Not merely physically but in another, more sobering way. She looked—contained, that awful feeling when you don't want anyone to know the size and the scope of the battle that's tearing you apart. What was doing this damage to her?

He remembered hearing something, some hoopla, years ago, from Massie about mysterious comings and goings. Ty coming unglued at the seams. Mereth going. So what was new? Systematically, one by one, with great forethought and greater skill, old Ty had driven them all away. Brit had left first, after Ty had threatened to "nail his Commie-pinko ass to the barn door."

The memory of the ugly scene sobered Josh and caused his own expulsion to pale in comparison. What was a fag compared to a Commie?

But Mereth? She'd always been Ty's favorite, literally the Golden Girl, fresh as morning, beautiful even as a child, laughing her way through every crisis and teaching others to do the same. What sin could she possibly have committed or failed to commit to warrant Ty's anger and expulsion from paradise?

Well, there was time to find out. For now, order coffee, dress and go down and apologize to all for any offenses you might have committed in your first few hours at Warrick. Also he was curious to find out what the hell was going on in the rest of this vast mausoleum. And what of Ty? Had he come home for a funeral or a death watch?

As the questions pressed down upon him, he felt that paralysis that is always a part of the sobering-up process, the lethargy which is, in a sense, the best part of any drunk, the release from action and reaction.

Now he stood in his stocking feet in the middle of his bedroom with only one clear desire in his head: why hadn't he insisted that Peter come along? Hell, Peter was better than he was at passing for straight. A business partner, that's how he would have introduced him.

Call him.

He sat on the edge of the bed and closed his eyes in an attempt to give the endless telephone numbers a chance to line up in his head, like obedient children.

He picked up the receiver and started to dial but heard a voice on the line, brash, aggressive, one he was fairly certain he had never heard before. Quickly he started to hang up when he heard:

"Oh, no, I don't know when I'll be back in town. The old man could go on like this for days. The worst kind, really."

Then there was another female voice.

"Dr. O'Rourke said he would recommend pulling life support in a few days."

"He can recommend his head off. There's a nigger woman out here, did you know that? Acts like she owns the place. Even old Buckner kowtows to her. And I mean she's a nigger."

There was a deep guttural laugh. The woman's voice fell.

"Boy, I pulled a booboo when I first arrived. I thought she was help, you know, and I told her to bring my bag up to my room!"

"Oh, Nellie, you didn't!"

"Swear to God."

"That's the old man's mistress!"

"I don't care. I don't like her."

Josh stared down at the thick brown carpet. Welcome home, he thought wryly.

"Got to go, Rita. Old Buckner's back. The house is filling up. All the grandkids and the cronies are coming in for a funeral. Boy, do I have bad news for them!"

"Well, it can't go on forever."

"Who says? He's strong as an ox in every way. Just his brain is busted up. Well, I gotta go. See you . . ."

The line went dead. Josh continued to hold the receiver for several minutes. It didn't require a lot of effort to figure out who had been talking. A nurse, obviously. No matter. He knew better now than to use the phones, unless he could find a private line downstairs. Apparently all the connections were joined.

"Just his brain is busted up."

He put down the receiver and stared at it as though it were an object of fascination. There had been a time when he would have made an effort to understand that level of mentality, but too many futile efforts had informed him that there really was nothing to understand. The same vision that saw Jo Massie as a "nigger woman" saw nothing else, was capable of seeing nothing else.

Dear God, if he didn't stop he'd pick up his bags and go right back out to the airport! But he mustn't. He was here for a purpose.

"He could go on forever."

That was distressing news. Ty might be able to go on forever, but Josh couldn't. He lay back, sideways across the bed, and stared upward at the ceiling. Suddenly, no matter how hard he tried, he could find nothing diverting or humorous in the ironies that threatened to overwhelm him.

"No grandson of Tyburn Warrick's is a fag."

"Wrong, old man, wrong!"

There was a knock at the door, muted across the distance of the sitting room and the entrance alcove. Mereth? He hoped it would be Mereth.

"Just a minute," he called out, fairly certain his voice had not carried. As he hurried through the sitting room he called out again "Just a minute!" and tried to put all negative thoughts behind him.

"Mereth?" he asked as he opened the door, and thus was surprised to see an altogether different countenance on the other side, a face which he'd known and loved since childhood, his surrogate mother, teacher, defender, best friend, the "nigger woman" herself.

"Not Mereth, I'm afraid." Massie smiled apologetically, and he saw tension in her face. "Granted, a poor substitute, but I do come bearing coffee." She stood back, indicating a tea cart, pushed by a young man in a white jacket Josh had never seen before.

At that moment two equally strange young women, each carrying neatly stacked linens, passed in the corridor behind Massie. She nodded at them and at the same time instructed the boy to push the tea cart into Josh's sitting room.

As Massie passed close on her way through the door, Josh hugged her, aware of the young boy eyeballing them.

"If we did this earlier," he smiled apologetically, "I'm sorry. I don't remember it."

"We didn't," she said, returning his hug.

"I'm sorry, Massie."

"For what?"

"For arriving . . . drunk."

He was conscious of the boy behind them. At the end of the corridor he saw the two young girls greet two others.

"Who are they?" he whispered.

Massie stepped back, the better to see. With the exception of red eyes, he thought she looked terrific, tall, svelte, a gorgeous green silk dress reeking good taste and expense.

"Oh, they're here to help," she responded. "Jobe's kids. Jobe's Jobbers, they call themselves." To the young boy she said, "I'll finish. Thank you."

Josh wondered if his failure to understand a word she'd said was her fault or his.

Jobe's Jobbers. Surely it was a joke.

"If you need anything else, Miss Massie, you just let us know." The boy grinned.

Josh stared, dumbfounded, at the closed door, then glanced back at Massie, who busied herself behind the tea cart, filling china cups with black, steaming coffee.

"Hungry?" she asked, motioning him toward a plate of sandwiches. "Dinner may be late. We're waiting for Brit."

He shook his head. "Maybe later. I am sorry, Massie, for my unceremonious arrival."

"Not necessary. I suspect the next few days will be marked for their lack of ceremony."

"And you. How are you faring? I'm sure you wonder what has become of your secluded rural life."

She shook her head and worked endlessly on her coffee, stirring, stirring.

"Ty's . . . so . . . ill."

"I know." Josh nodded. "Is there a nurse with him?" he asked.

"Oh yes. Two, as a matter of fact. A Miss Kent, nice, very professional. And a Miss Nellie, I believe her name is."

Josh recognized the name from the phone conversation.

"And doctors?"

"Horace Buckner, of course, and yesterday Jim O'Rourke sent out a specialist, though he didn't stay long."

Her thoughts seemed to drift and her voice along with them. Josh gave her all the time she needed, continuously reminding himself that while he hated the dying man, this woman had loved him and loved him still.

"Any . . . prognosis from all these medical wizards?" he asked.

She gave one sharp shake of her head. "Not much hope, Josh, I'm afraid . . . from anyone. Buckner said they might have moved him to the hospital but . . ."

"Come on, Massie, let's sit down," Josh urged, placing his cup on the table.

But she shook her head. "Can't. Too much to do. The house is filling up like a hotel. Red Pierson's here now, and Junior Nagle, and I'm sure Harry Beekman will be along and God knows who else. So much to do. I must . . ."

"Do nothing for a while," Josh scolded lightly. "Come on, we're going to sit over here," and he pointed toward the comfortable sofa, "and put our feet up here," and he gestured at the coffee table, "and in ten minutes I'll tell you all my activities of the last ten years and then you tell me yours, a year a minute."

She laughed and did not refuse his foolish invitation and took his arm and leaned against him and seemed so sincere when she said, "Josh, what would I do without you?"

And those words worked on his system like oxygen on a suffocating man. He snagged a pimento cheese sandwich on passing the tea cart and for the first time dared to think, Maybe it wasn't so bad being home after all.

Tulsa

ON THE WALK leading to her apartment, Mereth decided that what she needed first and foremost was to sit for a few minutes in Hal's safe, calm presence. Thus she resolved to call him immediately. Harry Beekman could wait, her clothes could wait, Ty could wait, even the past would have to wait. Hal was her anchor, that good solid weight that kept her from drifting too far out into the hazardous sea of the past.

Steady as you go. Concentrate on the day—

Hal. She smiled. How would it hurt?

But as she approached the front door she heard the phone ringing and for a moment was torn between a desperate need to find her key and gain quick access, or to stall, pretend that she wasn't here. The day was perilous, unscheduled ringing phones very real threats. A death message? Or worse. He was still alive—

She found her key with alarming ease, the key turned on the first try, releasing the lock, and she found herself confronting her shadowy apartment, silent except for the ringing phone.

She thought of one hundred reasons not to answer it. "Hello?" Yet she did, tossing her purse onto the coffee table.

For a moment, nothing.

"Hello? Massie, is it—"

"It's Hal."

She blinked once at the familiar voice she'd wanted to hear more than any other in the world and briefly contemplated the miracle of answered prayers.

"Hal, how good to hear your voice. I can't believe it. I was just— How did you know I was— Where are you?"

He laughed.

She'd been at Warrick for two days. Had anyone there laughed? Just once?

"Slow down, Mereth. You're safe."

A peculiar thing to say. No time, less inclination to understand it. "Hal, how did—"

"I called Massie. She said you were coming into Tulsa."

"Of course. Did she say— How was—"

"She said no change." There was a pause. Too long. "I had— hoped you would call me."

"Oh, Hal, I'm sorry, it's just that—"

For the first time she dared to relax and sank into the ivory cord chair beside the phone and from this angle looked effortlessly into her bedroom, the bed still mussed from where they had last made love. He was a good lover, Hal, always in control, playing within certain limits of time and then leading her from pleasant though inconsequential movements and rhythms into the paralyzing collisions of diverse individual wills.

The remembered sensation did sweet damage. She touched her breast in a self-caress. "Hal, I miss you," she whispered.

"Nonsense. Well, tell me, how are—things?"

"Terrible."

"In what way?"

"Ty won't die. He won't get well—"

"Which do you want him to do?"

A funny question. She stared at the arm of the ivory chair. "I—don't understand—"

In the ensuing silence she spied a loose thread on the creamy fabric. If she pulled on it, a seam would come loose.

"Mereth, you there?"

"Yes, I just didn't understand. What did—"

"It's not important. Are you well?"

She nodded and felt a harsh burning behind her eyes and wondered why she was so weepy? "Hal, can you come over for a few minutes?"

"Why?"

She laughed and wiped at her eyes and tried to cancel the burning. "Why? Do I have to give you a reason?"

"It would help."

Something was wrong. There was tension in his voice, some vague expectation.

"Hal, it's my turn. What's wrong?"

"I really can't come now, Mereth. I'm expecting a client at any minute. You understand—"

"Of course." She would not bawl again. For several moments neither spoke, and she tried to hold the conclusion at bay by allowing practical matters to absorb her mind. The small suitcase would do, one basic black suit, several pairs of slacks, hose—

"Mereth, you there?"

"Yes."

"I—"

"What is it?"

"I'm going to run up to Vail tonight for a few days."

She laughed. "It's April, Hal. There's no fresh snow at Vail."

"I'm not going for the snow."

She tugged on the loose thread. The seam weakened. Vail. His condo was behind the lodge, away from all commerce and traffic, tucked in a grove of high singing pine. She remembered the big

German mugs they'd bought in Berlin out of which they drank hot mulled wine. Cold noses. Warm hearts. Popping fires.

"Why are you going?"

Even as she asked, she knew the answer, and in less than an instant went over the three years she'd spent with him, and in every word, every action, she saw an expression of his love for her, and could not reciprocate with anything greater than sincere affection.

Quietly she leaned forward in the chair and suffered inward loathing of herself. His voice, when he spoke, was the same calm deep voice she'd longed to hear. Unfortunately she never dreamed he'd be speaking these words.

"I believe it's time, Mereth, don't you? Nothing that stagnates is good. I'd hoped once we were—going someplace. But we're not, and we both know it."

"No." She spoke the single word and pulled on the thread, the seam splitting open.

"You'll do fine," he went on. "If Ty dies, then Massie will need you. If he lives, he'll need you."

"You have it all worked out."

"For a change, yes."

"I don't want to lose you."

"Will you marry me?"

"I can't."

"Good luck, Mereth."

"Hal—"

But the connection was dead, the persistent buzzing of the phone joining the one inside her head. Mereth closed her eyes and bowed her head upon her arm, trying to hide her tears. He had every right. She had none. She had long suspected that he wanted something more permanent, and she had long known that she couldn't give it to him. With what remarkable speed life took giant steps forward. Or backward.

She stared with timid wonder at her arms wet with tears. A good relationship had just died a civil and very quiet death. It was over and she wiped angrily at her eyes and vowed no more tears and was pleased to realize that she could grasp nothing, could think of nothing, could feel nothing.

She was here to make preparation for a journey of uncertain duration. Then select clothes, pack a bag, make phone calls, await Chris's return—

Slowly she stood and wondered if this too was part of her punishment and realized only at that moment how savage a word punishment was and looked around in search of the first task that needed doing and found it in the bedroom, the mussed bed still heavy with dead passion.

It must be straightened, covered over and put to rights as though nothing had happened. No one must know anything. And with excessive energy, she threw back the covers and straightened the sheets. And straightened them, and straightened them, all the time weeping . . .

Her eyes tearing, her mouth and lips seared as though by a blowtorch, Mereth swallowed the red-tipped tostado, reached for another and plunged it into the picante sauce, undaunted.

"Really very mild," she lied, a noticeable breathlessness to her voice which she heard, along with the stunned silence coming from the opposite side of the table.

"I . . . don't believe it." Chris gaped, apparently genuinely impressed.

Actually Mereth wasn't doing well at all. Not that the jalapeños were bothering her. She'd been taught to eat the small green peppers at Ty's knee and thus had over the years developed both an appetite and a tolerance for the fiery sauce.

Rather it was Hal's abrupt announcement that had left her stunned and from which she was struggling to recover.

"I believe it's time, Mereth, don't you? Nothing that stagnates is good."

Of course he was right. Still, she would miss him and think about him and perhaps even regret that she had been unable to make the kind of commitment he wanted.

"Are you sure you're all right?"

She nodded to Chris's question, dipped another chip and looked about at Tio's Finest Mexican Restaurant. Chris was right. She hadn't known it was here, though she must have passed it a hundred times in all the years of her growing up.

In the oldest part of Tulsa, just the other side of the tracks, it was a low, squat, concrete-block structure wedged between and hidden by two huge and now abandoned warehouses; across the street a bulk candy distributing company was still in operation and down the street were several auto salvage yards, but the rest of the neighborhood was contemporary disreputable, awaiting the finality of urban renewal and the wrecking ball.

Another chip dipped into the sauce, and she took a brief inventory of Tio's interior. Small, no more than twelve tables—the best Mexican restaurants were always small—oilcloth table covers, what appeared to be a Mexican market on the west wall, tortillas, enchilada sauce, peppers of all sorts. Overhead at opposite ends of the room hung two faded, dusty piñatas. On each table was an arrangement of plastic purple flowers in empty chili pepper bottles.

Through the serving bar which led to the kitchen she saw a Mexican man and woman, beyond middle years. A younger man was at the cash register next to a platter of pralines. Every table was filled, and there was an admirably egalitarian clientele, grease monkeys from the salvage yards, button-down types from uptown Tulsa and a large table in the center of the room filled with men and women wearing shirts from the pottery factory on the other side of the river.

Now she saw Chris raise two fingers at the young man behind the cash register, who immediately nodded and disappeared into the kitchen. There was a feeling of cozy familiarity about the gesture and the response.

"You've been here before."

"My favorite place in Tulsa."

"Did you find Harry Beekman?"

"I did. He was, naturally, upset. He hadn't heard the news."

"Where and how did you meet Harry Beekman?"

Her question seemed to disappoint him. He leaned back in his chair, balancing precariously on the two rear legs.

"Are we going to start that again?"

"What?"

"You know damned well what." Suddenly he leaned forward. "Look, why don't you just tell me what it is you want to know? About me, about anything. If I can answer, I will. Okay?"

Lacking an answer to his anger, she was pleased when she saw the young Mexican from behind the register carrying two cold cans of Coors toward their table.

"Always thirsty, huh, Chris?" He smiled pleasantly, placed the beer on the table and left.

"You don't drink beer?" The question was Chris's and slightly accusatory.

"It's not my favorite."

"I don't think Tio's has a wine list."

"I didn't ask for one."

"Well, what do you want?"

"This is fine," she said and lifted the Coors and sipped.

A few minutes later Tio reappeared with two heaping platters which he carried gingerly with hotpads and placed before them with a warning. "Plate's hot. Don't burn."

Mereth found herself staring down at enough food to feed four hungry people. In the exact center of the platter were two golden fried chili relleños, and flanking them on either side were two enchiladas and moving out in concentric circles she encountered two tamales, a mound of Spanish rice on one side and a cheese-covered mountain of frijoles on the other.

"He has to be kidding," she murmured and looked up to see Chris already into his, pulling the stems off the relleños, sucking the batter clean.

"There's an author, an anthropologist . . . can't remember his name," Chris began, "who claims that peppers, jalapeños in particular, have hallucinogenic qualities. Have you ever hallucinated?"

"I may have," she replied. "So much of my life in retrospect seems like a hallucination."

For the first time he put down his fork. "Has it been that bad? Being a poor little rich girl, I mean."

She heard what she thought was resentment and foolishly thought she'd try to explain what it had been like growing up at Warrick.

"Hey, I'm sorry."

The apology came from across the table and she looked up, surprised. "It's good," she said after the first forkful. And they ate steadily, without speaking. A short time later, she passed the still half-filled plate to one side. "I guess we'd better be getting back."

"Coffee?" he asked. "Don't worry about getting back. I'll call Eddie and see what's up. He asked me to, anyway."

"Yes, coffee." She nodded, really in no hurry to return to Warrick. She had the sinking feeling that once she returned she would be unable to think of another reason to leave again for some time.

Tio retrieved the platters and accepted their compliments. Chris requested two coffees, then excused himself.

As he disappeared, Mereth had a peculiar sensation of being "free," and lost. For a moment she considered simply leaving the café, going out to her car and heading back to Warrick alone. She might have done this except for a brief recall of seeing him pocket the car keys as they'd pulled up in front of Tio's. So nothing to do but wait. Also, if he was calling Eddie she was curious for a progress report. With luck Josh was still sleeping. She hoped that Massie had retired to her rooms for the same purpose, and that Junior Nagle and Red Pierson had taken refuge in the terrace room for their favorite pastime, prolonged discussions of the ups and downs of the Warrick Corporation.

Not dead yet. Let go, Ty.

"I'm back."

She looked up, surprised by his quick return. Though she had a thousand questions for him concerning his phone call, her first was urgent and instinctive.

"Where did you leave Deeter this morning?"

He shrugged. "He was in the terrace room, wasn't he? Eating, as always. Why?"

She folded what was left of her paper napkin into a small square. "You know Deeter."

"He was sober. Don't worry. He's getting ready to leave for a few days."

"Where?"

Chris shook his head. "I never ask. He has several private hideouts."

"He doesn't think Ty's ill. He thinks that it's someone else in . . ."

"I know. We talked late last night. He loves Ty, that's all. It will be good for him to go away for a while. If something happens to Ty . . ."

"*If* something happens," she parroted. "Something *has* happened."

"I didn't mean . . ."

"Buckner told Massie this morning there was little cause and less hope for prolonging his life."

She saw the sober expression on his face.

"Buckner told her this?"

She nodded. "I don't think he was speaking on his judgment alone. The specialist yesterday must have conferred with O'Rourke."

He seemed to listen carefully to her words, as though searching for something to rebut or deny. Apparently he found neither.

"Eddie said we were to get on back," he muttered, as though just then remembering his phone call.

She too had forgotten. "What else did he say?"

"Nothing important."

As she made her way to the door, she noticed a few empty tables, the lunch crowd beginning to thin. It was a good place. She'd remember it. Brit used to enjoy good Mexican food. If he hadn't lost his appetite for it completely under the boredom of bland English cooking, she'd bring him here. He'd like this place. There was definitely the feel of the masses about it.

Outside a brilliant midafternoon sun temporarily blinded her. She walked slowly to the car, head down, feeling strangely cut off from everything and everyone.

"I have to fly up to Anchorage, Massie. Want to come with me?"

"No thank you. Alaska? Why?"

"A good friend died. Palmer Sutton."

"I've never heard—"

"He was my first rig foreman. Years ago. Went through some rough times, we did, and he never once lost faith in me. Makes me mad as hell when a good man dies. Covey is his wife of forty-three years. Imagine. I promised her I'd be at the funeral. Do you want to come with me, Mereth?"

"I'll come with you, Ty."

As she reached the car, she leaned with one hand on the hood for a moment's balance. She peered into the locked car and saw her luggage in the back seat, garment bag hanging near her window. For the first time she noticed a square parcel wrapped in plain paper, no adornment.

"What's in the box?" she asked Chris as he unlocked the door for her and stood back.

"Cigars. For me."

"I didn't know you smoked cigars."

"There's probably a lot about me you don't know."

In the car, she looked up at him, surprised. Not that his comment was said with any degree of hostility. To the contrary, he seemed only amused.

"You're right," she said. "Where do you go, Chris, and what do you do when you're not at Warrick?"

He angled the car out onto the street. Across the way she saw two old Indians shuffling along on the graveled shoulder. Six blocks to the north was modern, high-tech, oil-rich Tulsa.

"All right," he pronounced. "Direct answers to direct questions. I'm a graduate of Harvard. Harvard Law. Read law and history at Cambridge, and I've read law at the Inns in London. A few years ago I became disillusioned with both the letter and the spirit of the law. It seemed to serve a limited clientele at best. Deeter invited me to come back out here to—as he wisely put it—'Get out of my head.' Been coming out here since I was a kid. Now . . ." He shrugged.

She stared at him. His inconclusive "Now . . ." was the least of her worries. The greatest one concerned the truth. Her first instincts were to label it all bull and forget it. That had been no Harvard lawyer hitchhiking on the toll plaza of the turnpike.

"No further questions?"

She heard the sarcasm in his voice and ignored it.

He drove easily now up the ramp to I-44 and threaded his way into oncoming traffic with perfect timing.

She slid down in her seat and gazed blankly out of the window at the passing motels and restaurants, mock Camelot, mock Chinese gardens, mock Grecian isles, mock Italian villas.

Something real, please. Anything!

Ty was real.

And not dead yet.

Warrick

AT FIRST Red Pierson thought it was just the second floor of Warrick that smelled like a hospital. But when the antiseptic odor followed him down the staircase, Red found the door behind the draperies in the terrace room and stepped out into one of those mint-perfect Oklahoma spring evenings, the kind that songwriters write about.

A walk, then, down to the gazebo and back.

A plan of action had always been good therapy for Red. He

couldn't function without one, and now he covered the flagstones with renewed purpose, studying the new plantings around him.

If Ty died—

The words intersected his thoughts like an unexplored path, and he realized he'd not really taken Ty's stroke seriously until his conversation with Massie when he'd first arrived.

If Ty died, Red would not have a chance of talking him out of amending that last foolish codicil. What had possessed Ty, what whim, or fancy, or worse, ironic humor had caused this fatal lapse of judgment? If he died, Red would be left with no alternative but to march straight into court with what would surely be the most newsworthy sideshow in recent memory. The media would have a field day.

Of course Red might first try reason, though the breed he'd be dealing with was not known to possess great reasoning powers.

As new worries collided with old, Red walked more slowly, head down, concentrating on the muddled configurations of the flagstones.

Approaching the gazebo, he looked up and caught sight of a human form slouched on one of the padded cushions. The head was bent over, cradled in massive hands, the whole form resembling something lifeless.

Dusk was falling, though there still were significant pools of light here and there, rays that escaped capture by shadows, and though one such pool fell on two filthy, worn, dusty cowboy boots, the rest of the human shape remained lost.

No matter. Red had seen enough and knew who it was. It was Deeter, drunk or close to it, or well past it. Deeter sober had never held much appeal for Red Pierson, except insofar as a sideshow holds appeal, limited at best, repulsing as much as it attracts. Why Ty worshiped the old Indian, Red had never been able to figure out.

Then a subtle, silent detour back down the steps in the event—

"Is that Red Pierson? I know it is, so don't bullshit me." The voice was familiar, the speech slurred.

How did he—

"I've been watching you pussyfoot your way down here since you left the house. You walk like the earth is sour to your feet. Why do you do that, Red? It looks goddamned dumb."

Poised on the bottom step, Red decided the Indian might not be as drunk as he'd suspected, though to be sure he now caught a strong whiff and he knew that somewhere, tucked in those awful-smelling clothes, there probably was a bottle, maybe two, but at least the man was capable of speech.

"Come on. I want to talk to you, Red," Deeter concluded, suddenly serious, almost sad-looking.

In a bizarre way Red was curious. This was Ty's "pet," a very expensive pet too. There had been times in the past when Red had had to impose his own good judgment on Ty's generosity. Anything Deeter wanted, Ty provided him with, including that eyesore in Warrick's eastern corner, that so-called castle.

"Come on, you can make it, old man." Deeter grinned down on Red. His mouth glittered with gold teeth, interspersed with gray, decaying ones.

"Can't stay," Red said briskly, climbing the steps into the gazebo and moving instinctively to the far side, wanting to put as much distance as possible between himself and the unspeakably filthy Indian.

Still, there was something fascinating about the face opposite him, the figure half crouched in evening shadows, wholly consumed by age and dissipation. Son of the last great Osage chief, the result of a mixed marriage, and the product of ancient hatreds which he and Ty had converted into a lifetime of love and devotion.

Deeter lifted the bottle, took a swig and recapped it, cradling it like a baby.

"I'm going away for a few days, think it's best. But you got a problem. You know that, don't you, Red?"

It seemed an oversimplification of the impending chaos.

"Oh, I think we have several problems, Deeter. Which one did you have reference to?"

"Ty!" the old Indian exclaimed, leaning closer, his knees spread. Red noticed for the first time that Deeter's zipper was undone. Probably stopped off to take a leak behind a bush on the way down from the house. Red looked away before his embarrassment could register.

"Yes, Ty's a problem, I'll admit. But they are doing everything they can do. Or so I understand."

"What are you talking about, Red? He's been gone now two days," Deeter whispered conspiratorially.

"He's upstairs in his bed."

"Bullshit! That ain't Ty. Can't you see for yourself?"

For several moments Red seriously applied himself to the "mystery." Then it dawned on him. Deeter didn't want Ty to be in that room dying, and therefore he wasn't.

Enough. Red had to get back. He had the feeling that he was surrounded by unruly children, all looking to him for stability and decision.

"Hey, where you going?" Deeter protested, seeing him rise and trying to follow suit, but it was difficult to rise when the legs wouldn't hold. "Red, wait!"

"What is it, Deeter? Do you want to go back up to the house? I think it best if you go away for a while."

"Oh, I'm getting out of here all right, damn it!" the old Indian cursed. "Just want to find Ty."

There was something urgent, even lucid in his manner, despite all the booze. Red could not honestly contradict him because Red had not been granted entry into that second-floor master bedroom suite. Not that he wanted to go in. He could handle the fact of death. It was the act of dying that presented "a problem."

Now he turned away from the smelly mountain of flesh and thought he'd handled things well enough when suddenly he felt a viselike grip around his neck, and at the same time felt the sharp, hard angle of a knee drilling into the center of his back. The attack took him off guard. When was the last time anyone had touched Red Pierson? And violently?

"Deeter . . . what in . . . let me go! Turn me loose, you hear? What . . . ?"

He felt himself being led back to the cushioned bench where, unceremoniously, he was twisted around and pushed down hard upon the seat. He looked up into Deeter's angry face.

"Don't walk away from me, Mr. Red Pierson!" the big man warned with almost childlike simplicity. "I ain't got no one to talk to. I just need to talk to someone for a minute 'fore I leave. Is it asking too much?"

As two ham-sized hands held his shoulders flattened against the cushioned back, Red was unable to do anything but shake his head. "I'm . . . sorry, Deeter. I didn't know you had anything else to say. In fact, I . . . thought you might want to be alone."

"Shit! That's what I am all the time," Deeter said, shaking his head. "Sometimes Ty would leave for days at a time and don't come and see me, and that Chris, he shows up like a bad penny, when the mood strikes him."

Red rather liked Chris. The young man seemed bright and respectful and certainly seemed to have Deeter's best interests at heart.

"So what am I goin' to do?" Deeter mourned and slumped heavily beside Red, half pinning him with the weight of his body. "With Ty gone, there ain't nothin' left."

"Well, I think we'll find him," Red said quickly.

The old Indian appeared to be growing sleepy. Or worse, nostalgic.

"When we was kids," Deeter began, "there wasn't a square inch of this Warrick we didn't call our own. There weren't nobody around to supervise us, you see. I feel sorry for kids now. Everybody bosses them about, every goddamned body wherever he turns around. But not us. The smartest thing we ever did was to get out of the way of those two old wild men."

Suddenly Deeter laughed, a hearty, deep laugh, his eyes glazed with something other than the booze, and Red had the feeling he was seeing horizons not of this world as he stared out at the terraced gardens of Warrick.

"Once," he continued, his voice a whisper like a reverence, as though the past were a god, "we rode too far, Ty and me did, rode 'til our horses was lathered, looking for something that moved to shoot at. Anything. We weren't particular." Something crossed his face, a look akin to pain, and his voice when he spoke again was husky.

"I'll tell you something not too many people in this rotten world ever knew, a secret, Ty's best secret. When he was a kid, back then, you know, well the truth of it was that he couldn't stand to shoot nothing, let alone kill it. I mean *nothing.* I had to do all the shooting and cleaning and skinning. He said it like to kill him to see animals die, said they didn't know nothing.

"But his daddy, that meanest son of a bitch, got on to him, started calling him 'girlie' in front of all the cowboys, and when that didn't work he beat him real bad every night for a couple of weeks and—"

Deeter's voice fell. Slowly he closed his eyes, as though wanting to blot out that dead world.

"Course Ty got good, damned good, the best damned shot in the state until his eyes went. But like I was telling you, way back then, we was just two green kids wandered too far from home, cold and hungry, and we made camp somewhere over there, and we lit us a jet like we always did to keep warm and . . ."

Red was listening closely and had followed everything up to that point. "You lit a . . . what?" he questioned.

"A jet," Deeter repeated.

"A jet of what?" Red persisted.

Deeter sat up as though excited by the recall. "Well, what you do is, you sink a gun barrel down into the earth, wiggle it and pull it out and there's a hissing like a snake and you strike a match to the escaping jet and you got fire and light for as long as you want it."

Red stared. He'd never heard that story in his life.

"Where was this . . . jet?"

"Over there in them woods. Hell, my people been doin' it for years to keep warm."

Red sat slowly up, trying to separate drunken boast from fact. Natural gas, if the story was true. He'd heard countless stories and had seen for himself the sabotage the Indians had inflicted on the aboveground pipelines in the Osage territory, puncturing holes and lighting those jets to warm their cattle and melt enough snow for them to drink.

But these shallow deposits Deeter was talking about were certainly fiction. Producers and drillers in the state were sinking the world's deepest natural gas wells, 31,000 feet to date. Where in the world did natural gas lurk close enough to the surface to be tapped by a gun barrel?

"And you know," Deeter went on with circumflex eyebrows, "we, Ty and me, sat up all night warming ourselves and pledging our brotherhood, just like in the movies. You seen that movie with Glenn Ford, I believe it was, and, hell, someone else, I forgot, but we was doing it real and honest. Brothers we was and now I can't even find him. Course I know what happened. He's gone on ahead and left me behind. And he promised me, swore he'd never do that. Never!"

As the man's drunken ramblings continued and reached new incoherence, Red studied the strong profile. Despite the flabby dissipation and tracks of time, he saw the remains of what once must have been a remarkable face.

Well, two courses of action now. One, he must insist to Buckner that he be allowed a brief moment inside Ty's room. And, two, he wanted to repeat Deeter's crazy gun-barrel story for Junior Nagle and see what kind of an incredulous reaction it brought forth. It was certainly the melodramatic rambling of a drunken old man who'd simply lived beyond his time and his purpose.

Red's thoughts broke off as Deeter stood abruptly, lurched his way to the seat on the opposite side of the gazebo and withdrew a full bottle of Gilbey's Gin. He broke the seal, tipped the bottle and drank it effortlessly as though it were cool spring water on a July day.

"Deeter, come on back to the house with me now," Red ordered and stood up, ready to lend the man a hand if he needed it.

"Piss out!" the old man slurred and slumped down in the seat, clutched the bottle to him, closed his eyes and appeared to be asleep.

Red tried again but soon changed his mind. He wasn't this disreputable man's keeper, or any other. On more than one occasion he'd wondered why Ty had felt such a weight of responsibility. Guilt, probably. Crazy Indian, that's all he was.

On that final observation Red straightened his coat, adjusted his tie and proceeded slowly down the steps. And then, though it surprised him to admit it, he felt sorry for Deeter, felt sorry for all of them. The center of their respective worlds was ill, perhaps dying. A few, like Red and possibly Junior Nagle and old Harry Beekman, the good, hardheaded businessmen among them, would cope and adjust. All they would miss of Tyburn Warrick was his extraordinarily unique and diverse personality.

But Deeter and those worthless grandkids and even Jo Massie, who had allowed love to weaken her, and all the others who had failed to learn life's most important lesson, the need to ride strict . herd on that most destructive force of all, rampant and uncontrolled emotionalism, well, all those poor souls would not fare so well.

The truth, as Red saw it, was that the strong of this world cultivated this weakness in others, developed it and exploited it, thus forcing them into emotional dependency. Look about. In any relationship there was a weak and a strong. God, that's what gave the strong their strength! And Ty Warrick held many in this imprisoning emotional bondage. The most pitiful prisoner of all was that old Indian, starting to sleep off the numbness that had taken him all day to accomplish.

Just before Red stepped up onto the flagstone path that would lead him back to the house, he looked over his shoulder.

Jesus!

He held his position, stopped by what he saw in the diminishing light: old Deeter poised on the top step of the gazebo, legs spread, one hand perched rakishly on his hip, the other holding his penis, which was spraying a yellow arc the length of the gazebo steps.

Red started to call out in disgust at such a sight, but there was something in the old Indian's stance that suggested he was doing more than emptying his bladder. Red sensed, rightly or wrongly, a kind of defiance, an insult, a challenge to—something.

"Crazy fool," Red muttered, and turned his back. For some reason he was fully prepared for Deeter to call after him something tasteless and obscene and insulting. But all Red heard was the splattering of hot urine coming from the gazebo behind him.

Horace Buckner had never been so tired in his life. As he closed Ty's door, he decided he was getting too old for this sort of thing, watching his friends die one by one. Of course, most of them had had the good taste to do it quickly with that blessed element of surprise which always helps to deaden grief. He might have known Ty's death would be different, would resemble a circus.

Somehow, though it was the last thing he wanted, his memory instantly conjured up an image of the man he'd just left, senseless, in a coma, every orifice of his body tubed and wired. Such goddamned nonsense! Without it old Ty Warrick would have joined his beautiful Mary Beth by now and would be poking around the hills of heaven or hell for something hidden, something to search out.

Buckner stirred himself from his weary lethargy and found only one thought in his head worthy of giving thanks for: barring a crisis or the blessing of death, he would not have to reenter those bedroom doors tonight. His two angels of mercy, Miss Kent and Miss Nellie, had just sent him off for the evening while they curled up in Ty's sitting room with one of the portable color TV's, munching thick-slabbed roast beef sandwiches from the kitchen and watching some soapy TV movie-of-the-week.

Well, look to your own needs, a voice whispered in Buckner's ear, and at the moment those needs consisted of a couple of stiff drinks, a steaming hot shower to wash the smell of dying off of him, then a quick change and down to the carnival Massie had planned for them all this evening.

Hell, the company would be circus enough. Ty's "inner sanctum," his "posse" as he liked to call them, old reprobates like Junior Nagle and pricks like Red Pierson and the Warrick kids, three worthless excuses for the future if Horace ever saw them. And, thrown in for good measure, the Reverend Gerald Jobe, the greatest crook to come out of these parts since Jesse James.

And probably Eddie O'Keefe would be at table. He always was. Maybe even Ramona, the cook, and Jobe's kids, all those bright-eyed and bushy-tailed youngsters who appeared so uniformly bland that they'd probably join in the first "Sieg, Heil!" that came along.

And, of course, the great lady herself, Jo Massie.

Buckner hadn't meant to offend her when he suggested pulling the plugs. It was just that the man was already dead. Brain dead, at any rate, it appeared.

He could read the signals. If the foreigner had seen anything to save, Ty Warrick would now be in the ICU of St. Mark's. But if they couldn't do anything, they backed off as fast as hound dogs from a skunk hole, and everybody had backed away from poor old Ty, except for the vultures gathering downstairs, hoping to get a good bite of one of the richest pieces of carrion this country had ever produced.

Slowly Buckner shook his head. Hell, he was no better or worse than most of them. Human nature, that's all it was.

The thought comforted him and helped make him tolerant of what was happening here and got him moving down the corridor when he heard footsteps coming from the opposite end. He squinted into the sound, feeling protective of the dead man pinned to his bed.

No repetition of scenes such as Deeter had caused, though as the mysterious steps drew nearer Horace Buckner found himself in a peculiar mood agreeing with Deeter. That wasn't Ty Warrick imprisoned in that bed. At least not the Ty Warrick most of the oil world had come to know and hate.

"Why do they resent me, Bucky? What have I ever done to any of them?"

"For a bright man, Ty, you sure can be dumb. You've succeeded! That's enough to piss off the whole fucking, failed world."

"Who is it?" Buckner called out.

"Take it easy, you old quack. We ain't come for your dope."

Horace relaxed. Junior Nagle, Ty's partner, a darned good quail hunter. Not a bad sort, when he didn't get up on his high horse. He'd been a better man thirty years ago, before he'd gotten to be a rich one. Horace put his specs on and for a moment the lenses didn't do a lot of good; then, gradually, he brought Junior's huge frame into focus. Buckner had known him when he was pencil thin.

"You old bastard." Horace grinned and extended a hand toward the man dressed in his fancies, looking for all the world like a typical oilman. "I heard you were at Warrick. Counted on seeing you at dinner, not . . ."

He broke off, seeing for the first time another figure hovering in the shadows. As he squinted over Junior's fleshy shoulder, Junior said, "It's Red, Bucky. Red Pierson."

Then the man himself materialized, and Buckner put all his prejudices temporarily on the back burner. "Sure," he said, and he tried to muster the same size grin he'd given to Junior Nagle, but it was difficult. It wasn't that he actively disliked Red Pierson. It was just that he always felt awkward around him. Junior's facade of city slicker was just that, about a quarter of an inch deep. But Buckner suspected that with Pierson, the phoniness was bone deep.

"Nice to see you again Red," Buckner said. "I think the last time I saw you was . . . at the deer hunt."

"West Texas."

"Yep."

And that was it. Buckner had nothing more to say to him. The deer hunt had taken place last November at Ty's Texas place. He'd invited Red Pierson, his ultimate compliment, and while the fastidi-

220

ous little man hadn't really fitted in with Ty's oil bums, still he'd managed to hold his own, proving himself to be a fairly good shot, the number-one requirement for anyone in Ty's posse. Buckner always suspected that Red Pierson practiced like hell for eleven months out of the year to get in that one good shot in November. Now—

"I was wondering, Dr. Buckner," Red Pierson said, stepping ahead of Junior Nagle as though they had appointed a spokesman and Red was it.

"What's that?"

"We . . . feel it necessary to speak with Ty," was what Red Pierson said without cracking a smile. Otherwise, Buckner would have sworn he was making a poor joke.

"Look, Bucky," Junior broke in, something apologetic in his tone, "if it isn't convenient tonight, then tomorrow would do. We . . . Red and me and probably Harry Beekman, we need to know just precisely how it is that Ty wants us to carry on. You understand."

Buckner listened patiently through this tortured recital. "Junior," Horace began, as gently as possible, knowing it wasn't going to be easy, "there ain't nothing to see in that room," and he gestured with a jerk of his hand over his shoulder. "Oh, Ty's in there all right . . . what's left of him, which ain't much, Junior, I'm warning you."

"I . . . don't understand." Junior frowned, and for one awful moment Buckner believed him.

In the impasse Red Pierson stepped closer, too close. Buckner liked distance between himself and those he didn't trust.

"If it's not convenient to see him this evening, could we make an appointment for first thing in the morning?"

"Make an . . . appointment!" Buckner exploded and stepped back several feet from the two men.

"No need to shout, Dr. Buckner," Red hushed. "We can hear perfectly."

"Good for your hearing, Mr. Pierson. How's your understanding?"

"Our . . . ? I don't . . ."

"Mr. Pierson, to all intent and purpose, Tyburn Warrick is dead. Strokes are sometimes like God's bad jokes. Or better, bad jobs. Yeah, like sloppy workmanship. Like leaving a well 90-percent done. The Almighty killed off about 97.5 percent of old Ty early yesterday morning, and carelessly He's left 2.5 percent lying in that bed."

Junior turned away as Buckner knew he would. Red, on the other hand, seemed undaunted.

"Then what are we to do?" he asked idiotically, a slightly offended tone in his voice, as though Ty had behaved in this manner to spite them. "There are legalities that must be attended to. The corporation will be all right for a while, but there are other more personal . . . What I mean, we need power of attorney perhaps . . ."

Not that Buckner didn't fully understand his confusion and sympathize with it. Of all of Ty's "posse," Red Pierson in all fairness worked the hardest for Ty. It was not a job that Buckner would want. Even the Lord had trouble unscrambling and interpreting Ty's above-the-table deals. The Lord Himself probably had no full comprehension of what precisely went on in those shadowy just-this-side-of-the-law regions below the table.

For several moments the corridor was quiet, each brooding in his own way. Buckner was pretty sure they still didn't fully understand, but at least they'd taken that first difficult step toward realizing that a major transition was in the making.

"Dr. Buckner . . ."

The voice came from the bay window across the corridor. Red Pierson.

"Would you have any notion how long this . . . condition . . . will persist, based on experience, your medical knowledge?"

Now it was Buckner's turn to express bewilderment. "What 'condition' is that? I don't . . ."

"Ty, of course," he said with what clearly was mounting impatience.

Then came Junior's voice, as pleading and childlike as Buckner had ever heard it. "Just a couple of moments, Bucky. How would it hurt? We wouldn't ask him any questions. Just a quick look-see, let him know we're here, with him, ready to help. You know, that sort of thing."

Staggered by their respective denseness, Buckner at last understood. They were refusing to understand.

"Shit!" Buckner muttered to the floor and, although it was against his better judgment, he walked back to the bedroom doors. "Come on, the both of you. Now! You wanted to see Ty? All right, then go see Ty. Ask him anything you like, anything at all. Get on *in* there!" he commanded and literally shoved the two men into Ty's bedroom, overflowing with the smell of dying.

"Bucky, no!"

It was Junior's last plaintive cry before he caught his first clear glimpse of the man on the bed.

"Could we bow our heads in prayer to Jesus Christ, our Lord and Savior, and thank Him for all our many blessings, even in the midst of the great tragedy that has descended on this house?"

As Reverend Jobe's preacher voice effortlessly filled the large formal dining room, Massie bowed her head and knew she ought to be listening, knew she was in desperate need of any sustenance that she could get. But not now. Platitudes wouldn't work. There was nothing powerful enough to combat this terrifying feeling of estrangement, like a ship cut loose from its moorings.

Don't, she scolded herself, and heard Reverend Jobe ask Jesus Christ to grant everyone seated at the table the courage to face the rough seas ahead. Quite an order, even for Christ.

Next to her was Josh, who had been so apologetic for his drunken arrival. She'd tried to reassure him, but he'd persisted with that slightly haunted look, as though at any moment Ty might descend and assail him for almost everything.

Next to Josh was Mereth's empty chair. She was in the house changing, having just arrived.

"Thou preparest a table before me in the presence of my enemies. Thou anointest my head with oil . . ."

Please, Reverend Jobe, not a sermon now. Just reassurance that all of this has some sort of meaning, some purpose.

Beyond Mereth's conspicuously empty chair was Eddie O'Keefe, his head bowed so deeply it looked as if his neck was broken. It was good to have someone close who had not been wounded by the great benefactor himself.

Next to Eddie was the Reverend Gerald Jobe, his face lifted to the crystal chandelier overhead as though God were hiding out among the glass prisms. Her feelings for this man had altered in the last few years. In the beginning she'd viewed him as little more than an evangelist who exploited the ignorant and bilked the innocent.

But Gerald Jobe was different. Anyone who could win Ty over to a religious point of view and get him to donate a million dollars in the process was not a man to be taken lightly.

". . . and so, dear Christ, empty all those who sit at this table of self and fill completely with Thee. May we come to distrust our own strength and rely only on Thy power and wisdom and strength. In Jesus Christ, Your only Son, our Lord, we ask this. Amen."

"Thank you, Reverend Jobe," Massie said and looked from Jobe to Ty's empty place, then at Junior Nagle and Red Pierson and Horace Buckner lining the left side like three oversized, overaged schoolboys who'd recently been chastised. What had happened, she had no idea.

"Brit's plane is due sometime tonight," Massie announced, aware that no one had asked. Her voice drifted as the serving team appeared, armed with soup bowls and a large tureen.

Massie glanced at Ty's three cronies on her left. What *had* happened to them? Junior Nagle looked incapable of speech. Though Red Pierson was carrying on, she knew him well enough to recognize that imperious expression. It was what he hid behind when he sensed trouble. And Horace Buckner was the most puzzling of all. That normally gluttonous old man sat slumped in his chair, gesturing to the young girl that one partially filled ladle of lobster bisque was enough.

Soup served around, she was aware of all eyes on her and quickly lifted her spoon and set the table into motion, relieved in a way that the silence was now filled with the soft click of silver on china.

In an unguarded moment she looked at Ty's empty place at the end of the table. The discomfort lodged in her throat and might have been relieved by tears but, of course, they were out of the question.

"Dr. Buckner, no change I assume? In Ty . . . ," she said softly, hoping to communicate only with the man seated directly on her left.

But the question reverberated endlessly about the table. A few soup spoons hung suspended in midair between bowl and mouth, as though the common impetus had failed simultaneously.

At that moment the large double doors which led into the library opened and Mereth appeared.

Massie smiled. "Glad you're here."

As the pink in Mereth's cheeks deepened to a full blush, she ducked her head and Massie observed the long, silken hair done up in a meticulous French knot which nestled becomingly at the nape of a very slim neck. One of Reverend Jobe's young men drew back her chair for her.

"You look lovely," Massie said. "I trust Chris served you well?" she added.

"Very well, thank you," Mereth replied and concentrated unduly on arranging the napkin in her lap. "Where is Deeter?"

Massie shrugged. "Deeter moves in his own world and in his own time. I believe he said he was going into Tulsa for a few days."

Red Pierson placed his soup spoon beside his empty bowl and

contributed a clue. "I saw him earlier this evening in the gazebo. Drunk, I'm afraid. Let him go."

The announcement seemed to add a new strain to the table. As plate after plate was set before each guest, the tension grew and did not bode well for adequate digestion. It could not persist. Ty would not want it to persist.

Accordingly, Massie took a deep breath. "My friends," she began, "Ty would not appreciate this . . . wake. I beg you, relax and try to enjoy yourselves. If Ty were sitting there . . ."

She reached for her napkin and pressed it to her face, mystified by frightening feelings and powerless to alter them.

"Massie, do you want me to . . . ?" The voice was Mereth's. "Come on . . ."

Hands were assisting her out of this bewildering place when she heard another voice, male.

"Miss Warrick, if I may suggest, why don't you take your seat and leave Jo Massie where she is? We are not afraid of her grief nor are we embarrassed by it nor should you be. In fact, we share it and only by sharing it can we come to terms with it, understand it and thus be able to rise above it."

Reverend Jobe. The voice was unmistakable. Massie started to look up, for the Old Testament voice had successfully frightened away any tears that might have foolishly considered slipping down her face.

"Come on, Miss Warrick," Jobe's voice repeated in a scolding tone, as though he were accustomed to dealing with weak-willed children. "Take your seat. Jo Massie will be fine. She's a strong woman."

"What if she doesn't *wish* to be strong at the moment?" Mereth's voice was astonishing.

Reverend Jobe laughed. "Now why, Miss Warrick, pray tell me if you can, why would anyone purposefully choose weakness over strength?"

"Because both words are subjective and depend upon points of view."

"Oh, my! Hear that, Eddie? We have a humanist in our midst. Nothing is good or evil but only thinking makes it so."

Massie heard sarcasm in his voice, but it seemed playful, harmless. On the other hand, she felt Mereth's grip tighten on her shoulders.

"What's so dangerous about humanism, Reverend?" she asked, and Massie was pleased to hear a new control in her voice. With Jobe one had to be controlled, if nothing else.

"The dangers of humanism," he repeated. "You know, Miss Warrick, the question is so simple that one of my students here could give you an adequate answer in less than a minute. But I'm not going to ask them to because we have work here today. Later, Miss Warrick. For now, please partake of the delicious dinner provided by Ramona."

"I would rather discuss this point with you, if you don't mind—"

Jobe laughed. "Oh, that persistence. Massie, where have we seen that persistence before? And right here at this table, seated there at the—"

"Tell me about the dangers of humanism, Reverend Jobe, as you perceive them, that is."

More tension as Jobe blinked once and wagged his head and appeared to lose a degree or two of Christian patience. "I said, Not now, Miss—"

"Why not now? Because you have no response? At least none that makes sense?"

"Mereth. Please—"

"No, Massie, I want him to talk. He was the one who made the accusation, although a more foolish one I doubt anyone at this table has ever heard. What, in the name of God, and I mean that quite literally, is inherently wrong or evil in a philosophy that asserts the dignity and worth of man and his capacity for self-realization through reason? I for one see nothing lacking in that and want very much for someone to point out the flaws in such a philosophy. Is that asking too much?"

Everyone at table was listening closely, no fork moving. Massie joined them in close attention, secretly surprised and very pleased. For a moment she caught a glimpse of the old Mereth, the fire, the insistence upon understanding everything down to the last detail, every nuance. Ty had both encouraged it and been driven to distraction by it. Something had happened to that marvelous stubbornness several years ago. At least for a moment it was back.

"Well, Reverend Jobe, I'm waiting. We're all waiting. You have a captive audience. Please, I beg you, point out to us the satanic evil in a philosophy that does no more than try to improve the quality and state of being human. As none of us are gods, except in our ludicrous self-delusions, we must work with what we are. Human beings. Fallible. Perhaps perfectable. No more. No less."

Silence, though from where Massie sat she could see a pulse in Jobe's temple.

It could not go on. Massie had to put a stop to the battle. And with a nod of her head, she motioned for the girls to continue serving dinner.

As the young people passed baskets of freshly baked biscuits, Massie reached up for one of those tense hands still grasping her shoulders.

"Thanks, Mereth. I'm fine now. I really am. Please go back to your seat."

But apparently Mereth wasn't interested in going back to her seat. Instead—

"If you'll excuse me," she said and walked to the door and without another word was out of the room, leaving a deeper pall than before.

Massie debated whether or not she should go after her and at the same time heard the scrape of a chair directly to her right and sensed that Josh too was bailing out.

She begged softly, "Please, Josh, stay," and might have said more except, coming from the end of the table, his preacher's tones muted by a mouth filled with biscuits, she heard Reverend Jobe.

"Yes, please. Enjoy your dinners, all of you. I shall go to her shortly. I launched the assault; I'll tend to the apology. But not now. It would be a far greater sin to allow this gorgeous meal to grow cold."

To Massie's relief, she saw Josh reluctantly sit back down and she saw an expression on his face which suggested he was doing it against his better judgment.

The next grumble came from Horace Buckner. "A good red wine would be nice, Massie." He delivered this comment between sizable bites of prime rib.

"I am sorry, Horace. I'll . . ."

"I'm afraid the absence of wine is my fault," Reverend Jobe confessed wearily from the end of the table. "It isn't necessary for the full enjoyment of a meal or a life. The Epistle of Paul to Titus," he quoted, looking up at the ceiling, " 'We should live soberly, righteously and godly in this present world.' "

For the second time that evening Massie felt mutinous feelings coming from her left. Horace Buckner loved his wine, and its absence would not be taken lightly.

"Did anybody ever tell you, Reverend Jobe, that you are a first-class horse's ass?" he said. Buckner did not look up at the ceiling as much as he glared in a heavenly direction. "You want to play Bible verses, Jobe? All right, we'll play Bible verses. Let's see. Ecclesiastes, chapter 9, verse 7. 'Go thy way, eat thy bread with joy and drink thy wine with a merry heart for God accepteth thy works.' " Buckner still did not look down from the heavens, which he seemed to be confronting with great delight. "Now how about the First Epistle of Paul to Timothy, chapter 5, verse 23? 'Drink no longer water but use a little wine for thy stomach's sake and for thy other infirmities.' "

The first shock waves came from the young people standing at attention along the wall. The second came from Reverend Jobe himself, who gaped at the challenge. Then he threw back his head and laughed as heartily as Massie had ever heard him.

Buckner stared at the man with an expression of baffled curiosity. Finally he gave a huge shake of his head, pushed back in his chair, walked the length of the room and disappeared into the small serving pantry. A few moments later he reappeared and stomped his way back to the table, a newly uncorked bottle of Mouton Rothschild in one hand and three crystal wineglasses clutched in the other.

"For whoever wants it," he muttered, slamming himself down in his chair and filling the three glasses.

"Well, my goodness, if I had known . . ." Reverend Jobe smiled. "Massie, with your permission . . ."

Without waiting for her permission, Reverend Jobe left the table and disappeared into the serving pantry and reappeared a few minutes later, cradling a second bottle of wine. As he served the wine himself, he seemed impervious to the gaping. Once all had been served, he resumed his place.

"We are not here to sow the seeds of discord or discontent. A toast, if you will, to all of you, the men and women who must fill the vacuum left by Tyburn Warrick. I will pray for you."

Disarmed. The entire table. The presence of wine seemed to work wonders. Junior Nagle said something about the phenomenal growth taking place in Dallas, and Red Pierson politely asked for specifics, and Horace Buckner leaned toward Massie and asked if he might have a touch more beef.

The only one at table not engaged in pleasant chatter was Reverend Gerald Jobe, who sat with his eyes fixed and brooding on the flickering white candle directly in front of him, and Massie saw an expression on his face which she recognized instantly, having suffered from it so recently, so painfully.

Lost. Reverend Jobe had temporarily lost his way.

Tulsa

HARRY BEEKMAN had postponed this trip to Warrick as long as he could. Now, with the news hounds closing in and bank examiners crawling over every square inch of his Tulsa Petroleum Exchange Bank and, worse, with personal inquiries from friends in banking from New York to London to Mexico, he'd finished his dinner—always an ordeal since Josie's death four months ago—summoned his driver Bradley and now found himself in the back seat of his gray Lincoln, studying the latest stock-market reports on closed-circuit TV, wishing like hell he wasn't going where he was going and wishing he didn't know what he knew.

The bank examiners had kept him late, made him miss one of Ramona's delicious dinners. How Josie had enjoyed exchanging recipes with Ty's Ramona. And Massie. His wife had loved Massie, the friendship growing and deepening between the two over the last twelve years. Josie, one of the world's great opera fans, could sit for hours and listen to Massie's tales of her youth, visiting her mother in the wings of the Metropolitan Opera.

Josie dead. Harry still couldn't believe it. And now Ty.

Of course, there was always the possibility that Ty wasn't dying, that someone had exaggerated his condition and that, after a couple of days of playing "the grand invalid," he would come storming up out of his bed to take command of an empire that could not operate without his genius.

Harry stared out of the window at the passing night. Not much to see. Tulsa was an early-to-bed town.

With a blank hour ahead, Harry considered work, even though his briefcase on the floor was strangely empty. Funny how still

231

things got when examiners were about, everyone holding his breath.

No, no news, no work, no stock market.

Josie gone. Thirty-seven years gone. Ty had helped him to understand his grief.

"Take your time, Bradley," he called through the small sliding panel. "I'm in no rush."

The driver nodded and settled the Lincoln into a law-abiding 45 mph and Harry relaxed against the seat and tried to make his mind a safe blank.

Tulsa wasn't his true home. His father had come up from Beaumont in the early twenties. Having witnessed firsthand the Spindletop oil boom and seen the specific and expensive needs of a drilling oil industry, he'd proven himself a visionary and decided what Tulsa needed most was a bank geared to meet the needs of the oil man. The Tulsa Petroleum Exchange Bank had been born on June 7, 1921, and while it had been a going concern when Harry had inherited it in the mid-forties following his father's death, he had transformed it into one of the major banking institutions in the Southwest.

"If you need anything in seven figures, go talk to Harry Beekman at Tulsa Pet."

Of course, the major coup of his career had been in the late forties, when Ty had started deep gas drilling in Warrick's southern field. Everyone had thought Harry was committing professional suicide when he'd given Ty a blank check. A year later both their fortunes were sealed, as was their friendship.

Suddenly Harry felt a sneeze coming on, fished hurriedly inside his pocket for a handkerchief, withdrew one in the nick of time and exploded into it, covering his face in an attempt to corral the fury. He caught Bradley's eyes in the rearview mirror, noncommittal eyes, and blew his nose, wiped it and restored the handkerchief to his pocket and was left with the thought that had preceded the sneeze, that his forty-year relationship with Ty Warrick, both professional and personal, might be on the brink of termination.

The realization, following the exhaustion of the sneeze, left him sitting in a curious vacuum as though the Lincoln had fallen away, taking the highway, even Tulsa, with it.

" 'Bye, 'bye, Tulsi Town. Warrick, here we come!"

Ty's voice hovered close.

"Take my hands, Harry. Hold on tight. I know what it's like to lose a wife, not one of thirty-seven years. Still—"

"Dear God, Ty, I didn't know she was so ill. If I'd known—"

"Go on, Harry. Bawl. Bawl like a baby. I'm going to sit right here with you and somehow we're going to hold this old world together. Josie would want that. She loved you so much, Harry. You know what she told me once? She said her life really started when she met you. What a good thing to remember, Harry. You made her so happy. What more can a husband do? There is nothing so precious as the love that exists and grows between a husband and wife. Go on, Harry, cry. I'm crying with you. Then we'll drive out to Warrick and walk that long stretch of road that leads to the oil fields and turn around and walk it again and again and again until night falls and we can find Josie in the stars—"

Harry leaned forward and wiped his eyes and rested his head in his hands. How he loved Tyburn Warrick. Just the best friend he had in this world.

Still, he was worried about the examiners who had infested his daddy's bank, and the tenuous nightmare that everything was coming to an end all at once like Josie's death, without giving him a civil warning.

And what of grief? Shouldn't he cry? If Ty died there would be such a colossal collapse that circumstances would require the coolest of heads, the steadiest of hands and the driest of eyes.

Then that was his goal. Get all the mourning over with now, for that man who had claimed to have a nose capable of smelling oil at ten paces, gas at five.

Strange. Now that he'd set his mind to it, Harry was chagrined to find his eyes dry.

So Ty Warrick was dying. Dead maybe. It came to all men and wasn't always a curse; and was on occasion the rarest of blessings.

Warrick

"DO YOU SUPPOSE he's dead?" Josh asked and filled his brandy glass and offered the bottle to Mereth, who stood before the dead fireplace, looking as angry and as frustrated as when she'd left the dining room.

After dinner, and Jobe's embarrassment, the dining room had emptied hurriedly, everyone literally disappearing, as though if there was to be an announcement of death there would be no one there to receive it.

Now, in answer to the offer of brandy, Mereth smiled a no and paced off the fireplace.

"Are you cold?" Josh asked, pleased despite her mood that he'd escaped here, alone with Mereth.

"The bastard," she cursed.

"Jobe?"

"How did he get in here? Who gave him permission to— God, but I hate his breed, self-appointed guardian of the public morals— 'Oh my, we have a humanist in our midst.' "

As she did a rather precise imitation of Gerald Jobe's sanctimonious voice, Josh laughed.

"No, I mean it," Mereth persisted. She picked up a petrified cotton boll, a curiosity that someone had found years ago in the Warrick fields. For a moment Josh thought she was on the verge of hurling it. She was that angry, her breath that uneven, her hands trembling.

"Mereth, try to calm—"

"Ty would never have endured that man's stupidity for a moment and you know it. Then how did he get in here, who gave him—"

"When was the last time you saw Ty?"

The question was innocent, or so Josh thought. But the expression on Mereth's face was one of devastation.

"Mereth, when did you last see—"

Slowly she replaced the cotton boll, though her hands were still shaking. "Years—ago."

"Then he could have changed, right? Something could have changed him."

Carefully she nodded and looked lost, turning once in an aimless circle before the fire. She sat slowly on the sofa and closed her eyes.

Josh took note of this new mood and tried to understand it.

"Mereth, is everything all right? Here at Warrick, I mean."

She didn't look up. "I suppose. What do you mean?"

"Well, you're here most of the time and I'm out in California and . . ."

"I'm not here," she protested. "This is the first time I've been back in six years. I wouldn't be here now except—"

Abruptly she left the sofa. On the far side of the room, she came to a halt before a solid row of leather-bound volumes. She appeared to stare straight ahead at the bound volumes, a complete history of the Warrick Corporation, Ty's business dealings of a lifetime, every drilling project, every brilliant gamble, copies of every lease, every court litigation, every corporate venture. Ty had paid a small fortune to have it compiled and organized.

"Mereth, I'm . . ."

"I can't answer your question, Josh. If you really want an answer, you're in the wrong room. The men down the hall are far better able to answer than I am."

"Look, I'm sorry. I didn't mean . . ." Suddenly he resented her attempt to make him feel guilty. "What the hell, Mereth? It's your future too, you know. I assure you it's the only reason I came back, the money and you, and I think I can safely speak for Brit as well."

"I'm sure you can."

"But not you?"

It was several moments before she answered. "I want . . . nothing from Tyburn Warrick."

He sensed her exhaustion and was on the verge of offering another truce in a brandy snifter when she asked, "How's your life in California, Josh?"

"It suits me," he said. "Peter and I celebrated our fourteenth anniversary last month. Not many heterosexual marriages last that long. Or have been as happy."

"Congratulations!"

Funny, he'd hoped to shock her. Instead, she seemed pleased and more receptive.

"Tell me about him. Peter, I mean. And what do you do, what are your dreams?"

He smiled at her generous invitation to share his dreams. "Are you serious?" He took the chair opposite where she was sitting at the gaming table and didn't quite know where to start. "I've . . . directed a few films, mostly bad ones."

"Why bad?"

"Poorly written. Empty. No budget. No decent actors."

"Sounds grim."

"In Hollywood, like anyplace else, you need money."

"A universal law?"

"Absolutely. Still, I think you'd like it."

She gave him a skeptical look.

"No, I mean it, Mereth. Haven't you seen a film that you consider at least approaches an artistic achievement?"

She appeared to be thinking, and only then did he see the light of humor in her eyes.

"Well, watch carefully because your brother hopes to produce one."

Before she could respond, he saw Massie at the door.

"I wondered where you two were. We just received word. Brit will be in later this evening. Eddie will pick him up."

As Mereth hurried to the door, Josh felt disappointment amounting to pain and moved down toward the fireplace. He stared up at a large oil painting of Warrick's first oil field, a maze of derricks, black, symmetrical, too symmetrical. He remembered overhearing Ty tell someone that the things leaned when not properly anchored, but why bother? The point was to get the oil out as fast as possible.

Lost briefly in his own disappointment and that early Warrick field, Josh felt his mind glaze over. Why had the world never taken him seriously?

A drink? Sure. So that he wouldn't take the world seriously.

"Josh?"

He heard Massie call his name, then—

"What's funny? Why are you laughing, Josh?"

Was he laughing? He looked back at the two women.

"I was studying this," he said, pointing to the poor painting of the Warrick field. "Grimpen Mire," he laughed again. "You remember the old *Hound of the Baskervilles.* All those panicky peasants warning Dr. Watson, 'Do not go near Grimpen Mire,' and the good doctor replying with British panache, 'Nonsense!' And you know the rest. We all do."

Only Mereth smiled.

He started to say something else but felt suddenly drained and turned back to the painting of toy-sized and lifeless oil derricks. It really was a third-rate work. All those pumps were painted at exactly the same angle, not a sign of the continuous and hypnotic movements which, when looking out over an entire field, sometimes made one feel the queasy unease of seasickness. Obviously the artist had never taken the time to study a working field.

Suddenly Josh felt irrationally angry at the painting, the artist and the fool who had purchased it and placed it in such a prominent place to reflect absolutely nothing but his own lack of taste.

"Massie," he demanded suddenly, "who's responsible for this?"

"It's . . . Ty's favorite."

"No surprise. Everything third-rate in this house . . ."

Mereth nudged him in the vicinity of the ribs.

"Sorry," he muttered and slumped back down on the sofa, legs akimbo, and closed his eyes again.

"I'm sorry I interrupted," he heard Massie say.

Mereth thanked her. "I'll come down to the terrace room shortly."

No response that Josh could hear. Door closed. Silence. Count five.

Mereth spoke lovingly. "Do you work at being difficult, Josh? Or does it come naturally?"

"Are you in love with anyone, Mereth?"

"I don't think so."

"Have you ever been?"

She laughed. "Are my answers being recorded?"

"No."

"Then . . . yes."

"The sick kind?"

"I don't understand."

"Then you've never been in love. The love-as-illness metaphor, when you feel literally debilitated, when no act, no request can be denied the beloved, from eating feces to drinking piss."

"Josh, I don't think . . ."

"I didn't mean to shock you."

"You didn't."

Despite her denial, she moved away from the sofa and stood in a position directly in front of that awful painting. "It *is* bad."

"You never notice that about things you grow up with. Did you know that I learned most of Ty's important 'life lessons' right here on this sofa, sitting in approximately this position? They should bronze it or something."

Mereth laughed. "What were the 'life lessons' he taught you?"

"Really impressed, aren't you?"

"I don't know. I haven't heard the lessons yet."

"All right." He sat up straight, as though to face head-on that voice of authority that largely had made him what he was. "Ready?

Here goes. God gives a man balls to use, so use them. If you need more brains, buy them; everything is for sale."

"I had that one, too. That must have been a unisex lesson. What else?"

"The land would treat you good if you treated it good."

"Yes, I've heard that one."

"Pay no attention to the opinions of others; they matter only if you allow them to matter. No need to leave Warrick; it is paradise and thus contains everything a man could possibly want or need." He looked up at her. "Want more?"

She nodded.

"Oil is the only future for a man with balls. Oil requires the best and shit-cans the ball-less."

"Did he really use 'balls' all that much?"

"Constantly. Ask Brit. He was hung up on balls, I swear it."

Abruptly Josh looked up, a brilliant idea dawning. "Let's go get Brit," he proposed, the idea gaining momentum even as he spoke.

"You're drunk and I'm exhausted."

"A perfect welcoming party for a Commie brother."

"Brit isn't . . ."

"Hell, I know what Brit is and isn't. Generally he was sitting right here on this sofa with me, hearing all about balls and oil and paradise."

"Josh, it's almost midnight. The plane doesn't even get in until 3 A.M."

"The perfect hour. The only perfect hour in twenty four. Come on, Mereth. I'll let you drive."

He didn't bother to check Mereth for a reaction. He'd been at Warrick less than twenty-four hours and already he felt the suffocation of the place.

"Come on, Sister. We can party all night and sleep all day tomorrow. Don't you remember? It's the only way to survive Warrick."

"I'd better tell Massie."

"No. For God's sake, don't tell Massie!" Josh insisted, catching up with her at the door.

"Why not?"

"She wouldn't approve and you know it."

"Then Eddie. It might be considerate if he didn't have to make the trip in."

Josh thought on this a moment and then offered, "All right. You go change; I'll find Eddie. I'll meet you at the garage in fifteen minutes."

"You are crazy."

"Of course I am. I've worked hard at it all my life. It'll be good to see Brit, though. We can go to the Rodeo and sing 'The Internationale' all night while the shit-kickers do the two-step. Now how's that for dramatic contrast?"

Mereth looked as though she were trying hard to banish all second and third thoughts and better judgments.

Josh thought he might have a hard time getting her to the Rodeo, a half-acre nightclub on the outskirts of Tulsa, a duplication of Texas's mammoth Gilley's, with mechanical bucking broncos and bare-assed waitresses and no rules except "Piss in the urinals" and "Don't bleed on the floor." It was the favorite place of redneck cowhands and roughnecks from central Oklahoma.

"Fifteen minutes!" he called.

Then she was gone, and he felt a sudden draining of energy. He leaned against the door and felt his hands trembling and wished that Tyburn Warrick would do something simple and straightforward just once in his life, like dying.

Would it happen? And how would his life change if it did? And did he want it to? If there was no longer a need to grub for money, then one could see and perceive with terrifying clarity the size and value of one's creative gift.

He heard voices coming from the far end of the corridor and hoped it was Mereth coming back but knew better. He looked up to see Jobe's kids, an entire gaggle of them, heading upstairs, apparently for the night. One young man spotted him.

"May we get you something, Mr. Warrick?" he called. "Anything?"

Josh shook his head and waved them away and remembered his first homosexual encounter. He'd been about eleven. It had happened over at the ranch house, the field offices of the Warrick Corporation, a subtle encounter in the front seat of an old pickup while Ty and Junior Nagle conferred less than twenty feet away.

There was a foreman named Bobby McCasland, and Ty always liked Bobby to drive him around the oil fields. So it was Bobby sitting behind the wheel of the pickup that day and it had been Bobby who had reached between Josh's legs with perfect and rather graceful ease, had found his penis and stroked it, a smile on his face, bringing Josh to full and breathtaking release in less than two minutes.

The wet spot on his jeans and the seat had dried by the time Ty had crawled back in with the command, *"Take us to the fields, Bobby. Let's show this young greenhorn what it means to have balls."*

Bobby McCasland had had dirty fingernails and dirty ears and a dirty neck, but Josh had never been played to greater effect.

He bowed his head at the recall and whispered "Jesus!" and hurried down the hall, praying he didn't encounter anyone until his erection subsided.

"Problems, gentlemen."

Harry Beekman made his blunt two-word announcement and looked out over the terrace room. He swallowed the last of his brandy and looked at his watch. Midnight, and he felt midnight-tired and belatedly wondered if this was the proper time to inform Red Pierson and Junior Nagle.

He saw Red Pierson in close conversation with Junior Nagle by the bar, saw three girls clearing up the remains of the buffet and coffee cups.

Reverend Gerald Jobe appeared in the doorway which led to the small serving pantry. At first he took a quick assessment of the workers, then, with a snap of his fingers, he summoned the girls to him, and they obeyed that snap promptly.

241

Harry sat uncomfortably on the arm of a near chair, resigned to another brief delay. He had wanted this conference shortly after he'd arrived at Warrick, but there were so many people wandering through Warrick's halls and corridors—

He took advantage of the temporary delay to close his eyes, remove his glasses and rub the burning, and he felt like a hapless student left in charge of a schoolroom in the absence of a teacher.

The "teacher," of course, was Ty. Damn! He should go see him, even if Red and Junior both strongly advised against it.

Abruptly he looked up, realizing he was missing someone. Chris. Chris Faxon should be here. He had been here earlier, with Deeter Big Cow. It had taken all of their energies to get the old Indian out of the room and into the Jeep. Chris was going to deposit him in Tulsa for a few days.

He looked up from his brooding and saw Jobe make his way further into the room and ultimately manipulate his way into the conversation. On a note of resignation, Harry lifted his empty snifter and moved to the bar, past the men talking quietly.

Junior Nagle looked up at his passing. "You said something, Harry. You want a meeting? Problems?"

"Later." As Harry poured brandy into the snifter, he thought again on Ty's absence, which was proving to be more powerful than most people's presences. There were some immediate and pressing questions Harry had to ask him, providing of course Buckner gave his permission. Harry certainly didn't want to do anything that would impede the man's recovery, for if he was ever needed as the linchpin in his own empire, it was now.

"At last count we're clearing between eight and ten thousand a week," Jobe was saying, and Harry listened with his back turned, interested in Jobe's latest money-making proposition, Tulsa's newest embarrassment, the Faith-O-Mat.

Red expressed shock at the figures. "You can't be serious! I don't believe you."

"True," Jobe exalted. "And of course, it's almost one hundred percent self-operating and self-maintaining. Minimal outlay after the initial investment. It's a gold mine, that's what it is. We're making plans to install them all over the Southwest. I think they'd go particularly well in Dallas, don't you? Lots of money, lots of guilt. And where there is guilt, there I shall be also. Funny how the two always seem to go together."

Harry took a final look at the expressions of disbelief on Red Pierson's and Junior Nagle's faces, then walked away to the broad terrace window.

He hated night. Had always hated night since he was a kid. Bad things happened at night.

Bank examiners—

They were practically sleeping in the Tulsa Petroleum Exchange. What were they looking for? And would they find it?

He heard laughter behind him and tried to analyze just how he'd guided his always flourishing bank into these treacherous waters. Nothing unusual about it, just coincidence really. Ty had understood. His last words had been a passionate promise that together they could ride it out.

"Haven't we always ridden it out, Harry? We'll do it again." Unless he died.

The thought sobered him anew, and Harry looked over his shoulder and really didn't care whether Reverend Jobe relinquished the floor or not.

"If I may, I need these gentlemen for a while, Jobe. Business. Warrick business. I'm sure you understand."

Fortunately the Reverend understood. "I *am* sorry."

"Safe trip back to Tulsa," Harry added.

"I won't be going back to Tulsa, Mr. Beekman. Jo Massie has graciously arranged a suite for me here at Warrick. I stay here quite often, you know, chatting with Ty Warrick. He's such good company."

Jobe was halfway out of the terrace room door.

"If you're interested, Mr. Pierson, Mr. Nagle, I'll tell you more about our Faith-O-Mat in the morning. You may be interested in investing a few dollars. They are that happy and blessed combination of being financially *and* morally sound. That's a difficult combination to find nowadays."

He gave a mock salute to the three remaining in the room. "I'll pray for all of you."

Then he was gone, leaving the three of them looking at the closed door.

"Shit," was Junior Nagle's first reaction.

Red Pierson shook his head and came around the sofa and sat down.

"Why's he ranging around Warrick?" Junior Nagle asked.

"Why do you think?" Pierson said. "Money. What else? That's drawing all of them back with the unfailing attraction of a magnet. They smell money, Ty's money, and a powerful odor it is."

"Speaking of which," Harry said, coming rapidly to the sofa, "I think you both should know: bank examiners have descended."

Those four words captured their attention and delivered them to Harry like unprotesting prisoners.

"So?" Red rallied first.

"So we could be in trouble. Particularly if Ty . . ."

Junior sat up slowly, coming out of his slumped position, and said nothing, which made the silence worse.

"Of course, I'm trying to keep it quiet," Harry said, "but it's hard. Tulsa is a gossipy town. The last thing we need is a stampede."

"What precisely happened?" Junior asked.

Harry shrugged. "I don't have to tell you, Junior. Bad loans. Quick loans. Insufficient collateral. A few big loans. Like the Warrick loans . . . and too many others." Now he was angry that Junior had even asked.

"Good God, you don't think it's my fault, do you?" Harry exploded defensively. "The last thing Ty said to me was, 'Harry, we've been down before. What's fun is climbing back up.'" He paused. "It's always been Tulsa Pet's purpose to service oilmen and to provide them with the money they require, sometimes in a matter of hours. We've never asked too many questions. We've never had to. You both know that. It just . . . got out of hand. Hell, it happened in Oklahoma City, didn't it?"

The terrace room door opened, and Harry saw Massie standing in the shadows.

"Come on in," he invited, pleased that she had returned. She was smart, and he knew that Ty had confided in her, had perhaps told her things that he hadn't told anyone else.

The two others saw her, and both rose.

"Please, gentlemen, keep your seats. Has Dr. Buckner come down yet?" she asked.

"No, I'm afraid he hasn't," Harry said, trying to adopt a comforting tone. "We're talking business, Massie. I'd like very much for you to hear. Do you feel up to it?"

"This . . . business, it . . . can't wait . . . until . . . ?"

"I don't need decisions, Massie, of any sort. I just wanted you and Red and Junior to know that we may be in some trouble, at the bank I mean, Ty's business affairs, all of which may be in a very uncomfortable spot right soon."

Massie's face was a blank. Obviously Ty had said nothing to her.

"It's the times as much as anything," Harry went on, not certain if it was. "And we've survived bank examiners before, so I'm not going to get too excited yet."

"What are they looking for?" Massie asked directly.

Harry shrugged. "Look, Massie, the equation is simple. Warrick Field is a booming field; we all know that. But this continued recession is going deeper than anticipated. Interest rates are staying high. The global recession has dampened oil prices, and it's brought down prices at the producer's end. All in all, we're caught between a rock and a hard place."

The only movement was Junior Nagle's head bobbing up and down.

Harry went on. "At this point I don't know what to say to anybody. Ty owes a bunch. I don't know if you knew that or not. He's borrowed heavily. But that's all right. Even if the Warrick Field goes bust, he's still got the Warrick Basin. What he says is that it looks good."

Suddenly Red Pierson protested. "You can't count on an unproven field for liquid assets."

"No, of course not."

"And when in the hell are they going to start drilling?"

"Junior can answer that one."

Junior Nagle looked up. "No, no drilling in the Warrick Basin, not just yet."

"Why are you worried, Harry?"

The soft question came from Massie. Ty always said it was her ability to cut through bullshit that made her such a skilled businesswoman. Harry smiled at her. And lied.

"Like I said, I'm not really worried. Of course, bank examiners are to bankers like Judgment Day is to Christians, a serious reckoning. Sometimes we can play it fast and loose and get away with it. And we've played very fast and very loose of late. Especially in the eyes of the rest of the world." He moved to the edge of his seat. "But the rest of the world doesn't understand the psychology of the oil business or oilmen. They are a breed apart, literally, forgive the cliché. The conservative, the cautious, the careful men of reason and good sense have no business in oil. They generally don't last very long and certainly never succeed. In a way it has been the greedy, the stupid and the inexperienced who rushed in with the last boom and, in general, messed things up for everyone else. Ty Warrick once told me that to find oil, you have to sense that it's there." He remembered a story of Ty's and wondered if he should tell it. Why not? It was an old man's privilege to tell stories; young men didn't know any worth telling.

"Ty told me this once about Benedum and Trees, about 1904 I believe he said it was, and those two guys were out looking around for oil leases and stopped at a farmhouse for lunch. The farmer asked why they didn't lease his farm. Well, old Trees laughed and told him he didn't think there was any oil for miles around. The farmer, who was blind, asked to feel Trees's pulse. 'You're all right, young man,' he said. 'I'm going to tell you something I've never told anybody else. There's oil right here under this farm. Through my blind eyes I've seen it spouting over the top of that big maple tree out there in the back.' "

Harry paused, pleased by the rapt attention of his audience.

"Well, the partners drilled and the well roared in right over the top of that big maple tree out back for three thousand barrels a day." He felt the hairs on his arms stand up.

"I told that story to a bank examiner once, and you know what he said? Said that Trees was irresponsible and just lucky!" He shook his head. "Ignoramuses, all of them. But they can do us serious damage simply because they don't understand that the indispensable tools in oil exploration are freedom to disagree as to where oil may be hidden and courage to risk money to prove your belief. If the rewards are not commensurate with the gamble, courage to risk will be lacking in the same degree. Trees's reward on that first strike netted almost eight million dollars. If profit-making had been the only incentive, he would have quit. But he didn't."

Harry was aware of the mood he'd spun and didn't want to do anything to alter it. "The fact is that the bank has overextended itself; the fact is that Ty Warrick himself might be heading for rough seas; the fact is that every bad thing that can happen to the world economy in general and the oil economy in particular is happening; the fact is that new seekers have flooded the market, causing a rush on drilling rigs, a rush on borrowing money for drilling, messing up the fundamental economics, efficiency going down, costs going up—"

Silence again, everyone pursuing private thoughts, which Harry suspected were as splintered as his own.

He looked up to see Junior Nagle standing and stretching, his oversize belly straining against the confinement of his shirt.

"Of course," Harry said in the manner of an apology. "I'm sorry to have kept you all up so late."

"How long will they be there?" Red asked. "The examiners, I mean."

"Who knows?"

"And you believe there's real cause for worry?"

Harry let his silence suffice as an answer. If Ty were in good health—

"Come on, let's hit the sack now," Harry suggested. "Ty always said there wasn't nothing in the world worth losing sleep over."

Massie overheard his comment and came back and lovingly took his arm.

"Poor Harry," she whispered. "You must sometimes feel that the whole world is deserting you."

There was such compassion and understanding in her voice that for a moment Harry struggled to rein in his emotions. Before he could reply, she went on.

"You're not alone, Harry. You must never think that you are. We're a family, and we'll do what we have to do when we have to do it. And we'll help in any way we can. Do you understand?"

He nodded and heard Josie's voice in his heart.

"Massie is Tyburn Warrick's greatest treasure."

He put his arm around her shoulder and drew on her strength and, for the moment, felt strong.

———————

Every time that Brit flew home to Tulsa from anyplace, he always felt as though he were plunging into his own soul, never quite certain what he would find there, thick layers of filth, or pure, flowing springs. This trip was no different, and as the plane took off into the night sky from Oklahoma City, a scant twenty-five minutes to Tulsa, he recalled the wearying odyssey which had begun early this morning in London:

Two-thirty in the morning, approaching three. Notting Hill. He could still see the dead woman, hear the screams.

Was *he* dead yet, that old man who notched souls on his belt the way old-time gunfighters had notched lives?

He shook his head to the stewardess's offer of coffee. He was wired on the stuff already, his thoughts alternately lucid, then—

lunacy! While waiting at the Dallas–Fort Worth airport, he'd imagined himself an erstwhile Balzac going home to the provinces to "refresh his understanding of the passions."

Why had he made this trip?

There was that sharp state of regret that had plagued him since the 747 had lifted off over the unnaturally green English landscape. There had been a cold April drizzle. Sophie had wanted to drive him to Heathrow. He'd insisted no. The child had a feverish cold. Didn't know his name. Sex—male. Didn't know his age. Three years, perhaps four. In cases of malnutrition it was difficult to tell.

"Take him . . ."

All right. So that's why he'd come home: to fetch some good capitalist money to feed the nameless children orphaned by murdered parents, or indifferent ones.

Then it was an act of hypocrisy, wasn't it? He'd play a dutiful grandson, brother, hail-fellow-well-met, and then line up for the money bequeathed by the man he didn't love in a system he didn't approve of.

The thought stopped him. He *had* loved Tyburn Warrick once, with slavish adoration, had followed him everywhere, the nearest image to God Brit would ever need. And he had felt, rightly or wrongly, that Ty had returned that love.

There were memories poignant with pleasure and pain; the small boy curled up in Ty's comfortable lap, listening to that deep resonant voice reading all the characters in *Huckleberry Finn* and *Tom Sawyer*. And later—

"Tell me about Copernicus, boy. Remember, I read to you about that fight he had with old Ptolemy's theories? What was their difference of opinion, and who won the battle? Come on, sharpen your mind, Brit. It's a damn good one. Don't you dare waste it."

When had Ty stopped loving him? And why?

Abruptly Brit pushed back against the cushioned seat, smart enough to recognize the disastrous effects of self-loathing.

No more. Home soon. Let your mind play in whatever field it finds attractive. But keep it safe.

The plane was dropping a bit. He could feel it and wondered if there was anything he could do in the lavatory to improve his appearance, and decided no. The stubble of beard would have to stay, as would the wrinkled khakis and mussed cotton shirt.

What did he resemble? No answer.

All across the Atlantic the battle had raged, to the background merriment of a Goldie Hawn movie. Now Brit, with a bewildering sense that the true end was drawing near, though it was disguised as the beginning, leaned forward and lowered his head into his hands and did not pray. Nothing so simplistic and childlike as that. But he did look deep inside to see if possibly there would be enough tolerance and forbearance and understanding to make it through these next few difficult days so that everyone would emerge unwounded and intact!

To his pleasant surprise, some source which he was unable to identify assured him that it could be done. For the first time in over eighteen hours he dared to relax and wondered who would meet him. Perhaps no one. In which case he'd rent a trusty Hertz, if they were open for business. It *was* a late hour.

Mereth. He smiled at the name. It would be good to see Mereth again.

And Josh, all past wounds forgotten, an artist, or so Josh told him in his infrequent letters which arrived at Brit's box at the American Express on Haymarket.

And most fascinating of all, Massie, the beautifully liberated woman who'd imprisoned Tyburn Warrick with her love.

He smiled at the faces that paraded before his memory. But none of the images stayed long and were immediately replaced by his last glimpse of Sophie, a little scared for being left like that, promising she'd stay off the streets, cradling the undersized child in her arms, promising also to take him to the clinic if his fever worsened.

Suddenly the conflict exploded full force, and he felt a breathlessness as he tried to reconcile the memory of himself as a child, that spoiled little boy who had run through the luxurious corridors and gardens of Warrick, always overfed, overdressed, over-everything, unaware even that the world was capable of orphaning a child.

"Tulsa, ten minutes," came the tired voice of the stewardess.

"Fasten your seat belts, please, and remain seated until the plane comes to a complete stop."

He stared out of the window at the patchwork quilt of lights that was Tulsa at 3 A.M. Larger than Oklahoma City—or so it seemed from the air.

"Mind if I sit?"

The friendly voice was that of the stewardess. Brit had no objection.

"You look as pooped as I feel," she murmured. "This morning New York, down the coast to Orlando, then over to Big D, Tulsi Town, then bed, thank God!"

Tulsi Town. He hadn't heard it called that since high school, a corruption of the Creek Indian word Tallahassee. The Spaniards had mistakenly pronounced it Tallosi, and from there the corruption had moved on to Tulsi Town and ultimately Tulsa, although there were many old-timers who still and with a great deal of affection, Ty among them, called it Tulsi Town.

"Tulsa's your home." He smiled.

"How did you know?"

"Tulsi Town. Nobody knows that but locals."

"You too? From Tulsa, I mean."

"I live in London now but I grew up here, yes."

She gave him a it's-a-small-world look. "What's your name?"

He wished she hadn't asked.

"Come on," she coaxed.

"Warrick. Brit Warrick."

There was a moment's pause. "Warrick! *The* Warricks?"

He glanced out of the window.

"What brings you home?"

"My grandfather is ill."

"The old man? I'm sorry. That could mean trouble, couldn't it?"

He was puzzled by her statement. "What do you mean?"

"Come on! Remember, I grew up in Tulsa. There were two names whispered, like being in church. One: Phillips. Two: Warrick. How old is he now? Your grandfather, I mean."

Brit shrugged, not really knowing. "An old man."

"Well, anyway, welcome home, Mr. Warrick. I hope your grandfather is on his road to recovery now." With that she was gone, disappearing behind the drapes which led to the front cabin.

He rested his head against the cushion and closed his eyes.

He missed Sophie. She was one of those fortunate few who had solved the world, not by answering its most fundamental and baffling mysteries but by simply refusing to view any aspect of the world as mysterious.

"I thought you might be interested in this. One of the crew picked it up in Oklahoma City." It was the stewardess again. She handed him a folded newspaper. Then she moved toward the rear of the plane.

"We're landing now, folks. Five minutes. Make certain your seat belts are fastened."

Baffled, Brit took the newspaper and unfolded it.
WARRICK STRICKEN
The headline was huge, black and blunt. He angled the newspaper toward the dim light and read the second headline.

> Tyburn Warrick, Oklahoma oil multimillionaire, was stricken by a massive cerebral hemorrhage at his country estate of Warrick outside Tulsa . . .

Brit tried to read on but couldn't. He'd be on the scene soon enough.

"Thank you." He smiled, refolding the newspaper and handing it back to the stewardess as she passed by on her way from the rear of the plane.

"Oh, just keep it," she said breezily. "The pilots were through with it. Good luck. I mean it."

"Thank you."

Down, down and the plane screamed and Brit suddenly felt the pressure of descent. He stared bleakly out of the window, his feet pressed hard against the floor, helping the pilot fight the power of jet speed.

Home.

Fighting for our freedom, we are free.

A few moments later the plane touched down, skidded, gave one long shudder and reluctantly accepted its earthbound condition.

At last he reached beneath his seat and withdrew his single bag. He stood with calm despair and started down the narrow aisle, hauling his luggage behind him, knowing only one thing.

The survivors must have courage, and each one must try to save what he can.

Mereth led the way through the terminal, hurrying against time, against Josh's voice as he described the concluding scene of his new film property, something called *The Brothers,* which he'd talked about to Mereth, frame by frame, ever since they'd left Warrick.

". . . and it's in that cold, frozen, open field, you see, that the understanding first dawns on both of them that the desire for salvation is the essence of salvation itself."

Mereth nodded, not wanting to be rude but acutely aware that her watch said three-twenty and that Brit's plane had been due at three and, despite Josh's clear enthusiasm, she'd found the lengthy monologue a poor duplicate of *The Brothers Karamazov.* Dostoyevsky had done it before, only superbly.

"I swear to God, Mereth, doesn't it just give you goose bumps?"

"It sounds very good, Josh," she agreed, "though sometimes these things are difficult to translate into a synopsis. One needs the visual images."

"Damned right!" He nodded, his face flushed from the open bottle of Stoly's vodka he'd brought with him in the car.

She stopped in her haste and looked at him, this wounded older brother who had seemed to be merely an unhappy and sulky malcontent until he'd launched forth into his passion and then had come alive.

All the leaves are rotten, all the trees are sick, but the forest is magnificent.

She smiled at the remembered snippet. "I wish you the best with it," she said and took his arm, partly out of the desire for closeness and partly to propel him forward.

"There it is," Josh said, pointing toward the board. "Gate 41. I know the way."

Mereth smiled and followed after, enjoying this late-night escapade, looking forward to seeing Brit, though there was the outside possibility she wouldn't recognize him. One day years ago—she'd been in junior high—handsome Brit had left for Princeton and had never come home. She had a vague remembrance of Massie being quite upset, spending one entire day and night on the phone, something about a foreign embassy and the State Department, and Ty storming up and down the garden walk, announcing that the kid could rot in hell and good riddance as far as he was concerned.

"Well, look who's here!"

Josh's surprised voice summoned her back from the unhappy past to the early morning hour and the deserted airport and the sight of two male figures standing in identical positions by Gate 41, hands shoved into jeans pockets, shoulders lifted as though against a chill. She squinted, recognizing Eddie, Ty's driver, and Chris, who'd chauffeured her about and introduced her to Tio's.

"Did you forget to tell Eddie that we . . . ?"

"Couldn't find him."

She whispered, "Do you know Chris?"

"Of course, I know old Chris. He's been hanging around Warrick for as long as I can remember. Hey, Chris, how long have you been hanging around Warrick?"

"Long enough," came the reply.

Mereth stared after Chris as he walked toward the closed door which led to the narrow corridor down which passengers would shortly emerge. Eddie and Josh followed after like jostling school-boys. Only Mereth was left standing by the ticket counter.

She wished she'd stayed at Warrick. Too late, she realized the evening was taking on all the aspects of a stag party.

"Here it is!" Josh called excitedly over his shoulder, pointing toward the large glass wall, beyond which she could just see the blinking lights of a plane touching down at the end of the runway.

"Come on, Mereth," Josh urged further. "We're going to form a chorus line, really blast the old boy off his feet! Eddie, you on that end. Chris, you on the other and Mereth and I will . . . ."

He never finished what he and Mereth would do. No need. He grabbed her arm and pulled her into place next to Chris, whose embarrassment was being manifest in the storm of crimson which washed up his face.

"Now everybody keep your eyes open and the first one that sees him . . ."

A few minutes later the door swung open and a sleepy-eyed stewardess appeared. Mereth looked down the long corridor which led to the plane and saw a yawning man in a dark blue suit, tie askew, briefcase in hand, swinging it schoolboy fashion. He was followed by a young woman in blue jeans and jacket, sunglasses.

"Where in the hell is he?" Josh muttered.

There were two more passengers: a middle-aged couple, both wearing sheepish expressions for some reason, and then—

"Son of a bitch, there he is!" Josh grinned and Mereth felt his arm tighten about her waist.

Mereth saw Brit now as well, tall, fair, more Ty's grandson than any of them, at least physically.

"Okay, are you ready?" Josh whispered, about four years old.

"What are you going to . . . ?"

Long before she was ready, she felt the "chorus line" leap into a ridiculous rendition of *Ta-ra-ra-boom-de-ay, have you had yours today?*, legs swinging akimbo, splintered creaking voices shattering the night's relative calm, everyone looking at them with expressions of curiosity or condemnation.

The makeshift chorus line came to a slow, spluttering halt as everyone caught their first glimpse of the thirty-five-year-old man who looked—sixty!

"Jesus!" Josh whispered.

Mereth saw recognition in Brit's tired face, and she smiled and waved and felt a powerful surge of emotion for this brother, perhaps the rarest and best of them all. Not just tired, gaunt, as if he hadn't eaten, or was ill. Then she saw Josh going toward him, hands extended, both men grinning.

"We're going fishing, Massie, me and Brit."

"Which direction, Josh?"

"Probably over toward Deeter's."

"Be careful, and watch after Brit."

Apparently handshakes were no longer sufficient and, though it was impossible for Mereth to tell who initiated the embrace, they came together awkwardly as men do and ended up by patting each other vigorously on the back as though for a job well done.

She saw Brit glance toward Chris. Within the instant the two men embraced, warm, intimate, European. Mereth felt her own surprise mirrored in Josh and Eddie.

"Can't believe it!" were Brit's first words to Chris. "How in the hell did you get here?"

"Same way you did."

"When?"

"About three weeks ago."

"How did you know?"

"I didn't know. I came home to see Deeter."

Both men looked at each other as though listening to the silence. Suddenly Brit's attention was brought back to the others.

"Josh, it's good to see you! And Eddie, my God, it's been years!"

All three men seemed to close around Brit, shutting Mereth out. Suddenly the uneven circle broke open and she looked up and saw very clearly the ruin that was her brother.

But the smile on his face was dazzling, and in that split second she wondered what woman had been gifted with that smile looking down on her after sex.

"Mereth?"

Her name was an astonished question. Long before she was ready, as though it was part of his personality's unique power to catch people off guard, he was upon her. He kissed her forehead with a tenderness that reminded her how often he'd comforted her during the trials and hazards of growing up at Warrick.

She drew him close and buried her face in the warm hollow of his throat and tried to fight back tears and felt a slight stubble of beard and clung to him, eyes shut, wondering if it would be asking too much of him to hold her like this for the rest of the night and possibly into tomorrow as well.

"I love you," she whispered.

He held her face between his hands and wiped away her tears, and she saw up close the hollows about his eyes, gray hair at the temples. The whole world was his responsibility, always had been.

"Brit's gone, Mereth. I'm afraid he won't be coming home for a while. Don't cry—"

"You've grow'd up!" He grinned in a funny imitation of a redneck.

"So have you."

"Thank you for coming to meet me. I was hoping you would."

"Family reunion and all that. Compliments to T. S. Eliot."

"How is Ty?"

She shrugged. "The condition of his health seems to be a state secret. Old Doc Buckner is presiding in every sense of the word."

He started to ask another question.

"Come on," Mereth urged. There would be time enough for this when they returned to Warrick. "I think they have plans for you." She nodded toward the three waiting men.

"Okay, greetings over and on to the party!" Josh proclaimed.

"Where are we going?" Brit asked.

"I think you're going out to the Rodeo. I'm going home."

"No." The word was flat and delivered with quiet force.

257

In answer to Brit's "No," she smiled. "I think I would if I were you. One last fling before Warrick."

"Then you come, too."

"It's a stag party."

"Nonsense. There's no such thing anymore. Besides, I want to talk to you."

"At the Rodeo?"

"We'll find a corner. It's the only way I'll go."

She was surprised by the soft-spoken threat which nonetheless was a threat.

Eddie stepped forward. "Come on, Mereth. A couple of beers, that's all. I'll drive the limo. You can pile in and leave your car here."

"All right," she said reluctantly, "but I'll take my car. The rest of you go with Eddie. I'll meet you there."

"I'll go with her."

Shocked, she looked up, unable to believe the voice that had managed to penetrate the inarticulate protests.

Chris.

"Well, why not?" He grinned. "Josh and Brit have a lot of catching up to do. Eddie can chauffeur them, just like old times, and I'll show Mereth where it is."

"I know where it is."

"Sometimes it's tricky finding it at night."

"Tricky, hell. Just follow the red neon glow in the sky."

"Still, I think I'd better come with you."

Josh seemed to be in eager agreement. "It's best, Mereth," he advised.

She looked ahead to the broad fan-shaped terminal, still sleepy in the predawn hours, and said nothing. The three men came to a stop at the front doors. They all were talking, quite volubly now, easily and, she sensed, enjoyably.

"Hurry up, you two!" Josh called out. "Last one there is a rotten egg!"

As he pushed through the door, Brit held back. "Chris, take care of her."

"I will."

Brit touched his forehead. "See you soon," and then he was gone.

Mereth fished through her purse, found her keys and held them up. "I'll get us there, and you get us home."

"Deal." He nodded and strode ahead out into the night.

Mereth watched him, fascinated by his stride, the gravity-defying angle of his cowboy hat.

"You coming?" he called back.

She hurried off the curb before night devoured him.

Warrick

NELLIE FORSTER moved out of the easy chair in the sitting room, back into the sickroom and stood at the foot of Tyburn Warrick's bed and gazed down on the man. She thought that if only the world could see him now, that it was this common leveler of death and dying that had led her into nursing.

She heard Miss Kent snoring in the other room and started to awaken her to take her turn and thought, what the hell, whoever can't sleep gets the duty. Kent could pay her back later.

Feeling generous, she yawned, scratched her right breast and tried to decide where to start this midnight check. Actually everything but the catheter could be done visually from where she stood. What the hell difference did it make? The cerebral accident had been massive, and Nellie envisioned Warrick's brain as bits and pieces of confetti floating around inside a black balloon.

She looked directly at the patient's face, something she seldom did if there was the remotest chance the face would stare back at her. But with this one it made no difference. He looked dead now. She wondered how long Buckner and the family would let the charade persist.

Nellie sighed and decided she was hungry, always a good antidote to confusion. The catheter could wait. All she wanted now was a sandwich. And a couple of belts. She knew that Tyburn Warrick had damned good scotch around here someplace, if only she could find it.

Despite the pleasurable goal, she stood a few minutes longer looking down on him, not seeing the man but rather seeing what he stood for, money, vast amounts of money, more than most people could even comprehend, Nellie among them, poor people who worried from measly paycheck to measly paycheck. "Better not buy that; won't have enough to pay for that." Endless worry, killing worry, killing self-denial while bastards like that one, who ordered up the world with a gold fence around it, snapped their fingers and the money spilled from hundreds of sources. "You want it? Buy it!"

Strangely breathless from the pace and nature of her thoughts, Nellie gripped the end of the bed and thought calmly how much she loathed the old man in this monstrous house and these spoiled-rotten people and that black woman—mistress is what Kent had told her, though Nellie hadn't believed it at first, had gone to Buckner for confirmation. A god-awful mistake that, for Buckner had lit into Nellie like she hadn't been lit into since nurse's training.

"What Jo Massie is is none of your goddamned business and don't you forget it!"

Okay, back off, you old buzzard.

Still, as far as Nellie was concerned, the broad was a nigger, a rich nigger, which made her even more offensive.

Enough. Needed food. Needed to get out of this smelly room. Jesus, it could go on for weeks, months! Move it out.

Then she was moving toward the door and, as her thoughts accelerated to keep pace with her steps, she yanked open the double doors with such force that she failed to see the figure approaching from the other side, carrying something. Had it not been for Nellie's quick reflexes, the collision would have been awesome.

"I'm . . . so sorry," a voice murmured.

Nellie looked up in anger at the nincompoop who'd almost knocked her down and suffered an angry shock, followed immediately by embarrassment and then by confusion. It was the nigger herself, Massie.

She was wearing a green robe and her face was without makeup and her generally smooth black hair was uncombed, her eyes rimmed and puffy, and she looked god-awful and lost, though in her hands she carried a tray bearing a platter of sandwiches, a bowl of chips and, God help us, a bottle of Chivas Regal.

Nellie was stunned. She tried to speak and couldn't, her attention focused on the tray of food.

"I . . . was hungry," the nigger now confessed quietly, "and I thought you might be as well. Dr. Buckner told me you had the night duty and . . ."

As her apology drifted into new embarrassment, Nellie felt a collision of emotions. The black woman looked so ordinary now, not sleek and fancy like she'd looked earlier with her Neiman-Marcus clothes and fancy pearls. All that stuff was gone, and she looked just tired and scared.

Nellie stepped forward with an offer. "You want me to take that before it all slides onto the floor?" She took the tray effortlessly, Jo Massie putting up no resistance.

As Nellie looked around for a suitable place to deposit the tray, she decided upon the low round table in the alcove across the way. She looked up to see the woman standing in the open doors which led to Mr. Warrick's room, staring in at the man practically obscured by distance and bedding and tubes and standards. Nellie straightened after placing the tray on the table. Her first impulse was to yell for the woman to get away. After all, Buckner had made it clear: no visitors. But something prevented her from calling out, even though she knew damned well that the food probably was a bribe.

So what? Maybe the woman was entitled. If she'd slept with the man for years, then maybe one good look and she'd know she wasn't going to get any more and she'd better give up.

So let her look her fill and then she'd see for herself what probably even Warrick himself knew, that it was time for an ending, so let the ending come.

Slowly, never taking her eyes off the woman's rigid back as she walked forward, Nellie bent over and snagged a sandwich and chewed slowly.

The black woman moved with admirable resolution to a position about five feet from the bed. There she stopped abruptly as though she had collided with an invisible barrier.

She appeared to be transfixed by the sight, and that Nellie certainly understood. Go on, move closer, Nellie privately urged. For some reason she wanted the woman to see the damage complete, the spittle running out of the left side of his mouth, the opened mouth struggling for oxygen despite the tubes in his nose and throat. There would be no more oil deals created inside that brain.

Then there was movement, a brief step forward, a soft but discernible collapse which seemed to drag the woman all the way to the foot of the bed, where she reached out to the footboard for support, grasped it with both hands and leaned heavily upon it.

Good, Nellie thought. Now she'd seen it whole, seen everything. Get rid of the grief; say your good-byes . . .

Massie was not prepared. How does one prepare for a shipwreck? That was how she felt, looking down on the bed.

"Ty . . ."

Despite what she saw, she spoke his name as though he might open his eyes and push aside the tubes and needles and grin up at her—

"It's a fine day, Miss Jo Massie, and it's ours. How shall we spend it?"

She clung to the end of the bed as though to a piece of wreckage in a tossing sea.

"Mr. Warrick, my name is Jo Massie and I am more than qualified to do the job you hired me to do—"

"Bullshit."

Then a few years later—

"Did you want to see me about something, Mr. Warrick?"

"Yes, I need your help on this matter. Dallas is calling and I need a second opinion."

And later—

"Don't leave me, Jo. Just sit with me for a few minutes, please."

"Your wife is waiting dinner, sir."

And finally—

"It's late, Ty. I should be getting back to my rooms."

"Stay, Massie, please stay. The house is so empty, I feel empty after the funeral. Please stay. I need you so."

Silent tears flowed openly down her face. And she had needed *him,* his strength, his warm body, his tenderness, his consideration, his mercurial moods, his life, his genius. She had never known anyone quite like him, and she never would.

As Massie clung to the bed and gazed down on his ruined face, she knew and at last accepted that it was over. Ty Warrick was over, their love was over. But she still had her rich storehouse of memories, and she would feed on them for the rest of her life.

Curious, but at the moment of acceptance she saw him not as he was, wasted, blue lips, hollow eyes, imprisoned on the very bed on which they had made triumphant and deliriously happy love. Instead she saw Ty as he had been, his face alive with the rapturous delights he found in the world, an expression of innocence and youth despite the years, strong, dazzlingly white teeth, not a gray hair on his head, and his whole frame had a look of suppleness and hardiness and endurance. And she even heard his voice, that great peculiarity of his talk with its spontaneity and readiness. Yet out of the tragedy of his dying, she felt that the world that had been shattered was rising up now in her soul, in new beauty, on foundations that could not be shaken.

A kiss, Ty. One more. And in the sweetest of farewells she

moved slowly around the bed and bent low for her kiss and took it and was conscious of something pleasant and soothing and did not take her eyes off him, or her heart, and felt her jaw quiver and felt tears rising in gratitude that she had known and loved such a man.

Wait. What in the hell? What was she—

Quickly Nellie moved through the doors, alarmed by what she saw, the black woman seated on the side of the bed, bent over the blue half-opened lips, one hand pushing back the mussed hair while the woman herself leaned over and—

Nellie shuddered, repelled, but couldn't quite bring herself to turn away from the kiss. Jesus, they had a name for it, didn't they, making it with a dead man. Of course, the woman wasn't actually making it, just a long kiss that was obscene and inappropriate and wouldn't have been tolerated in St. Mark's Hospital.

It had to stop.

And then it did, the woman raising slowly up, her hand lingering on Warrick's face.

Nobody home, honey. Never would be. Never again. 'Bye, 'bye.

The woman stood erect beside the bed. She seemed to move differently, no longer bowed. She straightened her robe, reknotted the cord and, as she passed within the sphere of a lamp, Nellie was dumbstruck by the transformation. Jo Massie was smiling. Once she left the vicinity of the bed, she walked faster, heading toward the small arrangement of chairs in the alcove, where Nellie had taken refuge next to the tray of sandwiches.

Massie approached the silver tray, retrieved a glass with one hand, the bottle of Chivas Regal with the other, cradled the glass next to her body as she unscrewed the bottle cap and lifted glass to bottle and poured and poured and poured, half to three-quarters full before she showed the slightest inclination to cease.

She returned the bottle to the tray and drank.

And drank. And drank.

Drained the glass, at least five shots full, maybe more, and quickly lowered her head and placed the empty glass between her breasts and seemed to press it into her flesh and at last looked up at Nellie with a smile on her face, tears in her eyes.

"Good," she whispered.

Nellie fought against the impulse to giggle and failed, and as the giggle turned into a laugh she fought also against the impulse to like this woman. Not moderately or sanely or courteously, like most sensible friendships, but immoderately and with a complete lack of caution.

"Sandwich?" Nellie grinned and extended the tray to Massie and was absolutely delighted when she took one and settled back into a nearby easy chair as though for a long, intimate chat.

Tulsa

MERETH HAD been right. All she'd had to do was follow the red glow in the predawn darkness that led them directly to the Rodeo, a shit-kicking redneck nightclub that sat just beyond the question-able arm of Tulsa law and therefore was a place where anything could happen, and generally did.

"You've been there before?" Chris asked.

"A few times. It's like church; you have to pay your respects occasionally or you lose your Tulsa citizenship."

"Easy!" Chris warned as she swerved wide to give passage to an oncoming pickup. "What's the rush?"

"Let's get there and get it over with," she murmured. She nod-ded toward the dashboard clock, which said a quarter to four. "Massie will be . . ."

"Massie will be fine. She knows all of you are big boys and girls now. She knows it, even if you don't."

Mereth bent low over the wheel and saw the red glow burning brighter, the reflection of hundreds of yards of neon fence surrounding the large club, supposed to resemble a rodeo arena. She'd seen it once from the air and had been amazed that it actually had resembled a rodeo.

Now, on her left, she noticed a well-lit concrete acreage, the first mammoth parking lot.

"Did you say your parents are still living?" she asked, wondering where the question had come from.

"I didn't say," he answered, "but if it will make you feel better, my father's alive, mother's dead. There. Pull in there."

Intrigued by his response, she almost missed the turn. About twenty-five parked cars later, she saw the black Cadillac limo, flanked in front by a gray Rolls and behind by a white Lincoln Continental.

For a moment she wondered if her ancient little German convertible would rate a place next to these leviathans, but Chris rolled down his window and called with easy familiarity to the attendant, "Dave, can you manage one more?"

Dave squinted in the direction of the voice.

"Another Warrick car," Chris added in the nick of time before Dave shook his head in a resounding "no." Instead he bobbed it up and down in an enthusiastic "Yes."

"That you, Chris?" he asked, bending over the window for a better look. "Old Eddie just peeled in ahead of you with a couple of greenhorns. I asked where you were."

"Here I is," Chris joked as he climbed out of the low cramped seat. "The greenhorns are Warricks. Both of them."

As they approached the curb, Dave stripped off his cowboy hat, revealing thinning reddish hair. "Morning, Miss Warrick. Always our pleasure."

She smiled and headed toward the front doors, which were painted to resemble saloon doors. While she was still several yards away, the fake saloon doors were pushed open by a young woman wearing jaunty red Ultrasuede short shorts and a small fringed bra which struggled mightily and failed to contain 40-D breasts.

"Evening, y'all." She grinned and held open one of the saloon doors with a curvaceous hip.

"You must be freezing," Mereth murmured, straight-faced, and pushed open the opposite door. She waited on the other side, amused at how rapidly the girl readied all the big guns of her female personality for Chris, who apparently had looked ahead, seen the hazard and come to a dead halt on the pavement outside.

"Come on, honey," the girl coaxed. "I won't bite you, 'less you want to be bitten." The breasts heaved almost free of their hand-kerchief-size bra.

Mereth smiled and wondered how Brit, Josh and Eddie had made it so effortlessly past this keeper of the gate.

Then the girl stepped closer to Chris. "A bunch of queers just came in, you know. You can always tell 'em. Don't know what management expects me to do with queers . . . or *for* them, for that matter. But you're different."

Suddenly, to Mereth's surprise, Chris reached out and grabbed the girl and drew her close. He whispered something in her ear, then pushed her gently away and proceeded on through the doors, leaving her standing openmouthed.

"What did you say to her?" Mereth whispered.

Chris shrugged. "I said she was far too good for this sort of work, and I advised her to try to live up to her God-given potential."

"You told her *what?*"

"Come on," Chris urged, apparently unaware that he'd said anything out of the ordinary. "Hey, there they are."

He pushed through the second set of swinging doors that led into the cavernous club itself.

Mereth followed after him, her amusement dwindling as she confronted the Rodeo, a city-block long, one continuous mahogany bar, mirrored, running the length of the club.

The first time she'd come here several years ago, the place had been jammed and somehow had not seemed as large. Now the emptiness in the predawn hour made it appear like some gaunt cathedral minus worshipers, save for a few couples hanging disconsolately onto each other around the fringes of the dance floor, one small combo furnishing what was supposed to be music, most of the activity taking place along the bar, though even there people seemed to huddle in groups as though for protection against the emptiness.

"Hey!"

She heard Chris call out and saw him start toward a section of the bar where Brit, Josh and Eddie appeared to be conversing earnestly with one of the many bartenders, Josh saying something in anger to the man who was semibalding, middle-aged, with satin garters on his sleeves and a soiled apron which proclaimed LET'S RODEO.

Although the bartender turned away in a surly mood, Josh continued to stand in mute confrontation. Chris said something, less than three words, though they stirred the bartender into fresh anger, for suddenly he shook his dishcloth at them, a curiously inept gesture considering what he said.

"I said git!" he shouted. "The lot of you. I don't have to wait on fags and queers. Management says I don't have to wait on anyone I don't want to. So just git. Now!"

Mereth heard, along with everyone else in the huge club. Good. The order to leave was precisely what she'd wanted to hear, and she started back toward the swinging doors.

For some reason she was certain that everyone would be following. A few steps later she looked back to discover she was moving alone around the periphery of empty tables. Why were they waiting? Mereth suffered a splintered emotion for Josh, part anger, part sympathy.

He stood close to the bar, both hands gripping the edge. She saw several others drawing nearer, a mismatched crew of urban cowboys blending with real ones, the egalitarian philosophy of the Rodeo never more in evidence than in its clientele. It apparently could host and serve every kind and stripe and color of human being.

Save one.

Come *on,* Josh, a voice prayed inside her. It's too late for masochism and too early to try to raise his consciousness.

Josh stirred himself and demanded, full-voiced, two things: first an apology and second a bottle of champagne.

Mereth closed her eyes. She had the most peculiar feeling that Josh was playing a scene, relishing his humiliation, wanting to force the bartender into a more serious confrontation. For what purpose, she had no idea.

Even Chris seemed surprised and tried to draw him back. But Josh pulled away angrily and stood like a small misbehaving boy, watching the bartender closely, as though wishing he would respond.

And his wish came true. From where she stood, Mereth saw the man reach behind and pull the cord on his bar apron, all the while never taking his eyes off Josh.

Were they serious?

She continued to watch the drama, along with thirty, forty others who sensed the beginnings of their favorite nightly ritual, the sight of two adult men beating each other senseless over a matter of absolutely no consequence. She saw the bartender strip off his apron and drop it, uncaring, on the floor behind the bar.

Then she saw the bartender lift the hinged portion of the bar and slip beneath it and emerge onto the floor. Why did he look larger with every step he took, appearing full length now, a good six feet, maybe taller, husky though not one spare ounce of fat, all muscle.

By heart-sickening contrast Josh seemed suddenly to have shriveled. She saw Chris say something, but Josh stepped around him and took up a position about twenty feet away from the grinning bartender, whose friends shouted a creative volley of clever obscenities at him, all having to do with male genitalia.

If Josh heard, he gave no indication. Now several impromptu bookmakers passed among the crowd with small notebooks and wads of money. Brit and Chris joined Eddie on the sideline, resigned if nothing else.

Somewhere someone stopped the music. There was silence.

Mereth continued to watch the curious standoff around which the crowd had formed. Near the swinging doors she saw three men, dressed quite differently from the local types. These three wore expensive, tailor-made suits and gazed out at the impromptu battleground with grins on their faces.

Clever entrepreneurs. *Let the rednecks provide their own amusement. It's far better than anything we can give them. And cheaper.*

In that last moment of quiet stalking and sizing up, she thought how ironic that the only one who would have truly enjoyed this barbaric ritual was lying half dead in his hard-earned luxury at Warrick. Ty would adore this moment. He'd be right there in the front row, pulling for the stronger, no matter who that happened to be.

Then movement, each man encircling the other while Mereth was busy plotting what to do after the bartender had finished. The nearest hospital was St. Francis. She shut her eyes for a moment.

Suddenly an ear-splitting shriek filled the air, a male voice raised in an ungodly yell and she looked up to see Josh, legs spread, shirttail out, his right arm raised over his head, his hand rigid, standing over the bartender, who was on his knees, his head hanging limp. What had happened?

A hush fell over the crowd, no more jeers, as slowly, painfully the bartender rose, wobbling to his feet.

Baffled, she stared out at the unexpected tableau. Had the bartender slipped? Surely Josh had not—

But then he did it again, the entire assault preceded by that really silly, though impressive, scream, and he executed a movement so fast that Mereth was unable to see what had happened beyond the blur that was Josh's hand and arm crashing down on the man's neck, a damaging enough assault in itself but this time accompanied by a foot delivered with equal force and speed to the man's groin so that, while he was in the process of reeling backward from the neck chop, he was jerked reflexively forward in belated protection of his groin and the opposing movements sent him spinning off balance where, like a top running down, he twirled twice, then fell, revealing a nose streaming blood.

Or maybe it came from his mouth. It was difficult to tell anything for sure except that the bartender of the foul mouth and superior strength lay spread-eagled on the floor, breaking one of the two sacrosanct rules of the Rodeo by bleeding on the highly polished floor, while Josh continued to encircle him in that stupid spread-knee position, which for some reason looked even less masculine on Josh as he glared down on the man.

The crowd struggled to accommodate the discomfort of shifting loyalties and mistaken judgments. A few diehards from the back row yelled stupidly, "Come on, Herb! Quit spoofin' and git up!"

But Herb wasn't going to be getting up for a while. In the next moment, two bartenders pushed their way through the crowd, apparently to clear the debris.

But Josh had other ideas. Suddenly he stepped forward and placed his foot squarely in the middle of the sprawled man's back, hands on hips, the whole ridiculous pose reminding Mereth of old tintypes she'd seen of Victorian British officers in India, except in those photos the felled prey had been an elephant or a tiger.

Before this tableau, the two approaching bartenders halted, not through any real sense of intimidation but in genuine bewilderment.

Into the silent vacuum Josh took the plunge.

"My apologies to all who care for confrontations such as this even less than I do. I assure you I did not seriously injure the gentleman, though mind you, I could have . . ."

There was something both playful and threatening in this claim, as though he wanted to serve notice on anyone who might be entertaining the foolish notion of a second attack. Across the arena Mereth saw Brit and Chris and Eddie, all three with eyes wide in disbelief.

". . . but I assure you he was most offensive," Josh went on, speaking with the politeness of a prince about the man who lay senseless beneath his foot, "and I really see no reason for one man to demean another in that fashion or any other."

From the back of the room came a voice. "All he did was to call you a queer, which is what you are."

Mereth swiveled about in search of the voice. Josh lowered his head.

"True," he nodded, smiling. "And I respect the truth, don't you?" He addressed this hopefully rhetorical question to those standing nearest. "And that's not why I almost took his head off. He made me angry only when he refused to serve my party. Now that's unforgivable."

Suddenly one of the bartenders stepped forward. "Sir, I'll be happy to serve you and your party."

Josh smiled. "I'm very grateful. I truly am. We would like a quiet table if possible, assurance that we won't be disturbed again and three bottles, chilled of course, of Moët Chandon. Can you accommodate us with all that? If so, I'd be most grateful."

As Mereth looked back, the first face she saw was Brit's across the arena. He was laughing uproariously.

Then she saw Brit, Eddie and Chris approaching Josh, who still occupied center stage, though Herb had just been pulled from beneath his foot.

"Come, my children!" Josh exclaimed and opened his arms. "This gentleman tells me that we can have any table in the house that suits us." He grinned, winked and put his arm around Mereth.

Impressed, she smiled. "Where did you learn that little trick?"

"No trick. Kung fu. Peter's a black belt. We don't screw all the time, you know."

"Damned impressive." Brit smiled. "You'll have to teach me."

"I'll start a class. At Warrick. It's what we've always needed. Come on, I'm tired of the spotlight. You know what Andy Warhol said, 'Everybody in the country will be famous for ten minutes.' Well, I've just had my ten minutes and thank God it's over!" He led the way through the gaping crowd, bowing to the right and to the left like passing royalty.

Mereth fell into the parade and looked ahead to see his destination, one of the raised alcove tables near the far west wall. The obliging waiter was just lighting a red votive candle and brushing off the padded seats with a white cloth.

She heard Eddie adding his praise to the victorious Josh. "Never saw anything as fast as your hand! Some trick. You should box. Bet you don't have trouble anyplace you go."

"Right." Josh nodded. "Unless I want trouble. Sometimes a good knockdown-dragout is just what the doctor ordered. Pain is good for you." Then he led the way up to the large, round alcove table, which looked quite festive with its red candle.

"Champagne coming right up, Mr. Warrick," the bartender said, his polite manner increasing, and understandably so. Somewhere he'd picked up the name of the offender, and the name alone instantly softened the offense.

In the absense of any hostility, Josh seemed to go limp and sat on the nearest chair and looked disconsolate as he stared out at the rapidly emptying club.

"This place is only mildly depraved," he mourned. "You'd think they'd welcome a little homosexual activity. I mean, we could elevate them to new levels of decadence if they'd just let us in. All right, Brit, tell me about London and what the hell it is that you do over there and why you can't do it out in Los Angeles. Talk. This is supposed to be a reunion. Come on, everybody, let's *look* happy, anyway."

Slowly they all took seats, Josh, Brit and Eddie on one side, Chris and Mereth on the other. For some reason which she could not begin to identify, she liked the moment, the evening, this place and this bizarre company.

Josh made a lovable fool of himself just once more, and that was when the bartender delivered the bottles of champagne sans ice bucket which, as an offense, paled in comparison with the champagne itself.

"*California?*" Josh shrieked and held the bottle up as though it were unspeakable. "Moët from California?"

"It's our best, sir," the man protested wearily.

"I know," Josh mourned, "and that makes it doubly sad." He drew the bottle down as though it were a mentally deficient child that could not help its condition. "Truly sad," he grieved and reluctantly gave the bottle over for uncorking.

Mereth's eyes met Brit's and for just a moment there was an understanding, as though Josh's neurotic behavior served as a mirror for both of them, a kind of tacit reminder that shared neuroses might form a stronger bond than shared blood. Suddenly they were laughing and talking all at once, and the moment was good.

The bartender poured the wine, then retreated, and Josh lifted his glass and announced quietly, "A toast, if you will. To each of us, for we are alone." He stared at his upraised glass, at the flawed champagne, then added, "And to the exquisite languor of passive contemplation, which is the classic description of death, and to our renowned progenitor who will shortly, if he hasn't already, entered that blessed state. How I envy him!"

Then he thrust his glass higher. "To the old bastard himself!" In a rapid movement he brought the glass back down, spilling a few drops en route, tipped it to his mouth and drained it.

"Shit! Kool-Aid," he muttered but refilled his glass and commanded Brit, "Tell all. What do you do? How do you live? How do you account for your existence?"

Though the expression on Brit's face seemed to suggest it was a tall order, he took a swallow of champagne and smiled. "You know, frequently I ask myself the same questions."

It sounded like a conclusion, but Mereth knew it was a beginning and, though she wanted desperately to hear of Brit's life, she also heard a sentimental Kenny Rogers song. Chris leaned close and whispered, "Would you dance with me?"

Mereth required about one-half second to make her decision. "Yes."

"Come on, then."

As Chris led the way out onto the center of the almost deserted dance floor, she followed him, enjoying a good feeling of un-scheduled adventure, like a child playing hooky.

Suddenly he stopped and did not turn around.

Baffled, she stared at his back and thought at first he might have seen someone else he knew in the smoky distance. But when he continued to stand with his back to her about ten feet away, unmoving, she asked. "Chris, is anything—"

Slowly he turned, a smile on his face, hands shoved easily into his pockets. "One thing I've failed to tell you that perhaps you should know," he began, as though vastly amused by something.

"*One* thing," she repeated. "Make that one hundred and—"

"My name is Chris Faxon."

"I know that. You—"

"I'm Deeter's grandson."

She looked up, stunned, certain she'd misunderstood him. "You're—"

Suddenly someone struck the snare drums in the live combo, and as the resounding discord was taken up by the other instruments, she tried again to repeat his incredible claim but could not, and gaped up at him, suffering the frustration of a thousand unasked questions . . .

Warrick

"MASSIE, WAKE UP. I'm worried. The kids aren't home yet."

At the sound of the alarmed male voice, Massie reluctantly awakened from her good solid sleep, largely induced by good solid scotch, and for one blessed moment she did not recognize the voice or know where she was. Then recognition. Of everything.

The cramp in her back informed her that she'd slept curled in the large chair opposite Ty's room, the awful lingering taste of onions and mustard reminded her that she and Nellie had put away the entire platter of sandwiches as well as the once virgin bottle of scotch.

Tentatively opening one eye, she saw Dr. Horace Buckner standing over her, looking like something out of a Eugene O'Neill play, the five o'clock shadow too real.

"The kids didn't come home last night," Buckner repeated. "Did you hear me? I don't have to tell you, Massie, the last thing we need now is a goddamned bunch of publicity on the antics of those rotten, good-for-nothing grandkids, you hear? And someone's got to go out and talk to those reporters. That gate looks like a . . . And my head nurse has piled her ass up in bed to sleep off one that you helped her tie on!"

Slowly Massie raised up and remembered the countless early spring mornings she and Ty had walked out across Warrick. He would have preferred to ride but she loathed horses, so they'd taken dawn walks, early risers both, in the good days and sometimes they'd walk three or four miles, and they'd make small miraculous discoveries: the first wild violets beneath the rotting wood of a fallen tree, and always arrowheads, some simply lying on the surface of the ground like pointers to the past.

"Massie, you all right?"

"I'm fine, Bucky."

"Here, take my arm."

"Not necessary. And I'm sorry about Nellie. But I thought we both needed . . ."

"I need a sober nurse," he snapped.

Massie smiled. She couldn't remember what they'd talked about while shoveling in the sandwiches and the chips and the booze, but she vaguely remembered that the large woman had shared a litany of loneliness and rejection.

"Do you have any notion where the kids are?" she asked.

"Hell, I didn't even know where they went when they were

teenagers! I haven't the faintest notion where they'd go now to get into trouble."

She increased her steps to keep up with Buckner. "What should I tell the reporters?"

"You? You ain't going to tell 'em a goddamned thing. You're the last person in the world I want going out there."

The force of his response startled her. "Why? I'm the logical one."

"You're about as logical a spokesman as . . . Don't worry. I'll take care of it. You concentrate on finding the kids before they make the newspapers."

Ahead was the wide hall which led to the staircase. At the top, just starting down, she saw Junior Nagle and Red Pierson. Both looked dapper in business suits.

"Good morning, gentlemen. Did you sleep well?"

Junior Nagle nodded and started down the steps.

Red Pierson held his ground. "Very well, Jo, thank you. And Ty. How is . . . ?"

Horace caught up. "No change, but then, of course, we really didn't expect one, did we?"

Something about his tone caused Junior to look back. "How long will it go on, Bucky?"

Bright morning was the time for blunt questions. And blunt answers.

"Have you ever known Ty to give up? On anything?"

"What do I do about Dallas?"

"Whatever Ty would want you to do."

"We have problems."

"Damn right we do!"

Massie noticed Red Pierson listening. "I think, regardless of what Ty does or does not do, we must sit down and talk. You set the time, Massie; we will defer to your wishes."

"The kids aren't back yet," Buckner persisted.

"Where are they?" Red asked.

"I don't know. They left here to pick up Brit at the airport."

"Trouble, you think?" Red asked.

Massie shook her head. "I don't think so. They haven't seen each other for years."

"We don't need publicity," Red said.

"Neither do they," Massie countered. All at once she'd had enough. She had many things to do. She must dress and clear her head and carry on as Ty would want her to do, and she must check on Nellie. Without warning, she found herself thinking fondly of the large woman who had kindly helped her to tie one on last night.

"If you'll excuse me, gentlemen," she said, "I'm sure the children will arrive soon to sleep off a night of harmless family reunion. In the meanwhile, I have various tasks."

She'd managed a few steps down the corridor when Red Pierson called after her.

"When should . . . ?"

"This afternoon. About three, I think."

She continued walking, feeling the weight of their eyes upon her.

The ability to endure and prevail had always been the one characteristic she'd admired in others, mainly Ty, who had taken the art of simple endurance and converted it into a religion. Then she would endure as well, for Ty's sake.

Deeter's Castle

MERETH WATCHED Chris pour from the battered blue-and-white-speckled coffeepot and thought it the most normal thing in the world when he extended an open bag of Fritos with an invitation.

"Breakfast?"

She smiled. "Why not?" She sipped at the hot black coffee and looked into Deeter's living room, at the bodies scattered here and there at various angles and in varying degrees of unconsciousness.

Josh had made it as far as the brown sofa, had there fallen upon his knees and now lay, still on his knees, arms spread as though at prayer except for the awesome thunder of his snores.

Brit sat more or less upright in Deeter's oversized leather chair, his head resting at the center of the torn fabric, the jagged white stuffing resembling an exotic halo.

Poor Eddie had simply opted for the floor and lay curled on his side, arms crossed as though cold, before the dead fireplace filled with black, half-charred logs.

Permeating the entire room was the stale odor of greasy food and burned-down candles.

"What are you looking at?" Chris asked, settling into the chair opposite her.

"Looks like a morgue in there. How did *we* survive?"

"We did more talking than drinking."

She took another look at the various bodies and thought for the first time in several hours of Warrick. Someone there might be worried, and she'd have to do something about that in a minute. But not now.

"Did you enjoy yourself as much as I did?" he asked shyly.

Embarrassed, she reached into the Fritos bag and withdrew a handful of chips.

"Yes, though I still can't believe it."

"What?"

"That you're Deeter's grandson."

"I told you it would make a difference."

"No, of course not," she protested, sitting up and arranging a handful of Fritos on the edge of the table. "Why do you keep it a secret around here?"

"I don't keep it a secret. When anyone asks, I answer."

"But you don't volunteer the information."

"Why should I? Do you run around telling people that you're Ty Warrick's granddaughter?"

She laughed at the cliché forming in her head and decided to deliver it anyway. "You don't *look* Indian."

"I told you my mother was English."

"When I first saw you, I thought you were Italian."

"No, I assure you I'm not."

"Does Massie know?"

"Of course she knows. Ty and Massie visited us once in Cambridge. They always tried to talk my father into coming home."

"He didn't want to?"

"Oh, I think he did. He still does. It's not being American he objects to; it's being Indian that he can't quite come to terms with. Being Deeter's son, that's even more difficult."

"How long have you been coming back to Warrick?" she asked.

He drained his coffee before speaking. "Well, as I said, forever, or so it seems." He smiled at the empty coffee cup. "Unlike my father, I can never get enough of it. During winter term I can remember staring out at that cold, constant English rain and dreaming of this hot Oklahoma sun. Sometimes I would close my eyes and literally re-create the feel of it upon my face."

As though by way of demonstration he closed his eyes and lifted his face to an invisible sun, and the slow smile suggested that he was feeling the warmth. He lowered his head.

"Would you like to take a walk with me?"

"What about the others?" she said.

"What about them? They're content. We might as well be. Certainly you didn't plan to take them back to Warrick in that condition?"

"No." She hadn't. But again she had the feeling that someone should know where they were.

"Come on, we won't be gone long. Have you ever seen Deeter's hill, the one place within walking distance where this incompleted pile of stones actually does resemble a castle?"

As she passed by him at the door, she suffered a splintering of emotions, realizing that about twenty minutes from here Ty was ill, his business cronies in a state of confusion, phones ringing, Massie stricken, Reverend Jobe's squeaky clean kids informing everyone that God loved them, while here—

She looked back into the dim living room, shades drawn, and saw Chris taking time first to check on each sleeping body like a loving father. Then she drew open the front door and let in a flood of dazzling morning light, stepped out onto the path and looked up at the immense shell of Deeter's castle.

"This way," Chris said and cut directly across the high, blowing grasses.

She hurried to catch up and found her attention divided between the uneven terrain and the looming facade of the castle. "From a distance you don't realize how huge it is," she commented, looking up.

"The real one would fit inside. Deeter saw to it that his was just a little bigger."

"Will he ever finish it?"

Chris shook his head and continued to lead the way across open prairie, to the distant hill. "I doubt it. He's an old man."

"Would your father come home if something happened to Deeter?"

"My father *is* home. In England. He hates this place. In England he is different, and acclaimed and honored for that difference. Here he is ostracized and scorned. No, he won't come back."

She started to ask additional questions but changed her mind. They were approaching the end of the castle and, based on experience, she knew there would be a wind waiting for them on the open prairie.

She looked up at the multicolored beauty of early morning sun on the various grasses and earth and sky, most of the colors deepening with distance, mauves turning to purple near the base of the hill, pale blues growing darker, the stubby brindle of prairie grass altering to a rich ivory and, most dramatic of all, the delicate light green of spring seeming to come from no particular source, a clump of clover here, a fringe of willow there in that small draw.

"I've seen a hundred landscapes more dramatic, more cultivated, more significant, but I've never seen one as moving."

Her quiet tribute sat easily on the faint breeze.

"I do love this state."

"I don't believe you."

"Why?"

"Your brothers seem to hate it so."

"I'm not my brothers. They left. I stayed."

She walked ahead and brushed the tall grasses with the palm of her hand and gazed out at the landscape. "Of course I love it, and I suspect in their own way they do too. Sometimes it reminds me of a gangly adolescent, which is what it is, insensitive, occasionally stupid. And callow. But full of life and energy and promise."

"I'd say it has some growing to do."

"Yes, but consider where it's come from, what it once was, a land nobody wanted, given to a people nobody wanted, displaced Indians, dirt poor farmers and renegade outlaws—"

She laughed despite her rising emotions. "I love it so," she murmured. "Maybe it's because I feel a little displaced and renegade myself, but it's where I belong. No matter where I go, I'm always drawn back. It's where one fights battles and draws lines and makes decisions and takes command of life. It's . . . home."

She was aware of him standing close behind her, aware when his hands lifted to her shoulders, gentle hands that caressed her and turned her toward him. She looked up into his face and found it pleasing, saw a mirror image reflection of her words, a shared love for this unique land.

He smoothed back her hair. "Deeter once told me that Tyburn Warrick's wife, Mary Beth, was the most beautiful woman this world has ever seen and that you are her double."

"Deeter tells tall tales."

"I believe him."

"Chris—"

She went up on tiptoe and kissed him, shyly at first, though shyness had little to do with his response as he enclosed her in his arms. She opened her mouth and tasted salt and moist warmth and mutual hunger.

Suddenly she drew away, not wanting to move too fast. Passion was dangerous, must be checked, kept in control, watched.

As she walked ahead, she knew he was following and was sorry she had permitted the kiss and was sorry she had stopped it and wished she could understand why she wanted love so badly and yet was unable to give or receive it.

No answers, just new awareness of imprisonment within herself, a new defeat and loneliness. And before fresh despair paralyzed her, she searched desperately for a safe horizon and saw a thin, moving dust trail miles away, a Warrick pickup heading toward the southern oil fields to check on the rigs. To the right, also far removed, she saw a mass of white-faced cattle like one gigantic organism with frayed edges. The herd had just been released to spring pasture and was now eagerly fanning out and devouring the fresh green-sprigged grass so that they, in turn, could be devoured. Briefly her awareness of the cycle unsettled her.

She turned back and saw Chris looking down on a sun-bleached white cow's skull grinning up through the winter's stubble.

Josh had made a tidy sum during senior high by running all over Warrick in one of the company's Jeeps and collecting the grim mementos, selling cattle skulls to a roadside joint up by Grand Lake, near the Kansas border. Josh had done very well for himself, and might have done better if Ty hadn't found out. In one of the more traumatic memories of her youth, Mereth remembered the day Ty had come upon Josh with a horse whip, delivered several lashes to his back, tracking him around the broad drive near the house, ignoring his pleas for mercy, silencing the whip only when Josh had agreed to return the skulls to the places where he'd found them scattered about the prairie. Josh, still crying and with red lines slowly appearing on the back of his white shirt, had loaded his skulls into the Jeep and started off alone on his mournful re-delivery.

"Why would my grandfather object to those things being gathered and sold?'' she asked, looking at the skull, newly intrigued by the ancient mystery.

Chris shook his head. "I've no idea why Ty would object. Deeter would object like hell."

"Why?"

"Religious. Death makes a place sacred. It would be like grave-robbing."

"Osage?"

Chris laughed. "Deeter does things without knowing why he does them."

"Because they're right?"

"Because he believes in them. All this is sacred to him."

Before she could question him further, he drew ahead and seemed to hesitate before selecting the best route up to the small plateau. Bending into the incline of a washed-out gully, he reached for handfuls of long grasses to aid his ascent.

She made her way with little effort to the top of the plateau, which was as flattened as though a gigantic iron had pressed it down.

"It's beautiful," she said, surveying the land of Warrick from this unique elevation.

She walked to the end of the plateau and looked for landmarks. Could she see Warrick's red tiles from here? No. She saw instead the tops of derricks toward the south, the huge Warrick oil fields that had fed, clothed, nurtured and sustained them for as long as she could remember.

She raised her hand to shield her eyes against the brilliant morning sun and saw nothing to the west and remembered there were two substantial land rises between here and the western fields. Then north. What could one see—

"Good Lord!" she gasped and squatted slowly, gaping down on the incredible view, the huge and rambling facade of Deeter's castle in the near distance resembling much more than a facade, looking for all the world like a real castle.

"It works from here, doesn't it?" He smiled, coming up alongside her. "It is incredible. Stupid, but incredible."

She laughed and nodded. "Has your father ever seen it?"

"No. He hasn't been back since Deeter started it."

"Are there really bad feelings between them?"

Slowly he joined her in a squatting position and held it for about fifteen seconds and apparently found it uncomfortable and sat flat, his knees drawn up. "Not bad feelings," he mused. "Just no feelings. None at all."

What he said seemed to sadden him and, respectful of his mood, she sat flat on the earth as well and, without intending to, mimicked his position, knees drawn up, hands clasped about them.

"You know what baffles me?"

She shook her head.

"Why do you remember everyone from childhood except me?"

At first she wasn't certain if the question was rhetorical or not. "Did you come over to Warrick often?"

She rested her forehead on her knees, then looked up grinning. "Mystery solved. I went to camp every summer. From about six on."

"Did you like it? Camp, I mean."

"I hated it. I never wanted to go. My grandmother thought it was a safe place for me to spend the summer. She was terrified of kidnappers."

"And you?"

"I always had a feeling they just wanted me out of the way for three months."

For several moments he joined her in looking down over the castle.

"I don't think I'll be leaving here for a while," Chris said.

She wasn't certain how she was supposed to respond and said nothing.

"Deeter's getting old," he added.

"I'm sure he enjoys your company."

"He enjoys having someone to drink with, to buy the beer. But if Ty died . . ." He broke off. "Were you very close to your grand-father?"

"I don't think you could safely say that Ty was close to anyone, except perhaps Massie."

"But you," he persisted. "Will you miss Ty?"

She felt a sudden compulsion to move away. "I would hope I would feel the loss of any death." A dust trail was coming close, moving at a high rate of speed. "Someone's coming," she said, nodding down on the tiny black car which had just emerged from behind the rise of land, bringing the dust trail with it.

He squinted in that direction. "That's a Warrick limo," he said. "But who's driving?" Puzzled, he rose slowly. Then suddenly, "Come on," he ordered and reached a hand back to her.

"You go," she suggested, annoyed at the tone of command in his voice. "Do you know who it is?"

He looked back down. The car was approaching the fork in the road which led around the handsome and useless, black wrought-iron gate. "I told you. It's a Warrick limo. I can't see who's driving. Red probably. Or Junior. I have an appointment. I'd forgotten. Harry Beekman has called a meeting at Tulsa Pet."

"Why?"

"For God's sake, Mereth, come on. I have to . . ."

"Well, then go!"

"I can't leave you here."

"Why not? I know the way home. I'll gather up the others, don't worry."

In the last minute she had an urgent question of her own.

"Why Junior and Red?"

"Business. Deeter's."

Over the wind she heard the distant scream of a horn. Someone was growing impatient.

He waved one last time, then she saw him break into a trot and then a jog, his long stride devouring the distance back to the castle.

Clearly the passion of the kiss was over for both of them, as was the pleasant respite atop the plateau. Well, it was for the best.

Deeter's grandson in conference with Junior and Red? What was going on?

Was Ty dead?

"Will you miss him, Mereth?"

She bent over and rested her forehead on her knees.

"My only desire is to make you happy. Will you let me?"

"It's cold, so cold. There's brandy somewhere."

Voices again, dangerous and blending. She bowed her head lower and suffered a painful splintering of emotion. She saw herself sitting alone atop this high plateau and realized that this had been her position for the last six years of her life, removed, set apart, isolated.

Sometimes she felt as if it were killing her, this aloneness. Yet she felt powerless to alter it.

Gone now, Chris was, safely inside the black car which was moving slowly away from the castle, ready to retrace the road back around the useless gate.

"Just be a good girl, Mereth, and don't cry."

"You'll love camp. Of course you will, and summer won't last forever."

Tulsa

THE ACCIDENT was a bad one, and Harry Beekman had come upon it right after it had happened, a small sports car crushed by an overturned truck. From where he sat in the back seat of his car, he could see a dead dog.

Now, less than six blocks from the bank and in desperate need for haste, he was forced to wait in his car and listen to the scream of sirens and the sound of a blowtorch—someone trapped and dying —and wonder which files the bank examiners were working over now, and could he get there in time to try to answer their questions, and more important, could he clear a path through the wall of examiners for Junior and Red? There were certain hard facts of life they must know now. It couldn't wait any longer.

"Cleared, sir, at least one lane is, but take it real easy."

"Thank you, Officer."

Harry heard the exchange between his driver and the policeman and felt the limo ease forward, and purposefully he averted his eyes from the wreckage and the ambulances and wished he hadn't seen the dead dog.

Despite his bleak mood, it always gave Harry a thrill when his driver guided the gray Lincoln out of busy Tulsa traffic and into the graceful curving drive which led to his Tulsa Petroleum Exchange Bank.

Stanley would be there curbside as always, in his smart gray uniform—Josie's idea a couple of years ago to accommodate the steady flow of Eastern bankers who wanted to get on the merry-go-round. Harry had hated the uniform at first but now he liked it, particularly since Josie's death, liked old Stanley's black face split in a wide, white grin, stooping to open Harry's door.

"Mornin', Mr. Beekman. It's a fit day."

Stanley had been saying that to Harry for over thirty-five years, with or without the gray uniform, snow, rain or blast of July heat. Harry still didn't know what a "fit day" was. No matter. He appreciated men like Stanley, good men who did their jobs well and served loyally and understood their position.

Ty's philosophy as well.

The unexpected thought of his dying friend further dampened his spirits.

He felt the car pull up the incline that led to downtown Tulsa and looked out of the side window, as he always did, for the towers of his bank. Art Deco, some architect said. In the same class, and maybe better than, Boston Avenue Methodist Church.

And there it was, less than three blocks away, to the right of the square-blocked Mayo, then Williams Place to the left, then—the Tulsa Petroleum Exchange Bank.

He rubbed the side of his nose with his knuckle and killed the strong emotion before it got the best of him. He caught one good clear glimpse of the white limestone-layered towers, a sweetheart of a bank, unique in every way. And that's one thing the big bank boys from the East Coast would never understand. Texans could because they had their own equivalents, institutions where an oil operator could go and borrow almost unlimited funds and use his handshake as collateral. Of course, that handshake had to be made with the right man.

Harry closed his eyes to rest them. Hadn't slept worth a damn, since Josie died.

He felt so tired, his hands trembling. Drained, and no respite in sight. It would get a lot worse before it got better. Josie would tell him—

"You need to go look at the mountains."

And they would run up to Colorado for a couple of weeks, and he would look at the mountains and play golf and come down feeling ten years younger.

There was no one to look at the mountains with now. He might as well sell the house in Evergreen. He wouldn't dare go back. It would hurt too much. Dear God, he'd never felt so alone. Josie gone—

And Ty gone?

The flamboyance gone, the daring to plunge ahead, throwing good money after bad, borrowing up to his neck and always coming up with the brass ring in the form of not just a producing well or two but a whole damned field! Dozens of them.

Eyes open now, Harry remembered the recent newspaper headlines proclaiming the failure of the Penn Square Bank in Oklahoma City and the threatened closing of several banks in West Texas that specialized in energy loans. Harry knew all too well the details of the Penn Square debacle, knew that the bank had been run by amateurs to serve the new "oilies," as they were called.

"Amateurs," he blurted out and felt the heat of embarrassment as he caught his driver's eye in the rearview mirror.

Steady. But the potential for disaster was enormous, and now he felt cold perspiration on his forehead. As he reached for his handkerchief he saw all too clearly what might occur at his own bank. The collapse of Penn Square was sending shock waves throughout the entire financial industry, and a worldwide recession didn't help matters. So now prudence and caution were being preached. But where was the prudence and caution during World War II and where were they after the war, when this country had rebuilt the world to run on oil? No one had given a damn about prudence and caution then.

He looked down to see his handkerchief wadded and crushed into a ball inside his fist.

Relax. This would never do. He was a professional banker with over forty years of experience. He was not responsible for high interest rates, the oil surplus or the entire economy. He was responsible only for the Tulsa Petroleum Exchange Bank. After all, what had he done? He had granted large loans to some of the most trusted men in the oil industry, but for some time he had deferred the interest due on these notes, and in addition the collateral was less than adequate.

How great was the deficiency in collateral, and how much interest was due on these notes? Harry had ordered an internal computer readout to be waiting for him this morning. Then he'd know, only a step before the bank examiners.

Harry lowered his head and again closed his eyes. He knew even without the report: the bank was going to be short huge sums of money. The examiners could force the collection of the interest payments or the calling of the notes. If the notes could not be collected, the bank would be required to foreclose on drilling equipment, which in today's depressed energy market would not bring thirty cents on the dollar. Ty would be ruined and so would Tulsa Pet.

Dear God—

He cut the thought short and abandoned it for the dangerous thing that it was. He wasn't going to put any pressure on any of his customers.

These men were his friends, personal friends, and the whole world needed what they were busting their butts to get.

Oil.

"Mr. Beekman, we feel your institution must be a little more diligent in policing your accounts receivable."

He stared fixedly at the red traffic light. Nervous Nellies, the lot of them. Butterfly collectors trying to understand elephant hunters.

As the car pulled away from the light, Harry thought of the grim wake that now was Warrick and for the second time suffered a stab of unexpected pain that accompanied grief and transition.

Lord, he could remember the Christmases he and Josie had spent at Warrick, the ones that Mary Beth and Ty used to stage for the "posse," Warrick filled, a full staff including imported chefs, a tree flown in from Oregon that touched the ceiling in the entrance hall, gifts covering the entire area, clowns for the kids, laughter, shouts of delight and—presiding over it all—Tyburn, more alive, more successful than any man had a right to be.

"I wish we could have had children, Harry."

"You're all I've ever wanted."

"The time will come when one of us will be alone. A child would help to ease the loneliness. Look at what little Mereth means to Ty. He dotes on her."

"Anyway, when the time comes, we'll go together. I'll arrange it."

"Not death, Harry, you can't arrange death."

Another traffic light. Harry sat in the silent, enclosed womb of his car and hurriedly wiped away the tears. He'd better get ahold of himself.

"Meet me at the bank around twelve noon."

High noon. Gary Cooper shootout. Bank examiners.

The car glided to a halt before the bank. Harry Beekman looked out and saw a grinning Stanley hurrying toward it.

"Morning, Mr. Beekman. It looks like it's gonna be a fit day."

291

Slowly Harry crawled out of the backseat. "Stanley, every morning for how many years, you've been standing here greeting me with a grin and a handshake, and you always say, 'Morning, Mr. Beekman. It looks like it's gonna be a fit day.' "

"Yes, suh."

"Well, what I want to know is: what is a fit day?"

Old Stanley looked confused for a moment, then a grin threatened to split his face in half. "Well, suh," he said, "what it means is that a day is gonna be good to a soul, ain't gonna trip him up in any way, hurt 'im. You know."

Harry nodded, reached into his coat pocket and withdrew a fold of new bills. He licked his index finger and peeled off a twenty-dollar bill.

"Then let's hope it's truly a fit day," he said and stuffed the bill into Stanley's pocket and walked straight into his bank.

Warrick

AFTER LESS THAN twenty-four hours at Warrick, Brit had the feeling that he'd never left, that the spiritual, emotional and philosophical growth he'd worked so hard to accomplish the last few years had been nothing more than a self-delusion.

"More coffee, sir?"

A cheery, nameless female voice contributed to the illusion.

Brit said no and looked toward the far end of the room, where Mereth was sitting alone at the gaming table. In a chair near the door he caught sight of Josh's slouched figure, legs spread, head nodding to one side.

"Happy families are all alike. Every unhappy family is unhappy in its own way," Tolstoy had said.

Not much help there, Leo. Brit looked about the room for a rescue party. Massie was generally pretty good about stirring them into some sort of family unit. But Massie was missing. The posse was missing as well. Junior Nagle, Red Pierson, Harry Beekman, all gone into Tulsa. Was Chris Faxon with them?

A rattle of dishes from the buffet caught his attention, and he looked up to see Doc Buckner filling his plate. Ah, rescue! Brit had not yet had a chance to greet the old man or make civil and private inquiry after Ty.

Slowly he started toward the buffet and caught Buckner just as he was turning about in search of a place to put his heaping plate of ham and potato salad.

"Dr. Buckner, good to see you," Brit called out cordially, or so he thought. Then why the scowl on the old man's face? It had been years.

"I'm Brit Warrick, Dr. Buckner. I . . . ."

"I know who you are. Last time I saw you, you were about sixteen and I was treating you for jock itch. Trust you learned how to take care of yourself after all these years."

A blush fanned out over Brit's face. Unfortunately he caught Mereth's eye at the end of the room and saw her turn away in a soft collapse, stifling a laugh.

"Well, have you?" the old man blustered further when Brit still had not replied. "That stuff can be pernicious, you know, like athlete's foot, those little blisters just tuck themselves up around the testicles and the scrotum and hide out as if . . . ."

"I'm *fine*, Dr. Buckner," Brit at last interrupted, more to silence the man than anything else.

"Well, I certainly hope so."

"How is my grandfather, Dr. Buckner?"

The old man looked up. For a few seconds the chewing stopped.

"Your grandfather's a dead man. Oh, I don't mean literally. I wish he were—dead, I mean. He's as good as, but you know Ty. He always does everything the hard way."

293

Brit gaped at the man, hearing love somehow in that fractured diagnosis.

"So tell me about yourself, Brit. I lost track of you."

"I'm . . . afraid I'm more concerned about Ty."

"Why? And when did this 'concern' first begin to plague you? Plague any of you, for that matter." He looked, annoyed, over his shoulder in an all-encompassing glance which included the entire terrace room.

"Come, Brit, over here, and the rest of you as well. Let Uncle Bucky tell you a few of the facts of life, just like I did when you were minnow-size." With one wobbly gesture he covered all corners of the room. "Well, come on!" he bellowed, leaving no doubt in anyone's mind that he meant business.

Being closest to the sofa, Brit arrived first and stood at the far end. At the same time Mereth started forward, nudging Josh, who dragged himself wearily out of his slumped position and followed after her.

"You've always been a bastard, Buckner, you know that?" Josh's voice sounded tired, almost loving, as he delivered himself of this indictment.

"I know. It's my natural role," Buckner replied. "Now sit yourselves down before you fall down, and I'll try to make this as brief as possible for all our sakes." Buckner leaned forward. "Ty would have liked to have been here, but the truth is that Ty won't be joining us in this reunion. Not today, not ever."

Apparently Mereth did not approve of the diagnosis and spoke up angrily. "Why are you saying this?"

"Because I want you all to understand that Ty won't let go voluntarily. The thinking, reasoning, communicating Ty Warrick is dead, over, a thing of the past. But . . ."

It was an ominous "But . . . ," and more than filled the silence. The only disturbance was a strange one coming from outside the door, a series of thuds as though someone were moving furniture or shifting something about.

Buckner looked up, annoyed. "Someone coming?"

When no one seemed inclined to move, Brit volunteered. "No, sir, I don't think so."

Josh apparently felt compelled to keep him on track. "Why are you telling us this?" he demanded. "What do you think we can do about it?"

"You goddamned idiot, didn't you just hear me? That . . . torture can go on up there for weeks, months."

"What are you . . . suggesting?" Brit asked cautiously.

"I'm suggesting that we pull the tubes, turn off that blasted respirator."

"No." This first rejection came from Mereth. She looked frightened. "You have no right."

"Agreed." Dr. Buckner nodded. "I'm simply the unlucky bastard who must watch him die."

A car door slammed, distant, muted, out on the drive.

Buckner heard the disturbance and looked up like a man under siege.

A thought occurred to Brit. It wasn't just their decision.

"Massie. Have you . . . ?"

Buckner shook his head. "Won't hear of it, though she's seen him."

Josh sat up from his slumped position. "If the old man is already dead, then why persist?"

"Josh, no!" Another protest, coming from Mereth. Suddenly she stood and hurried away from the sofa and gained the far end of the room and looked out over the gardens. Brit thought she might speak, say something in her defense or Ty's. But she said nothing and continued to stand at the farthest point in the room, as though all she could do was disassociate herself from the others and the discussion.

"All I ask is that you think about it," Buckner said. "Maybe God will intervene, you know what I mean, show the good sense and love for Ty that we apparently lack."

With all the calm Brit could muster, he suggested, "Dr. Buckner, let's talk about it later."

"When later?"

"When everyone is present."

"Everyone is here."

"No. Massie . . ."

"Massie is of no help."

"Still, she must be consulted."

"I'll bring you a list of doctors tomorrow. Pick one. Horace Buckner's getting too old for this."

"Dr. Buckner, please . . ."

Suddenly the exhortation was interrupted by a knock at the door.

"Dr. Buckner, are you in there? Please answer. You must come. Something . . ."

As the hysterical message penetrated, Brit saw Buckner blink at the door. "Who is it?" he called out.

"Nurse Kent, sir. Please, you must . . ."

In response to such apparent need, Brit started toward the door and at the same time saw Mereth move from her position by the window.

The knock came again. "Please come, Dr. Buckner."

Brit drew the door open and saw on the other side a distraught nurse.

"Dr. Buckner . . ." she faltered.

"What *is* it, Miss Kent?"

"It . . . concerns Mr. Warrick," she murmured. "He's . . . gone!"

Buckner frowned. "Expired, you mean."

"No, sir!"

This strong rebuttal was followed immediately by tears. Brit started toward her to offer her comfort but she backed away, rejecting all assistance.

"The patient was sleeping peacefully at noon. I had changed the I.V., checked the catheter, done b.p. and pulse, and recorded everything when it occurred to me that Nellie might be stirring and in need of coffee." Fearful that she'd ventured off in the wrong direction, she quickly returned to the proper track.

"I started to call for one of those nice young people, but they're awfully busy, aren't they? So I left the room and was gone no more than, I swear it, fifteen minutes, and when I returned . . ." Her voice broke. "He's gone, sir, gone, missing from his bed, not in his bed. All the I.V.'s are pulled loose, the catheter, the monitor, everything just . . . oh, my God!"

At last, as though the full impact of the macabre message had just dawned on her, she covered her face and took refuge out in the corridor and wept against the wall. And that weeping was the only sound, for her difficult message had turned everyone in the terrace room into mannequins, temporarily beyond speech, beyond reaction, beyond movement—

Tulsa

CHRIS FAXON sat off to one side of the meeting which was taking place in Harry Beekman's executive suite and thought if any of them told one more Ty Warrick quail-hunting or deer-hunting story, he'd slip away and steal a few winks in the backseat of the limo.

"And Ty said," Junior remembered, "that when a man is exploring for oil the only reality is the next elephant hunt. He lives so completely in his undiscovered wealth that the struggle to pay his bills is what seems like a dream."

Chris sat slowly up in his chair at the far edge of the vast office and wondered when the subject had switched from prize hunting dogs to Ty's philosophy of hunting oil. He eyed the melting ice in the bottom of his glass.

Mereth.

The name approached slyly on the blind side of his conscience, caught him off guard.

"He knew Bob Kerr, you know. Personal. Liked him immensely. Said the senator was the best friend the oil industry ever had."

It was Junior again, forming one point of the sprawled triangle swallowed by the brown velvet circular sofa. All three men rested their feet on the low glass coffee table, ties askew, coats missing, several bottles of Chivas on the table. No niceties of ice or jiggers or stirrers, just three glasses. But even those had been abandoned, and now each man lifted his own bottle upward and swallowed and made a face at the good booze and remembered even more about Tyburn Warrick.

Chris suddenly understood what was going on here. This was a premature wake for their dying friend. In calling the meeting, Red Pierson had no intention of talking business of any kind. The fact that he'd insisted that Chris come along was simply his way of telling Chris that he'd read Ty's will and knew what was coming.

He suspected Harry Beekman had his own news, but for the moment all that had been forgotten in the pleasurable, drunken recall of the three men who, next to Deeter, were Ty's closest and oldest associates.

"Anticlines. Anticlines."

The repeated, slurred word came from Junior Nagle.

Chris was becoming fascinated by the compatibility of these three, their easy recall, the exchanges which, like "anticlines," were executed almost in code, for following Junior's double delivery of the word, the other two, Red and Harry, commenced nodding vigorously.

Even Chris knew how the word applied.

Ancient geology, that's what an anticline was, following fast on the heels of divining rods and doodlebugs. It was a place where rock strata arched, dipping or inclining in opposite directions from a ridge, like the roof of a house. Every major field in Oklahoma had been formed on an anticline. Of course, there were many anticlines that had yielded nothing and that's where the gamble came. Just because an explorer found his ridge of land didn't mean a damned thing. Most oilmen lucky enough to make the big strike felt only awe at the realization that they had triumphed over stubborn and unyielding Nature, forcing her to give up some of her treasures.

"Ty believed in them," he heard Red mutter.

All their reflexes were being considerably dulled by the scotch. Still, no one seemed to mind. Their observations held. The rhythm was their own and suited them, and they were of the generation and breed of men who, in all cases, established the rhythm that suited them and changed it only when they wanted to change it.

For a long moment Red's words seemed to reverberate around the room.

Then Chris noticed Junior lift his feet off the coffee table, rise awkwardly from the sofa and make his way across the room to a wall covered with framed photographs.

"Look at this," Junior exclaimed, his voice hushed.

Everyone's attention shifted clumsily toward the photographs. The one that had captured Junior's attention was a large picture of a dozen or so men, all standing knee deep in oil before a derrick, surrounded by what appeared to be a lake of oil. Nearby the trees appeared as blackened skeletons.

"That's the No. 1 Mary Sudik." Junior smiled. "I remember Ty and me had a dozen rigs going around Maud in the Seminole field, and we were about three days from hitting the Wilcox sand when old Mary went wild. Ty come to me and said, 'Let's go over to the city and see that thing. I think it's something we ought to see . . .'"

Chris saw everyone nod, the memory a shared one.

Then it was Red's turn. "I was recording mineral deeds for Ty in Cleveland County when old Mary blew, and when I came out of the courthouse that afternoon it was raining oil. It ruined the 1928 Packard I was driving. Can you imagine? Raining oil in Norman, twenty miles away."

Everyone stared at the yellowed photograph which represented the untamed, unregulated past.

"Those were good times," Junior mourned.

A pensive mood seemed to settle over the group. Harry Beekman sat slowly in the swivel chair behind his desk. "You know, it was Cities Service that drilled the Wild Mary Sudik, and this bank handled twenty-five percent of the financing for that field. We made a bundle and so did Cities Service. They became one of the giants."

Harry reached behind and raised the venetian blinds near his desk. "Look down there," he instructed, and the others moved slowly to the window. "What do you see down there about two blocks southwest, right across the street from the old Mayo Hotel?"

Red Pierson squinted against the sunlight. "Appears to be the foundation of a new building."

Harry nodded. "That was to have been the new fifty-story headquarters of Cities Service. But they got caught in a financial bind and were absorbed by Occidental, and now the building probably will never be finished."

Junior looked back out of the window, where something else caught and held his attention. "Look at that son of a bitch," he whispered, eyes leveled and accusing. "That one right there with the briefcase, just getting into the silver Mercedes."

They all followed the direction of his gaze until they found his target.

"That son of a bitch is wearing clothes that are made from petrochemicals and he is driving a car that burns gasoline, over highways paved with asphalt, so that he can get home to suburbia where he has fertilized his lawn with petroleum products, and this evening he and his wife will have a backyard barbecue and cook steaks on natural gas and serve them on plastic plates made from petrochemicals, and that same son of a bitch is probably against the depletion allowance and in favor of the windfall profits tax! The dumb bastard never stops to think that that raises the price of everything he uses."

Everyone looked until the gray car disappeared around the corner and into traffic. Then slowly, as though newly defeated by their inability to understand, they moved back to the sofa and sank down and drank deeply from their bottles.

Junior belched. "Course that one son of a bitch ain't nothing compared to the assholes we got in Washington. Now we're talking world-class assholes, willing to regulate every goddamned thing in sight with their goddamned computers and pocket calculators. A man can't get a hard-on anymore without Congress regulating the size of it!"

Red agreed and openly longed for the past. "It's too bad old Sam Rayburn and LBJ and Bob Kerr aren't still around."

"And Tyburn Warrick," added Junior Nagle.

The addition of Ty's name to the list of distinguished obituaries prompted another deep swig from all the bottles.

"Ty may be dying in more ways than one."

This strangely sober announcement came from Harry Beekman, the drunkest of the lot.

"Examiners still here?" Red asked.

"You know they are."

"Any reports?"

"Not directly. Lots of hearsay, lots of rumors."

"Bullshit, all of it. Pay no attention."

Junior placed his bottle carefully on the edge of the glass coffee table. "Well, they're taking it seriously down in Dallas. Damned serious."

Harry Beekman looked straight across at Junior. "How . . . did Dallas know?"

"Don't be so goddamned naive, Harry," Junior snapped. "How in the hell do you think they found out? Ty farts and it's heard all the way to Saudi Arabia. Dallas gets the first whiff."

Harry blinked at the crudity and asked a faltering question. "What are they saying?"

Junior breathed a deep sigh, which didn't seem to satisfy his need for air. "That all the shit in the world is going to hit the biggest fan in the world pretty soon, and none of us are going to come out smelling too good."

"If they'd just leave us alone . . . ," Harry protested.

"Well, they're obviously not." Junior waved his large beefy

hands in the air. "No matter, boys. Like we said, Ty always has something up his sleeve. All this will blow over, and I predict that in two months we'll be drilling in the Warrick Basin and Ty Warrick is going to knock the whole goddamned oil world on their asses. Again!"

No one had interrupted Junior. All he'd done was look up at Red, and apparently he'd seen something in that face that stopped him dead.

"Come on, we've got to get the hell out of here," Red said brusquely.

"Why?"

Red placed the bottle on the table and made an attempt to straighten his necktie. "If they can't get to Ty with their questions, wouldn't you say that we'd be the next best bet?"

Junior said, "Hell, they've got enough to do without bothering us. Besides, they ain't finding anything. Are they, Harry?"

Chris observed Beekman nervously opening the top drawer of his desk and removing what appeared to be a computer printout.

Junior, impatient for a response, rephrased his question. "Your house *is* in order, isn't it, Harry?"

The question was quaint. Harry tried to manage a smile. "My 'house'—I mean Tulsa Pet—is in 'trouble.'"

"How much trouble?"

"A billion dollars."

"Jesus."

Chris heard the ominous edge in Junior's cracked voice and realized that if the Tulsa Petroleum Exchange Bank was in trouble, then Ty Warrick was in trouble. Apparently Red Pierson had come to the same realization. He grabbed the computer report from Harry's desk and shuffled frantically through the stack of paper while Junior continued to mutter "Jesus—"

Within seconds Red became impatient and slammed the computer sheets back on the desk, staring anxiously at Beekman. "Bottom line, Harry. How much of the shortfall belongs to Ty?"

"Three hundred million."

The sound of Harry's voice and the gravity of his statement seemed to reverberate around the office.

Chris closed his eyes, realizing that his own hopes were tied to Warrick and now those hopes seemed in jeopardy.

"They don't understand." This plea came from Harry Beekman. "They can't expect me to . . . It doesn't work. Not that way . . . not for men like Ty, you trust or you . . . It's a conspiracy! Tulsa Petroleum Exchange is not Penn Square. We don't have bank officers loaning themselves money to cover gambling debts and committing fraud. All we've done is defer the debt service on the oilmen we've served for years, at least until we get through this recession. How is that different from Chase Manhattan and the Eastern banks loaning billions to nations that can't make payment? It's an East Coast conspiracy, that's what it is."

"Come on," Red commanded, a new gentleness to his voice. "We'd better be getting back to Warrick. That's where . . ."

But Harry made a stubborn, childlike, negative drunken movement. "No, you two go ahead. I'll have to deal with the examiners sooner or later. Might as well be . . ."

"Not like that," Red scolded. "That's all we need is to turn those guys loose on you now. No! When you do see them, I'll be on one side and Junior there will be on the other. Right, Junior? As of now we have nothing to worry about and little to do except to return to Warrick and nurse Ty back to health. Like it or not, as long as Ty breathes, all our asses are safe. Right, Junior?"

Slowly and mysteriously, all three men, it seemed to Chris, were returning to their respective states of inebriation.

"Chris!"

He looked up to see Red looking directly at him.

"I need your help."

On his feet now, Chris started around the sofa. While he was still en route, Red said:

"There is a door on the other side of that room which leads to a small corridor which in turn leads to a freight elevator, which in turn makes its deposits street level, rear of the building, on Fourth Street."

Chris wondered who was going down in the freight elevator. Red answered with obliging speed.

"I doubt seriously if any one of the three of us should be seen in our present state. Not drunk, mind you. Just . . ."

Of the three, Harry Beekman seemed to be faring worst. He had not looked up for some time, and his hands continued to obscure his face.

"Dumb thing to do," Red muttered. "Don't know what I was thinking of."

"You mentioned a freight elevator," Chris prompted gently.

"We will take it down, the three of us. If you'll be so good as to take the main elevator down and fetch the car and bring it around to the back, to the Fourth Street exit . . ."

Chris glanced down at the two other men, who had yet to stand. "Do you need help?"

"We're not drunk. We just . . . remembered too much."

Without another word Chris closed the door and started through the outer office.

"Mr. Faxon." The female voice was hesitant and came from behind.

He turned on it and found a prim, middle-aged woman, tastefully dressed.

"My name is Gypsy Walters. I'm a bank officer here and a friend of Jo Massie's. We're very concerned, all of us, and I was wondering if you could . . . ?"

"I'm sorry, Ms. Walters. I assume you are referring to Mr. Warrick's condition?"

She nodded.

"When I left Warrick, there was no change. He remains pretty much as he's been since the initial stroke."

She appeared grateful. "The newspapers tend to be hysterical."

He hadn't seen a newspaper report but now had a question of his

own. "Things here, Ms. Walters, how are they? Are the examiners
. . . ?"

"They're everywhere," she said, lowering her voice. "It would
be very helpful if Mr. Beekman . . ."

Chris smiled. "I don't think Mr. Beekman can be much help to
you at this moment."

She caught the innuendo. "He hasn't been any help since Mr.
Warrick took ill." She broke off as though aware she'd said too
much. "They ask about him, you know, the examiners. We can't
cover for him forever. Sooner or later he's going to have to—"

"Let's make that later. Right now, I'd better go."

"Tell Massie I'm thinking about her. Gypsy Walters. She'll remember the name. And if there's anything I can do . . ."

"I'll tell her."

"And give Mereth my love as well."

Chris looked back. "You know Mereth?"

"Oh, yes. She's generally in once or twice a week."

"I'll tell her. Now I must go. They are . . ."

"I know your grandfather too, Mr. Faxon, and I know who you
are. I know most of the Warrick family, and it is out of this familiarity and concern that I speak. We are in trouble here, Mr. Faxon.
The consequences could be devastating and far-reaching. Everyone's caught up in it, and with Mr. Warrick's . . . illness, no one
seems to be at the wheel. I'm afraid that—"

She was interrupted by a shout from an unexpected source, Red
Pierson clinging to the doorway of the executive suite, the agitation
in his voice unprecedented.

"Chris, thank God! Come quick!"

That was all he said, and without hesitation Chris started back
toward the door, his heart accelerating along with his speed, suffering a series of wild conjectures.

Not until he was approaching the doorway did it occur to him
that he'd left Gypsy Walters standing there. But as he looked back,
he saw the elevator doors just closing, caught a glimpse of the

305

tailored gray pin-striped suit and then the doors were closed and the red light glided silently downward.

"Chris, hurry, please!"

He took the door running and saw first Harry Beekman, collapsed on the sofa where he'd left him, with Junior sitting beside him.

Then he saw Red Pierson at the far end of the room, behind Harry's desk. Red held out the phone receiver. "Hurry, something's wrong."

"What?"

"How in the hell should I know? It's Mereth, and the bitch won't talk to me. She wants you."

Chris took the receiver and was aware of the taut silence coming from behind him. He cupped the receiver close to his mouth.

"Mereth?"

Warrick

MERETH WISHED she'd closed the door to the telephone room, but it was too late now.

Outside the door she heard running footsteps. The entire house had gone topsy-turvy since Kent's announcement that Ty was missing. Mereth still couldn't believe it, even though she'd seen it for herself, had been a part of that melodramatic procession which had streamed out of the terrace room following after Dr. Buckner who, like some reluctant pied piper, had led them straight up to Ty's room—Josh had laughed the entire way—only to be presented with the empty bed, truly empty, though it bore the mysterious imprint of a body like some embryonic shroud, tubes dangling from nearby standards, I.V. bottles dripping onto the carpet. Even the catheter and the bottle half filled with pale yellow urine had been shunted to one side, a bizarre vacuum which had reduced all of them to a state of mute paralysis, and Josh had stopped laughing.

Then chaos, everyone talking at once, and Mereth had slipped out of the hysterical room, aware that someone with reasoning powers still intact had to be notified.

"Chris, is that you?"

"Sorry I took so long. I was at the elevator."

"Chris, something has happened."

"I figured. What?"

"Ty's . . . gone."

There was a pause. She listened to see if she could hear background voices. She knew he wasn't alone. Red, Junior, Harry were there someplace in close proximity.

"I . . . don't . . ."

"Not dead," she said and felt his confusion mount. "I don't mean dead, Chris. Do you understand? He's *gone,* missing, not here."

Aware of her raised voice, she pleaded softly, "Please get back here, Chris. Something's happening."

"Mereth, I don't understand. How could he be . . . ?"

"I know you don't understand, and it's difficult to explain over the phone."

She closed her eyes and cupped her hands about the receiver and spoke slowly, starting with Miss Kent's first announcement.

"He's not in his bed, Chris."

"That's not possible."

"Oh, but it is. I swear it."

"He was dying."

"He either found strength to leave on his own or he had help."

"I'm on my way," Chris said at last. "It may take a while. They've been . . . toasting Ty's health."

She understood. One or all were drunk.

"Chris, hurry," she whispered. "Things are really crazy here."

"Mereth, don't talk to anyone outside Warrick."

"No, of course not."

"One more thing, Mereth. Are there still reporters at the gate?"

"They were there when we came home late this morning."

"As many?"

"More. Ty has always been news."

Then on the line she heard a voice. Red Pierson was her guess. Apparently Chris had held him at bay long enough.

"Well, I'll go now," she heard him say above the insistent voice. The line went dead.

A voice from behind startled her, and she looked over her shoulder to find Brit's face, looking more lined than ever after the sleepless, drunken night.

"I think Massie needs you up in Ty's room. The good Reverend Jobe has caught up with her and is suggesting the empty bed represents . . . a miracle."

"Who let him in?"

Brit laughed. "His troops are everyplace. Come on, let's see if we can throw a little compassionate atheism on that awful, unintelligible god up there before he totally destroys Massie."

"Where's Josh?"

"Where do you think he is, an old ham like Josh? He's in Ty's room, of course, relishing every moment."

"Dr. Buckner?"

"On the phone."

"Who's he calling?"

"Ask him. Here he comes."

As they reached the top of the stairs, Mereth saw a very harried Buckner hurrying toward them.

"Dr. Buckner, what . . . ?"

"Not now," he snapped. "I've called Jim O'Rourke at St. Mark's. He told me to call the police immediately."

"Don't talk to anyone outside of Warrick."

As Chris's warning reechoed in her ear, Mereth confronted the old man directly. *"Have* you? Called the police, I mean."

"On my way. Can't get an extension out. Someone is really messing up the lines."

"Dr. Buckner, wait."

"Can't wait. What we have here is kidnapping, and I'm not talking about plain Joe down the street. I'm talking about Tyburn Warrick, kidnapped from his deathbed by the most villainous and wretched animals you ever . . ."

"Dr. Buckner, please!" she called out. "Let me talk to you."

"I said no time, girl. Didn't you hear me? Do you have any idea of the magnitude of what's happened here?"

"What *has* happened?" she asked with a bluntness which she hoped would stop him.

He turned back. "Good God, Mereth, you've heard, surely!"

"I've heard nothing. Nothing except that my grandfather is not in his bed."

"Well, ain't that enough?"

"To charge kidnapping? No."

The old man blinked up at her, as though trying to decide whether or not to dignify her ignorance with a response.

"Well then, precisely what does it make it?"

"I don't know, but I think before the police are brought in we should . . ."

"What? Wait until the trail gets cold? You know this has happened before, don't you?"

Now it was her turn to express shock. "What?"

"Threats to Ty's life, threats of kidnapping. Happens every day all over. Getty kid lost an ear. Terrorism, blackmail." Out of Buckner's age and fatigue and fear came incoherence.

Mereth felt sorry for him. None of them had asked in this life to be placed in close proximity to Tyburn Warrick.

Now, in an attempt to ease Buckner's fear, she gently took his arm. "I called Tulsa a minute ago. Red, Junior and Harry, and Chris as well are on their way out. Why don't we wait until they arrive before we call . . . anyone?"

The old man gestured helplessly in the air and looked at the bottom of the stairs, where Eddie O'Keefe had just taken the doorway running.

"What in the hell is going on?" Eddie demanded. "That crowd out there at the gate has about doubled. They say they want to talk to a member of the family, to Massie."

"Massie has nothing to say," Mereth said. "Nor does anyone else."

"What in the hell is wrong? Something is, I know."

In defense against his instincts, Mereth moved down a step. "Eddie, where have you been for, say, the last hour or two?"

"I've been in the office," he said, as though she should have known.

"Did you . . . what was the last car you saw going or coming into Warrick?"

A simple question for someone who had spent the last few hours in the garage office. From its vantage point to the right of the large covered drive, anyone seated at the desk would be in a position to see every car that entered or left via the main driveway.

"The last car," Eddie repeated, "was Red Pierson this morning. He had Junior Nagle with him. Going in to the bank to meet Harry Beekman, or so he said. Not come back yet."

"And coming?"

"Easy. Reverend Gerald Jobe about an hour ago. His driver's out there now having coffee."

"And that's all?"

He ducked his head, grinning. "Well, we . . . we came in, remember? But that was earlier."

She started to thank him when something caught in her memory. "Wait a minute, Eddie. We didn't get back until after Red had left, because they came by Deeter's and picked up Chris. How would you know when they had left Warrick?"

"The log," Eddie said without hesitation. "Junior and Red both know they have to sign the limos out. I checked it when we got back. Mereth, what is it?"

"Nothing now, Eddie. Later, I promise."

310

She looked back to see old Buckner sitting dejectedly on the top step. Without words she assisted him to his feet.

Once up, the man managed on his own and now conceded the wisdom of her suggestion. "You're right," he muttered. "The last thing we want out here is a bunch of uniforms. But, Mereth, where is he?"

"You heard Eddie. No one has left since Red Pierson."

He walked slowly beside her, head down, as though feeling the full weight of the loss.

"Dr. Buckner," she asked, looking ahead down the corridor toward the cluster of people outside Ty's rooms, "are you certain my grandfather was incapable of moving himself, of walking away?"

"Of course I'm goddamned certain!" he exploded.

Down the hall, several looked their way. From this distance she could see Brit and about four others, all unrecognizable, Jobe's kids, she imagined, and she heard a familiar droning voice, well modulated, with just a hint of Bible Belt dialect.

Praying? Why was he praying?

Massie.

Concerned, Mereth eased into the circle tightly formed about the doors and looked into the room, trying to blot out the melodramatic voice of the man who stood to the right of Ty's empty bed, holding a mussed pillow up in the air in one hand, his other hand pressed down on Massie's head where she sat, bent over, hands obscuring her face, in one of the bedside chairs.

But the voice was insistent, as was the man himself, the upraised face of Gerald Jobe, his expensively tailored silk suit straining against the distorted angle of his body, which was as nothing compared to the distortion issuing from his lips.

". . . so we dare not ask for understanding, Jesus Christ. It is not our right to understand. We ask only for the strength required to have faith that You have called Your son, Tyburn Warrick, back to the bosom of Your heart, that You will welcome him as a prodigal and that You will pass a forgiving judgment upon him for all his sins, that You will . . ."

311

Mereth closed her eyes. As always in any confrontation with fundamentalism, she felt herself going mute.

The voice soared.

". . . I believe in God, we all do, no heathen here, Lord, I swear it, and we believe that You are a loving Father and an all-powerful one, capable of lifting a man up to Heaven . . ."

Mereth started to ease back away from the madness when she heard a giggle and a slightly suspect "Praise the Lord!" coming from somewhere in the room. She looked around and saw Josh seated atop a large eighteenth-century mahogany cabinet, legs drawn up, a look of sheer rascal delight on his face.

". . . and we ask Your guidance, Jesus Christ, for Thou are the hope of sinners. The power of Thy love has made others brave and strong and pure. We ask Thee to cleanse all evil from these lives that You may use them as instruments of Thy will and spread the word of Tyburn Warrick's resurrection, tell all that the stone has, once again, rolled away . . ."

On and on, so many words, so haphazardly and carelessly arranged, the worst cant, the worst dogma, and the most simplistic.

She was on the verge of turning away, of going back to the terrace room and waiting for Chris and the others to arrive—she wasn't certain what was going on here, was only certain she wanted no part of it—but just as she turned, she saw Massie make a curious move, a slight wrenching upward as though the weight of Jobe's hand upon her head was causing discomfort. As Massie tried again to move, Mereth saw Jobe clamp his hand down with renewed strength and stand closer to the chair as though literally holding her a prisoner in that subject position.

Didn't anyone else see it?

Apparently not. Then it was up to her.

As she passed on her way to the atrocity, Miss Kent whispered, "Oh, Miss Warrick, I'm so . . ."

But at the moment Mereth wasn't interested in apology. Her central goal was to cleanse the room of the poison that Jobe was spreading.

312

". . . we have many confessions, oh, our Lord, and if Your action today was by way of punishment, we must confess those sins for the sake of our loved one. We all must confess. Now."

"Please stop it."

Stunned by how weak her voice sounded in comparison to Reverend Gerald Jobe's "preacher" voice, Mereth was ready to repeat her request in the event he hadn't heard the first time.

Clearly he'd heard, but he started again.

"We ask Thee to cleanse us from evil and pray that Thy mercies will . . ."

When had it happened, this man's influence over this house?

"I asked you to *stop* it, please," Mereth repeated.

". . . and that the temptations of wealth which have assailed every member of this house . . ."

Mereth was less than ten feet from the chair in which Massie sat, pressed beneath the weight of the man's hand. If Mereth couldn't stop the man, then she would try to remove the victim of his obscene prayer, and now she started forward, reaching out for Massie, pulling her away from the man's hand.

Jobe felt the vacuum. The praying voice ceased and he looked down at Mereth, who gave him only the briefest passing glance.

At the same time she heard the bizarre sound of solitary applause and looked up to her right to see Josh, still sitting on the cabinet at the far side of the room.

"Cavalry to the rescue!" He grinned from his perch and lifted his hands to his mouth and gave a discordant imitation of a trumpet sounding.

Mereth thought she saw him preparing to jump down, but she didn't linger. All that mattered was to get Massie to a place of relative peace. To that end she slipped her arm around Massie's shoulders and led her unprotesting toward the doors, not stopping, not even when Jobe called after them.

"Miss Warrick, my only intention is to serve, to offer comfort to . . ."

"It's all right, Massie," she whispered, trying to urge the collapsed woman to postpone complete disintegration for just a few more moments.

Then she heard Josh as he hurried past, both hands waving toward the tightly packed knot of people in the door. "Move back. Please. Show's over. Let's go."

To Mereth's relief, she saw a passage open. Once out in the corridor, she looked across the alcove and saw Dr. Buckner and Brit.

"Come on, this way," Buckner ordered firmly.

Mereth looked ahead, curious to see where Buckner was leading them. Ty's suite was at the extreme west end of the second-floor corridor. There was nothing beyond his rooms of significance except—

Then she remembered. The nursery had been down here, the large sunshine-filled gallery where they'd spent their childhood.

"In here. All of you."

As Dr. Buckner drew open the old nursery door, Mereth fully expected to see the bright yellow walls and white trim and hardwood floors on which she'd taken her first steps. But as she and Massie entered she saw a large room done in muted shades of brown and gray and ivory, an office suite, a massive desk situated directly in front of an immense wall map, a flattened world. Here and there, punctuating the map, were clusters of gold-headed pins.

Dr. Buckner called out, "Bring her over here."

Mereth obliged with Brit's assistance, the two of them helping Massie to a leather couch where they lowered her gently, Buckner hovering like a mother hen, concerned yet speaking with reassurance.

"She's all right. Not a superwoman, though she fancies herself one."

Mereth backed away, intent on leaving them alone for a moment, and glanced toward the door to see Josh still standing there, gaping at the new office.

Every place Mereth looked she saw crystal, gold, etched glass, leathers, velours, orientals. But it was like a model room or a stage set, for there wasn't the slightest evidence of anyone working or living here.

She saw Brit wandering around in the same sort of fascinated inspection.

"Sure beats the old ranch house, doesn't it?" he asked, sizing up the desk. The surface was devoid of papers, pencils, machines, dictaphones, the various pieces of small equipment necessary to run an office.

"And here we are," she heard Brit say and looked up to see him standing before the wall-sized map of the world.

Josh headed toward the wall map.

"Unless I'm mistaken, this should light up the world."

He reached into the corner where two walls intersected and flipped a switch, which in turn caused all the gold pinheads to light up.

For several moments no one said anything, the dazzling display holding their attention. It was the Warrick empire, every gold head representing a producing well. And there were gold heads everywhere, vast clusters of them in West Texas, Kansas, North Dakota, Wyoming, California, the Gulf Coast, even a few scattered about the sandy stretches of Saudi Arabia, which did not mean ownership, of course, but did mean collusion, perhaps secret partnership.

But far and away the largest congregation of gold pins was in Oklahoma, south central, the enormous Warrick fields less than ten miles from this room, that sea of pumps and drilling rigs.

"Jesus!"

The whisper came from Josh.

"Is that for real?" he asked further, and no one seemed inclined to answer him.

"This room used to be the nursery, right?" Brit said.

Mereth nodded.

"There was one wall . . . that one, I think." Brit pointed toward the north panel. "And on that wall we could write anything we wanted to, remember?"

Mereth remembered, recalling the expanse of white newsprint

that Mary Beth had tacked up daily on which they could write, print, draw, color, anything. Gone now that one expanse of free expression, and in its place—

"No, I beg you. I'm all right, Bucky. I really am. Please, just . . ."

This gentle protest came from the couch and Mereth saw Massie sitting upright, a handkerchief pressed against her lips.

Still Dr. Buckner hovered. "I think you need—"

"I need nothing, Horace. I promise you. It's just the shock. I can't understand. Where could he . . . ?"

As the mystery swept over Massie again, the incoherence increased, but she seemed more in control now. She asked first that Buckner leave them alone for just a few minutes, a reasonable request, followed by, "And Horace, please try to find Reverend Jobe and . . . apologize."

She never specified what he was to apologize for and even Buckner looked dumbfounded, though he said nothing and started for the door. His docility was another matter, most uncharacteristic that, but in a way Mereth understood. The world and everyone in it was off the track somehow. Nothing was happening as it should, and no one was behaving in the manner prescribed by nature.

The door slammed. Mereth looked over her shoulder to find Brit seated beside Massie on the couch, holding her hand, their heads bent together in comforting closeness. At that moment Massie looked up, and Mereth thought she'd never seen her so undone.

"Mereth, you look as lost as I feel. Come, sit down beside me."

She saw Massie extend her hand. As she took it, she felt the flesh cold and dry, and suddenly felt a compulsion to hold Massie tight, and did. Predictably, the warm embrace seemed to stimulate fresh tears and, dabbing at her eyes, Massie drew back and sat up.

"Come on. This is the last thing we need, isn't it?"

"What's the first?" Mereth smiled.

Massie called out to Josh, who was still examining the map, "Hey you, come on over here. We need to hold a family powwow."

Josh came immediately, though his eyes were glazed and there was a fixed grin on his face.

For a moment Massie seemed pleased by their closeness.

"If only we had done this earlier, under happier circumstances, how pleased Ty . . ." She shook her head. "No. Enough bawling. What we need to do is talk. Any ideas, any suggestions?"

Silence. Then Josh contributed a non sequitur.

"This used to be the nursery."

Massie agreed. "It hadn't been used in such a long time. Ty needed an office close by. I told him he couldn't run over to the ranch house all the time. The winters have been fierce. How much better, I thought, to have his files, his needs close by." She laughed and shrugged.

"So he told me to go ahead, find him a spot and fix it up, and I did." At this she looked around the spacious, elegant, unused office. "Of course, I don't have to tell any of you what happened. He sat at that desk exactly once and has never been near it since. He still makes runs over to the ranch house. Once, twice, sometimes three times a day." She stood.

"When I heard that he . . . was gone, I called over to the ranch house, thinking . . ." She walked toward the center of the room. "But the men there hadn't seen him."

"Did you tell them that he was missing?" Josh asked.

"Yes. If he left on his own, if he was all right, he eventually will turn up at the ranch house. He loves it there, much more than here."

Mereth too abandoned the short-lived family circle. Something was threatening her, closing in. She found it difficult to draw enough air into her lungs. Move away before anyone noticed.

She made it as far as a safe corner and waited out the mysterious discomfort. The ranch house. Hazards there, something waiting for her. Why would Ty go back? Surely he was as fearful of it as she was.

Yet Mereth could not deny the accuracy of Massie's words. The ranch house was situated at the exact center of Warrick and represented Ty's beginnings. His father had built the core of the rambling white frame house, then Ty had added on to it and spruced it up, and he and Junior Nagle had put together their first field from that tiny "office" off the kitchen.

"Massie, when was the last time you saw him?" The question was Brit's.

"Late last evening," Massie replied.

"Were you alone?"

"No, Nellie the nurse was with me. She wanted me to . . ."

"What?" The question apparently was difficult, the answer more so.

"She felt . . . we should allow Ty to die peacefully."

Then it was Mereth's turn. Restored, she looked back from her corner. "Massie, was Ty alone when you and Nellie left his room?"

"Yes, of course."

"And where did you go?"

"We . . . didn't go anyplace. We sat in the alcove. I'd brought up sandwiches for Nellie. And a bottle."

"Then you both were in a position to see if anybody else went into Ty's room?"

"Yes. But who would go into Ty's room? Everyone was asleep. Or gone."

Silence again as every potential clue seemed to unravel in their hands.

Massie shook her head. "I don't understand any of it, but I swear to one thing: he was not capable of walking away on his own. Someone else was involved."

Then it was Josh's turn again. "Who else was in the house last night, Massie?"

Brit answered for her, "Who wasn't in the house? There are people everywhere."

"Jobe's kids," Massie murmured.

"Did Ty know Gerald Jobe well?" Josh again.

"Oh, yes, very well. They were good friends. After all of you had gone and left him alone, there were some rough spots. He needed someone to talk to. Gerald Jobe was here, was always here."

Only when the silence persisted longer than necessary did Brit ask an intriguing question. "Massie, did Ty know he was ill?"

Massie seemed temporarily at a loss. "I don't know. I don't think so. He never said anything, but then he never complained. Perhaps he was beginning to believe his own legend, that he was indestructible. Everyone kept saying that stupid thing to him. Oh, I don't know." Massie fell silent for a moment. "We were growing apart, you know. Something was coming between us. I thought it was business. Maybe it was something else. Poor health."

"Why would you think it was business?" Josh asked.

"Because there were business problems, Josh. Enormous ones, I'm afraid. The strange thing is, he knew I knew everything and yet he refused to talk to me about it."

She broke off, which was too bad, for she had a rapt audience.

Josh persisted. "Can you tell us, I mean if it isn't confidential, the nature, in the broadest sense or the most specific, of Ty's business . . . complications?"

With difficulty, Massie tried to answer his question.

"Josh," she began, "the business problems are varied and complicated. You see, Ty, like so many other oilmen, believed that oil prices were going up to forty-five, even fifty dollars a barrel in the next few years. He bought more equipment, acquired more leases and hired more drilling crews, all at inflated prices and higher interest rates. Then the recession came, oil prices dropped along with demand. Two years ago a hurricane in the Gulf destroyed three of Ty's rigs. Two others were lost by fire in West Texas six months ago. The insurance couldn't begin to cover all the losses, and lately his crews have been hitting a lot of dry holes. Normally I would say not to worry, Ty'd been in hot water more than he's been out of it. But now—"

Clearly the thought sobered her, and she paused before speaking again.

"As you know, the Tulsa Petroleum Exchange Bank is our principal lender, has been for years."

"Harry Beekman?" Josh asked.

Massie nodded. "Bank examiners have been with Harry for three months now," she went on. "You all must understand what that means, not just in terms of their presence alone. Bank examiners investigate banks every day, but few teams stay this long and fewer still . . ." Again she broke off.

"Bankruptcies everyplace, of course," Massie went on at last, her tone strangely light considering what she'd said. "Ty said last week a man his age should be reading the obituaries to keep up with his friends, but in his case he could keep up quite well by reading a list of the weekly bankruptcies." As humor, it died a quick death and left her staring down at the desk again.

"What we fear is that Tulsa Petroleum Exchange, as the Warrick Corporation's principal lender, will demand immediate payment of in-bank loans and interest payments."

"Harry Beekman wouldn't do that to Ty," Brit protested.

Massie nodded. "Harry wouldn't, no, of course not. But it is a demand that could be forced on him by the examiners, and he would have no choice."

Mereth wondered who would have the courage to pose the next question. It was Josh, though suddenly a shy, almost reticent Josh.

"Massie, do you know how much . . . ? I mean, precisely what is the figure we're talking about?"

Massie met this most crucial question without flinching. "Harry called earlier. The immediate payment that would be demanded is approximately three hundred million dollars, and the corporation has not yet issued its full financial statement."

"Three hundred . . . !" Josh tried to repeat the figure and couldn't. Brit bowed his head.

Confronted with their shock, Massie rallied. "All of you have been around the oil industry and your grandfather long enough to understand such a figure."

"Was he in it alone?" Josh asked.

"He let in a few friends, industry independents, a few elephant hunters, but if Warrick doesn't have the resources for exploration, you know very well no one else does either."

Josh stood and began to pace in an aimless square in the center of the room.

Massie watched him for a moment and then added, "I think what Ty feared most was that the bank would exercise its right of offset."

"What in the hell is that?"

"It means the bank has the right to tap the company's deposits, even Ty's personal accounts if need be, to satisfy the indebtedness."

Josh stared at Massie, an expression of disbelief on his face. "Fuck!"

Into this tension Brit spoke, a gentle and hopeful voice, considering the black despair of the moment. "Is this all . . . speculation?"

Massie shook her head. "As of yesterday morning only speculation, although something is coming. Everyone knows that."

"Even Ty?"

"Ty more than anyone." Massie smiled. "In the last few years Ty has ventured off more and more on his own like he used to do, I assume, when he was a young man, responsible to no one, capable one way or another of covering his own debts, his own liabilities. I tried repeatedly to tell him, as the others did, that times no longer permit such private exploration. The Warrick Corporation is multifaceted, and the left hand must always know precisely what the right hand, indeed what the entire sovereign body, is doing at all times. But Ty . . ." She shrugged.

"He wouldn't listen to me, wouldn't always listen to Junior. Consequently, he committed large portions of his capital to ventures and risks without doing proper homework. Some worked out, but I'm afraid most didn't. And his indebtedness has continued to climb until . . ." She broke off, suffering a new weariness.

"Please excuse me and I'll go make myself presentable."

Mereth tried to convey reassurance and love, and started toward the door after her. She'd had enough of old nurseries and failed hopes.

"Oh no, please," Massie protested. "You stay. You three need some time alone. You've grown apart. Take a few minutes to discover those things which bind you together. I suspect that your only strength in the coming difficult days will be your unity. Without that, they'll devour you."

Then she was gone.

"Appropriate setting, wouldn't you say?" Brit smiled. "The nursery, I mean. I remember this was the place where I heard for the first time there was no Santa Claus." He laughed and looked up at the ceiling. "I think we just heard it again."

"Bastard!" Josh said, still pacing, though his circle had expanded to include Ty's desk and the wall map beyond, with its clusters of gold.

Mereth felt their disappointment. Apparently their trusts were insufficient. Obviously they both had come home hoping for Ty's death and a division of the estate.

"All right, where are these damned bonds that are supposed to bind us together, and what in the hell did Massie mean when she said it would be our only defense?" This belligerence from Josh, who apparently had tired of the map, the room, the day, the place and the circumstance.

As no one seemed willing or able to answer, Mereth held her position by the door, still planning to leave at the first reasonable opportunity. "I think what she meant was that if Ty is not found, is not declared legally dead or alive, an already bad situation will be thrown into chaos."

"Which means we might as well pack and book the next flight home. Well, what the hell! We had a good time at the Rodeo, didn't we?" Josh grinned as though to reassure them that the trip had not been a total waste.

"Where do you suppose he is?" Brit asked. "Do you think he walked away?"

"No, he did not walk away," Mereth replied quickly.

"Then what? Kidnapping?"

"Possibly."

"Who?" Josh asked.

Brit posed a more interesting question. "Why?"

Josh turned. "Why? You have to be kidding!"

"No," Brit insisted. "If what Massie says is true, if bankruptcy is an imminent fact, if his death was imminent, why would anyone want to kidnap a dying and bankrupt old man?"

"Nobody knew he might go bust," Josh said. Then his expression changed. He smiled. "Bingo! Brit, you get the box of Crackerjacks. How do we know Ty didn't stage this whole damned charade, fake the stroke with the help of old Doc Buckner and his nurses and arrange his own kidnapping?"

Now it was Brit's turn to play dense. "Why?"

"To win sympathy and stall for time, to dodge bankruptcy. Don't you see how the press will be handled? TYBURN WARRICK KIDNAPPED FROM SICKBED. Then Ty hides out while Red Pierson and Company obtains legal delays and orchestrates the media until interest rates come down or some international crisis causes oil prices to rise."

"Look," Mereth said, "I don't know any more than you two, and apparently even Massie—"

"Massie's changed." This flat statement came from Josh.

"Chris is bringing the three men in from Tulsa, and they might be able to shed some—"

"Don't you think she's changed, Mereth? Massie, I mean."

"I suppose we've all changed, Josh."

"Do you see her often? Massie, I mean."

"Not lately. When I left Warrick, I . . ."

"How long ago was it that the youngest chick finally found the nerve to abandon the nest?"

Mereth kept her hand on the door, not certain exactly what it was she heard in Josh's voice. "About six years."

"Why?"

"Why what?"

"Why did you leave?"

She let go of the door and looked back at Josh. "What is this? A star chamber?"

"No," Josh protested amiably. "It's just . . . we've both been gone for a good many years, and things do seem changed, and even when you left you managed to get only a few miles down the pike, as it were, and I was just wondering . . ."

"I know no more than you do, Josh. Geographical distance from Warrick is simple to accomplish. Emotional distance is harder."

Get out, a voice warned, before they ask the wrong questions. She started through the doorway. "I'll see if Chris has returned, and the others. Maybe they can answer your questions. I can't."

So swift was her exodus that she did not see the human obstacle standing in her path until she collided with it.

"Go easy, child," the familiar voice counseled, though curiously enough it was not the voice that brought about recognition. Rather it was the slightly spicy perfume which always seemed to saturate the air around Reverend Gerald Jobe.

"Please . . . ," she faltered and tried to pull free of the hands which held her. "I need . . ."

"God knows your needs, and at the moment they are indeed sufficient. That's why I came to fetch you, fetch all of you . . ."

She looked up through her distress. Did the man know something? "Ty . . . ?"

He shook his head. "No, still walking a secret path with God."

"I must . . ." Again she tried to pull free from his grasp.

"Come along, Mereth," Jobe urged. "You're not alone."

"No," she said.

"Why not?" he questioned softly. "A few of the young people feel the need for a prayer circle. They gain sustenance from it, and strength. A circle is a strong bond." He drew her closer beneath his arm, a gesture part paternal, part something else. "Awareness of such strength should be innate within you. Our ancestors, yours and mine, frequently used the circle in defense against the red man. There's no need to be afraid."

"I'm not afraid."

"Then join us. Massie's already downstairs. It was her suggestion that I—"

"No!" With a strength that surprised even herself, Mereth pulled away. "No, thank you, Reverend," she repeated, struggling for control over fatigue and fear, grief and worry. "I must . . . there are, you see . . . I . . ."

She surrendered to incoherence and looked about, desperate for an escape. She found it in the partly opened door to her left, which she took without thinking.

It wasn't until she had darted into the room and closed the door that she could see where she was. When she did, she commenced shaking her head in a slow, childlike denial, mouth open, not enough air, tears forming, her head pressed back against the door, her hands as well, as though once inside her fortress she now wanted more than anything to escape from the sight directly in front of her: Ty's massive, mussed bed, the various pieces of life-sustaining medical equipment pushed uselessly aside, an I.V. standard lying on the floor, the bed empty, the room empty, the suite empty, a vacuum of such enormous proportions that for a moment she felt in danger of being pulled into its center.

"Ty, please."

"Of them all, you are my best."

The collapse was simple. Her knees seemed to curl to one side, and though the inner fall was total, the shell of the woman continued to sit upright, hands curled lifelessly in her lap, her eyes fixed on the empty bed of the missing man who had stolen her life and spirit as he had stolen everything else, with flair, with dignity even, as though the act of theft were a virtue.

Turnpike

NEVER BEFORE had Chris Faxon felt such an air of disaster, as he herded the black limo back down the turnpike toward the Gilden exit and Warrick.

He lifted his head from the oppressive feeling to check on the Three Stooges lounging in various states of inebriation in the backseat. Red Pierson sat behind Chris, looking appropriately sobered, even though Chris knew better. All of them, Red, Harry Beekman and Junior Nagle, had been hitting the Chivas Regal since before noon.

In the boring stretches of the turnpike Chris found himself looking backward more than forward, allowing the powerful car to take itself home.

That wasn't Harry Beekman sprawled unconscious and exhausted in the backseat. That was the Tulsa Petroleum Exchange Bank. The institution had bankrolled every major oil exploration since the Sinclairs and before. Why had it worked, capitalism at its best, for fifty years and why was it now suddenly in danger of failure? In Chris's judgment, before the week was out the bank examiners would pronounce the death sentence on Tulsa Petroleum Exchange and the shock waves would reverberate all the way to Chase Manhattan in one direction and Bank of America in the other.

Why?

What had Harry Beekman, Jr., done that Harry Beekman, Sr., hadn't done before him? Oilmen needed funds, needed them quickly with few questions asked.

Ty Warrick. There was one major clue, though precisely how that fit with the disaster itself, Chris wasn't certain.

Gilden ahead about five miles. Keep your eyes on the road.

Ty missing.

The bastard! How long would he continue to engineer and control the entire damned scenario? Christ, he was ancient! Time to die, old man.

A Warrick pickup truck rattled past, horn blaring, summoning Chris out of his woolgathering. He didn't recognize the driver. Some hot dog. Inside the limousine, the pickup's horn sounded like little more than an angry insect.

If Tulsa Petroleum failed, after the first shock would come the foreclosures on the Warrick equipment needed for the drilling: cranes, ninety-ton tower gantries, three-hundred-ton crawlers, sucker rods, steel-bolted and welded tanks, winch trucks, flatbed trucks, oil emulsion treaters, and on and on and on, a multimillion-dollar inventory, to say nothing of the huge rigs themselves.

"Better watch or we'll end up in the ditch."

He searched the mirror for the calm speaker and saw Red Pierson directly behind him, the only one of the three alert and conscious. Chris reached back and slid the glass panel open.

"Do you want to come up?" he asked the rearview mirror and the eyes staring back at him.

"Why not?"

As Red Pierson struggled forward in the deep plush seat, Chris eased the car onto the gravel shoulder and brought it to a halt.

After all maneuvers had been accomplished, Chris looked to his right to find Red slumped in the seat beside him. He eased the limo off the shoulder and back onto the turnpike, looking ahead to the Gilden cutoff less than a mile away.

"Go the roundabout."

Puzzled, Chris asked, "I beg your . . . ?"

"The roundabout. Take the roundabout. It'll get us close enough. Better than trying to get through that mob of reporters at the gate."

"This . . . roundabout, where do I find it?"

"I thought you said you knew Warrick."

"The parts that matter."

"All of Warrick matters. Turn right."

"Where?"

"There." With one solitary jab of his right hand, Red indicated what appeared to be no more than a cattle trail, two grassy tracks.

"This car won't . . ."

"Turn!"

This command came so forcefully that Chris obeyed, braked and tried to ease the low-slung car over the washboard culvert and felt the undercarriage scrape and at last bounce forward onto the grassy track itself.

"Follow it," Red instructed.

"I hope this improves," Chris muttered.

"It doesn't."

"How did you know about . . ."

"Anyone who knows Warrick knows the roundabout."

With this last, Chris felt an attempt had been made to put him in his place. So be it. If this washboard enabled them to avoid the crush at the front gate, then he'd follow it.

"Did Mr. Warrick use it often?" he asked, struggling to keep the heavy car aligned within the ruts.

"Whenever it suited him."

Chris bent low for a more comprehensive view out of the front windshield. The grassy tracks seemed to encircle one of the few plateaus of Warrick. They were heading west, and he could not see the end of the trail and could not even begin to guess at what point they would emerge.

"You know what's happening, don't you?"

Chris glanced over as he heard this question, unable to determine its meaning.

"The bank, the Tulsa Petroleum Exchange could be going under. You know what that means?"

Chris kept quiet.

"Everyone thinks Ty has the golden solution in his pocket."

Carelessly, Chris struck a deep hole squarely on and heard the undercarriage scrape and remembered then that in the melodrama of spiriting the drunken president out of his bank, he'd withheld the latest incredible news from Warrick, that Tyburn Warrick had disappeared. At that moment it was as though Mereth's message had just penetrated his own consciousness.

"For Christ's sake, follow the ruts!" Red shouted. "They're all you've got!"

Chris jerked the limo back into the tracks. Perhaps he'd misunderstood. Maybe Mereth had meant something else. Missing? Or dead? How missing?

Unable to solve the puzzle, Chris decided that now might be a good time to share it. "Mr. Pierson, that phone call back in Harry Beekman's office was from—"

"Do you know what this road was used for?"

Interrupted, Chris took the coward's way out. He'd share the bewildering message later. "No, I don't know."

"When they were building Warrick, the heavy machinery found it easier to come this way."

Chris looked to his left and saw that they had completely encircled the small plateau.

"You might do well to remember that you don't know everything about Warrick," Red said quietly. "No one does. Ty went to great pains to see to that. He kept us all carefully compartmentalized, denying anyone the privilege and advantage of an overall picture." Red smiled. "I wouldn't be surprised if he doesn't, at this moment, know precisely what's happening."

There was a steep incline which Chris thought he could take head-on. But he saw that such an approach was out of the question, and angled the limo to the left in an attempt to try a more gradual approach. At the same time he gunned the motor for the difficult ascent and heard the rear bumper scrape on the incline and heard a loud groan coming from the backseat, someone objecting to the rough passage.

As he tried to determine who had groaned, he heard Red Pierson's sharp command, "Keep going! Keep going! Lose speed and you're lost . . ."

So he did, with little choice, and for a few moments the front half of the car angled straight upward as though it were trying to become airborne, and Chris found himself staring at the April sky, unblemished except for a thin trail of gray smoke which snaked lazily upward an indistinguishable distance away.

"Easy and down," Red ordered, sitting on the edge of his seat in defiance of gravity, grasping the dash for balance.

In a delayed reaction, Chris thought, Smoke? Again he peered through the front windshield in search of that solitary finger of smoke he'd seen curling.

"What are you looking for?" Red Pierson exploded.

"Nothing. I just thought I saw . . ."

"Well, keep your eyes on the road. I don't think either one of us is up to hauling those two out of here on foot from this distance."

Beginning to grow weary of the tiresome little lawyer who fancied himself a cut above the rest, Chris nodded. "Yes, sir."

Chris drove silently down the old graveled track, keeping an eye on the thick stand of native trees on the right from which he'd detected the smoke.

"Ty *was* decent, no matter what anyone says," Red muttered now, in a disjointed eulogy. "To everyone, even the full-bloods. He fought like a tiger in 1915, when all the big boys started labeling the Indians as mentally defective. Ask Deeter. He can tell you about Ty Warrick."

No need to ask Deeter anything. Chris had grown up on Deeter's legends of Ty Warrick.

"Did you ever hear about the time that Ty met with the Osage under the big elm in Pawhuska?"

Chris stared straight ahead.

"Oh, other companies were there, but the full-bloods had come only because Ty Warrick called them. It was morning, the old men with their rainbow-hued blankets and buckskin leggings and beaded moccasins, their iron-gray hair hanging in long braids over their shoulders. And the squaws, you know the squaws were seldom seen in public and were fully blanketed, like the Arabs." The man's voice now came in an uninterrupted stream of recall.

"It was a high-stakes game for Osage oil, the last well coming in at five thousand barrels a day, which quickly had increased to nine thousand barrels a day, which quickly had increased to nine thousand four hundred. Just Oklahoma's biggest gusher. The lease was to be auctioned off that morning. How much would the gusher be worth on the block?

"When the sale ended, Warrick Oil had bought the greatest number of west-side leases and an additional seven hundred thousand dollars was in the Osage treasury. Included in the lease purchases that day was a large parcel of unexplored and undeveloped land known thereafter as the Warrick Basin."

Chris gripped the wheel and tried to seek out the invisible holes before they did too much damage to the limo. In the distance he looked for the red-tiled roof of Warrick and couldn't find it and wondered briefly what precise state of disintegration he would find when he arrived, and toyed with the idea of not going in at all, but rather depositing the three old men at the house, retrieving his Jeep and returning to the castle.

But he couldn't do that. Not yet. There was far too much unfinished business. For one, someone in this car must be told. Now.

He waited a polite moment for the tale of the past to settle back into Pierson's memory. Then—

"Mr. Pierson, I think you should know."

"What?"

"That was Mereth Warrick who phoned Harry Beekman's office."

"And?"

Chris drew a deep breath. "Tyburn Warrick is missing."

For a moment there was no sound except for the limo scraping over rough passage.

"I—don't understand," Red managed.

Chris shrugged. "That's all she said."

"Ty—is—" Red tried to repeat the word and couldn't.

A few seconds later, Chris glanced in that direction and saw the man still looking at him, on his face a fixed expression of speechless bewilderment.

Warrick

MASSIE SAT in the prayer circle in the terrace room and tried to concentrate on Reverend Jobe's words, and felt the uncomfortable pull of crossed arms, the two young people on either side grasping her hands in a death grip of sweat and zeal. Despite the overwhelming spiritualism surrounding her, she felt herself thinking, with closed eyes, not of God and His divine power but rather of the first time Ty had made love to her.

". . . and forgive us all our sins, O Lord, and make it possible for this grand house once again to know the peace and serenity of Thy holy spirit . . ."

She'd been doing the books, the job for which she'd been hired. Mrs. Warrick had been dead about six months.

"You busy?"

"No, Ty— Well, yes . . ."

". . . fill us, we pray Thee, with Thy light and life. Help us in our penance that we may show forth Thy wondrous glory . . ."

"Massie."

"Yes, Ty, I'm here."

". . . grant that Thy love may so fill our lives that we count nothing too small to do for Thee, nothing too much to give and nothing too hard to bear . . ."

"Miss Jo Massie, how did you get so smart?"

"I'm not all that smart, Ty."

And she remembered it as clearly as though it had happened yesterday, how she'd folded the upper right-hand corner of the account book she'd been working on as he'd touched her face.

"Will you come with me?"

And she had gone with him, to his rooms, had waited, less than patiently, as he'd unbuttoned her blouse. And as his lips had closed around her nipple, she remembered looking down and seeing his thick white wavy hair in contrast against her flesh, and thinking how beautiful, the contrast. And she remembered his strength as he'd carried her to the bed, remembered how, without warning, that strength had turned into vulnerable gentleness, such loving thoughtful gestures: the way he'd arranged the pillow beneath her head, the whisper of thanks for her comfort, her company, her sweet presence, how he had looked down on her as though she were invaluable and irreplaceable. No man had ever looked at her in that manner before, and she remembered how he had eased himself between her legs, how he had—

". . . so teach us, Lord, to serve Thee as Thou desirest to be served, to give and not to count the cost, to fight and not to heed the wounds, to toil and not to seek for rest, to labor and not to seek for any reward save that of knowing we do Thy will."

"Amen!"

The chorus came from all around, and only then did she realize the prayer was over.

"Ty . . ."

Gone, the memory gone.

"Miss Massie, would you like to sit down? You look . . ." Reverend Jobe grasped her elbow and led her out from the quietly milling young people.

"Here, sit. You'll feel better," Jobe commanded.

"I'm . . . fine," she murmured and shook her head and looked out over the gardens.

Two figures caught her attention in the late afternoon sun, Brit perched on the railing of the gazebo, Josh visible over the soles of his shoes, which were propped up on the railing.

"We must talk, you know, Massie," Reverend Jobe whispered. "We can't go on like this. Authorities must be notified. And soon."

"Not yet," she protested.

"But Ty's absence must be reported. A kidnapping . . ."

"We've heard from no one. No ransom demand. I don't think it was that."

"Then what? We can't just pretend as if nothing had . . ."

Again she moved her head, though this time she said nothing. Ty had disappeared. That was the given. The bed upstairs had once contained a dying man. Now it was empty. Why must anything be done? How palatable death would be if the body just disappeared.

Massie looked back down to the gazebo, where the boys were talking. They'd had so little use for each other as children. It was nice to see them sitting as adults in Ty's gazebo—

—chatting as though nothing but years had come between them.

"Red Pierson and the others are on their way out," Massie said with unexpected sternness. "When they get here, then we'll decide."

"Whatever you say." In this submissive phrase there was a thunderous accusation that ricocheted about the quiet terrace room.

She disliked the feeling that she had made the wrong decision. "Then what do you suggest?"

"First," he began, "I think we must call the police."

"No."

"Why not? What else can we do under the circumstances?"

Suddenly she stood, unable to face either his questions or the image of the Highway Patrol swarming all over Warrick. There had to be another way.

Would she be intruding on Josh and Brit if she went down there? They looked so attractive, like a muted nineteenth-century watercolor, two pampered young men in white shirt-sleeves, in a white Victorian gazebo.

Reverend Jobe touched her arm. "Let me call a friend in Tulsa, a discreet friend. I promise he'll know what to do."

"No."

"You have no choice."

"Reverend Jobe, you are . . ."

She'd started to say "overstepping your bounds," something pompous and silly. Instead, as she viewed the man up close, she saw an expression that briefly disarmed her, the angles and features scarcely resembling a man, more like one of those gruesome carica-tures of Hogarth's, an artist who had seen humanity too clearly and painted it accordingly.

The sense of suffocation came slowly at first, with the need for a good deep breath. "Excuse me, Reverend. I have things to do."

It was a polite exit considering the circumstances. She expected him to call her back, and he did.

"Massie."

But no power on earth was strong enough to draw her back into isolation with that man.

The doors were before her now, and beyond the doors she felt the first cooling balm of the April evening on her face and knew instantly she'd made the right decision. Wait for Red, Junior and Harry, men who'd known Ty forever.

Brit and Josh and the gazebo, that was her destination. She hoped she wouldn't be intruding. If she sensed that she was, she'd leave. With Ty gone—

"Why do I love you so, Miss Massie?"

"Why do I love you so, Mr. Warrick?"

Had he been the wisest choice she'd ever made in her life? Or the gravest mistake?

It was a foolish question, always had been, making it sound as if she'd had a choice.

The damned graveled roundabout road had stopped short of Warrick by at least a mile and a half.

Now as Chris traipsed through the woods, he tried to use as his beacon the glimmer of sun on the red roof. Good sense had dictated that Red Pierson stay behind with the others. Harry Beekman had never fully revived, and Chris suspected that human will had as much to do with it as Chivas Regal. The man knew his bank was probably headed for collapse, knew the full consequences better than anyone.

Chris stopped to get his bearings and his breath, and found himself making plans. Return to Warrick, find Eddie O'Keefe and Brit, better still, Josh with his surprising strength. Get help, then get the old men back to civilization where they can sleep it off and—

Listen!

He froze, head down. The silence was suspect, filled with nature's sounds, those that belonged here. Crickets, birds, a crow someplace, the natural hum of uninhabited places.

And something else.

Slowly he lifted his head, his eyes moving rapidly across the monotonous sun-dappled tableau, lingering now and then on a tree trunk that seemed theatrically shaped to mimic the human form.

What he'd heard had been only a slight sound, a footstep perhaps, the crack of a rotten limb. He stood still a moment longer, then glanced behind. Red Pierson might have followed. But the tableau behind resembled the one in front, monochromatic and unmoving except for shifting shadows.

There it was again! Something out there. Something moving with stealth. He dropped down, thinking, wild animal? But no self-respecting coyote or bobcat would come this close to the mansion. Then what?

He stood for a moment longer, listening for the mysterious noise. Then he started off again.

Keep moving.

And he did, though he continued to look and listen for unseen faces and unspoken words.

Mereth rallied from her brief collapse in Ty's empty bedroom, succumbing to the need to get out of the room, out of the second floor, out of Warrick itself. Hazardous in all ways. Filled with family and friends and ill-wishers.

Jobe.

The man was a fraud. What he said sounded stale and hollow, like a tale told by someone who knows it only by hearsay and can't quite believe it himself.

Run away!

If she stayed in this room, she'd give in to the desperate need for a confessor, someone to whom she might speak, or perhaps only hint that there were things about her which no one knew.

Run.

And she did, peering cautiously out of Ty's empty room. Where was everyone? Down the steps, doors straight ahead. It was as though she were alone in the house.

Grandmother always put the Christmas tree there, and Ty directed the whole undertaking perched mid-step, about here, where she was standing, his boots muddy from his daily trek into the oil fields, his rugged, handsome face made ruddy by cold biting December wind, and always an open bottle of bourbon tucked in his pocket which he'd nip at from time to time, all the while shouting instructions.

"Get up here, Mereth. I need your advice."

And the child, no more than seven, running, pleased, up to the man and slipping between his legs, feeling those powerful arms go around her like a vise, holding her fast—his face scratched her cheek—a unique cocoon of such magnitude that it had rendered all other shelters in her life incidental.

Once past the unexpected obstacle of Christmas memories, Mereth reached out for the doors and drew them open to find the covered porch and driveway beyond also blessedly empty. Where was everyone? Why had she been left alone in this place?

Run away!

The command sounded the alarm bells inside her head.

Not east. She couldn't go in that direction, not toward the gate crowded with reporters.

"Come on, Mereth, let me tell you about the gambling spirit and the language of oil."

Then west, toward the woods.

Slowly she backed away from the concealed brick wall. Above her was a flagstone terrace which went portico fashion around the west wing of the house.

At the end of the terrace she took three steps down, ran across the lawn and saw the woods drawing nearer. She reached out for a nearby tree for support and debated the wisdom of the woods.

Then where could she go? How was it possible to feel trapped on over a hundred thousand acres of land? She took one tentative step into the woods and proceeded on until, looking back, she could see only a limited area of red-tiled roof.

Ahead about ten feet, she saw a fallen log. It looked reliable and, as she sat, something small rustled in the fallen leaves at her feet. Patiently she waited out the rustling of a lesser thing fearful of her presence.

Slowly she leaned forward and supported her forehead in both hands.

In the shelter of her hands she closed her eyes and skillfully re-created memories: the smell of rain, the sound of the storm, dim light, the fine purple iris at the centers of his eyes.

She couldn't catch her breath, coming faster, something happening, a crescendo of enormous proportions, something right, something shared, something wrong—

She laced her hands across the back of her neck and pressed her forehead into her knees. Suddenly there were tears, though they were silent and none seemed to spring from remorse.

Dr. Horace Buckner did what he'd done for the last seventy-five years when faced with a crisis too great to solve: he took a nap. The end result might not be a solution to the crisis, but at least it made one feel better in the midst of failure.

Now, just waking up in the mussed bed, he heard rude knocking at his door on the third floor of Warrick and reached blindly for his glasses, as though sight was a necessary requirement for speaking.

Specs in place, he called out angrily "Who?" and raised up on one elbow.

"Now who do you think? It's me, Nellie. I need to speak with you. Now."

"Hold your horses!" Buckner yelled back, cursing the day he'd ever sent for Nellie. Once he'd hoped she'd serve as bodyguard. Bullshit! She'd served as exactly nothing.

All the way to the bathroom he tried to clear his head of sleep and, as he did, the various problems came crashing down. He stared at the toilet water turning yellow and thought of Ty.

Where in the *hell* was he? Had Massie even ordered a search of Warrick?

A few moments later he turned on the hot water faucet and breathed in the steam and amused himself with visions of Junior Nagle in Dallas, addressing the board.

"Gentlemen, I must tell you, a funny thing happened out at Warrick last week . . ."

The joke died in the vigorous scrubbing of his hands, as though he were thirty again, a promising young surgeon.

What in the hell had happened to that promising young doctor? The answer was near.

Ty Warrick had happened, that's what.

Another knock and the harridan voice.

"Dr. Buckner? There's very little time . . ."

"I said I was coming," he shouted at the reflection of the door in the bathroom mirror, and at the same time he held his hands beneath the water and washed away the clinging soap, along with all regrets.

"Miss Nellie," he said, smiling with false warmth as he drew open the door to confront the immense woman on the other side.

"I must speak with you, Dr. Buckner."

"I gathered as much. Has anything—"

"No. That's why I'm here. Kent and I have been talking."

"Where's the family?"

"Unless Mr. Warrick's . . . disappearance is reported immediately—"

"Where are the others? Massie?"

". . . that is, we feel we will be held responsible . . ."

"Nonsense!"

"But he was in our charge."

"Have you seen Massie?"

"Dr. Buckner, we want you to assure us, in writing, that—"

"Goddamn it, you have my reassurance!"

The double-tracked conversation finally got the best of him. "Come on, Nellie," Buckner ordered and dragged her across the threshold.

Funny, it had never occurred to him to question Nellie or Kent before. In looking back, they all had acted as if Ty had simply risen from his deathbed and gotten into that old beat-up Jeep and gone for a turn through the fields—a quaint euphemism which meant an eagle-eyed inspection of all his drilling wells.

"Nellie, tell me, if you will," Buckner began patiently, "exactly what happened this morning. When was the last time you saw Mr. Warrick, and what—"

"I didn't see him at all this morning, Dr. Buckner. Kent had the night duty. She said she stepped out of the room about 6, 7 A.M., said she was gone about twenty minutes and when she returned . . ." The woman lowered her head, her face a map of confusion.

"Will you absolve me of all responsibility, Dr. Buckner?"

"Of course," he muttered.

"Will you put it in writing?"

"Nellie, have you lost your senses? What do you mean, will I put it in writing?"

"Just what I said," she replied, meeting his anger.

340

He was on the verge of blowing again when coming from some deep personal reservoir of memory he heard Ty's voice.

"To hell with funerals, Bucky. Has man ever conceived of a more barbaric ritual? You know what a funeral is, don't you? It's a religious ceremony designed for garbage disposal."

"Dr. Buckner, are you all right?"

The concern came from Nellie.

"Why, y-yes," he stammered. "Must find Massie."

"They're in the garden," Nellie said, "the lot of them, as though nothing has happened."

For the first time he heard condemnation. Poor Nellie. She didn't understand the Warricks. Not many people did.

"Don't worry, Nellie. No one will have your ass for this, I promise. Tell Kent the same."

"We must do something. We can't just . . ."

"I know. I'm headed that way now." He passed through the door.

"Remember, Bucky. No funeral."

"Don't talk like that, Ty."

"Hell," he had said, pointing, *"there are my memorials."*

The memorials were his oil fields, row after row of black derricks, the pumps like squat fanciful animals kissing the earth in perfect rhythm.

He looked over his shoulder, suddenly self-conscious. Nellie stood in the open doorway watching him. She was right on all counts: something had to be done. Massie had to notify the authorities.

Oh, Christ!

The projection was almost overpowering, the sirens, the hordes of reporters storming the gates, the endless phone calls, all the various investigative agencies turned loose on Warrick.

Damn you, Ty! Couldn't do anything simple, could you, not even die?

The repressed anger propelled him forward down the long corridor, and he was puzzled by the deep and surrounding silence.

The fact that she was sitting still, curled over on herself in the shadow, caused Chris to pass her by. Then it wasn't a visible awareness of another human presence that drew him back, but rather the sense of a heart beating, and an instinct for silent grief.

"Mereth?"

Her hands moved in two quick motions about her eyes, her back straightened, and he saw engines of self-control gathering heads of steam, all defense mechanisms taut and in place.

"We seem to meet in the strangest places."

She looked about as though seeing the woods for the first time, a convenient movement that enabled her to turn her back on him, thus completing the repairs to her face and eyes. When she looked back, she was almost restored.

"What are you doing here?" she asked.

He put a foot on the end of the log and felt the rotted wood crack. "I'm on a rescue mission." He pointed in the direction of the abandoned limo. "About a mile and a half from here you'll find Ty's personal lawyer, Ty's closest business associate and Ty's personal banker."

She glanced in that direction. "What are . . . ?"

"Drunk," Chris broke in, "at least two of them. Harry Beekman passed out before we got out of the bank. Junior, I think, is just dozing and Red is fairly alert, though even he—"

"Why?" she demanded, suddenly annoyed. "Massie's waiting for them. Couldn't you—?"

"No, I couldn't," he said gently to her accusations.

He hesitated, not knowing how much he should tell her. Not that it mattered. She'd know everything soon enough.

"Tulsa Petroleum Exchange is in trouble," he said bluntly. He'd expected a moderately shocked reaction. Instead, she walked a few feet into the woods.

"Chris . . . he's still missing." She turned back. "He was dying. Buckner said so. A dying man can't . . ."

342

Either she hadn't heard or hadn't fully understood his announcement concerning Tulsa Petroleum. No matter. In time she would hear and understand. For now it was plain that the source of her despair was here.

"I have to get back," she said in a sudden reversal of mood. "What are you . . . ?"

"We ran out of road," he explained. "Tell Eddie I need help. Beekman can't even stand up, and Junior isn't much better. I was hoping that Eddie, maybe Josh, Brit . . ."

He waited for her response. When none was forthcoming he asked, "What happened?"

"I don't know," she murmured. "Kent left the room for only a moment."

"When?"

"Sometime this morning."

"Who was in the house?"

"Everyone was in the house, I suppose."

"We weren't. We must have still been at the castle."

"Why—"

"It's important to determine who was in the house," he said. "Ty was dying, not just according to Buckner, but others had made that judgment as well. Therefore, if we assume he didn't get up and walk out by himself, we must then assume that someone . . ."

"But who?" she persisted. "And why?"

They were stymied by both questions.

"Chris, how well did you know Ty?"

"Not as a bona fide member of the inner circle. I knew him from a distance. As Deeter's grandson, I won a nod from him now and then."

"Were you ever alone with him?"

"Once," he confessed, beginning to suspect that her questions might be leading in a specific direction.

"When?"

"A few years ago."

"For what purpose? What did he say to you?"

343

Deeter had always called Mereth the smart one, more like Ty than both the boys put together.

"Nothing important. Nothing that I can remember," he lied.

"Did he ever discuss business with you?"

Chris looked up. "Business? Not really. As I recall, he was interested in the international scene, and as I had just come from London . . . Why are you asking me these things?"

That seemed to catch her off guard.

"I suppose we'd better get Eddie to give you a hand. Why didn't you just—?" She broke off in mid-sentence, as though she'd provided herself with an answer.

"Go in the front gate?" They'd both taken refuge in a question that could be safely answered.

"Never mind," she said. After a moment she drew a deep breath and suggested, "Let's go get the Marx Brothers out of the woods and back to a pot of strong coffee. Surely between the three of them they'll know what to do."

For a moment they stared at each other in the shadows. They made their way to the edge of the woods and the dying sunlight. As they started across the grass the silence was shattered by a young and very insistent shouting voice. "Miss Warrick! Miss Warrick! It's important. Phone . . ."

Both looked up and saw a boy's face, appearing decapitated from the angle at which he peered out of the high second-floor corridor window, one of Jobe's kids.

"Miss Warrick, telephone! Something about your grandfather. Hurry!"

Mereth started off at a dead run.

"Wait!" Chris called.

But she didn't, and he ran after her.

If Ty Warrick had been found, where had he been found, and was he still alive?

Running after Mereth, he knew that he'd worked too hard and come too far to have anything happen now, and he suspected that

Ty Warrick's granddaughter was not as helpless or as uninformed as she appeared to be.

"The waves of an ancient sea had lapped the edges of the uplift, and a giant sandbar formed along the beach. At least that's what Ty always claimed and, Jesus Christ, who am I to doubt him?"

Junior Nagle tried to stretch in the backseat of the limo and bumped into the still unconscious Harry Beekman in one direction and the black padded door in the other. He released the door handle and angled his cramped legs toward freedom.

Still wobbly, he grasped the top of the door, aware of Red waiting on the other side of the limo for him to complete his geological description of the Warrick Basin.

"Where in the hell are we?" Junior muttered.

"The roundabout," Pierson said. "Thought it best with all the reporters at the gate and Sleeping Beauty back there."

"Poor bastard!" Junior muttered.

"Go on," Red urged. "You were telling me about the basin."

"Who got us this far?"

"Chris, Deeter's grandkid. Do you have any other geological confirmation?"

Junior gaped at the stupid question and wondered when Red Pierson had gotten so dumb. "What in the hell are you talking about? Since when does Ty Warrick need further geological confirmation? The basin is his. He didn't even let me in on it, which was okay. I've got enough gravy."

In the falling dusk Junior thought Red looked like a mole, a balding, red-faced, squinty-eyed mole. His eyes were too close together.

It was getting dark fast. If they were going to be stuck here for a while, they'd need light. "Red, punch open that glove compartment. See if there's a flashlight."

Red pushed a button and the glove compartment fell open.

Whoa," he muttered. "What's this?" Carefully he withdrew a snub-nosed blue-black revolver.

Junior dismissed it. "Standard equipment for a Warrick limo. On Ty's orders. You never know. I'm afraid we need a flashlight more. Anything?"

Red returned the gun and closed the compartment.

Annoyance mounting, Junior snapped, "Where in the hell did Chris go? Why did he just leave . . . ?"

"He went for help. We can't haul Beekman back by ourselves. Go on. You were saying something about a sandbar."

He stabbed at his shirttail and ventured away from the support of the car. "Then gradually the sea covered the bar, and when it subsided millions of years later, the bar became a thick layer of porous sandstone tilted against the uplift, a trap for a lot of oil which had been forming from marine life."

He grinned down with pride at the rough stubble underbrush at his feet. Ty's basin, the gem in a long career that rivaled Hunt and Getty, though he might leave both those boys behind to eat his dust when the Warrick Basin exploration commenced.

"Where in the hell did Deeter's grandkid go?" he asked of the balding head and squinty eyes which watched him over the top of the limo.

"I said to get help. We can't haul Harry . . ."

"What in Christ's name is wrong with him?" Junior grumbled, peering in the back window at Harry Beekman.

"Drunk."

"He didn't drink that much. No more than we—"

"If I were Harry Beekman, I wouldn't want to sober up either."

"Well, how in the hell long are we supposed to wait?"

"Until he gets back."

"What's that?" Junior pointed north to the smoke curling upward into the evening sky.

Red dismissed that which he couldn't explain with a gesture.

"Junior, you might as well know," Red began. "We've got trouble back at Warrick."

"Don't you think I know that?" Junior snapped.

"Now listen," Red commanded. "While we were in Harry's office the girl telephoned, Mereth, and said that Ty is missing."

Junior blinked down on the man. "Ty is missing . . . what?"

"He's . . . missing. Missing from Warrick."

"You've got a screw loose. He's in bed."

"He *was* in bed. He's gone now. He's no longer there. Flown the coop. Gone!"

This last word was a bellow of anger and frustration.

Junior blinked. At last he'd understood. "Who called?"

"I told you. Mereth."

"When?"

"I told you!" Red's anger was rising again. "At the bank. Chris took the message, then got us out the back way."

"Smart kid."

"What are we going to do?"

"Let's go."

Junior was out of the car when Red called, "What about Harry?"

"Harry's handling this better than any of us, with the possible exception of Ty himself."

At the thought of the name, he saw Ty as he'd last seen him, eyes closed, a blue tinge on his lips.

Abruptly Junior stopped, needing reconfirmation of Red's astonishing news. "Pierson, are you . . . sure?"

"That's what Mereth said."

"Come on, then."

By Junior's estimate they were only a couple of miles from Warrick. Keep looking left for a beacon of light.

Ty missing. Ty missing.

Junior found himself repeating those two words over and over again like a litany until they formed a rhythm of their own and he could match his stride to it, could feel a strength he had not felt for years.

"Hello? Hello?"

Mereth grasped the receiver as though to hold the male voice which was fast fading, either through static or a broken connection or both.

According to the young boy, who'd met her at the top of the steps and accompanied her in a run down the corridor, "The phone rang. Someone for you, about your grandfather."

"Did you recognize the voice?"

He shook his head.

"Hello?" She grasped the receiver, thinking she'd heard something on the other end. For some reason she thought: long distance. "Who is it?"

She looked up at Chris's voice. "No one. Just static."

She held out the receiver for him to listen. He placed his ear close to the telephone and questioned the boy.

"What did they say?"

"Said I was to get Mereth Warrick, that it was about her grandfather and that's all he said, and I went running." The boy left the room.

Mereth heard nothing but the damned static.

"You might as well hang up," Chris said.

For some reason his insistence that she give up annoyed her.

"Someone called," Chris said, "and lost his nerve."

"Why?"

"Kidnapping's a serious charge."

Beyond Chris, Mereth saw the bed, still mussed, I.V. standards hanging unused on both sides, the oxygen setup on the left near the pillow. Suddenly she shivered.

"Put the receiver down, Mereth."

She looked away from the empty bed, still resentful of his propensity to give orders.

"Have you sent Eddie and the others back to the car yet?"

"No. I came up here after you."

"Hadn't you better find them? From what you say, one of them might be in need of help."

He backed away. Apparently he sensed her resentment. "Look, I'm sorry." He smiled. Then he left the room.

Mereth listened to the muffled tread of his steps down the hall until she could hear it no longer, could hear nothing but the muted static coming from the telephone.

"Hello? Hello?" She spoke twice into the receiver and, at last giving into that anger which she'd successfully held at bay for so long, slammed the receiver down and leaned heavily over Ty's ancient and scarred desk.

"You stay away from that, little girl."

"Stay away from what? Just some old mussed papers."

"Look close. See that map? What do you see?"

Mereth stared down at the desk as though in search of the ghost voices. Instead she saw the clutter, the unanswered letters stuffed into a green plastic letter-holder, several brown manila folders stacked crookedly atop one another, a tin can stripped of its label, holding ballpoint pens. She suspected that none of them worked. Behind the tin can she saw a brown glass ashtray, chipped and old, the glass bowl filled with an assortment of arrowheads picked up from Warrick land over the years.

Now, feeling more at home in the past, she pulled out the straight-backed chair and sat and reached for the arrowheads and examined three in the palm of her hand. Small game heads, rabbits, belonging either to the Poncas or the Osages.

"It was Indian land first."

"The hell! What did you Indians ever do for it?"

"We left it alone."

"Deeter's a crazy blood. You know that, Mereth?"

Fondling the arrowheads, Mereth listened to the voices. What a marvelous love affair the two old men had with each other, a relationship based on the perpetuation of total misunderstanding. Each took endless delight in pretending not to understand the other, a devoted war that had raged all their lives, since their fathers' inconclusive battle over who owned what portion of Warrick.

Deeter. Safe in Tulsa, thank God.

Beginning to relax, she opened the drawer directly beneath the desk's surface. It was a treasure trove of a mess. Obviously no one had been permitted in this inner sanctum for the purpose of tidying. Among the old green ledgers, crumpled newspaper clippings and empty stamp books, she found a neat stack of half a dozen brown loose-leaf notebooks.

Carefully she eased the top notebook free of the others and held it in her hands. On page 2 she discovered Ty's slanted handwriting, a spidery script which at first made as much sense as a foreign language. But as she deciphered the words, their meanings became clear.

These notebooks were private diaries, this one dated 1936–37 and entitled "The Ranch." She took the five others out of the heavy rubber band, wondering if there was any sort of sequence.

Apparently there wasn't. The earliest was dated 1930, the latest 1982. Quite a span. But if they had been written at random, were they to be read at random? Why was the notebook bearing 1982 in the center of the stack? Nineteen thirty-six to nineteen thirty-seven had been on top.

After a short time she put together the meaning of the notebooks. If the bound leather volumes in the library were the accounts of the completed empire, these childishly scrawled diaries were rough-hewn accounts of how to create an empire.

A knock at the door. Mereth felt like a trespasser, or worse.

"Who is it?" she called out, trying to gather the books together again.

"It's Josh."

The simple announcement brought her a degree of relief. Josh, more than anyone, would understand mildly unethical behavior.

"Come in," she said, continuing to restore the notebooks. One of the pages had fallen out. It was a map, yellowed, with notations in Ty's hand.

"Better be careful, sitting in that chair. He didn't like any of us near his desk."

"I'm doing more than just sitting," she said, smiling. "I'm snooping."

"Well, if the old bastard's alive and within hearing distance, that should bring him roaring back."

She was in the process of sliding the books into the top drawer when Josh appeared on her left.

"Gutsy bitch, aren't you?" He grinned down at her. "My palms are sweating just standing here."

She closed the drawer quietly. "You still afraid of Ty?"

He shrugged. "No more than I'm afraid of cancer, terrorism and thermonuclear war."

"I think he's dead."

"Don't count on it. I mean, who's going to want him? Even Lucifer has to maintain certain standards."

Mereth looked over her shoulder, startled to see Josh stretched out across Ty's mussed bed, hands laced behind his back, staring up at the ceiling.

"Speaking of gutsy," she said.

"Beds are always holy places to women," Josh said. He turned on his side, facing her. "What were you doing up here?"

"There was a phone call from somebody about Ty."

"Who said?"

"One of Jobe's kids."

"Who was it?"

"No one."

"Suspect as hell, if you ask me. Mereth." Josh looked at her for a moment. "The son of a bitch spent it all, didn't he? Or lost it?"

She remembered his dream to produce the special script he'd found.

"I'm not certain. He may have overextended a bit."

"Christ, how do you 'overextend' hundreds of millions of dollars?"

Suddenly Josh sat up. "I'm ready to go home. I miss Peter. Crap, but this is a godforsaken place! How in the hell do you stand it, Mereth?"

351

"I don't. I don't live here, remember?"

She recognized his rage. "Don't go back to California yet, Josh, please," she asked, starting away from the bed. From the door she looked back. "Where are the others?"

"Roll call time," he said and left Ty's bed. "Brit has gone on the rescue mission with Chris. Massie is with Jobe. Those pubescents are running amuck, polishing everything that stands still. And poor old Ramona and her kitchen crew are trying to get everyone herded toward the terrace room. Would you believe it? They tell us it's time to eat again. What is this *eating* fetish?"

Mereth watched him as he muttered his way down the hall.

From the far end of the corridor she heard a distant, good-natured shout.

". . . and don't worry, Mereth. I wouldn't think of leaving, not until I find out what has happened to the old bastard. Best goddamned drama I've seen in ages."

She waved at the diminished Josh and hoped there was no one in the downstairs hall to hear his words. She wanted to go down those same steps in a minute and out the front door, and she didn't want to pick up company along the way. While Chris was running his rescue mission, she had an errand of her own, to locate the one person who might have an idea.

Mereth waited until Josh disappeared. Then she hurried down the corridor, took the steps two at a time and was out the front door.

She saw her car parked about a hundred feet away. The keys were in the ignition where she'd left them.

With a great sense of having escaped, she guided the car in a slow turn, her mind racing ahead to the second hurdle, the front gate and the reporters. Maybe some had grown hungry and fled to the Dairy Queen in Gilden for a quick hamburger. Whatever. The security guards would clear the way for her.

In the final approach to the gate she saw that the crowd had increased. The guard waved her through, and she noticed several of the reporters in the path of her car, either refusing to move or thinking that she would stop. When she didn't, they jumped to one side, one scarcely clearing her fender, and glared at her as though trying to see if she was newsworthy or not.

Obviously she wasn't, for no one gave chase and within a few minutes she was driving silently across Warrick, following the beam of her own headlights to the first section line. She tried to relax behind the wheel and clear her mind of the madhouse.

Deeter. Maybe he had returned from Tulsa.

Again she tried consciously to relax, took a deep breath. The window was down and the night air was cool.

"Ty?"

No ghost voice this time. She spoke his name aloud as though he were capable of response, as though he were riding in the car with her.

A short time later, still following her headlights, she angled the car to the right and circumvented the black wrought-iron gate and took her chances on the bumpy terrain of open country before swerving back to the graveled road which led to Deeter's castle.

As the ruts of the road required more of her attention, she gripped the wheel and thought how bizarre it would be if she found Deeter and Ty at the castle, sitting cozily in Deeter's little cinder-block bunker within the castle's facade, beside the old pot-bellied stove, both men drunk and happy and reliving the past.

"Go get him, Mereth. He's over at Deeter's castle."

"Come on, Ty. Massie says, 'Enough.' "

"Tell Massie to go to hell."

She pulled the car over and turned off the ignition.

"The greatest single element in all prospecting is the man willing to take a chance."

She could hear Ty, and for one eerie moment as she walked slowly toward the castle she could smell him, that unique blend of pipe tobacco, scotch and his own essence, indescribable, not altogether unpleasant, a faint smell of new oil as though it ran in his veins.

Approaching the door, she called, "Deeter, it's Mereth. Are you . . . ?"

She let the torn screen door shut softly behind her. The front room was its usual blend of chaos: a lumpy sofa which served as Deeter's bed, an off-white, soiled pillow which still bore the large central indentation of a head, while a Navajo blanket lay pushed back, revealing equally lumpy sofa cushions, as though someone had just risen.

Near the kitchen she saw a large pile of old canvas, cut for some reason, the pieces pushed aside, revealing jagged edges as though someone had grown weary of the slow path of the knife or shears and had simply grasped the two sides and ripped them. Someone had been here recently.

Nearer to the kitchen she smelled something. Through the doorway she saw a small bucket filled with thick black creosote. The surface of a flat spatula bridging the top was covered with the black and shiny substance. For several moments she peered down at the mess and tried to make sense out of it.

Then she saw other things which compounded the mystery: the refrigerator door ajar, several beer cans scattered across the counter, a box of Cheez-its fallen on its side, a half-eaten sandwich on the floor in front of the sink and—most mysterious of all—a sound she could neither locate nor identify. A low buzzing, like an alarm clock running down, or a timer, or—

A telephone with the receiver off the hook, the frantic beep-beep of a distant computer as it tried to signal the resident.

She replaced the receiver and saw the scattered peelings of an orange, a half-eaten Twinkie oozing marshmallow filling. She touched it. It was soft and fresh, as though someone had just put it down atop that old map.

She moved around the table, her head turned at an angle in an attempt to see the map. Old, that much was clear. Red marks on the expanses between section lines, but one wide square with two scrawled words beneath it: FIRST CAMP.

A real antique. She leaned closer and saw another designation to the right of the large section line, a triangle with a bizarre notation, crudely penciled like the others: DEETER AND TY.

She frowned down at the map and at last fought the frustration by moving the food to one side, lifting the map and spreading it out on the floor in front of the door. She felt the edges tear under the velocity of a slight movement. Printed in faded script on the bottom right-hand corner were the words INDIAN TERRITORY.

Pre-1907, then, the date of statehood. It *was* an antique.

Primitive designations indicated certain natural landmarks on Warrick, such as the twin wavy lines in the lower left-hand corner. That would be the little stream that ran only during a rainy spring. And there, that childlike rendering of many trees would be the only sizable stand of timber on all of Warrick, the one due west of the house.

She looked closer. The red triangle was situated in those trees, along with the words DEETER AND TY.

Slowly she sat back on her heels.

What did it mean, that triangle? It was the only one on the entire map. Nothing else even remotely resembled it. To the left or east, spread out over a large area, it said OSAGE COUNTRY, but no triangles, no designations of settlements.

Only this one triangle.

She tried to imagine the woods, amazed that it was the second time the shadowy place came to mind, one that she'd not thought of since childhood. The limo, Harry Beekman, Red Pierson and Junior Nagle were all waiting there for rescue. Maybe Chris, with Eddie's help, had escorted them to safety by now.

Then what was she doing here? She should be helping Chris rescue those three old men. They had to advise Massie on what to do. No one else was qualified.

Then get on with it. In the event all the available manpower couldn't escort the drunken party on foot back through the woods, her car might be helpful. She could pick up the roundabout this side of the toll booth and follow it to the dead end a couple of miles from the house. She assumed he'd wanted to avoid the reporters at the front gate. Now they might have to return that way.

Thus resolved, she refolded the map along its old weak lines, thus weakening it further, and took it with her. She paused for one more look at the interior of the cinder-block apartment.

Triangle—Deeter and Ty.

"Harry's drunk, passed out. The other two aren't faring much better, need help."

"The greatest single element in all life is the individual willing to take a chance."

Mereth turned her back on Deeter's chaos and stepped out into the night and noticed she'd left her headlights burning. Perhaps her battery had been drained and she would not have to take the car to the deserted roundabout in search of three drunken old men.

But it proved a vain hope, for at the first twist of the key the motor turned over and purred.

For several minutes she stared transfixed into the beam of her headlights. The storm of the past continued to push against her and was capable of drawing everything living into itself. The only escape seemed to come by pressing forward.

This she did by heading slowly away from Deeter's castle, into the black night, to the beginning of the roundabout, where ideally she would find nothing more alarming than snakes and a heavily rutted road and three old men who had noplace to go and who belonged to no one now.

———

Harry Beekman really wasn't drunk. He'd merely suffered a glimpse, without illusion, of everyone around him, and they all had seemed safely ensconced in a self-evident world order in which the words "incompetence" and "failure" did not occur at all. The only major flaw on that world's horizon was Harry Beekman.

Thus his defense was to feign sleep, and he continued to hold this painful position, the side of his face pressed against the seat cover, his spine twisted into a pretzel shape by the weight of his own body.

Still he heard everything, as he'd heard everything since they'd left Tulsa.

Oh, he'd put away quite a bit of Chivas, but he was far from drunk. The last time he'd really been drunk had been with Ty a few weeks ago, when they'd been led to believe that the Warrick Corporation's principal creditors would work together for an indefinite period to try to help the company restructure its debt, thus making it possible for Tulsa Pet to stay afloat. They had really tied one on that night, so drunk that Massie had assigned Eddie O'Keefe to "watch them" and to keep them out of everything with four wheels.

Despite his cramped position and his acute pained awareness of himself, Harry smiled.

"Hell, we've had problems before, haven't we, Harry?"

"You bet, Ty."

"And survived to bury all the other bastards."

Inadvertently he made a sound and now froze for fear Red and Junior would look back from their front seat conversation. What were they talking about so earnestly? His bank, what else?

So it was going to collapse and take Tyburn Warrick with it. And there wasn't a thing he could do about it except thank God that Ty had had his stroke and pray for some similar good misfortune of his own.

Josie might have made a difference. She was always telling him to have more faith in himself, in God's mercy and in His guidance.

"We get lost, Harry, only when we wander too far afield from the hand of our Lord."

Then Harry had wandered very far afield. Not that the caliber of his faith had ever matched Josie's. Harry played at church, feigned it often, appeared in the role of "prominent citizen," little more. It was Josie's heart and soul and blood.

"Oh Josie, I need you so much."

Over the tumult of his thoughts, he heard the front car doors slam. He held his feigned drunken-sleep position, trying to determine where the voices had gone and wondering why he couldn't see anything clearly. Belatedly he realized that someone had removed his glasses.

Slowly, aching, he tried to ease himself up and felt the side of his face pressed against something wet and cool, and realized that in his semiconscious state he'd been drooling.

"Your boy Harry doesn't have it, Mr. Beekman. It's that simple."

"Hell, Harry, everybody's old man was a bastard. I guess you showed him, didn't you?"

What was the matter with his head? The voices were there, inside. *"All right, Mr. Beekman, I believe I can assure you and Mr. Warrick that the upstream banks will see to it that you secure a substantial new loan. But you must swear to abide by the new restructuring."*

"Can't you see, Harry? They've got their fucking eyes on the Warrick Basin. They think there might be something in it."

"I know, Ty, I know. But what can I do?"

No answer.

Against the devastating silence, Harry tried again to lift himself from the damp seat and this time succeeded and looked carefully around for any telltale shadow and listened for any voice that didn't belong there.

But he was alone, had been left alone, and he knew why. The rest of the world would know tomorrow. But at least he could be spared that.

Curious how earnest a human soul can truly be, and Harry felt his soul to be in earnest.

But not yet. Though at the precise moment he postponed it, he was totally convinced of its inevitability, here in this place, Fate having thoughtfully provided both the means—his eyes moved to the black leather glove compartment—and the privacy for such an act, which more than any other human act, including copulation, demanded privacy.

He sat for a moment in a childish position, his arms resting atop the back of the front seat, chin resting on his arms, legs spread.

The roundabout, that's where they were. End of the road. All those aggregate stones and bricks that now formed Mary Beth's gardens had been hand-hauled by cart from this point in.

What was that Red had said? Ty gone? Then thank God he was dead.

Abruptly Harry lifted his head in need of air. He had to go to the bathroom. All the booze had at last drained into his bladder, and the pressure was building.

Once out of the car he didn't bother to find a place of concealment in the surrounding woods. He simply unzipped his fly. Not until he felt moisture running down his leg did he realize he'd not been paying any attention and had wet himself.

No matter. It didn't matter. Nothing mattered.

He returned to the car, opened the front door on the passenger side and sat sideways in the front seat.

Headlines tomorrow.

Failed. Failed bank. Failed man. Failed—

He grasped his head as though to contain the litany, but it couldn't be contained. He'd had such a different ending in mind: successful, loved, a long, long funeral cortege.

No, this was the proper end, the right one, sitting alone in Tyburn Warrick's abandoned limousine at the end of an abandoned road, abandoned and failed.

"Tell us, Mr. Beekman. Did you know personally of the lack of collateral, that your officers were, in essence, giving away large amounts of money?"

"Of course I knew it. How else do you think we're going to put oil in your speedboat or fly your wife and kids to Disney World?"

He stared down at the damp earth at his feet, momentarily distracted from his anguish.

"Come on, Harry. Faith. We still have the basin."

The basin had become for Ty like the promise of Heaven. The fact that he needed vast amounts of money to develop it seemed not to matter to him.

"God looks after old oilmen, Harry. Reverend Jobe says . . ."

Harry sat up straight and looked at the night and saw nothing but shadows and wondered with good clinical objectivity what would he truly miss in this life, in this world?

Well, good scotch and good beef and those gauzy, smoke-smelling November mornings, quail hunting with Ty. And what else? Ty gone— Josie gone—

Baffled, he looked up at the night sky.

Then move on, Harry. If you hurry, you can still catch up with Ty and find Josie.

He was talking out loud, keeping himself company as he pressed open the black leather glove compartment.

Slowly, with the respect it demanded, Harry withdrew the gun, closed the glove compartment and checked the revolving gun barrel and found it fully loaded, as he knew it would be.

A little scary, the moment was. Why couldn't Fate have been as kind to him as it had been to Ty? One exploding blood vessel in the brain, one clot creeping up in a major cardiac artery, one good, hard, malignant growth on a vital organ, how would it have hurt Fate?

But all those things had been denied him, and he had found himself out of step with Divine timing and unable and unwilling to see what Destiny would do.

He angled the gun until he was staring down the barrel, one black, round eye which stared impassively back at him.

"Josie, I tried. I really did—"

Slowly he cocked the gun, drew back the hammer. A nice piece of equipment. For Tyburn Warrick, only the best.

Christ, make it stop! Enough cowardice, enough lies. One honest act. One sincere confession, though who would understand?

Earlier there had been an impulse to weep like a woman. Now nothing, and though his hand shook as he lifted the gun, he lifted it anyway, placed the barrel inside his mouth and closed his lips around it as though he were sucking it, asked for forgiveness from all those he had offended and tried to forgive all those who had offended him, prayed for courage here, at least at the end, and wished only that he didn't have to leave his garbage lying about for others to clean up.

Perhaps he—

———————

Brit heard the single sharp report, like a distant gun. He'd heard similar sounds recently at Notting Hill, with tragic results. Somewhere close by—had life ceased?

But when neither Chris nor Eddie commented on it, Brit decided perhaps he'd heard something else and tried to remain upright as he stumbled through the woods, listening to the good-natured argument between Chris and Eddie concerning the difference between a torch and a flashlight.

"I don't know why," Chris said. "That's just what the English call them. Right, Brit?"

Brit nodded and listened to the echo of the report that no one else had heard. He thought of Sophie in London and missed her, and wondered if the child had survived the fever. What was he doing here? He was needed there.

"You coming, Brit?" The inquiry came from Chris, who aimed the flashlight back into Brit's face.

"Right here," Brit nodded, squinting. "Did you hear that? Sounded like . . ."

"A Warrick pickup." Eddie nodded. "One of the old vintage. Mr. Warrick lets the roughnecks take them into town at night. Nobody maintains them. The boys just drive them into the ground. Get three or four of them on a road at once and it sounds like the Fourth of July."

"Listen!"

Brit heard it as well, a disturbance coming through the foliage, stumbling, though nothing was yet visible.

"Who is it?" Chris called out.

"Goddamned son of a bitch! Can't see . . ."

Eddie grinned. "That's Junior Nagle. I'd know his 'goddamns' anywhere." He reached back for the flashlight in Chris's hand, and

Brit saw its light pick up the pair. Junior Nagle was in the lead and Red Pierson followed, both looking the worse for wear. One missing. Hadn't Chris mentioned a trio? Harry Beekman.

After a brief discussion, Eddie was to lead the two old men back to Warrick while Chris and Brit went on into the woods in search of Harry. Now, as Eddie herded his little troop back past Brit, the flashlight caught bizarre angles of their faces, distorting their features.

Brit watched the ragtag caravan and the bouncing eye of light and realized that Chris had relinquished the flashlight. But in the next few moments he discovered that peculiar illumination that can often be found in total blackness and discovered as well that he saw more clearly the farther the light moved away from where he stood.

Sophie.

Suddenly, standing alone in the midst of this wilderness, he missed his life in England with an ache akin to physical pain. Somehow in the chaos around him, he'd reached a decision. He couldn't wait here any longer. He would make it a point to talk with Red Pierson in the morning, would be more than willing to sign over a portion or all of his inheritance in exchange for ready cash.

For now he needed to return to London with as much workable cash as he could raise. He might even suggest to Sophie that they buy a place outside of London where the kids would have trees and flowers, breathing room.

"You home to stay, Brit?" The question came from Chris, who apparently had not an inkling how far off the mark his question was.

Brit laughed. "No," he said and moved so far ahead of Chris that the shadows appeared to devour him. Then—

"There it is!"

All questions were momentarily tabled and Brit hurried toward the black limousine that sat alone, spectral and silent at the dead end of the roundabout.

Twice Mereth lost the road altogether and found herself bouncing the car across rough open country.

Even back in the ruts she had to maintain a fierce grip on the wheel, and she wondered belatedly if this was the right thing to do. Her instincts answered yes, otherwise how could Chris and the others transport those three old men back to Warrick?

A few years ago Junior Nagle might have made his way through these woods. But as for Red Pierson and Harry Beekman, their idea of an outing was a trip via Lear jet to Ty's deer lodge in West Texas.

Ty.

As she drove, the single syllable intersected her thoughts. Damn him! Why was he doing this to all of them?

Ahead she saw the thick stand of timber drawing nearer like a solid rim around the edge of the world. If she remembered correctly, the roundabout veered south just this side of the trees, followed alongside them for a while, then moved into their center as though taking refuge from the wide Warrick prairies.

The timber was drawing nearer, though again all semblance of a road disappeared and she saw only the brown, stubbly, prairie grass in her headlights, interspersed here and there with fast-growing spring rye, even a few wayward shoots of wheat.

"We've had some good times, haven't we, Mereth?"

"Massie's waiting."

"Damn Massie."

The voices wouldn't leave her alone. As the inner tempo mounted, she felt a dull throbbing in her left temple. She saw straight ahead a discernible turn in the ruts, south to the left, the timber straight ahead.

Turn here. And she did.

"Damn!" She cursed aloud as she heard the undercarriage scrape against the rough terrain. She should have gone back to Warrick for a Jeep.

"At the very moment you are convinced beyond any doubt you must turn back, push on."

"The entire American oil industry is but the lengthening shadow of the independent oilman, like Tyburn Warrick, whose form and substance are stamped indelibly over its entire structure."

A tribute. From someone. On some occasion. Mereth couldn't remember.

"The greatest single element in oil prospecting is the man willing to take a chance."

The road here was better, rough gravel. She was heading due south, now traveling parallel with the woods. For the first time in too long, she relaxed her grip on the wheel and wondered how far ahead she'd find the abandoned limo with Ty's three old friends, drunk and equally abandoned.

She smiled at the image and remembered younger days, raucous poker games, Massie constantly railing against the awful mix of oil and sand that stuck to their boots after a day in the fields. She could see the four of them, the men who'd created an empire out of daring and random chance. Ty said once, in one of his bursts of oratory, *"No glamour in oil and Indians and Oklahoma, just a burgeoning dream capable of destroying a man or lifting him up to a seat with the gods."*

She caught a glimpse of her face in the rearview mirror and wondered how much further and what she would find when she got there. Possibly Chris and Eddie and Brit had already arrived.

She looked to her right, thinking she'd seen something in the unbroken blackness, a glow, like a small fire off the road.

She wondered if she'd misunderstood Chris concerning the location of the limo. She'd thought he'd said at the end of the roundabout, which should be straight ahead. But perhaps the old men had built a small fire for warmth while they waited.

She stopped and eased the car into neutral and pulled on the hand brake and pushed back against the seat, the better to see around the obstruction of the windshield post. Better yet, get out.

She was on the verge of doing this, her hand on the door, when a stray wisp of better judgment intervened.

Hitchhikers, maybe. No. Too far off the turnpike.

Hunters? Nothing much to shoot here except rabbits and possum and skunk.

Then what? And who? Go find out. At last she crawled out of the car, reached back and switched off the lights. Good thing she'd remembered. Hers was the rescue vehicle. Wouldn't do to have a dead battery.

But in the instant the lights went out, she looked up into a world gone wholly black, no accommodating haze or glow from any part of the night horizon, as though time and place had fallen away at the exact moment she'd extinguished the car lights. She was left only with a touch of steel beneath her hand as she groped her way around the hood, waiting, thinking that at any moment she would be blessed with night vision, at least to the extent that she could proceed.

Slowly she started forward and found the distant glow of the fire again.

How far? Why was it so difficult to tell? It was as if the dimension of the fire itself altered.

Keep moving toward it. Keep your eyes on it and if it disappears from your vision, find it again before proceeding.

Mereth walked at a steady pace, still keeping her eye on the small orange-red glow erupting like a primal eye an indeterminate distance ahead.

No more thoughts, no memories, no dread of the past. She was alone in this place, without light or sense of distance or direction, heading toward something she could not see or identify. The moment was everything.

The fire was coming closer. She could smell it, as though the wind had shifted. And beyond the fire she saw a strange structure.

Poles of some sort. High poles. Four. Supporting something, a platform.

One red triangle crudely drawn but recognizable on Deeter's ancient map. A guide to—

From this angle she saw something else: a humped, square shape seated upon the ground, head bowed, if it had a head, perhaps not a human form, cutoff tree trunk, something thick.

Now the distance was discernible. Something was becoming clear, something not of this time or this world.

She stopped momentarily, seeking cover behind the last protection of trees before entering the clearing, which appeared larger than she had judged from the roundabout.

Stripped of trees on some ancient date, only the low-growing foliage had grown back. Here and there a reed-thin sapling clung to the earth and might, a hundred years from now, match the older specimens such as the ones behind which she was hiding. As for the rest, it resembled an old campground, the arena cleared for a special purpose, although she had yet to get a clear look at the humped figure seated just the other side of the fire close to the four poles and platform as though keeping watch on something.

As she entered the clearing, less than twenty feet from the fire, she thought she recognized that humped, square-block figure with the torn plaid shirt seated cross-legged upon the ground.

"Deeter?"

She spoke the name softly, not wanting to startle the old man out of his sleep, not certain what he was doing here, or why his phone had been off the hook, or why—

"Deeter, it's Mereth."

Any moment now the old man would turn and scold her for "creeping up."

"His hearing is gone. Sad for anyone. Tragic for an Indian."

"Hell, Massie, Deeter's about as Indian as I am."

"Deeter, are you . . . ?"

When there was no response from the seated figure, she moved around the fire.

"The stupid old blood can sleep anyplace. Once he fell asleep atop his horse."

But now her attention was not focused on the unmoving old blood, but rather on the four poles, the poles topped by a sort of platform of stretched and taut canvas. And resting on that canvas—

"That ain't Ty Warrick in that bed. Don't know who it is, but it ain't Ty."

The ghostly voices continued to create a patchwork of the past in her head, not Ty's voice this time, but Deeter's, only a few days ago.

She knew now what she'd stumbled upon: the ancient campground of two small boys who had "hid out" while their fathers had beaten each other senseless over a rich and stolen land.

Slowly she closed her eyes to rest them from the swirling, stinging smoke. Sooner or later she'd have to see what it was wrapped in that heavy canvas, resting on the platform, suspended at the top of the four poles.

"Blood ways are the best, Ty, honest, you know."

Where was the stepladder? It had to be here. Again she turned, almost feverishly. Raising the poles would have been hard enough. Deeter could not have lifted him up by himself.

"Where did you hide it?" she asked, accusing him out loud, not caring whether she awakened him or not. Probably he wasn't asleep at all, probably just drunk. Yes, she could smell it, like all the bars in the world.

"Massie, he's drinking himself right into his own Happy Hunting Ground."

"He's alone, Ty."

"He's not alone. He has me. He's always had me."

"Deeter, where is it? I need it. Where did you . . . ?"

As she spoke aloud to the old Indian, she saw it propped up against the front of the Jeep. Stepladder, small, no more than half a dozen steps. But half a dozen would suffice. Now, having found it, she'd stared at it as though accusing it of something, as though it were the culprit that had forced her to this point, this place. She reached for the small ladder and carried it past the man and the fire, which for some reason seemed to be blazing brighter, as though when she hadn't been looking Deeter had thrown on another log. The extra illumination served her well. Three more steps—impossible for Deeter, drunk, to make this climb carrying—

"The purpose of the burial ground is to place the wrapped body high above the reach of prairie predators: wolves, coyotes. Also the Great Mysteries will be sure to see a departing spirit placed so conspicuously to attract His attention."

Top of the stepladder now, her hands hurt, eye level with the tightly wrapped body, which reminded her of a mummy.

"Everything connects, Mereth. If you just look hard enough and are clever enough to see, everything connects."

One hand, trembling from the duress of the climb and the moment, ventured halfway toward the upper portion of the wrapped body, then stopped as though better judgment had intervened.

Confirm the image and do it quickly, and deal with questions later, when Deeter is sober and can recite his own tale.

Accordingly her fingers fumbled with the crudely knotted ropes drawn tight around the neck and, with mixed feelings, she felt the knots give easily under her insistence. They might have been kind and resisted.

She felt the binding rope grow slack and, beneath it, the canvas. Reaching across, she found the flap and *knew.*

"What is 'dead,' Ty?"

"Don't bother your little head about that, Mereth. You're a long way from worry about that."

She saw the far side of his face first and was appalled by its whiteness, like an effigy expertly carved in heavily veined marble.

Had he been dead before Deeter took him from his bed, or had he died later? And if so, what were those implications?

"Crazy blood . . . murderer!"

The voice screamed inside her head, though there was no visible manifestation except the persistent burning caused by the smoke which the wind lifted and blew into her eyes.

His hair clung to the white-marble face, eyes closed and sunk in black hollows, mouth open slightly as though in protest.

"Ty."

She spoke his name as though, by the mere speaking of it, she could awaken him and free him from this peculiar bondage, even though she knew that he had already been freed.

Somewhere in the tightly wrapped cocoon was his hand. She wanted to touch it, to hold it.

"Against blood code, to unwrap a body."

"Deeter, he wasn't a blood, damn you! Why did you . . . ?"

She continued to address the slumped Indian seated upon the ground, as though at any moment her voice would penetrate his drunken stupor. But it didn't and she grew weary of her precarious perch atop the stepladder, whose legs creaked from time to time and sank deeper into the unreliable earth.

Besides, there was nothing to stay for. With the recognition of this body wrapped in this tight canvas, she felt all the life force engines grow still within her, the important fuels of love and hate gone, nothing to stoke, herself as much a dead body as the one before her, though less fortunate in that she still had to perform the pretense of life.

Over. How simple. One minute the object of concern and the next—

She reached out one hand to the flattened, still damp hair. There was nothing very complicated about it. In all her life, including pre-life and afterlife, she had loved, would love only one man. There would be rote motions and deep affections and fierce loyalties and treasured friendships, but as for love in the purest sense of the word, there had been and would be only one, and for this lifetime at least he was gone, well ahead of her, though she'd catch up, for they always more or less kept pace.

She felt as if everything vital to rationality had been loosened. She realized that she'd probably slipped civilly, unobtrusively into a harmless state of insanity. But who was here to tell.

Slowly now, because she perceived her head to be heavy and injured, she lowered it to rest on the wrapped body.

She lost track of time. There was no system of measurement sufficient to the occasion. Twice she shifted her awkward position atop the stepladder, never out of fear of falling. There were no additional depths to which she could fall.

"Do you want to see the big elm that we used as a marker for the exact center of Warrick?"

As it turned out, she had been climbing the elm for years, unaware. Not far from the old ranch house, it was. She'd perched in its heavy upper branches on hot May days and watched the big oil transports rumbling in and out of Warrick and, from their massive size and from the frequency of their visits, she'd begun at an early age to perceive the importance of being a Warrick, the importance of this land.

Tired. She turned her head, pushing lightly against the wrapped body.

"Look for the anticlines, Mereth. That's all you need to know."

It was over. For now, one bizarre conclusion had to be reported to the others and to the world. It would be interesting to watch them deal with it, each in his own way. Poor Massie.

"Deeter, come on! Time to . . ."

Carefully she made her way back down the stepladder, the small of her back aching from bending over Ty's body. Once on the ground, she looked back up at the macabre sight. Nothing orthodox for Ty Warrick, not even his death.

"Deeter, I need your help. We must . . ."

She approached the man as gently as possible, still not wanting to startle him.

She pushed against his shoulder once, twice, and on the third time the old man, without muttering a word of protest or apology, toppled lightly to one side, like one of those roly-poly children's toys with weighted bottoms. As he fell, his body seemed to unfold, one arm swinging wide, landing dangerously close to the fire, which was burning well and casting a sufficient glow on the old face she'd grown up with.

"Ty, can I ride over to Deeter's castle? I'll be right back."

"Tell him to come for dinner tonight, Mereth. He never eats right."

The once rugged and strong face was dead.

"The two little boys ran off and hid and played while their fathers tried to kill one another."

"Deeter?"

Denying what she knew was true, she called to him, protesting not so much the death of Deeter Big Cow—

"I'm part Christian, part heathen, and I've never been able to figure out which part is which."

—protesting only the epidemic of death, protesting as well the effortless passage from this world to a better one of these two ancient friends, protesting most of all her own terrible sense of having been abandoned by both.

"Deeter, damn you . . . !"

And she nudged him again and again, striking him openly once upon the shoulder as she used to do in play as a little girl, though she noticed the impassive old eyes were open, the expression on his face one of utter pride.

He'd accomplished what perhaps was the greatest feat of his life, his death, perfectly timed, without a taint of cowardice or suicide, walking with his old friend out of this circus of a world and into a better one.

She thought she heard laughter and halted in her assault on the dead man and knew where the laughter was coming from and where she'd heard it before. It was coming from the ghosts inside her head, and she'd heard it countless times as a child growing up in Warrick, generally coming from the game room where Ty and Deeter did their most serious drinking, the two men free to be as raunchy, as obscene, as irreverent, as drunk as—

"Damn you both!" she cried aloud in an attempt to cancel the sound of their laughter.

"Let me kiss them good-night, Massie. Ty and Deeter."

"No, you don't belong in there. Go right to bed."

She sat back heavily and glared angrily across Deeter's sprawled body. "You bastard!" she cursed, then tears rushed, provoked by her abandonment and loss.

"You know what my daddy, the old Osage chief, said once?"

"What, Deeter?"

"He promised us that the white man would never come to this land."

Mereth looked back and forth between the two dead men, hearing their voices in death more clearly than in life, and her own loneliness increasing with every second.

She wept, and went forward on all fours and looked up from this curiously primitive position at the underside of the taut-stretched canvas platform and saw the weight of Ty's wrapped body in perfect outline. Not wasted, as robust as ever.

She stood and lifted one hand and touched the back of the still muscular leg.

Her hand brushed across his back. Let this hollow shell go. The man himself had long ago escaped and now occupied her fully, like a marauding army, and would continue to do so until the day of her death.

All that remained was to inform the world of this ancient campsite and the two young boys who used to escape here and play together and who, once again, had escaped and gone off to play.

Not once did she look back as she left the clearing.

"What are you up to now, Mereth?"

"She's female, Ty, and not to be trusted."

"You're both bastards!"

She spoke aloud to the night and moved steadily though with new and indescribable weariness toward her car. A few minutes later she slid behind the wheel and leaned slowly forward, resting her head against it, her left hand caught beneath the press of her body and pushing against the horn, which cut through the night in a feverish and passionate alarm.

"Mr. Beekman?"

Chris called out to the man, having spotted the glitter of chrome. He paused about ten feet from the limo, waiting for Brit to catch up. "I can't seem to rouse our . . ."

But Brit walked past him and continued in a straight line toward the limo, peering in the window and then standing back, as though he'd collided with an invisible barrier.

"Brit, what . . . ?"

"Wait."

But Chris didn't wait and, as he approached the limo, Brit reached in on the driver's side and an instant later the overhead light illuminated the interior of the car.

Long before Chris was ready for it, he saw everything: saw Harry Beekman sprawled across the front seat, his relaxed position not unlike the sleeping pose he'd assumed coming out from Tulsa. Yet there were differences.

Chris saw too the black revolver resting on the driver's seat, dropped there as Beekman had fallen, saw a large and slowly growing stain on the cushion, saw in the dim light Beekman's ruined face, the upper half gone, blood and tissue and bone splattered everyplace.

"I heard the shot," Brit said simply.

For several moments Chris stared down at the violence, unable at first to comprehend the act itself. He'd contemplated it a couple of times. Who hadn't? Melancholia, melodramatic lapses in good judgment and, on occasion, terminal boredom.

"Are you all right?" The gentle inquiry came from Brit.

Chris stepped back, trying to clear his mind. "I don't suppose we have to spend a lot of time on why he did it."

"No."

"We'd better . . ." Chris broke off, not certain what it was they'd better do. He thought he heard something. "Do you . . . ?"

Brit looked over his shoulder. "Sounds like a horn."

It was faint, far away. The shifting night breeze seemed to affect it.

"All right," Chris said with dispatch, as though the diversion had provided them both with the momentum to make certain decisions. "I don't think we should disturb anything."

"No."

"Which means one of us will have to go back to the house and call the authorities."

"Massie won't . . . ."

"Massie will have to," Chris cut in, sharper than he might have wished. "So who stays and who goes?"

"I'll go," Brit volunteered.

"Call the police first. Tell them what's happened, and you might meet them down on the road where the roundabout begins."

"I'm off," Brit said. "Will you be all right?"

Chris nodded. "Just veer left as you go back," he added. "You should see the lights of the house not too far."

Brit looked back toward the car containing the dead man. "He gave all of us gold piggy banks for Christmas years ago. Told us it was never too early to learn the rules of prudent living."

Then the short memory was exhausted, delivered without inflection, and Brit was gone, leaving Chris alone with only the echo of his passage, and ultimately that too faded. Even the night breeze had gone silent.

The air was chilly and growing more so. While there was always the backseat of the limo, Chris rejected it and began to walk.

Not too far. Just keep moving to stay warm. Surely Brit wouldn't linger.

He ran in place for several minutes until he was breathing hard and felt warmer. It would take Brit at least twenty minutes, maybe longer, to get back to Warrick and another ten to make his way to the phone room in the first-floor hallway. Then how long for the Tulsa authorities to organize and get a move on? Impossible to say. Thirty minutes to an hour was his conservative guess.

So he was looking at approximately one dead hour, probably longer. The bleak perception settled heavily around him, and he looked back at the car and for the first time wished that Beekman had not blown off the top of his head. They might have held an interesting conversation, here on the back road of Ty Warrick's empire. But as it was—

Listen.

He heard again that peculiar distant horn, still so faint as to be scarcely discernible. Coming from that direction, north, the direction of the turnpike. A hapless motorist, no doubt, waiting for help.

What the hell? He might as well take a walk.

One hour, probably more. Better than standing around here. Harry Beekman would stay put.

The gravel crunched beneath his boots as he walked away from the car, more than willing to leave death behind. Something suggested that he enjoy the calm while he could.

"A gold piggy bank and our first lesson in prudent living."

Chris smiled at the irony of Brit's recall. The Warricks could be accused of many things, but prudent living was not one of them.

Mereth. Maybe she'd learned the lesson best of all.

The sound of the stuck horn was growing louder or else the breeze had shifted, carrying the sound with it.

Mereth knew what she was doing, knew she was sounding an alarm that quite possibly no one would hear, could hear.

No matter. For some reason, the persistent hysteria of the horn comforted her.

She turned her head, which was not a good move, for now she could see the clearing about fifty yards away and recall how mysterious it had been from this distance when she'd first happened upon it.

Now she knew precisely what those four poles supported.

"Not dead yet. Stroke, you know."

In echoing memory she heard Massie's voice a lost number of days ago, taut with grief. Though Mereth remembered the morning, she found now she had trouble remembering the world.

She had an apartment someplace. Where? A job. What?

"It's part of the magic of Warrick that in its beauty and luxury one tends to forget the rest of the world."

An effusive newspaper piece done several years ago. Ty had

hated it and thereafter had closed the doors to all "nosey-assed reporters."

"They've never seen a world like Warrick, Ty."

"Let 'em go make their own goddamned world."

Still staring sideways at the clearing, she closed her eyes and wondered how long the fire would burn, how long the horn would sound, how long the news would go unreported, the grief unexpressed, the anger—

"Mereth?"

The voice, despite the blare of the horn, sounded real, though how could it be real? She was here with two dead men.

"Mereth, are you . . . ?"

The light touch on her shoulder was real, and she jumped with a spastic suddenness, wondering for a moment which dead man had come back for her.

As she pushed away from the wheel, her body released the horn and the siren deserted the night air and plunged the limited world into an eerie silence that somehow seemed to thicken, so that even when she recognized Chris Faxon, she could not at first speak.

"Are you all right?"

She tried to see his face, see if he knew what the clearing around the fire contained.

"What are you doing?" he asked.

"I came to help."

"Why did you stop here?"

"I went to Deeter's and . . ."

"Was he there?"

Their sentences spilled out on top of each other, and she felt a tremendous need for movement. She pushed hurriedly out of the driver's seat, past Chris.

"Why did you stop here?"

She moved a short distance away and might have gone farther except his question caught her off guard. She decided to let him discover the text of the night for himself and was about to direct him toward the dying fire when he spoke bluntly.

"Harry Beekman is dead."

She looked up.

"Suicide," he went on. "Red and Junior left him asleep, or so they thought." He paused and for the first time looked around at the surrounding woods. "What's that?" he asked, his voice still strained from his announcement.

Harry Beekman dead.

"Mereth, why did you start a fire?" Slowly he walked away from the car, his eyes seemingly fixed on the light.

She considered warning him before he reached the grisly scene, feeling sorry for him, for the discoveries he would make in a few seconds. Abruptly she lost track of him through night and the thickness of trees and, despite her own reluctance to reenter the clearing, she started after him. She'd taken no more than half a dozen steps when she heard his first fearful call.

"Mereth!"

She saw Chris halfway up the stepladder, one hand grasping the top half of the canvas shroud. She heard only his silent shock and walked a few steps closer, pointing down at the shadow which lay curled in on itself near the fire.

He spoke his grandfather's name, and Mereth hoped only that he would come to the same quick acceptance, if not understanding, that she had reached. It wasn't wholly satisfactory, the simultaneous death of the two old friends, but perhaps—

"Deeter!"

This call had none of the hesitancy and quiet shock of the first. This was angry and accusatory.

"Mereth, did you . . . ?"

She nodded, and wished he'd leave her out of it. If he had a quarrel, it was with the old Indian.

"Mereth!"

"I saw."

Then she heard his grief. "You damn fool! You crazy son-of-a-bitch Indian, why did you do it? You had no right. No right! No right!"

377

There was something besides grief in Chris's voice, a rage that made him sound demented, and she saw him kicking the dead man, each kick punctuating what he was saying, an angry diatribe assailing everything from the old Indian's intelligence to his integrity.

Stunned, Mereth watched until she could watch no longer. Not that the assault was serious. The blows were scarcely disturbing the body. But the greater damage was being done to Chris, who appeared to be on the verge of losing complete control, all the while relieving himself of a lifetime of hurt and confusion and love.

"What did you think you were going to accomplish?" he shouted down at the dead man. "I told you it wouldn't be long. Do you remember me telling you that? We talked. Did you forget that?" For a second the despair in his voice seemed to settle heavily around him, rendering him inarticulate.

"You waited this long, why couldn't you . . . ?" Chris broke off and started away from the monologue with a dead man. Then something drew him back.

"You didn't *have* to do this, you bastard!" he shouted again. "You really didn't. This wasn't the time for your goddamned Indian theatrics. You give me a pain, that's what you do. You always have. My father's right, you know that? He said you were certifiably insane, and you are. Not just colorful or eccentric. Insane!"

Mereth watched him grow inarticulate with fresh outrage as he turned away from the body.

"Deeter, why?" he begged. He looked up toward the four poles and the rigid canvas cradle and the wrapped body. In the distorted shadows, she saw him close his eyes and what she heard next was part cry, part wail, part animal, part human, delivering fresh and potent anger while one visibly trembling arm pointed toward the poles.

"You crazy bastard, that isn't even Osage! Did you know that? Poncas bury their dead that way, not Osage. You don't even know who you are or what you came from! You know nothing! You contribute nothing! You accomplish nothing! You . . . !" The rage in the voice broke, as did the voice itself.

She watched from a safe shadow near the edge of the clearing and felt his grief more acutely than her own and saw his slow collapse, the physical and spiritual depletion of energy, until finally he dropped to his knees, close to Deeter, and for several moments seemed content simply to kneel there, head bowed.

She didn't think he would weep for the dead man.

But he did.

From her bed Massie set most of the elaborate machinery into motion, and by noon the next day she sat up against propped pillows and double-checked her list in the small, green leather notebook.

Bustling quietly on her left, gathering up the luncheon tray, was Ramona. "You didn't eat a thing, Massie," the woman scolded. "You know the next few days aren't going to be a picnic."

Massie nodded and smoothed the tassel of her bathrobe cord around her finger, aligning each small silk strand.

At least it was over now, for Ty, for Deeter. While she had no precise image of the next world, whatever, wherever it was, it would be a more interesting and colorful place with the arrival of those two. In a way she envied them their eternal companionship. She had already told Ty good-bye and now silently, in her mind, she bid Deeter a loving farewell. They would look after each other, she was certain of it.

And poor, dear sad Harry. In a way he had died four months ago with Josie's sudden and tragic death. What a lovely and unexpected place to find a great love—in a thirty-seven-year-old marriage that started in a Tulsa bank.

"Good-bye to all," she whispered and returned to this world.

Mereth and Chris had called from Deeter's castle to inform her of the multiple deaths. At that time apparently they had been surrounded by various authorities. They had tried once to get back through the gates but had been unable because of the flood of reporters. She assumed they'd try again this morning.

Now Ramona rearranged the coffeepot to keep it from sliding. "Need to ask," she said. "Reverend Jobe suggested sending all the florist trucks back to Tulsa to distribute the flowers to hospitals and nursing homes. There are hundreds, and more coming."

Massie gave her consent, then added, "I'll need all the cards."

"I'll have one of my girls keep track of them."

"Has Mereth come back?"

"They say they can't get through."

There was a sharp rap on the door and a male voice said, "Massie, I need a moment."

Eddie O'Keefe. Massie had given him several important phone calls to make.

"Just a moment, Eddie," she called out and caught Ramona as she lifted the luncheon tray and started toward the door.

"Ramona, wait," she begged quietly. "What's going on down there?"

Ramona shook her head. "Not much. Mr. Pierson and Mr. Nagle have been at the phones all morning. Reverend Jobe has organized a prayer vigil in the library for the support of the family." She smiled down on the tray. "But the family seems to be doing very well. The boys are in the terrace room. Josh is getting drunk, I'm afraid." Ramona paused as though trying to remember whom she'd left out. "Buckner is with someone from the medical examiner's office." She looked down at Massie. "Are you sure you're all right? You've been on that phone all night and most of the morning."

Massie patted the white telephone resting beside her leg on the bedcovers. "Ty always said there's nothing one can't do from his own bed if he has a telephone, a strong voice and a clear line."

For a moment her eyes rested on the white phone, which seemed to blend with the ivory silk comforter. Only one thing really bothered her: she wished she had seen Ty just once more, even in death. But Mr. Hoving, the funeral director, had sent his ambulance directly to the roundabout and retrieved the bodies and was now preparing them for burial, Harry's for a very public funeral in Tulsa, Ty's for a very private one here at Warrick, with interment to follow in the family mausoleum beyond the garden. A delegation from the Osage tribe had arrived early this morning to retrieve Deeter's body. As the son of a chief, he would be given full ceremonial rituals and buried in the Osage cemetery.

A knock again. Eddie growing impatient.

Massie, disliking what her mind did when left alone, said, "Let him in. I'll be down shortly."

"We can manage."

For a moment the two women stared at each other over the length of the mussed bed.

"You okay?"

"I'm fine," Massie replied too quickly. "Ask Mereth to come and see me when she gets back."

Ramona balanced the tray expertly with one hand and opened the door with the other.

From the bed, Massie saw Eddie O'Keefe framed in the door looking melodramatic in his good blue suit. She heard a whispered exchange between Eddie and Ramona, and a moment later Eddie was standing there alone, looking miserable.

"Come in, Eddie."

"If you're not feeling well, I can wait."

"I said I was. Please. Come."

He stepped in and closed the door.

"I did just what you told me, Massie. Everything. The complete list."

Massie leaned back against the pillows and tried to remember what had been on that list. She'd asked him to send personal wires to twenty-six of Ty's intimate friends and associates in various parts of the world who would not be immediately exposed to American newspapers. Then she'd asked him to invite Reverend Jobe to take charge of the services tomorrow. She wanted no part of it, except for one request, that it be kept short and simple and private in the mausoleum.

"Did Jobe agree?" she asked.

Eddie nodded. "Oh, of course. He'll obey your wishes to the

letter. He said he's sketched out a plan and will show it to you later today."

"It'll be fine, I'm sure." Again she looked at Eddie, so stiff and distant and out of character in his sober suit.

"Eddie, why did you get all dressed up today?" she asked, wanting the old informal and always good-natured Eddie back.

He looked down self-consciously at his apparel. "Something wrong, Massie?"

"Oh no, no," she reassured quickly. "You look fine."

"Reverend Jobe's idea," he explained and continued to look overdressed and miserable. "He said someone should be at the gate to answer questions. He said none of the family would be there."

Massie heard the accusation and let it pass. "What's going on at the gate?"

"A mess, that's what's going on. Those vultures aren't interested in Mr. Warrick's passing as much as they are in that damned bank. That's really what's got them excited."

Puzzled, Massie let the question show on her face.

"Mr. Beekman's bank," Eddie explained. "It was closed this morning, just collapsed flatter than a pancake. I tell you, it was a mob scene and all the while poor Mr. Beekman was dead in the front seat of my car with my gun . . ." He shook his head and turned away.

Massie understood. Eddie felt responsible, "his" limo, "his" gun.

"Eddie, it's not your fault," she soothed. "Harry Beekman would have found the means."

"But it was my gun, and they left him alone." He withdrew his handkerchief and blew his nose. "If one of them had stayed with him, they could have helped him."

Massie might have argued but didn't. Of greater interest to her was the state of Harry Beekman's bank.

"Have all accounts been closed?" she asked.

"Yes. There was a long line this morning. It stretched clear around the block as far as Williams Plaza. Police all over the place, trying to keep 'em quiet and happy. Someone sent out chairs for the old folks. And the rich ones. But nobody seems to know how long everybody's going to have to wait." He shook his head. "It looked like those old newsreels from the thirties. When I went to work for Mr. Warrick, I opened my account there. Now everything's gone."

"Oh, Eddie," Massie sympathized. "No, not gone. I'm sure certain accounts will be covered, the ones under a hundred thousand."

"Well, that more than covers me."

Then suddenly he looked worried again. "What about Mr. Warrick? He had some bucks in Mr. Beekman's bank, didn't he?"

Massie gaped at the ingenuous question. "Yes, but don't you worry. Tell me about Mereth and Chris. Have you heard from them this morning?"

Eddie smiled and looked pleased. "On their way. Since I couldn't get a car out of the gates, I phoned Security over at the fields. Got Leroy on the car phone. He was patrolling the south field, but I told him to knock off and make a run over to Deeter's castle and bring those two in. Don't worry. Leroy will get 'em home."

"Good. Thanks, Eddie. I don't know what I would do without you."

He blushed under the weight of the compliment. "It's not Mereth and Chris that's giving us a hard time, Massie. It's the rest of the family."

"I don't understand."

"No one else does either. And Reverend Jobe thinks it's setting a real bad example for the young kids around here. If you know what I mean."

"Josh and Brit?"

He nodded broadly and she sensed someone behind Eddie's indignation, a vocal someone who pointed self-righteous and judgmental fingers casually, easily.

"You know where they are?" he asked.

From the tone of his voice she assumed the question was rhetorical.

"They're in the terrace room, and Dr. Buckner's there too and that nurse Nellie. Anyway, they're all getting drunk out of their heads and telling dirty jokes. And none of them are dressed proper. I mean, Josh and Brit are still wearing those things they were in yesterday." He made it to the door, hand on the doorknob, when he turned back.

"Massie," he asked, not looking at her, "why did Deeter take him? Why did he do that to him? You know what I mean. Reverend Jobe says he was a heathen and didn't know any better, though I spent lots of good evenings talking to Deeter and he wasn't much of a heathen, you know."

"Deeter Big Cow was not a heathen," Massie said, her voice controlled despite her anger, "and he did nothing to Ty, nothing, you understand, but love him in the only way he knew how, to the very end. And you make it clear to all those downstairs that I will not have a harsh or derogatory word spoken against Deeter. You tell them that and you make them understand."

At the end of her tirade Eddie closed the door behind him.

Feeling exhilarated by her explosion, Massie stood, confronting the door. Well, enough. Apparently there were several pockets of need downstairs. For now she'd shower and dress and then meet Red and Junior in the library to see if there was anything they knew that she should know. And vice versa.

Then, if there were no objections coming from any quarter, she would join Josh and Brit in the terrace room, have a drink, listen to a few jokes, tell a few of her own, miss Ty—though she was certain that in such a setting he would be very close.

Red Pierson looked around the telephone room at Warrick. Hitler's Berlin bunker under siege. Red was alone here now. Junior had just excused himself for his forty-eighth trip to the bathroom down the hall. Diagnosis: nerves. After a full day on the telephone, the two men had determined that although it was Ty's funeral tomorrow, a lot of people were going to be buried with him.

Weary, Red got up out of the hard metal folding chair. To one side was a platter of smelly, half-eaten tuna sandwiches. There was a dull burning in the center of Red's stomach, and the foul odor was beginning to add to his discomfort. He looked longingly out of the window. Heavy clouds. Rain soon.

Slowly he leaned forward until his forehead was pressing against one of the telephones, an appropriate headrest.

Whom had they forgotten? Between them they'd placed calls all over the world, trying to soothe business connections, insisting to friends that the service was strictly family, strictly private, but that perhaps later Massie would consent to a memorial service of some sort.

Junior had talked to the newspapers, east and west and abroad, so it was only a matter of hours before the world learned of the death of Tyburn Warrick.

Red blinked once. He still couldn't believe it. Not just Ty's death, but the enormous transitions that were ahead for everyone. He daydreamed, hearing Ty's voice in his ear.

"Are you sure you've got it down just like I said?"

"I do, Ty, but—"

"No buts. I'm the trustee and I know what I'm doing."

Red's eyes blinked open.

"You take care of it, Red. I'm depending on you."

And he'd taken care of it, the last and final codicil carefully attached to the formal document. He tried again, as he had tried so many times before, to imagine what the reaction would be, but couldn't.

In the meantime, Harry had certainly muddied the waters by committing suicide. Who would have thought it? Exactly how long it would take the bank examiners to sort through the colossal mess that was now the Tulsa Petroleum Exchange Bank, Red had no idea.

Regardless, it would be his responsibility, as Ty's personal attorney, to gather the family together immediately after the funeral and go through the will, all clauses rather predictable save for that one last piece of paper which Ty had added only a few months ago. What had gotten into him, Red had no idea.

Footsteps coming.

Damn! Someone had trapped Junior.

He listened, trying to determine who. Then in the next moment the door was pushed open and Junior appeared, his face flushed, his eyes apologetic.

"Red, need your help here," he said gruffly and stood aside to make room for his escort.

Reverend Jobe's jackal face appeared in the doorway. Everything about the man was maddeningly self-possessed, as though to suggest that nothing out of the ordinary had happened here, certainly nothing as grim and imponderable as three deaths.

"Mr. Pierson, need to ask you a few questions."

"We're busy, Jobe. Ask Massie your questions. She . . ."

"Massie is trying to help the boys. Josh's solution to the present problem seems to be complete inebriation."

He was speaking in his most sepulchral tones, his eyebrows circumflex, the whole phony-baloney routine that Red could scarcely tolerate under the best of conditions.

"I won't bother you for long," Reverend Jobe promised.

"What is it that you need?"

"Your assistance," the man cut in and sat with deliberation on one of the high stools.

Junior Nagle leaned against the doorframe, head down, as though he knew they'd been trapped.

"What is it, Jobe?" Red asked. "We're really quite busy here, and I—"

"We're busy everywhere." Reverend Jobe smiled. He reached into his vest pocket and withdrew a white envelope and studied it a moment before making a ridiculous announcement.

"These are the names of people in the religious community of this country who would appreciate being personally notified of Brother Warrick's passing. Shall I do it or do you want to?"

Red blinked, his mind having snagged on "Brother Warrick."

From the door Junior said, "The . . . religious community?"

Jobe nodded enthusiastically. "Oh, yes, Mr. Nagle. In a way I suspect Tyburn Warrick led a double life. He was one man around you and your friends, and quite another among his church friends."

Red drew a deep breath and reached for the envelope. At first glance he determined that there were about eighteen names on the list. At second glance he saw that every name was preceded by the designation "Reverend."

He looked up to see Jobe watching him carefully. Then Red heard voices coming from the terrace room. A moment later the commotion increased, as did the sound of footsteps. He saw Josh stumbling down the hall, followed by Brit and then Eddie, who was protesting something.

"Hey, Josh, wait! No need to meet Mereth at the gate. I've sent a security guard over to Deeter's for both of them. Brit, stop him. He's drunk . . ."

But Josh was adamant and made one powerful effort and again broke free and started off down the corridor.

Red Pierson saw a peculiar expression on Brit's face, part resignation, part concern. Then he saw Brit break into a run.

Who would win? Red had no idea and little desire to find out. Eddie had gone back into the terrace room, and Red Pierson was left with Reverend Gerald Jobe and the list he had handed over.

And resentment. While Ty's two worthless grandsons got drunk and played games, Red Pierson was trying to keep their inheritance safe, if there was one, after Tulsa Pet—.

"Preachers?" he asked Jobe and at the same time tried to hide the contempt he was feeling.

"Men of God."

"What's their interest in Ty Warrick?"

"Concern for his soul."

"Or his bank account."

He expected indignation and denial. Instead Reverend Jobe smiled.

"Only insofar as Mr. Warrick gave generously, freely, as an offering of thanksgiving to God for his many blessings."

Stymied, Red studied the list, tried to manage his anger and recognized a couple of names. TV preachers, phony as three-dollar bills. He absolutely refused to believe that Ty had given these men the time of day, let alone sums of money.

"Call them yourself," Red muttered and shoved the list back at Jobe.

"What shall I tell them?"

The question at first sounded stupid. Only in echo did it begin to sound loaded.

"What do you mean, what should you tell them?" Red snapped. "It's your idea to call them. Tell them what you want."

"The truth? God's truth?"

"I don't . . ."

"How he died, where he was found, who he was with. That sort of thing."

Red had had enough. "Go make the phone calls, Jobe. Tell them what you like. It makes no difference to me."

"Did you know, Mr. Pierson, that over the last three years Mr. Warrick had very generously donated funds to all aspects of our ministry?"

"Delighted to hear it."

"These men consider him a saint."

"That's their problem."

"I'm sure the ones within traveling distance will want to attend the funeral."

Red shook his head vehemently. "They won't get past the front gate. I can promise you that. I have given the guards strictest . . ."

"On whose authority?"

Red blinked at the challenge. "On the express wishes of Massie and the family. Now go on with you. We've work to do here. I'm sure you can understand."

"Very well," he said, too agreeably. "I'll simply notify my colleagues of Mr. Warrick's passing and let them read accounts in the newspapers."

"You do that."

Jobe reached the door and turned back. "One last question, Mr. Pierson, if I may."

"Whatever."

"The will. Is it affected by the collapse of Tulsa Pet?"

"That is family business."

As Jobe stepped out into the hall, Junior Nagle stood back, leaving Red to combat the silence alone.

"Come on in, Junior, and close the door," he called, ignoring Gerald Jobe, who stood framed in the doorway, a mildly triumphant smile on his face.

Junior did so, leaving Jobe shut out on the other side, the envelope bearing the names of the men of God still clasped in his hand.

Red turned back to the table. "Come on, let's finish here. This place is driving me crazy. Who's left?"

"You get the ones in Dallas and I'll try New York again. Then . . ."

As Red lifted the list of corporate names to be notified on the East Coast, he saw instead, curiously superimposed, that long list of Reverends. What in the name of God had Ty gone and done now?

Oh, well, it wouldn't make any difference. It was one of the privileges of being a lawyer that he knew precisely how and when to skim the cream off the top.

Something was heaping guilt, making Mereth feel like a criminal. Either the fact that a stern-faced security guard had been sent to bring them safely back into Warrick, or the fact that she was alive and Ty was dead, or the fact that she'd left Josh and Brit to look after everything at Warrick for too long, something, everything was making her feel repentant.

As she sat tightly wedged between the security guard and Chris in the front seat of the Warrick pickup, she thought of how few words they had exchanged all night and now well into the day, a silent healing interim while each tried to adjust to the discoveries of the night.

After they had sounded the alarm and waited for the authorities to arrive, they'd made it around in her car as far as the gate. But the crowds of reporters had caused them to turn back. The approach to the main gate had been totally occluded with TV trucks and story-hungry media. As the roundabout had been cordoned off by emergency vehicles and the authorities, all access to Warrick had been closed. They had taken refuge in the castle, where they had spent what remained of the night.

The truck bounced over the rutted road, and she tried to brace herself. Memory blurred, became clear and then blessedly blurred again as her mind shied away from the canvas-shrouded body which had not contained Ty Warrick at all but merely useless flesh and bone, a noble house of original design, now deserted by its tenant.

"Come here, little girl, tell me your name."

"I'm Mereth, Grandpa. You know me."

Something hurt, and she thought irrationally that she must return immediately to Warrick and hurry up to his rooms and retrieve something of his, nothing of real value, just something that still bore his scent.

"Are you all right?"

Chris looked sideways at her and shifted the ancient leather portfolio in his lap, the only piece of luggage he'd not allowed the security guard to put in the bed of the truck.

She glanced down at the old leather portfolio which, intentionally or not, he'd clasped in an embrace, holding it in his arms as though it were the most treasured object of his world.

She looked out of the window. Not far now to blacktop, then ten miles to the section line, then ten, fifteen minutes after that start looking for the red tile roof. She closed her eyes, frightened.

No cause, she tried to reassure herself. A simple, private funeral in the mausoleum. Next to Mary Beth. See to it that Massie is all right, then bid her brothers good-bye for another ten years and

390

return to Tulsa, to the girls at Oakhurst and the moss-covered verses of Emily Dickinson.

She felt like a nail being hammered into a piece of wood by her own despair.

For a moment she suffered a painful splintering of personality. Surely there were two women, one who taught American literature in a civil and genteel setting, green ivy on red brick, silver tea service gleaming. And a second woman who crawled about, animal-like on all fours and succumbed to base instincts and discovered primal burial grounds in the middle of a night and wore no shoes and lived in cellars.

No hope for reconciliation between the two. One was so much stronger.

Blacktop ahead. Good. The endless bumping of Deeter's washboard road was beginning to get to her. Conversation would have been nice, but obviously there was no safe subject and Chris certainly seemed to prefer silence, clutching his portfolio.

Without warning, she saw in memory the clearing, the small used-up fire casting a shadow over everything.

She heard Chris questioning the security guard.

"Is it bad? At the front gate, I mean."

"There's a crowd, if that's what you mean. Word's come down from the big house that no one gets in unless with one of us."

Mereth looked up through the windshield at the sky. A storm threatened, purples and grays devouring the blue day. Early spring storms. Treacherous.

"Will we have any trouble? Getting through, I mean," Chris asked.

"Naw, I don't think so. But it's a mess, I can tell you. When I was over there earlier, there must have been seventy-five, a hundred people, TV trucks and equipment, radio people. Don't expect it's improved much."

Suddenly the security guard interrupted excitedly. "There he is, my point man."

Mereth looked down the long blacktop road and saw a second

Warrick pickup parked right in the middle of the deserted intersection. Chris sat up further on the edge of the seat.

"What's he doing there?" he asked.

"That's Doug," the security guard said. "Ain't no one gonna get past him that hadn't oughta get past 'im." He looked over at them. "And I'm Leroy."

Mereth felt the car slow again and saw Leroy roll down his window, his arm hanging out as he came up on the passenger's side of Doug's pickup.

"What's up?" he asked in studied, cool fashion.

"Looks like rain's comin', and that's gonna make matters worse."

Leroy peered up at the gathering clouds, daylight diminishing. "Reckon we'd better get started."

Doug nodded. "I'll ring ahead and tell 'em you're on your way."

Then Leroy shifted gears and Mereth felt the car roll forward and heard him shout through the window.

"Make your call and tell 'em we're coming in in about fifteen minutes. I just hope we can beat the rain."

At the moment he said it, Mereth heard the first drops strike the top of the car, saw the light of afternoon fade, the sun obscured by a typical Oklahoma April rain shower.

Then the pickup truck accelerated and, as Leroy turned out and around Doug's truck, he made the tires squeal. Mereth tried to relax and watched the rain coming down in a steady sheet and saw Chris, on the edge of his seat, his left hand grasping the portfolio.

"May I ask you a question?" Mereth began quietly.

He looked at her.

"What's in the portfolio?"

"Just some of Deeter's papers, that's all."

"Why are you taking them to Warrick?"

"I didn't want to leave them at the castle."

"Why?"

"It isn't safe."

He peered straight ahead through the driving rain.

She waited patiently to see if he would say more, but for the next several minutes they drove in silence except for the rain, the windshield wipers struggling to keep the deluge cleared and not always succeeding. The pavement was rapidly growing slick, visibility diminishing. A few minutes later she saw up ahead a glow like twin beacons.

Recalling the warning of the other guard, she watched Leroy for a hint of what he'd do. Cars were parked on both sides of the road, empty, the drivers unable to get any closer to the gate.

At that moment she heard Leroy on the radio cutting through the static, identifying his truck number. She couldn't understand the muddled voice and was suddenly overcome by the absurdity of it all, barred from entering a place she did not want to go, to prepare for the funeral of a man who, though dead, would never die.

Warrick

BRIT CAUGHT up with Josh at the front door and saw beyond the covered portico to night and the solid sheets of rain. He reached out and tried again to dissuade him from his foolish rescue mission.

"Come on, Josh, this isn't necessary. It really isn't."

"Mereth needs—"

"Mereth is with Chris."

"She found them, Brit, those two old dead men. God, how awful for her."

"I know. And when she returns we must be with her and help her."

"Mereth needs us."

His childlike insistence came in mournful repetition over the staccato of the rain. Brit released his grip on Josh's arm and slipped it around his shoulder, a more affectionate gesture, less restraining.

If he could only get him to sit for a moment, to reconsider, to concede his state of drunkenness which undoubtedly was exaggerating in his mind the drama at the front gate.

"Come on," Brit urged gently and shivered in the wet night air and realized that neither of them was dressed for a driving spring rainstorm. Still, it was worth a try to force a delay and perhaps even as they talked, Chris and Mereth would arrive and Josh would relax.

"Here," Brit said with studied concern and at last eased Josh down on the middle step and glanced toward the chauffeur's office in search of Eddie and belatedly remembered they had left him in the terrace room with Massie and the others.

Once down, Josh seemed to settle in more ways than one; first his shoulders collapsed, then his head hung loosely over, then he covered his face with his hands and drew a deep shuddering breath.

From behind this fortress he spoke. "Can you believe what's happened, Brit? Ty couldn't just pop off in his bed like normal folk. No, that wouldn't do for Tyburn Warrick. Let's make a bloody spectacle with every man and his dog turning over every bloody leaf—"

His voice dwindled for lack of air, and he shook his head weakly several times and was quiet.

Brit moved closer. "I don't think it was Ty's idea. Deeter's the one. And even then, I suppose in a way it was an act of love, nothing more."

Josh looked at him sideways, a broad expression of bewilderment on his face.

"You know as well as I," Brit went on, "that Deeter would be lost on this earth without Ty. *He* knew it better than anyone and so arranged for them to depart together."

Josh sat up from his bowed position. He seemed more sober, listening. "Did you love him? Ty, I mean? Really love him?"

The question caught Brit off guard. He looked at Josh and saw loneliness in his face, a tempest equal to that of the storm raging just beyond the covered portico.

"Love," he repeated and smiled and thought of Sophie and the children and the need. "I'm not sure that Ty wanted us to love him. I think he would have been far happier if one of us had emulated him."

"I hated him," Josh muttered, and again there was that plaintive childlike tone and Brit suspected that, as was always the case with hate, it did far more damage to the one who hated.

"No, Josh," he said gently and reached for his hand with a sweet intimacy and felt it cold. "Not hate. Ty wasn't understanding of any of us. But then neither were we of him. It was as if he had sailed for many years over a great turbulent sea and at last had come upon a fair haven and had created a paradise. I think the fact that none of *us* saw it as paradise filled him with unspeakable anguish. But he was a rare man, and if he did injury to us, I'm sure that in our own unique way we did equal injury to him."

"Brit," came a near whisper. "Let's never drift quite so far apart again. Please. I need you. I need my family."

"No." He smiled. "We must not drift away from each other again. None of us." In all ways Brit had enjoyed his time with Josh on this trip home, the two of them growing closer than ever before. And Mereth too. As children, their competition for Ty's approval had kept them apart.

"I'm so damned weak," Josh muttered despairingly. "That's what Ty despised more than anything."

"Not despised. Didn't understand," Brit said. *"You're* not weak. You have purpose."

"And doubt, more self-doubt than you can imagine."

"What do you do in London?" Josh asked.

A large question. "I try to help children who need help. It seems that all my life I have followed the ideals that other people by their words or their writings have instilled in me and never the desire of my own heart." He looked at Josh and smiled. "In London I follow my heart."

"May I come and see you sometime?"

"Anytime. I'd be so pleased."

Josh nodded. "Good. You know, I'm not so old that I can't learn." He stood and stretched and looked out toward the storm and the dull glow of lights coming from the end of the driveway and the front gate. "Come on, Brit. Let's go. I believe Mereth needs us. You said yourself. We are a family. Let's act like one. One for all and all for one— How good to be needed by someone, anyone."

The drunken flamboyance had returned. Josh was on his feet now, proclaiming to the night and to the storm. And before Brit could stop him, he ran forward and cleared the portico and was fast disappearing into the hazardous night.

"Josh, wait—"

But Brit's cry was useless. He stood for a moment and knew that Josh shouldn't be alone, not in his state, not on such a night.

Well, then—

He turned up the collar of his jacket in meager protection against the rain and felt suddenly tired. Strange questions, the ones that Josh had asked. Brit only hoped he'd answered them with care. He had always tried to do what he thought best. His ideals? To make an intricate and beautiful design out of the myriad meaningless facts of life. Of course, he had not yet succeeded. But there was time, an entire lifetime to love, to mold, to accept, to grant, to understand, to nurture.

As for Ty, Brit regretted that they had not had one last conversation. So much might have been accomplished toward healing the old wounds. But regret was absurd. As absurd as hate.

"Josh, wait up—"

Then he was running after his brother, into the storm, deeply touched by his close proximity to life and death and love. He understood so little. But no matter. The future was before him, rich with possibilities.

Warrick

ABRUPTLY THE truck stopped.

"When I give the word, Miss Warrick, duck down and hold on tight. You hear now? The rain's making it worse. But we'll do it."

"I assume the chances of us just driving through like normal people are out of the question?"

Leroy craned his neck about, a look of incredulity on his face. "You kidding? See those vehicles over there?" He made a stabbing motion at the cars parked along the rain-smeared road. "Their owners left 'em there 'cause they couldn't get any closer. All right, get your heads down, you hear?"

She saw Chris slide to the edge of the seat, his long legs folded up accordion fashion, the leather portfolio still clutched in his arms.

Then she felt a slow acceleration, Leroy whispering an ominous "We're coming through," and at the same time the rain yet increasing.

On either side of the road in a wet blur, she saw the lines of cars and trucks. The estimate had been right, eighty, perhaps a hundred people up ahead, partially hidden from view by enormous umbrellas, some wrapped impromptu fashion in shiny plastic bags, all heads bowed before the steady rain. Also she saw spotlights shining directly on Ty's gate, the gate itself guarded by two men on the outside and one on the inside, or at least as far as she could tell from this distance and through the hazards of the rain.

Though the pickup was still moving at a cautious 30 mph, the crowd ahead seemed unaware of their approach, more concerned with the rain and keeping their equipment dry.

"Leroy, they don't see—" she tried to warn, but either the man couldn't or wouldn't hear her.

The speed was steady now, and she saw a few of the reporters and photographers at the edge of the crowd look back through the streaks of rain, surprised at the truck coming toward them. Then the entire milling and soaked crowd seemed to perceive the hazardous situation and reacted instantaneously and moved quickly back.

With less than fifty yards to go, Mereth clung to the dash and saw the high gate just parting, the first man dragging his gate back toward the security house, the other—

What was the matter with the other? He seemed to be pulling on his side of the gate, but it refused to go with him.

"Leroy, watch . . ."

It happened at the exact moment she cried out, the grating collision against the right front fender as it struck the stubborn gate and hurled it open, the sound of breaking glass, crumpled metal, a heavy thud, accompanied a few seconds later by the sound of a woman screaming.

As Leroy struggled to bring the truck under control, he used the thick row of evergreens as a point of soft collision.

Then it was over, a pronounced silence after so much noise, except for the rain, and that now seemed diminished as though it had served a purpose. Even the woman's screams had ceased, and Mereth heard nothing save her own breathing.

"What in the—"

This muttered half-question came from Chris, who struggled upright, looking through the rear window to the scene back at the gate. He opened the door and crawled out backward, oblivious of the rain. Despite his awkward movements, not once did he take his eyes off the road behind at the gate and the now eerily quiet crowd of reporters and curiosity seekers.

Then it was her turn. She heard Leroy in the driver's seat moan and rub his head and push up from his slumped position over the steering wheel. Mereth crawled slowly out on uncertain legs and felt the first cool drops of rain splatter against her face. Using the open door for support, she looked back toward the gate.

The two spotlights mounted behind the crowd rendered them all in silhouette, no one clamoring to get in although the gate was open, one side pulled properly aside, the other twisted and crushed back upon itself, no one moving in the nightmare scene save one: Chris hurrying toward something on the pavement next to the twisted gate.

She saw Chris go down beside the form. What was it?

Though she still was about fifty feet from where Chris knelt, she could see, despite the rain, a subtle collapse of Chris's head and shoulders, and she moved closer and saw the figure on the ground, the legs and shoes and trousers, an unnatural distortion to the lower body, a twisted position impossible to assume unless—

"Mereth, get back. Go on up to the house. Send . . ."

The rain was diminishing. She felt only a gentle spray on her face now.

"Who is it?" she asked.

"Please," Chris begged.

She kept on coming. Someone had failed to get out of the path of Leroy's pickup.

She was standing directly over Chris, who glanced up at her once, an expression of surrender and apology on his face.

"Please. There's no . . ."

"Need" was what he was going to say, but obviously there was a need. Slowly she reached down toward the obscuring jacket, an element of recognition already dawning.

"I'm so sorry, Mereth."

The apology accomplished nothing. But she knew who it was even before she lifted the jacket and saw the sandy hair, intermixed with rain and blood, warning her to stop investigating.

But she didn't and foolishly lifted the jacket the rest of the way.

"Mereth, please go."

She wasn't certain who it was who asked her to leave, but it was out of the question. First she had to cleanse the face of blood, which continued to pour from the gaping cut which ran like jagged lightning lengthwise across his forehead.

"What you are running here is a company town, Ty, worse than the feudal system."

"Get out of here with your Communist ideas. Get out! You don't belong at Warrick."

Why had Brit come to help open the gate? Brit was designed for more than opening gates.

She knelt beside him, this brother who had laughed with her, carried her on his shoulders, told her about boys and kisses and sharing and forgiving and never once, to the best of her knowledge, resented her or patronized her or considered her to be anything less than she was.

With her hand she tried gently to wipe the blood away from his face.

She looked up for help and saw Josh standing a few feet away, a terrifying expression on his face, his hair plastered by the rain across his forehead. His lips were moving, but no words were coming out.

Someone was pulling at her from behind. She turned about to see Eddie hovering close, his good, plain Irish face stricken.

"Eddie, it's Brit," she whispered. "He needs help."

"Come on, Mereth. Please."

More footsteps, running.

Mereth knew that Massie was there, could sense her grief, her shock, her sense of waste, of tested endurance and of limits surpassed.

And then there was Dr. Buckner. "All right, clear out, all of you. Come on, get her away." As though following his own command, he knelt over her. "Come on, Mereth. That ain't accomplishing a goddamned thing. Get up and let me . . ."

She felt support on either side lift her away from Brit's battered face, and she wished she might continue upward into the sky, higher and higher until Brit, this driveway, this house, this land, this world was no more than a speck in her vision.

Why was she shaking? It was as if she'd caught a sudden chill. Her teeth struck together and no matter how she clenched them, she could not hold them steady.

Suddenly there came an unearthly shriek, so awful that Mereth covered her ears with her hands, but the scream persisted and she saw Josh, his face breaking, lunge for the driver of the pickup, his hands already outreaching, hungry to do as much damage as they could.

Someone screamed, "Josh, don't, stop him," and there was more running and Mereth's hands were shaking and she felt certain that she had passed the furthest limit of her own ability to endure. And the scene was still unchanged, death on a rampage, no one safe, and she fell to repeating in a whispered prayer, "Help us help us help—" and she tried to prepare her mind to bear resolutely on what was before her, without allowing herself even to think of what was to come, or how it would end.

But she knew she could not bear it any longer. Something wanted to push her over the edge and in that second, kneeling beside Brit's body, hearing Josh's guilty grief someplace behind the rain, all the ordinary conditions of life, without which one can form no conception of anything, had ceased to be.

She lost all sense of time and place and knew only one thing for certain: she had to get away from here, from this place of dying, where her heart was breaking.

"Mereth, wait, where are you—"

But she didn't wait. Whatever was ahead for her in the hazardous night was better than this. Stumbling only once, she ran blindly around the security gate and slid down the muddy ravine and saw shadows ahead and the shining black reflection of rain on leaves and ignored for the last time the voices calling her back.

The strained cord snapped. Sobs which she had never experienced rose up with such violence that her whole body shook. But they did not prevent her from running from the mystery of death, accomplished once too often before her eyes and in her soul . . .

Relying upon a sense of order that had served her all her life, Massie looked about at the nightmare scene and decided: first, let Mereth go. She needed to be alone. Second, Dr. Buckner would have to attend to Brit. Third, the one who needed her most was Josh, whose fierce attack on the driver had been halted by Eddie and three security guards. Josh stood now, arms still pinned behind him, looking up at the night sky, weeping.

"Eddie, take him to my rooms. Wait there with him until I arrive."

Relieved, she watched him go, passive now, as though something vital had been drained from him, a willing prisoner, hungry for punishment. In a way it reflected her own mood. As she saw Buckner bending over Brit's lifeless body, her reassuring sense of order briefly faltered. How and who had they offended to bring this down upon them?

Enough! No solution there, less comfort. The world and its spotted history was a vast landscape of random violence and tragic senseless death. No point, less purpose in trying to understand. The challenge was in finding the strength to accept.

She let Eddie and Josh take the lead by several yards. She wasn't ready yet to confront Josh's grief. She looked back and made brief eye contact with Doc Buckner and told him, without words, to do what had to be done here. He now was in charge of this Hellgate.

Then she walked slowly back up the drive, head down. On either side she was aware of movement, people running about as though a major disruption in balance and unity had occurred in the world with Brit's death.

Brit's death—

The words, incomprehensible, screamed in her ears and with rapid steps as though to leave the screams behind she reached Warrick and found the doors opened and looked ahead to see Josh and Eddie just disappearing at the top of the steps.

To her left, coming from the terrace room she heard weeping,

Ramona, she guessed, and the girls from the kitchen. She should go to them, but later.

"Massie, why do we have everything we want and so many others have so little?"

"I don't know, Brit. We must try to understand it, though."

Halfway up the steps, she faltered and reached for the banister to wait out the pang. Josh first, then find Mereth. Perhaps in helping them she would find a degree of relief for herself. Sometimes it worked in that fashion.

Long before she was ready, she found herself standing before her open door, looking in at a tableau: Josh seated on the sofa, his face covered by his hands, unresponding to Eddie's offer of a brandy.

As Massie appeared, Eddie looked at her and she saw relief in his eyes, grateful that she was here. Perhaps she could deal with the statue of a man who only moments before had been ready and willing to kill.

"Thanks, Eddie," she whispered and stood back as he thrust the ignored brandy into her hand and left the room. She saw the strained distortion of his face. There was need everywhere. This time death had struck with a sudden, bold and clamorous blow, had left everyone clinging desperately to whatever wreckage they could find.

She closed the door, looked down at the brandy, lifted the snifter and drained it in two swallows and closed her eyes against the good burning that accomplished its purpose, seemed to clear her head.

She drew a deep breath and slowly approached the sofa. "Josh—"

Carefully she knelt before him and pushed back the rain-wet hair clinging to his brow. Clutching his chilled hands in her warm ones, she tried to see his face.

But with a suddenness that startled, he stood up and brushed past her and took refuge on the far side of the room, and stood with his back to her, looking out on the rainy night.

"Josh, I need your help," she murmured. "Please don't walk away from me."

"It's for your own good," he said over his shoulder in a voice she didn't recognize, hard, flat, without inflection. "I can't help you. Look at Brit. Brit needed my help, and look at him now. Did you see him up close, Massie? Did you? His head is split—"

He turned toward her briefly, but the edge of despair broke in his voice and he went all the way to the window and pressed his forehead against the glass, and she could see him trembling with unspent grief.

"Josh, you must listen," she began, slowly rising. "It's not your fault."

"Then whose in the hell is it?" he demanded, turning toward her again with his swollen and agonized face. "Tell me, Massie. If not mine, then who gets to wear this one on their soul?"

She started toward him, no more than a step or two when new rage surfaced.

"I do think it's fitting that the murderer was an ignoramus security guard and the weapon a Warrick pickup. Fitting, though slightly redundant, wouldn't you say? Ty killed Brit the first time years ago, didn't he?"

"Josh, please don't," she begged, understanding what he was doing but disliking it intensely all the same.

"Why?" he demanded, confronting her with cruel persistence. "Oh, I'm sorry," he added with mock regret, "I keep forgetting your mystifying loyalty to the bastard. It's your one character flaw, Massie. Did you know that?"

As the attack continued, she reminded herself that sometimes it helped to ease the hurt by hurting someone else.

"I mean really, Massie, we've all tried at one time or another to figure it out. How *did* you stand the bastard?"

Josh was drawing nearer as he spoke, his face contorted. She watched him and held steady.

"I mean when he touched you, didn't you just want to cringe? How could you listen to all that crap he dished out, all that egomaniacal bullshit about balls and guts."

He was standing directly before her, with red fever spots rising on his cheeks, with an expression on his smug face that screamed to be removed.

The blow came with speed and accuracy, Massie's hand lifting with only one objective, to stop that tongue before it did lasting damage to both of them. She struck him directly on the left cheek-bone and saw him spin around in pain and surprise, grasping the side of his face and stumbling toward a near chair, still bent over where he collapsed, and she heard fresh weeping and thought good.

Though her hand hurt, she felt a sudden rush of tenderness and pity and again knelt before him.

"Josh, please listen to me. It serves no purpose to speak like that." She bent low and saw his lusterless eyes. On the side of his face was a reddened imprint of her hand. "Please forgive me," she whispered, caressing the wounded area. "We can't ease our grief by spreading poison."

"Brit is dead."

"Yes."

"It's my fault."

"No."

"Then whose?"

She closed her eyes in prayer before the question. "No one's fault, Josh."

"I can't accept that."

"You must."

"The fault is here, in Warrick. Brit knew it." He looked up at her, out of an expression of new suffering. "Don't get angry, Massie, but how did you stand him? Ty?"

On her knees, she bowed her head. "I loved him."

"What in the name of God was there to love?"

"A complex, generous though uncertain heart. He was a man who was not afraid to grow and change."

"I don't believe you."

"I know you don't, and you must." Slowly she stood, feeling a need for distance from Josh's grief. "Will you listen?"

She wanted no response, not now, not for a few minutes. "When I arrived here over thirty years ago, I shared your opinion, only mine was far worse. I remember I wrote home to my father and told him simply that Tyburn Warrick was the most bigoted, racist man I'd ever met."

He looked pleased by her confirmation.

"But he changed, Josh. Slowly, painfully he changed. Once in the sixties, I wanted to go to Washington to King's peace march. Ty flatly said no. I went anyway and vowed never to return to Warrick."

She had his attention, and for that she was grateful. In a way it eased the pain of the present by talking about the pain of the past.

"What happened?" he asked, rubbing the side of his face.

"After the march I went to Cambridge, to my parents' home. Ty called several times, and finally he appeared on the doorstep. I told him I'd come back on two conditions. One, that he never again tell me what to do and two, that he establish full academic scholarships for black students at nine Southwestern universities."

Josh smiled. "I think they call it extortion."

She nodded. "In the beginning, yes. I'm far from perfect. I thought you knew that. But now there are thirty-six such scholarships, all anonymous, at seventeen universities, all established by Ty over the years, without the slightest prompting from me."

She paused, moved by the past and her treasured memories. Josh looked at her, almost vacantly. He sat mute and passive.

"I'm not defending his attitude toward you and Brit, nor am I denying that he drove you away. He was wrong in that. He was hoping to find an oilman between you. Instead he found a poet and a dreamer." She smiled. "Naturally he was disappointed. But he was growing toward a reconciliation with both of you. Jobe was helping in his own way."

"Giving the devil his due?"

"Yes. As Ty used to say, the message is valid, only the messenger is a little nuts."

"And Mereth? No reconciliation there?"

Massie shook her head. "No. Ty wouldn't even allow us to mention her name."

Massie felt haggard and exhausted by the mystery of what had happened between Ty and Mereth. She must finish here and go and find her. "You have to remember, Josh. We all are in the process of becoming. No life is completely stagnant, without movement in one direction or another. What Ty was fifteen, twenty years ago was very different from what he was striving to become. So it is or should be with all of us."

Then it was Josh who spoke in an unexpectedly soft and compassionate tone. "I don't know what he was or what he was becoming, but I do know he was fortunate to have you. We all are."

His kindness proved her undoing and she felt the burning of fresh tears, saw his hand extended to her and accepted it, and for several moments they clung together.

Massie recovered first. She wiped her eyes and gently guided Josh down until his head was resting in her lap. She smoothed his hair. They had sat like this years ago as she'd eased his passage through one minor hurt after another. This one was not minor.

"Josh, I can't explain the violent and senseless deaths that occur in this world. They happen daily, hourly, and no Divine voice fills our ears with reason and logic. Yet I do know that we can't lose faith in the order of things. The world is not a disorderly, devil-ridden chaos. Because we can't understand it doesn't mean that it is without understanding or meaning. We must guard constantly against disillusionment, which is a living death. You must have a longing for life and go on living in spite of logic."

He was quiet.

"—and try for your own sake to be more patient with people. Try not to view them as golden ideals, fit only for seats on Olympus. Because they're not, none of us are, not even you. We're human beings, flawed, frail, very vulnerable and, most of us, very frightened."

She sensed release and a degree of relief in spite of what he said next.

"Brit was the best of us all."

"Perhaps. Then help to make his memory live by nurturing that goodness and striving to achieve it."

"I miss him."

She kissed the side of his face. "I do too, and will for the rest of my life."

He turned and clung to her while her trembling hands embraced him and though there were tears again, they were of a different nature, death not wholly turned back, just held at bay until love and life could gain a fresh foothold.

Massie closed her eyes, grateful for the strength that had come from some illogical source. She heard the rain increase outside the window. A new nightmare filled her heart.

Mereth. Where was Mereth?

Mereth knew where she was despite her rough passage through the black night, knew well this path that stretched between Mary Beth's civilized Warrick and Ty's old ranch house, having raced it, ridden it, skipped it, walked it all her life.

"Get your horse, Mereth and go and fetch your grandfather."

The rain stung her face and pelted against her bare arms, and she considered turning back. But didn't. Death was back there.

"The Warrick core, Mereth, that old ranch house. My Daddy started here with a dream and a dugout."

She ran with the sense that something was following her, beating in heavy rhythmical strokes like her heart.

"Ty, Brit's dead. I need you."

Noisy clamor all around in the rain, in near thunder, in distant cries and car horns. On horseback this passage could be accomplished in less than twenty minutes. On foot at night, in a driving storm, cutting across ravines, if she was fortunate, she'd never make it at all.

She was thinking that despite her speed and the treacherous footing, she must preserve her balance and at that moment she fell, her feet entangled in ancient roots and dried bramble.

Incessant whispering in her head, cold mud on her arms. No new happiness, not for the soul.

"I'm sorry, Massie."

The trouble with night was that you couldn't see the storm clouds, and thus you couldn't read them. It was important here to read clouds.

"Mereth, come on. Massie's gone to Tulsa for the day. She's abandoned us, so we'll abandon her. There's so much I want you to see: two new wells, both beauties, and your favorites, half a dozen new calves. Grab your hat and get your coat, leave your worries on the doorstep."

Having said this, the sunburnt, tall, handsome god with dark eyes crooked his elbow high in the air in a jaunty gesture, stroked his imaginary mustache and put his hand to his hat.

Death ahead. Death behind.

She pushed up out of the mud with a fine vigorous gesture and felt her shirt clinging to her back under the pressure of cold rain. On her feet again she looked back, expecting to see what was pursuing her. She could feel it coming closer, or perhaps it was ahead of her. But she could see nothing. Even Brit had disappeared into this night.

Pain engulfed her with extraordinary power and left her clinging to a nearby tree trunk. While she waited out the hurt, her head filled with unseemly sounds, scuffling, drunken, husky gasping, labored breathing.

"Ty, Brit is dead. Come quick."

With her forehead pressed against rough bark she sensed a massacre somewhere nearby, the air reeking with death, screams of pain, hundreds of mutilated lifeless corpses, a discordant uproar of disorder.

"You crazy, Mereth? It's April warm. Not a cloud in sight. Come on, you're acting like an old woman at twenty. I don't need another mother. Massie does enough of that, thank you."

She saw him then in sun as clearly as though he were standing before her, his thick white wavy hair gleaming, his muscles straining against his white shirt, his massive hand capable of enclosing both of hers, so alive, such great freedom of movement—moving like a god, as if the world fit him, as if he had assisted in its creation and thus understood its subtler working parts. When she watched him, which was always, she suffered elements of feelings she couldn't identify but which left her feeling weak and good.

In him all things were miracle. She awakened in the morning with only one thought: where was he and what was he doing? Her only goal was to see his face as soon as possible, to hear his voice before the first bird call started, to be wrapped in the sacred embrace of his arms, his name alone unutterable without causing her heart to falter.

"I love you, Ty."

"And I love you, Mereth baby. Now grab those reins and let's race."

"Ty, a storm is coming."

"Bullshit, you're just afraid that nag of yours can't keep up."

"He can beat the hell out of yours any day."

"He who speaks the truth better have one foot in the stirrup."

Mereth pushed carefully away from the tree trunk as though something was in danger of breaking. She moved slowly but steadily in what she hoped was the right direction, affecting composure. Just a brief respite in the night, alone, to find a new direction; then she'd return to Warrick and try to live with the novelty of new truths: that Brit was dead, that Ty was dead, that passions could not be uprooted, only redirected to a more noble object.

Ranch house not far. She could sense it. The matrix—

"Ty, damn it, I told you. Look at the clouds. Twister colored." And suddenly it was so cold, as if arctic doors had swung open and released a world full of frozen air to sweep down the central corridor of prairie and hurl against them, unprepared and vulnerable.

The horses were frightened, and they'd had to walk the last several miles and she had followed him, as she had followed him every day since her first step, as she would joyfully, willingly follow him over the edge of the world.

Now she attempted to climb out of a small ravine and slid back and tried again, gradually regaining her momentum though at some point the rain had increased, and for the first time, without hint or warning, she suspected what she was about to do and knew that she couldn't, and knew that she must and knew it would be anguish for her and that made her the more certain that it must be inevitable.

If only she'd been able to fix the furthest limit, to be able with confidence to say, three years, five years, twenty-five years from now it will be finished and I won't remember it or think on it again. But even then it would still be unchanged and she would still be bearing it, because there was nothing to be done *but* bear it, every instant, every sensation, every feeling.

Time shifted as she knew it would, and her sense of helplessness increased. Grief was disfiguring her. Brit was a human creature who once had existed, loved, given and now was no more. Time was not extraneous and superfluous. To each there was an allotment.

Despite the soft voice murmuring in her ear, keeping up a rhythmic whisper, she stirred herself out of this black wet void and into another. There was a ringing in her ears and a dimness before her eyes, and like a woman sinking under water she saw the ranch house loom before her, that place of beginnings and endings, a decrepit, ancient frame Victorian gothic, no paint left, the gray undercoat visible like the surface beneath peeled skin.

"Hurry, Ty, there it is, let me have your horse, you go on in and get warm, quick, you're shivering."

She bent into the rain and tried not to see his colorless face, blue-lipped with cold. They had been riding the southern boundary of Warrick when the wind shifted, the capriciousness of spring on the prairie, a driving, churning black whirlwind of clouds that had obliterated the late afternoon sun. They had spotted a twister cutting across the western horizon of the world. Nothing could survive its power. Nothing could escape.

Above the screaming wind she cried, "Hurry, Ty, get inside," and she watched as he stumbled up the steps, trying at the same time to steady the frightened horses and trying to steady her own fear as well while the black finger dipped and dropped lower.

Something had happened to Ty; he was not a god, not invincible. Something was happening now. With the first sheets of driving rain, his teeth had started to chatter. He'd kept his head down and had seemed suddenly to grow weak.

But they were safe now. And she waited until he made his way inside the ranch house, then she led the horses to the barn and secured them and bolted the door behind and ran back through the night-swirling afternoon sky.

Running now, she saw the ranch house as she'd seen it then, in gauzy obliteration, like a specter fading, then reappearing from the depths of the unconscious.

Brit dead. Ty dead.

"Ty, where are you?"

And she took the steps two at a time and pushed open the door and found herself in musty-smelling blackness, the odor of closed trunks and old pantries and aging ledgers.

"Ty?"

No answer, but she expected none. He'd lived on this prairie longer than she and knew precisely what to do.

Despite the shadows, her eye moved with unerring accuracy to the low door on the far wall, beyond his office to the steep descent that led to the storm cellar, that first dugout of almost a hundred years ago.

"Ty? You down there?"

Shivering, she pushed open the door. And saw nothing, but heard breathing, labored as though someone was struggling to push back the realm of delirium. She rallied all her forces and felt her way down and with comforting familiarity groped like a blind woman along the splintered edges of old canned goods shelves and fought in her heart the vague sense of something shameful and found a thick tallow candle and, stretching deeper into the recesses of dill-smelling wood found a tin holder and matches and glimpsed first a red ring of light round the candle and heard a rustling of cockroaches.

"Ty—"

Then she saw him, and everything from memory floated to the surface with extraordinary clarity and force. He was sitting on the edge of the mattress, the mattress itself on the sod floor. His arms were wrapped about his body in weak defense against his rain-soaked clothes. Spasms were wracking his shoulders. He looked up at her once and tried to speak but couldn't for the terrible chattering of his teeth.

"Oh, Ty," she whispered, and quickly, with the aid of the candle, she launched a search and found the stack of old blankets under which she sometimes had played fanciful childhood games in the cellar while waiting for Ty to ride back to Warrick for lunch. She remembered following his footsteps across the ceiling, wishing he'd fall through to her or she rise to him. Now she pulled at the blankets and shook them loose with trembling hands, all the time hearing his breathing grow more labored.

Someplace down here was whiskey. Josh had found several jugs once, had taken a swallow despite Brit's warning, had spit it out, claiming it was nothing more than cheap "shine."

She looked back and saw Ty bent over on himself and at that moment felt for and found the half-gallon jug and knelt before him and held his head back and forced the bottle to his lips. As she touched his forehead she felt fire, a fever raging despite the persistent and worsening chills.

"Ty, can you stand? I have to get you— You're ill. What—"

And there was panic, as she tried not to consider life without him, and ultimately she decided his wet garments were doing the harm and supported him as she would support a child and got his arms out of the frozen white shirt and quickly wrapped his body in one of the blankets, then helped him down onto the mattress and with effort removed his wet boots, unbuckled his belt and drew off his trousers and clamored about him, carefully tucking in the blankets, securing them with the weight of his body.

413

Breathless with effort, she forced another swallow through his lips, then another and held his head and felt the fever increase, alternating with chills and she was filled with terror and prayed, "God help, please," and as time went on, the more agonizing became his sufferings and her feelings of helplessness before them.

Delirium set in. He called out a name, "Mary Beth," and thrashed inside the cocoon of blankets and Mereth wept with fear, frozen herself, not knowing what she should do. If Massie was at Warrick, she'd know to send out searchers and help. But Massie was not at Warrick and there was no one to help them and Ty was dying for lack of warmth while she wept useless tears and watched him.

She had just started off in search of additional blankets when suddenly a pitiful moan sounded from the mattress, a name again, Ty calling for Mary Beth. Mereth stood still and for several minutes fought against understanding.

Then "Forgive me," she whispered to the cold night and repeated the words and at that instant knew what she was going to do and felt a peculiar concentration of her physical forces and waited for her intellect to catch up with what she had to do and instinctively knew not to wait any longer, for there were dual purposes to be served here, and though cold herself she felt her body flooded with a healing warmth as she slipped off her own wet garments and went down on her knees beside him and quickly drew back the blankets and covered him with her body and closed her eyes against the glorious pain of the first sensation, feeling his flesh hot against hers, experiencing shyness and terror and radiant longing.

"I'm here, Ty," she whispered and held his face and kissed him. "Mary Beth is here."

In simplicity and nakedness she became the woman he had loved and he looked up at her, his face flushed though now alive with happy recognition, and he pulled her quickly to him until she felt his breath hot upon her breasts, his hands moving down her back, caressing her thighs, pressing her to him while she understood for the first time the unique pain of hunger and longing and need for this miraculous closeness.

No regrets then. At some point she became Mary Beth, and while her only objective had been to cover him, now it was to ease the pain of emptiness deep inside her, and as her resolve grew stronger, so did his and without considering or anticipating anything, she felt the strength in his arms and hands increase, felt his weight shift, and she made room for his knees between her legs and looked up at the flush on his face in candlelight, his shining eyes, gazing passionately down on her and saw a peculiarly innocent childlike look such as she had never seen before. He enclosed her in his arms with a swift, supple youthful movement and dropped down upon her and when he was ready, she was ready and she closed her eyes as he pushed into her and with a moan of pleasure she felt the emptiness filled and clung to him and allowed him to take possession of her, as he'd taken possession of her years ago.

The rhythm commenced, causing greater pleasure, and she began to work with him, with a force, cleanness and depth that sent every nerve ending spiralling. And still the rhythm continued, all the faculties of her soul clearer and more active, the most diverse ideas and images possessing her mind at the same time: holy images and high walls and cockroaches rushing over tables and tallow candles with great smoldering wicks.

The pain of release caused her to cry aloud, and she clung to him and suffered a glorious paralysis of unbearable sweet agony. Oh, to prolong it just a moment longer. And he shuddered upon her and breathed deeply and she felt a pulse in the pit of her stomach, felt his heart beating against her breast, felt his flesh damp though no longer feverish.

Still breathless, he called her Mary Beth again and said how much he loved her and thanked her for marrying him and promised she would never regret it, that he would make her proud of him.

And Mereth kept quiet and held him and loved him and concentrated all her attention on her new happiness and finally fell asleep in his arms, grateful for what had been revealed to her of the mysteries of the world.

Morning then, the brink of dawn and calamity. She awakened to find him dressed, standing over her, horrified.

"You were—ill," she tried to explain, "—and cold—"

"Don't talk about it."

"I love you."

His face looked terrible. He looked down on her as though she were an offensive stranger. In his tone, in his eyes, she saw that he did not forgive her for her victory. And she knew that beside the love that bound them together, there had grown up between them during the storm of the night something evil which she would not exorcise from his heart.

She lifted her hand to him.

His hand closed to her. He turned away. "I think it best if you leave Warrick immediately."

"Ty, I love you. Did you hear me?"

"Leave us alone. Did you hear *me?*"

Then he left her sobbing amid a conflagration of grief and guilt from which she would never fully recover.

With a feeling of confusion and self-pity and loathing Mereth watched him go, listened to his step move across the old ranch house floor, and covered her head with the blanket and sobbed piteously and wanted death, yet knew she would have to seek some other, more painful way out.

———

Now she sat cold and alone on the bare mattress in the storm cellar, wrapped in a blanket, staring at the burned-down candle.

It was over. She had faced it, confronted all aspects of it. And she was still here. No judgmental bolt from God, no lasting punishment of hellfire and damnation. Then why guilt? What had she done that was so awful in the grand scheme of this world? She had loved him, made love with him, warmed him, warmed her. Nothing more. She rubbed her cold hands and looked out into the silence. Suddenly from the mysterious and faraway world in which she'd passed this night, she felt herself, all in an instant, borne back

416

to the old everyday world, glorified now by a new peace. She was not evil. Her only crime had been to love, and she still loved him and would forever. But the screams ceased, the accusatory ones, the paralyzing ones, the ones filled with self-recrimination. She closed her eyes. It *was* over.

Now with a curious sense of ritual, she stood wearily and carefully folded the blanket under which she'd taken shelter from the storm, placed it gently at the foot of the mattress and remembered Brit dead and knew there would be new despair ahead. But never again would she allow herself to be senselessly, hopelessly defeated, frozen by the past. Out of all the shadows of night and memory she had a presentiment of something good. From now on she must lay down her own individual and definite path in life. Brit's death was a powerful lesson. Determine a cause of action and follow it, without hesitation. Don't wait.

And she slowly climbed up out of the storm cellar and saw a warm morning sun beyond the open front door. To one side was Ty's old office, and out of curiosity and relief she went in, noticing first on the wall to the left, the coiled horsewhip that had belonged to Ty's daddy. Ty had whipped Josh with it once.

Inside the small, crude room there was evidence of the man himself, as though he'd recently been here: the cane-bottom rocker and rolltop desk and lopsided stacks of musty yellowed geological maps and old letters, though one did not look so old and, curiosity increasing, she flattened the fresh white sheet of stationery and saw Ty's curious slanted hand.

"Dear Brit—"

A letter of reconciliation.

"Dear Brit,

"Don't all theories of philosophy do the same, trying by the path of thought to bring man to a knowledge of what he has known long ago, has always known? It seems to me that where we went wrong was—"

End of letter, end of thought.

Carefully, lovingly she touched the incompleted letter, amazed at the man's ability to surprise, endless twists and turns, endless mysteries of soul and spirit contained within one rare human being that she had been fortunate enough to know and worship and love.

Nearby in the same sprawled script, she saw Josh's California address. More bridges to be mended? More hearts to be healed?

Nothing for Mereth? She found nothing to suggest that Ty's healing extended to her. Pain dug at her.

"Ty—"

She spoke his name and folded the unfinished letter and placed it, along with Josh's address, in the drawer for safekeeping. She wasn't quite ready for this yet, and she must get back to Warrick now where she was needed. But she'd come back here one day and explore at leisure this place, this man, this major portion of her heart and soul.

Outside the door the sagging old front porch creaked beneath her feet and she found herself in a glorious warm morning, no sign of the storm. Directly ahead was the massive elm, the "heart of Warrick," the one she'd climbed repeatedly as a child, to watch the big oil transports rumble in and out of Warrick.

Could she? Why not? And feeling grateful for the glories of this world, she hurried down the steps and got a running start and reached effortlessly up for the first limb and pulled herself to a higher level and settled on a sturdy branch and gazed up into the cloudless sky, then looked out over Warrick and found it beautiful beyond description and with both hands brushed the tears that swam in her eyes.

Off in the distance she saw the diesel trail of an oil truck, life and energy paying no attention to the epidemic of death. She smiled.

There was the key.

She settled comfortably into the crook of the old tree.

Ty was close by. She could feel him.

It was enough . . .

Warrick

"WHAT HAVE we forgotten to do?"

The hour was twenty minutes past midnight. The toneless voice was Massie's. The question was unanswerable.

Massie looked around the terrace room at the benumbed faces and decided: let the question go unanswered and order them all to bed.

Though she knew it probably would be the most unpopular request she could possibly make, she made it anyway of the man who stood at the door as though guarding it, in a strangely quiet mood, head bowed, obviously moved by the escalating tragedies that had descended on this house.

"A word, Reverend Jobe," Massie requested softly, "before we all retire, to see us to morning."

Prematurely defensive, she glanced up, expecting pained looks from all quarters, certainly from the bar where Josh and Chris sat hunched over, an empty vodka bottle between them. And if no reaction was coming from that quarter, then surely from Mereth, who had returned early this morning from someplace and who had immediately inhabited Ty's chair and throughout the evening had sat with her back to the group, saying nothing.

Massie felt that the others in the room would go along with a brief prayer, Junior Nagle and Red Pierson, seated at opposite ends of the sofa, heads slumped in identical positions, perhaps asleep for all she knew. And Dr. Buckner was still at the buffet table, picking over the fruits and cheeses and biscuits that Ramona had brought up several hours ago. He wouldn't object for the simple reason that he wouldn't listen.

"Please, Reverend Jobe," she repeated. "Help us to try to understand."

"I'm not . . . certain," he faltered and appeared to want to say
something else. Then he bowed his head, lifted his right hand mid-
way up into the air and spoke so softly that Massie had to strain to
hear.

"Our Lord, Jesus Christ, we come to the matter of our human
will in confrontation with Your divine one. Give us the strength to
accept Your coherent pattern, even though from our flawed state
we cannot perceive it, and lead us steadily toward Your enlighten-
ment. Amen."

And it was over, the simplest and most eloquent prayer Massie
had ever heard from Reverend Gerald Jobe.

He looked at Massie and said, "If you'll excuse me now, the
greatest tests are yet to come. Good-night to you all."

And he was gone.

Chris raised himself up laboriously from the bar. "What did he
say?"

Josh muttered, "He said we were all going to have to take a test
tomorrow. What on? Does anybody know?"

Massie ignored the two, who were feeling no pain. The one who
interested her sat at the end of the room in Ty's chair.

"Mereth? Are you all right?"

Mereth looked directly at her. "Will we all be buried in the
mausoleum?"

Massie felt the silent tension in the room increase. "If you want
to be. If not . . ."

"I don't think Brit wants to be."

"Did he tell you so?"

Mereth smiled. "No, we didn't talk of such things. I don't think
I've ever had a conversation with anyone about where I wanted to
be buried. Have you, Josh?"

Abruptly Mereth leaned forward in Ty's chair and looked over
her shoulder at Josh, who was returning her gaze with matching
intensity as though he understood.

"Actually, yes," he confessed. "But then I have a thing for death, you know. I always have."

Now Mereth turned about in Ty's chair and knelt on the seat like a child and rested her elbows on the back, quite at ease. "You, Junior," she proposed, and apparently didn't see the look of consternation that crossed over those usually dispassionate features. "Where are they going to bury you?"

Massie stood up, sensing the need for a diplomatic go-between. "Come on, Mereth." She smiled. "We can discuss ideal burial locations later. Right now it's late and . . ."

"Chris, you. Where are you going to be buried?"

It was as if Massie hadn't spoken. Mereth seemed determined to play the game to its end and, because this was a Mereth that Massie had never seen before, she stood up and backed off. Maybe there was no harm.

But if Chris heard Mereth's question, he refused to answer and held his position at the bar, head down.

"Chris?"

Josh shook his head broadly and placed a finger to his lips. "Tuckered out, old girl. He really is. Ask him in the morning and I'm sure he'll tell you." Then, despite his own wobbly legs, Josh slid off the barstool. "Come on, Mereth," he invited in a conspiratorial fashion, crooking his finger at her. "Come along. I want to tell you about my plans. Mine and Peter's, that is. Most creative and imaginative, they are. I promise you'll love it."

And Massie watched, grateful, as Josh, drunk or not, coaxed Mereth into movement.

Then they were gone, the eldest and the youngest, never close before, now drawn together, perhaps even a little surprised to find the blood bond so strong.

Massie looked about and decided that Chris could take care of himself. Let him sleep it off on the bar. It was the other two, the old men, who might need her assistance.

"Red? Junior? Come and I'll walk . . ."

"Need to talk, Massie." This brusque announcement came from

421

Red Pierson, who had yet to look up from his contemplative position.

Now Massie felt fatigue beginning to move in. "Could it wait,
Red, until later?"

"The will. Ty's will."

She looked up, glad that almost everyone else had left.

"Problems?" she inquired.

He nodded. "Perhaps."

"Then what?"

"Day after tomorrow. Here."

"What about probate?"

"Just a preliminary reading. Certain procedures need to be set in
motion."

Silence. Massie tried to understand the curious conversation.
"I'm sure that will be fine," she said now in answer to his proposal.
"Again, is there anything wrong?"

Red pushed slowly up out of the sofa. "Nothing that can't be
remedied, but I think we must get on it right away."

He was speaking in riddles and had to be aware he was speaking
in riddles. Apparently he saw the confusion on her face.

"Oh, come now, Massie. Surely you knew that the will would be
contested."

No, she didn't know that. "By whom?"

Red laughed, a curious sound in this setting of gloom. "Not
singular, Massie. More than one contestant. Very, very plural."

Now even Junior showed an interest. "What the hell are you
talking about, Pierson?"

"Confidential. You'll find out soon enough."

"Hey, wait!"

As Red left the room, Junior struggled after him. "Pierson, I said
wait!" he shouted to the empty door. "Listen, Massie, see if you can
get Jobe to hold off tomorrow till we get back. Twelve-thirty at the
latest. Please. Eddie's driving, so . . ."

She looked up, surprised. "Where are you . . . ?"

"Beekman's funeral. I should be there. Pierson, too. You, too, but everyone will understand, I'm sure."

Dear God, she'd forgotten Harry Beekman, the one who'd started this epidemic!

"Of course, Junior. Twelve-thirty will be no problem. It's just us, the family." She moved closer to the door, deriving comfort from the old man, Ty's "right hand" for as long as anyone could remember. She smiled and kissed Junior on the cheek. "Get some sleep. I'll need you tomorrow."

Her expression of affection seemed to undo the man. He turned brusquely away and started out of the door in pursuit of Pierson and left Massie with a sense of relief, alone except for Chris and—

"Need something to help you sleep, Massie?"

This gruff inquiry came from the buffet. Horace Buckner was now eating grapes Roman fashion, one at a time, holding each grape suspended above his mouth. Before she could respond to his first question, he proposed a second.

"Bet you're sorry now, aren't you?"

"Sorry? For what?"

"That you answered that ad thirty years ago from the Warrick Corporation for an accountant."

She smiled, pleased that old Buckner could always be counted on for the unexpected.

"Sometimes I'm very sorry." She nodded. "Other times I feel I would have ended up here, one way or another."

"Rough times ahead," he went on succinctly, tossing the grapes back on the platter, apparently full, or bored.

She nodded. "Is . . . Mereth . . . ?"

"Fine," he interrupted. "She's steel at the core, like Ty. It's not often that she lets being female get in her way."

Massie turned away from the buffet and saw Chris sitting up at the bar now, a filled shot glass before him.

At that moment the door opened and she looked back to see Eddie, out of breath, his jacket off and hanging from one finger over his shoulder. Then she remembered. He'd come from the mausoleum.

"Is everything . . . ?"

"—under control," came the exhausted reply and, at the same time, Eddie stepped all the way into the room and looked about as though in search of a drink.

Chris held up the vodka bottle. Buckner closed in on one side and Eddie the other.

"Would anyone object if we had another one of these?"

"Well, of course not." Massie smiled, suspecting that an all-night drinking session was in the offing for the three disparate men. But there was always the outside hope that perhaps they'd get so drunk they'd forget their differences and celebrate Ty's and Deeter's and Brit's lives, instead of mourning their deaths.

Massie hoped so.

———

Mereth led the procession back through the sunlit gardens from the blessedly short private services in the chill mausoleum and did her best to hide a smile at the conversation between the two men directly behind her, Josh deliberately argumentative and irreverent on this morning, and Reverend Jobe at his pompous worst again after his recent and mysterious lapse into good taste.

His dual eulogies for Brit and Ty had been simple and eloquent and moving. He'd painted a comforting picture of the glories of life after death. But who was she to challenge it? If it brought solace to the living, that was all that mattered.

"So you see, Reverend," Josh said in good humor, "nothing can persuade me that 'in the image of God' applies only to man. In fact, it has always seemed to me that mountains, rivers, trees, flowers, even animals, far better exemplify the essence of God than men with their ridiculous clothes, their meanness and hypocrisy, their vanity, mendacity and abhorrent egotism, all qualities with which I am only too familiar in myself."

No response. In fact Mereth glanced behind to see if by some chance she'd lost her procession. As she turned, she caught a glimpse of a startling sight: everyone walking in exactly the same posture, heads down, all clad in black, all silent, all—

Fellini. Or Bergman. Either man could film it as it was, naturally surrealistic, all those black and faceless figures moving through this sensuous, spring green ripeness.

Now, in answer to Josh's persistent line of questioning, the Reverend cleared his throat. "There is an objective truth in the word of God that does not leave itself open to opinion or interpretation."

"Oh? I see. And what would that be, sir?"

Again Mereth tried to conceal her amusement. She considered turning back to see how Massie was faring. But no need. Massie had been a rock during the brief service, and now Eddie O'Keefe was walking with her. Mereth would check later.

As the sun rose past the midday position, she felt the black wool upon her back begin to itch and cling. In a few minutes she'd be home.

"Hey, Mereth, wait up!" The voice was Josh's, giddy, good-natured, as though they all were only on a summer picnic. "Reverend Jobe here just asked me a question that involves you."

She stopped. At the rear, just approaching the gazebo some distance away, she saw Junior Nagle lean into the support of one of the black uniformed men who'd come out with the hearses. Red Pierson was walking by himself, a stylish red rosebud in his lapel. The others were scattered between here and there, Massie and her support group, Ramona and Eddie, and several of the longtime Warrick employees, like Elaine and Emanuel. And Horace Buckner was there, just starting up the path.

One was missing. Chris. Mereth had seen him at the service on the opposite side of the mausoleum.

The Osages had buried Deeter in the tribal burial ground early this morning. Chris had returned just in time for the twelve-thirty service here. Now, where was he?

"What Reverend Jobe has asked and what I cannot answer by myself is, why did we all leave this paradise?"

Postponing the search for Chris, Mereth looked at Josh, certain he was joking. But he wasn't, and neither was Gerald Jobe, who appeared to be making the climb easily, clutching his well-worn Bible under one arm.

"I *am* interested, Miss Warrick." Jobe smiled, drawing even with her. "I've always had trouble understanding why any young person would willingly leave all this." He gestured broadly, theatrically, to the surrounding gardens. "And Ty, what a rich influence he would have been on anyone who . . ."

Josh drew near. "Well, speaking for myself, Reverend Jobe, I left because I'm a homosexual and Ty's philosophy concerning homosexuals is that we all should be hanged by the neck until dead, which, as I'm sure you can see, makes this considerably less than paradise. For me, that is."

Quickly Mereth looked down at the flagstones and concentrated on the slow progress of a flatworm and again resisted the impulse to smile.

"I . . . shall pray for you," Reverend Jobe said and looked uncomfortable.

"Oh, please do," Josh said with baffling sincerity.

At some point Mereth had lost the rules of the game. They *were* playing, weren't they? Then why all of a sudden had everyone gone so serious?

"All right, you Mereth," Josh insisted. "Your turn. Why did you leave paradise?"

Surprised, she looked up to see both men, curiously allied, staring at her, waiting expectantly. Her impulse was to anger. What right did either of them have? Instead, she tried to dismiss the question lightly, without giving too much of herself away.

"One can't make a living at Warrick, and we all must work at something."

For several steps she thought she'd satisfied them and then she heard, directly behind her:

"You were a source of comfort to your grandfather, Miss Warrick. When you left him, he was devastated."

426

Again she turned on the meddlesome man and for one insane moment considered answering him honestly, as Josh had done. Better judgment intervened, although at the same time she felt unexpected grief.

"Mereth, are you . . . ?"

The concern came from Josh and Reverend Jobe who, despite their differences, hurried to her side. For a moment the gardens became steamy as a jungle, the black suit heavy, her breath limited and the flagstone footing uncertain.

"Come on, let's have that jacket," Josh demanded, and off came the hot wool garment.

As the breeze struck the dampness of her soaked blouse, she was stunned by a new perception of the past.

"You'd better sit down—"

"No, I'm fine, just warm."

"You went white. Did you know that?" Josh whispered, "You really looked . . ."

"I'm fine," she repeated and took his hand as they climbed toward the house.

"Why don't you go on up and rest for a while, Miss Warrick? It's been a difficult morning."

She nodded to Reverend Jobe's suggestion and tried to pull ahead of both men.

Ty.

Now every place she looked she saw surfaces that hid nothing, beginnings that were meant to be continuations, coherent accidents, failures that solved problems. She knew very well how the human mind reacted to the threat of its own destruction, but how would it react to the sure and certain knowledge of its resurrection?

She had fallen in love with Tyburn Warrick while she was still a little girl, had been in love with him all her life, had made love with him and would never cease to be in love with him. No need to apologize to anyone nor suffer guilt forever. For anything. In the end she, like everyone else, was an event which could not judge itself and which no one else had a right to judge.

"Hey, what's your hurry?" Josh called out, and for the first time she looked up, aware that she had pulled far ahead. The portico was in front of her, the glass door leading to the terrace room open.

Josh puffed his way alongside her and warned, "Here they come," and stood with her at the railing, both of them looking down on the stragglers.

"I've got to get out of this monkey suit. I'm roasting." And he was gone.

"Josh," she called, "we were going to call London, remember?"

But he merely waved a backward hand in parting, and she was left with the sense of a difficult job yet to do and the awareness of Reverend Jobe watching her carefully.

"May I be of assistance?" he offered and bridged the distance caused by Josh's sudden departure.

"No, I'm . . ."

"You mentioned telephoning someone."

"We don't know who, I'm afraid. All I have is a number," Mereth responded, backing away from the man and keeping her eye on Massie, who was just approaching the top of the steps, Eddie on one side.

Mereth had no idea what the order for the rest of the day would be and hoped it was nothing that included her. She felt a need for privacy.

"Massie." She reached out a hand to the woman, stylish even in widow's black, who now looked up through her veil as though surprised by the voice.

"Mereth, I lost track of you. Where did you—?"

"I came ahead with Josh."

"Where is he?"

"He went in to change. It's hot."

Massie looked up at the sun-filled sky with Mereth. "Ty loved to sit out here on days like this." Suddenly Massie's voice broke.

Mereth started to her side and saw Eddie draw close, and she stood helplessly back as he led Massie into the terrace room.

428

"She'll do fine." Reverend Jobe smiled. "That is one unusual black woman."

Mereth looked incredulously at the man, baffled once more by this latter-day madness in Ty's life. She started through the terrace room door and might have made it except for a voice calling to her from the garden path.

"Miss Warrick?"

She looked back to see a flushed Red Pierson just reaching the summit, a handkerchief grasped in his hand, patting his forehead. She still felt that awkwardness with Red Pierson she'd felt as a child.

"Yes, sir?"

"Need a moment." As he reached the top he leaned on the railing and, seeing Jobe nearby, became annoyed. "Isn't there something you have to do?" he asked with a rudeness that surprised Mereth.

If Reverend Jobe was aware, he gave no indication of it.

"Not really. May I be of service?"

"Not to me you can't," Red snorted.

Mereth wondered if perhaps she'd misjudged the prim little lawyer.

"Come. Walk with me, Miss Warrick," Red Pierson commanded and took her arm and led her away from the terrace room door and the gaping Reverend Jobe.

At first Mereth was afraid the preacher might follow them, but he didn't. Instead, he appeared to watch wistfully for a moment and then he disappeared inside the terrace room after the others.

"Good riddance," Red muttered and led her down the long stone terrace toward the east facade of Warrick. For several moments they walked in silence.

Mereth was acutely aware of her sloppy state, jacket off, white silk tie undone and hanging loose, while beside her Red walked, equally as warm but the picture of sartorial order.

"Why don't you loosen your tie?" she suggested.

"It isn't my tie that's bothering me," Red snapped and continued to lead her to the end of the terrace, where the crosswinds from the north had whirled a mixed debris of winter-dead leaves into the corner where they remained. From this point it was also possible to see the end of the driveway, and the peaked roof of the security house and the gate. The damaged half had been repaired and rehung.

Brit.

Again she felt the stab of grief for Brit. Just the beginning, she feared.

"This is far enough," Red said abruptly and came to a halt at the heavy stone balustrade and seemed now to peer into the distance, a strained expression on his face. "I will never claim to have understood Brit," he said coldly, "but I am sorry for this."

It probably was as close to mourning as Red Pierson could come. Mereth could think of nothing to say.

"The service was just awful, didn't you think?" he went on, more garrulous than she'd ever known him. At least he'd never talked much with her. Perhaps with Ty and Massie—

"I'm afraid I'm not an expert on funerals."

"One doesn't have to be an expert," he scolded. "You don't dismiss a man like Tyburn Warrick with ten minutes of Bible drivel." He seemed to flare into genuine anger in a remarkably short time.

For the first time Mereth sensed repressed grief. Still baffled by the purpose of this impromptu walk, she kept quiet and decided to let him take the lead, as he would anyway.

After several seconds of brooding, Red Pierson asked, "What are your plans?" and looked directly at her.

She faltered. "I . . . don't . . ."

"What are your plans?" he repeated. "Will you be returning to Tulsa? I assume you won't be staying on at Warrick."

"Permanently? No. Why?"

"You . . . teach, don't you?"

"Yes. At Oakhurst. Nineteenth-century American lit."

430

His eyes brightened. "Good school. Daughters of several friends of mine went there. I used to serve on the board."

"I went there. Ty was on the board."

"Of course."

"Mr. Pierson, what is this?"

"I think we'd better get back. Look . . ."

As he pointed down the terrace, she saw Junior Nagle just struggling to the top, where he was met by Horace Buckner, who put his arm around the man and tried to lead him into the coolness of the interior.

"Thank you for your time," Red said as he hurried away.

What was that all about, she wondered, and admitted she had not one idea.

Ty.

The name continued to inhabit her memory as the man inhabited her soul. What she'd really like to do was to go back to the mausoleum just by herself in comfortable blue jeans and a shirt.

Then after that, she would have to see if she could find whoever it was that Brit had left in London. Surely there was someone. Brit did not function well alone. There must be friends, people who loved him, who needed him.

Then there was a new mood of despair to be conquered. It wasn't the deaths or the grieving that was wearing her down. It was the endless effort of trying to transcend both and move beyond them, and trying to comprehend what lay behind the pain.

Slowly she turned and started down the stone terrace. The sun was high, the smell and feel of imminent summer upon her.

"Will you be returning to Tulsa? I assume you have a life there."

No, not really, Red, not life, not in Ty Warrick's sense of the word. She did have a profession that did not demand too much, a life-style that did not deplete her bank account, a freedom that did not free her, a future that did not challenge her, a life philosophy that did not sustain her.

It was a mountainous pile of negatives. If that was life, Red, then she had one.

The following morning Red Pierson arose early, feeling that unique excitement of a special day when he could play his lawyer's role to the hilt.

Now he was waiting for Junior, a brief pre-meeting meeting. He looked about at the terrace room. Was this the proper setting? At one end the girls were preparing the breakfast buffet. At the far end he saw the overcast day and Emanuel's gardeners. Distractions to the right, distractions to the left. No, this room would not do.

Thus resolved, he started back down the corridor. As he approached the entrance hall, he stopped, debating. Straight ahead was the small dining room, various guest rooms and the auxiliary kitchen. Veer right and there was the library, imposing, massive, intimidating. For this ritual, intimidation was a good characteristic.

With that in mind, he made his selection. The library, and wondered if he had to clear it with anyone and decided, no, for there was in Warrick this morning the decided sense of a runaway wagon, a cart without a driver, a plane without a pilot.

He closed the library door quietly and turned about to face the perfect setting.

Through the two large, leaded glass windows he saw a gray turbulent sky, more rain threatening. At the exact center of the room, surrounded by floor-to-ceiling walls of books, was a comfortable arrangement of sofas and chairs and several good strong reading lamps. It would be a simple matter for Red to occupy that desk right there and rearrange the other chairs until all were facing him, proscenium fashion.

How many chairs? Just the family. And Massie. And a few others. There were many bequests, but Red could deal with them later. For now all he wanted was to take the first legal steps, clear the way for the preliminaries and get the thing into the courts. Even then it would take time.

Yes, the library would do quite nicely, and now all he had to do was to find Junior Nagle and enlist his help in getting the others moving on this difficult morning. He looked at his watch. Ten after six. Everyone still in bed, no doubt.

"In here, sir. I believe I saw him. Oh, there you are, Mr. Pierson."

Red looked up. Eddie O'Keefe was ushering in a very puffy-eyed Junior.

"I saw you come in, sir," Eddie explained. "Mr. Nagle here has been looking . . ."

Junior interrupted him by pushing past with an expression which seemed to say, Get rid of him so we can get to work.

"It's all right." Red nodded. "Would you do a couple of things for me, Eddie?"

"Of course."

"Tell Massie that we'll be meeting in here at ten o'clock. That is, if she has no objections. And, if you would, spread the word to the others."

"What others, sir?"

"The family, Reverend Jobe and the permanent household staff."

The door closed behind Eddie, and Red heard nothing then but the wind rising outside.

"Coffee would be good," the old man sulked, seated uncomfortably on a low chair.

"We'll go have breakfast in a minute," Red promised as one would promise a child. "All right, what do we have?" he asked, moving directly to the heart of the matter.

Junior looked up on a yawn, which was followed by an expression of bewilderment.

"You *did* talk to Burton?" Red prodded.

"Of course I did. I said I would, didn't I? According to Burton, it don't look good. Old Ty was playing fast and loose at the very end. Burton's suspicion is that Ty knew and conveniently had his stroke. God, I'd give anything for a cup of coffee!"

Red listened carefully, trying to separate fact from fiction. "A complete accounting when?" he asked, trying to keep Junior on the track.

433

"When? About the day after hell freezes over."

"Did they give you a debt estimate?"

"Couldn't. Approaching three hundred million and still counting."

Junior was sinking into the confines of the leather chair.

"Don't get yourself too excited too soon," Red soothed. "The Warrick Basin is separate from the corporation. It is bound in an irrevocable trust, and Ty was merely the trustee. The corporation is liable for its own debts, but the trust is unencumbered. The creditors can't touch it. It was Ty's ace in the hole, and very shortly it will be ours." Red faltered slightly. "If reason prevails."

Junior struggled up out of his chair. "What do you mean, if reason prevails?"

"Well, there's always the unexpected."

"The unexpected? Lawyers! Shit!" Junior started toward the door, then stopped and turned back. "Listen, Red, between the two of us we own twenty percent of the stock in the Warrick Corporation. My expectation is to *keep* it and even enlarge on it. I'm now going to the terrace room, where I *expect* to get a cup of coffee, and before this day is over I *expect* you to see to it that goddamn reason prevails!"

Red heard Junior leave the library and made no attempt to stop him or join him. He moved slowly away from his uncomfortable perch on the arm of the sofa to a chair and looked out at the boiling gray clouds, the trees beginning to bend and dip under the force of the approaching storm. Twister weather. One good tornado funnel and no more worries.

But the infantile nihilism was so ludicrous that within moments he was back on track again, dragging himself up from the chair where he would sit shortly and tell his rapt audience precisely how things were going to be from now on.

No. Correction. *He* wouldn't be telling them. Ty would be telling them.

"Tell Mr. Pierson I'll be there as soon as I can," Mereth said over her shoulder to Eddie's persistence. Then to the receiver she shouted, "Hello? Hello? Who is this?"

Again static interfered, cutting off the faint voice, female or so Mereth thought, coming from Brit's London phone number.

"Yes, operator, try again." Slowly she hung up.

"I'm telling you, Mereth, Pierson's getting hot," Eddie warned through Ty's bedroom door. "Everybody's waiting."

Doubly annoyed, both at Eddie's insistence and at the image of what he'd just described down in the library, Mereth rested her forehead in both hands and stared down on Ty's desk, at the multidigited London number she'd taken from the address book in the terrace room. Why she'd chosen Ty's room, she wasn't quite certain. It was empty and quiet, and she felt close to Ty.

"Mereth?"

"Tell them to go ahead," she said.

"Red Pierson won't do that."

"Then he'll have to wait, won't he? Brit left close friends, I'm certain, someone, people who care. We must tell them . . ."

When she least expected it, she felt new grief.

"How long do you think?"

"I have no idea. The operator's placing the call again."

"Couldn't someone else . . . ?"

"No." She delivered the single word with a finality that she hoped penetrated. "Why don't you go on down, Eddie, and tell Red Pierson that . . ."

"Because he told me to come up here and not to come back without you."

She looked up slowly. "I . . . don't understand. Why do I have to be there?"

"The will," Eddie said.

"I don't care. It doesn't concern me."

"It seems everyone has to be present."

Mereth leaned back in Ty's chair. "How is Massie?"

"Fine," he nodded. "A rock."

435

"Who else is down there?" she asked.

"*All* the rest," Eddie said with emphasis, "and old Pierson's about to have a fit."

"I don't . . ."

"Reverend Jobe's there. Planted himself in the front row. Of course, why not? Mr. Warrick promised him . . ."

"What?"

Eddie shrugged. "They were good friends. I heard Mr. Warrick tell Reverend Jobe once that while he hadn't always done the right thing in this world, he'd see to it that he did the right thing in the next one."

Mereth blinked at the childish statement, unable to believe that Ty had said it.

She turned back to the phone, to the desk, Ty's clutter.

"Eddie, why don't you go on down? Tell Mr. Pierson to give me ten minutes."

Then he was gone, and for several moments Mereth stared at the door. It didn't hurt so much today, and for that she was grateful.

The phone rang. Answer it. Someone somewhere loved Brit. From now on, love must be served, not ignored or condemned.

"Hello?"

Static, not so bad. "Hello? This is Mereth Warrick. Who's there, please? Hello?"

Finally she heard a voice, small, distant, female, frightened.

"It's me. Sophie."

Chris sat in a straight-backed chair near the north wall of the library, close to the window. A good location. Not attracting the attention of anyone.

He looked down on the cracked leather portfolio resting on his lap. All his life, it seemed, he'd been waiting for this moment. Was every victory always marked by regret? He was here alone. Deeter should have been with him.

He turned sideways in the uncomfortable chair and looked out of the leaded glass window. Rain. Just starting. A pleasant background sound.

"Ah, Miss Warrick, I'm glad you could join us."

At the sound of Red Pierson's voice, Chris turned around in the chair and saw Mereth just coming through the door. She looked sleepy, distant, her blue jeans and loose-fitting shirt in sharp contrast to Massie's stylish attire. Now Chris saw Massie motion Mereth forward to the leather sofa, to the empty place on Massie's right, which apparently she'd saved for her.

On Massie's left sat Josh, and only then did Chris see it for what had been intended, a unified family portrait. Clever of Massie, Chris thought, and watched as Mereth started toward her appointed place.

Suddenly she appeared to change her mind and walked toward the back wall of books, no chair, just a heavy oak table which obviously had been pushed out of the way to make room for this new arrangement of furniture. Mereth sat on the table, pulling herself up and allowing her feet, bare feet, to swing in the air.

Chris struggled to hide a grin as Massie continued for several awkward moments to wave Mereth forward, but apparently Mereth was comfortable and content where she was and that's where she would stay.

At the newly created "front" of the library sat Red Pierson, to one side Junior Nagle, studies in contrast, Red dapper and groomed and pencil thin, Junior sloppy, coatless, collar of his white shirt wrinkled.

The rest of the company consisted of Horace Buckner, in the overstuffed chair, his feet lifted to the ottoman, coffee cup in hand and a large platter of assorted breakfast pastries on the table to one side.

And Gerald Jobe was there center stage, seated directly in front of Pierson, looking the most dapper of all in his gray silk suit that gave off an expensive shine. He wore makeup this morning, a visible layer of rosy pancake. As he had explained to everyone with profuse apology, he must leave here shortly and go directly to the television station for the live broadcast of his weekly show.

And Ramona Evans was there, hovering by the door on the pretense of refilling coffee for anyone who wanted it.

And Eddie O'Keefe holding a self-conscious position back at the door with Ramona, as though uncertain whether he should stay or go.

Now Chris looked about the large, impressive room to see who, if anyone, had been overlooked in this unique roll call. All present and accounted for.

Then he saw Red Pierson lift a large brown briefcase to the table, open it and withdraw a blue leather folder and place it reverently on the table.

Chris felt a tremor of excitement. It was about to happen, what Deeter had waited for, what Deeter's father had fought for and what Chris had longed for.

"Miss Warrick, are you sure you won't come closer?"

It was Pierson again, apparently displeased by Mereth's selection of a seat.

"No, Mr. Pierson. I'm fine."

"I can't see you in the shadows."

"I can see you."

Impasse. Give up, Mr. Pierson. Ty Warrick may be dead and entombed, but his stubbornness lives and is seated over there on that table, swinging bare feet.

"Then let's begin," Red Pierson said as though the next few hours were something only to be gotten through.

Mereth couldn't quite believe the monstrous and amusing drama that was taking shape before her eyes, a large, wood-paneled library, motley collection of family and beloved friends and trusted servants, the meticulous solicitor on one side, slightly rumpled and suspect business partner on the other. Even the weather was playing its proper role. The early morning sun had taken refuge behind

438

black, brooding clouds which she could now see through the high leaded-glass window. Spring rains in Oklahoma were known for their theatrics.

As Red Pierson arranged the papers before him, Mereth suspected he was enjoying himself to the maximum, suspected that most lawyers must live for these moments.

With the demise of the Tulsa Petroleum Exchange Bank and Massie's hints at trouble, the Warrick pie had probably dwindled to a cupcake. And for that she was sorry, for Josh's sake and anyone else's who had great hopes and greater needs.

She braced her arms on the table and stared straight down at the highly polished wood floor. Sophie. Sophie Randel, she'd said, identifying herself. Cockney-sounding.

"I'm so sorry, Miss Randel. Brit is . . ."

Somehow the woman had known, even before Mereth had spoken the word. After that she'd sounded simply newly defeated, one more blow in a lifetime composed primarily of blows.

They'd talked. Mereth had heard children in the background, laughing, apparently unaware of the nature of the call. They had not been married, no. Nothing so bourgeois as that, but there were children. Oh, no, not their own. Stray cats, you know, puppies and mudlarks in the old Dickensian sense.

"Are you with us, Miss Warrick?"

The terse question came from Red Pierson and jarred her back to Warrick and away from Brit's London world.

"Yes, of course."

The London matter wasn't over. She'd given Sophie this Warrick phone number as well as her private number in Tulsa. They would speak again.

"Well, then," Pierson began, rising from his chair like some harried schoolmaster.

Mereth saw the rest of the gathering straighten to attention as well. On the far side of the room, but at an angle compatible with her own, Chris was looking serious, and she felt sorry for him. He looked out of place, as though with Deeter's death his position here had become even more marginal. And, of course, his presence this morning was understandable. Deeter's heir. Something worked out behind the scenes long before Ty's death.

"First of all," Red said, fingering the edge of the blue leather folder, "I want everyone to realize that this is only Step One. With an estate the size and complexity of Warrick, it could take months, years, before final resolutions are reached. I would be less than honest with you if I didn't tell you this in advance."

As Red Pierson rambled on about probates and time limitations and federal requirements, state requirements and a variety of "fiscal obligations," Mereth struggled to keep her mind on the matter at hand.

The disposition of wealth, Ty had once told her, was the only truly boring aspect of acquiring it. The challenge, the development, the pursuit, the treasure hunt, these were all. The rest was garbage.

The only true miracle was how clear that voice still sounded inside her head, as though he were sitting on the edge of the table with her, swinging his feet with hers.

You see that, Ty, that man there in the front row, Reverend Gerald Jobe?

"Oh, I see him, Mereth. He's a clever bastard, that one is."

You gave him money.

"One million, to be exact. And there's more to come."

Why?

"Why not? He'll filch some, squirrel some away for himself, but some will fan out and do some good."

I miss you, Ty.

"Listen, Red's about to strut his stuff."

"Without waxing too poetic," Pierson was saying now, "I'm sure that every one of us will feel the effect of Tyburn Warrick in our lives for the rest of our days. In fact, I feel him here now, at this very moment, in this very room . . . ."

Mereth smiled.

"So let's commence."

Mereth closed her eyes to the droning voice, to the black clouds and fierce wind and sheets of rain and unseasonable chill.

"Aren't you interested, Mereth?"

No, not really.

"Where do you want to go?"

Anyplace. With you.

". . . and on the seventh of March," Red Pierson intoned, "he added what has now turned out to be this final codicil."

She looked up and tried to make sense out of Pierson's monotonous voice, but couldn't and found of much greater fascination the taut, strained expression on Chris's face as he listened closely. The storm had almost obscured all daylight and now forced Red Pierson to lift the heavy document filled with fine print from the desk and ultimately call out for—

"Light!"

Massie wanted nothing, was expecting nothing. She and Ty had had their "talk" a long time ago.

"I'm giving you cuts of the corporate pie now, Massie, because when I'm gone, you won't be able to trust any of them."

She had not believed him at the time, had in fact even scolded him for his cynicism. Now she was glad that that part of their relationship was over and had been over for many years. He'd been generous with her, but she'd known what to do with it, and now her position in the library on this morning was primarily one of responsibility to Ty's grandchildren.

"Your attention, please," Red commanded foolishly, for never had the communal attention in the room been more his. "As we all know, Ty's indebtedness over the last few years has been enormous. What you may not know is that he divided portions of his empire long before his death in the form of irrevocable trusts. The one exception is the Warrick Drilling Corporation. In point of fact, part of his indebtedness at Tulsa Pet came about as a result of paying extravagant gift taxes on sums of money and property he had set in trusts rather than by drilling misadventures, although there were plenty of those."

He ranged freely back and forth in front of the table. "I realize that many of you have been apprehensive recently because of the problems confronting the Tulsa Petroleum Exchange Bank. Let me now reassure you that the irrevocable trusts are completely safe and beyond the reach of that disaster. The Warrick Drilling Corporation, however, is rather seriously involved in debt. Seriously, but not hopelessly, and with proper and prudent administration, the Drilling Corporation will not only survive but flourish. My only regret is that I was, until today, unable to dispel your anxieties. The confidentiality of Ty's will had to be respected until all of Ty's heirs could be present or represented."

Massie listened more closely, hearing this for the first time. She had no idea.

Red went on. "In essence, Ty for years has been trustee to his own heirs, and now that he is dead the trusts are dissolved and the assets distributable. Important among those assets are of course Warrick, the estate and everything in it. It was Ty's express wish that Warrick, the house and all that it contains belong and quite rightly to Jo Massie."

Massie looked up, unable to speak. Red appeared to be searching for something on the page of the will.

"Ah, here it is," Red said and looked over his glasses at the gathering in general and Massie in particular. "I wanted to find Ty's words and here they are, concerning Massie and Warrick. 'To do with as she pleases in small repayment for the years she loved me and humored me and kept me strong.' "

The voice droned on, but Massie didn't hear the specific words, couldn't.

"*Ty, there's too much here. Let's open it to the public at least one day a week.*"

"*No, I won't have it, can't have it. When I'm gone, you can do with it as you like.*"

No tears. Not now. What she felt now was the beginning of a

steady, though bearable pain which she knew she would feel every day of her life, the loss and separation of a vital part of herself. Like an amputation. One never fully adjusted. The best one could hope for was accommodation.

"Are you all right, Massie?"

The soft inquiry came from Josh, who sat now with his arm about her shoulders. "We're all pleased," he whispered further. "It's exactly as it should be."

Then it was true. It was hers.

She looked up, alive with plans. First thing she'd do would be to combine all of the artwork into one ground-floor gallery, build a new annex, a separate entrance wouldn't be a bad idea, except for security which could be reworked, open to the public, free of charge, and then all of the garden clubs of the state should have a day, maybe two.

Then accommodations should be made for the handicapped, the elderly, an easy-access parking and additional sanitary facilities. No charge, of course, and Massie would oversee the entire operation and at last the special beauty of Warrick would be available to all. How appropriate.

The profit of the earth is for all. Ecclesiastes.

"Massie?"

Red's inquiry brought her back to the library, where the only sound was the rhythm of the rain upon the windows.

"I'm fine, Red." She smiled and was a little amazed and pleased to discover that she was.

"Then we'll proceed to the other bequests," Red went on, all business.

Massie longed to look back at Mereth, but couldn't do so without calling too much attention both to herself and to Mereth. She was being quiet for too long.

"For Joshua Warrick and for Britton Warrick, in compensation for the cross of bearing the Warrick name, I bequeath to each five million dollars."

Massie felt the tension around her escalate to excitement. Josh whispered something under his breath, a joyful obscenity, and clasped his hands together. He could build a very comfortable future on such a foundation.

Brit. Dear God, what would she do with—

Suddenly all thoughts ceased save one. Something was wrong, terribly wrong. Only two names had been spoken.

Massie turned about and looked directly back. Mereth continued to sit on the high table.

At that exact moment, everyone in the room seemed to perceive the terrible omission. Reverend Gerald Jobe turned slowly and looked back sympathetically, as did Chris. Josh made matters worse by standing and looking at her.

Silence.

What had happened between Mereth and Ty? Why the awful separation which seemed now to extend even beyond Ty's death? How many times in the past Massie had asked herself that question. She dared not ask it of anyone else. Still, what had happened?

"Look at her, Massie, isn't she something? Come on, Mereth, my baby."

Mereth had taken her first step into Ty's arms and had continued to move in approximately the same direction every day of her life until—

"Mereth and I are going riding, Massie."

"Come on, Mereth. Need company on the plane to Dallas."

"Where's Mereth? Can't find her."

"Mereth, get your hiking boots on."

"Massie, she's mine."

"Red, I . . . don't understand." Massie's weak inquiry did further damage to the already stunned room.

Slowly Josh sat back down on the sofa beside her. Reverend Jobe studied his hands. Chris fell into a close examination of his portfolio and Red Pierson started to read again, a long listing of Warrick employees and the amounts bequeathed to each, ranging from a generous one hundred thousand dollars for Ramona, which immediately prompted quiet weeping from the door, to a grand half a million for Eddie, which prompted an audible "Dear . . . God!"

444

Still nothing could quite annihilate that sense of injustice which had permeated the room with the reading of two names instead of three.

What had happened?

"To Tulsa Christian College, Mr. Warrick bequeaths the interest in the following three producing wells . . ."

Massie glanced toward Reverend Jobe, who sat now with his head pressed back against the cushion, eyes lifted heavenward, an expression of pure light on his face. He appeared to be at prayer. A generous gift it was, Massie thought, and perhaps one of the most difficult for Ty to make.

Ty had a curious attitude toward his wells. The oil in the raw natural state was his, his possession, his treasure. But once it entered the pipeline and was translated into dollars per barrel, then he lost interest in it. Now, to bequeath to Tulsa Christian College interest in three top producers—

Still, Massie was pleased.

As Red's voice droned on with lesser bequests to various men in his organization who'd served him well over the years, Massie tried to think of ways she could explain it to Mereth. Of course, she would make it up, give her something of value from Warrick itself.

Had Ty lost his mind?

"Now to the last two trusts."

Red's tone of voice altered and recaptured everyone's attention. Something to do with one of the corporations, no doubt, some personal arrangement worked out with Junior Nagle or—

"Most complicated, these, executed only a few months ago."

Again Massie looked up, puzzled by Red's hesitancy.

"I humored Tyburn Warrick at the time," he went on, in a personal confession that was out of place. "But it had been his habit of late to make several changes regarding this piece of property, and there are those in this room who'll be grievously disappointed, but I beg you, reserve all challenges, all objections for the courts. For now, this is as Tyburn Warrick wished it to be."

He lifted the last trailing codicil from the table and supported the bulk of the document with one hand and turned to the very end and read:

"To Deeter Big Cow, I bequeath the land on which his castle stands, three million dollars as small payment for a lifetime of love and companionship and all surface rights to the northeast corner of Warrick known as the Warrick Basin. In the event of the death of Deeter Big Cow, all of these bequests shall move intact to his grandson, Christopher Faxon."

Silence.

Then—

"No!"

The shout resounded throughout the stunned room and Massie saw Chris on his feet, one hand thrusting the leather portfolio up into the air.

"No. That can't be. Warrick said the basin was Deeter's. *All* of it. I have proof. A signed letter. What good are surface rights? There's nothing of value on the surface of the Warrick Basin."

Massie had never seen him so distraught, and as she looked toward Red Pierson to see how he would handle the man, she saw that he already had his hands full with Junior Nagle, who appeared equally upset, on his feet, his face as red as Massie had ever seen it, his voice rising.

"Ty told me that the basin—"

"Wait a minute, everyone," Red commanded. "There's more."

As the room fell silent once again, he shifted the codicil and read further:

"It is my wish that all subsurface rights to the Warrick Basin, including all mineral rights, be given to Mereth Warrick for the purpose of exploration and development and that this ownership extend in perpetuity to her heirs so long as the earth survives. In addition, this codicil awards to her 65 percent of the stock of all Warrick corporations, which gives her the financial control needed to develop the Warrick Basin, with one final note: that should she be unable or unwilling to assume these responsibilities, the Warrick estate including the Warrick Basin should be held in trust and jointly administered by my business associate Junior Nagle and my personal attorney Red Pierson and the Trust Department of the Dallas Commerce Bank. In the event Mereth Warrick refuses or is unable to assume this bequest, I leave her five million dollars."

Again silence. Deeper this time, no one speaking, no one moving. From where Massie sat she saw Chris take his bewilderment and disappointment to the high library window and the rainy day. He said nothing further, as though the defeat had exhausted him.

Massie turned and looked back at Mereth. Subsurface rights. If what Red Pierson had read was true, and if Mereth could fight any and all contestants and win, and if she had the wit and intelligence and courage and daring to know what to do with the basin, and if it was her desire to do so, then she could well become one of the richest women in the world by the end of the century.

If. Many ifs.

She saw Mereth smiling now, still perched on the edge of the table, still swinging her bare feet in midair.

She *did* look less bored.

What in the hell was the girl smiling for? Didn't she know what had happened?

As Red Pierson caught a fleeting glance of Mereth Warrick, he thought he saw an unexpected resemblance, that calm reaction under stress that reminded him of Ty. Ty was always smiling at the wrong moment, throwing his enemies off, disarming his competitors.

"I know, Junior. I know." Red now tried to soothe.

"No, I mean it, Red," Junior Nagle warned seriously. "The corporation was counting on the development of the basin. Hell, that was Ty's dream and God's creation, equal to the entire Gulf Coast of the United States. It is simply one of the richest basins in this world, under Ty's uncompromised control, and it is totally undeveloped." He paused, forced to catch his breath.

Red filled the vacuum. "And he had placed it in trust, Junior, several years ago. It is inviolate. The corporation can't touch it unless Miss Warrick yields."

"Mr. Pierson, I would like for you to look at these." Then there was Chris Faxon thrusting a handful of yellowed documents at him.

Between Junior's threats and Chris's entreaties, Red struggled to meet the demands of the moment.

"All right," he said, doing a little shouting of his own. "I said, all right. Now wait just a minute, both of you, and the rest of you quiet down as well. I mean it."

Gradually he heard a cessation of the voices around him, everyone returning reluctantly to their places. "Now I want to make it clear," he said and raised his voice over a deafening clap of thunder. "This is, in every sense of the word, a legal and bona fide document. Ty saw to that. Signatures of witnesses are in order, everything, so that it isn't the legality we are challenging. We want that clearly understood. What we are—examining—"

At the last minute he indulged in a little semantics—"to examine" was softer than "to challenge."

"What we are examining here is not even Ty Warrick's judgment. He must have had his reasons to which we were not privy, nor should we have been."

Red was aware that he was making the worse sort of lawyer noises, awful equivocation. But then, what was he supposed to do? It was a delicate matter, to start talking someone out of a great fortune and yet try to make it sound as if it was for her own benefit.

Massie spoke up as though beginning to suspect his ulterior motives.

"What precisely is it, Red, that you're trying to say?"

"What I'm trying to say is this," he repeated, "that there might be the possibility, that there would be no cause for us, any of us, to go near a court of law. You know what Ty always said about the courts . . ."

He broke off, realizing that what Ty had said about the courts could not be repeated in mixed company.

"Well, anyway," he went on, wishing that the girl perched on the table at the back of the library would look up, thus giving him at least a fighting chance to read her expression and judge his chances of winning. "Perhaps Miss Warrick wishes to express an opinion. What I'm trying to say is, perhaps she'd be happier with the money, something less demanding, something more immediate."

Chris spoke from the window, still bewildered.

"I'm not certain why you have even raised such a point, Mr. Pierson, when I now hold in my hand a signed letter giving Mr. Deeter Big Cow *full* ownership to Warrick Basin."

Patiently Red tried to jar the young man back to a semblance of good sense.

"The codicil I just read was dated and notarized two months ago. As a legal instrument it takes precedence over every other . . ."

"And what about original rights?" Chris suggested quietly.

Red didn't even try to answer that one, still concentrating as he was on Mereth Warrick.

"Well, Miss Warrick, could we dare to ask for a comment from you?"

The silence of the room was matched by the silence on the young woman's face, a peculiar silence which seemed to conceal a deeper, more private dialogue, something in her eyes, a distance and an intimacy that Red found strangely moving.

Ty had placed in her hands a large piece of God's earth that contained vast riches.

Now there were only two valid questions in Red's mind. One: was the young woman aware of the gift and all its potential? And Two: what was she going to do about it?

———————————

"I think it best if you leave Warrick, leave us alone."

The angry words seemed to evolve out of the rain. Mereth bowed her head against the focus in the library, all eyes on her.

"Mereth?"

She looked up. Strangely, the real voices were less real than the one ghost voice.

all right?''

Josh who ignored the tension and led her to a comfortable
chair and took the one opposite her, still impervious to the
communal stares, the tense waiting.

"If I were you," he whispered, "I'd take the money and run.
There are too many vultures in this room, and not enough dead
flesh to go around. I have only one sister. I don't want to see her
become a sacrificial victim."

Mereth smiled, touched by the awkward expression of love.

*"To Deeter Big Cow I bequeath . . . all surface rights to the northeast
corner of Warrick known as the Warrick Basin. In the event of the death of
Deeter Big Cow, all of these bequests shall move intact to his grandson,
Christopher Faxon . . . It is my wish that all subsurface mineral rights to
the Warrick Basin . . . be given to Mereth Warrick for the purpose of
exploration and development . . ."*

When she'd first heard Red Pierson read those words she'd
thought he'd been joking, thus her smile. It had been several moments later when she'd remembered that Red Pierson did not joke.
About anything.

"Miss Warrick, are you interested in talking with the group
now?" Pierson's overly polite, prim inquiry only compounded her
bewilderment.

"About what?"

"About this." He thrust Ty's will up into the air in her direction.
"Come on, Mereth, get the Jeep. I want you to see the new well."

"Miss Warrick? We're waiting."

The voices collided, the one in her head and the ones in the
room.

"Miss Warrick?"

To her left, Josh slumped in the deep chair and eyed her over the
tops of his fingers, which formed a tent obscuring the rest of his
face.

Take the money and run.

Not bad advice perhaps.

She turned away and found herself confronting the walls of books consisting of the bound Warrick files.

"I don't, for the love of God, see the point, Massie. Who gives a damn how I did it?"

Carefully Mereth ran her fingers along the books, remembering Ty's endless complaining . . . All Massie had wanted was access to his old files.

"I wish you could have seen it, Mereth. That first Oklahoma field was forty-three miles long and from three to twelve miles wide in places."

Red Pierson started slowly away from the table and the company of the others, as though he knew it was time to force a decision.

"Hell, Mereth, old H. L. Hunt won his first lease in a poker game. All you need is the gambler's instinct."

"Miss Warrick, I believe the time has come to talk."

Briefly she shut her eyes and wished that one or the other voice would go away. It was difficult trying to respond to both.

"Now, Miss Warrick, it would save everyone an enormous amount of time, energy and money if right here and now we reached some sort of understanding."

"Success comes not from determination alone, Mereth. The imagination to grasp a new concept must come first, then the courage to try it."

"Are you listening, Miss Warrick?"

"I'm listening, Mr. Pierson."

"Five million dollars. A comfortable foundation on which to build a future, wouldn't you say?"

Mereth wasn't saying anything for the moment, but she was beginning to understand. It was Ty again, as much a presence in this library as all those of flesh and blood, manipulating them in a masterly way, as only Ty could do. At last he had righted that ancient wrong, *his* father's thievery of Osage land. Now it was Ty's wish that there be cooperation, partnership.

With Chris owning all surface rights to the Warrick Basin, he owned as well all rights of access. Without his permission the heavy equipment needed for exploration and development would be blocked. Mereth knew she could go to the Board of Adjustment

se and after a year, perhaps two, after the involvement
Bureau of Indian Affairs causing further delays, she might
n luck be granted a variance in her favor. But she knew now that
Ty wanted it to work another way.

Ignoring the silence and all those carefully watching eyes, she
walked with deliberation the width of the library, to where Chris
stood staring out at the storm.

He heard her approach and turned, his expression guarded.

She looked up at him. "You know this means we would have to
work together," she said, part statement, part question.

He rubbed the back of his neck. A quiet smile barely separated
his lips. It was more a smile of the eyes. "Nothing would give me
greater pleasure."

Mereth held his gaze for a moment and was pleased. He would
be a good partner, informed, strong. As a beginning it wasn't bad.

Well then, a decision. It was time. Past time.

The Warrick Basin.

It was all there, along with his private papers. And it wasn't as
though she was a complete novice. She'd been privy to more conversations between Ty and Junior Nagle than Red Pierson could
imagine, and with their help had learned the language of oil. She'd
accompanied Ty on oil-field inspections, had joined in poker games
with the drilling crews and had tasted core samples along with
strawberry lollipops.

"Miss Warrick, will you cooperate? It's such a simple matter. All
you have to do is sign this, accepting the bequest of money and
relinquishing all rights to the Warrick Basin and your troubles are
over."

The Warrick Basin.

Somewhere on Ty's desk she'd seen the geology report. Final
studies on the Warrick Basin. Not isolated pools. One huge pool.
There was something hidden beneath that poor soil.

*"If only one fourth is recovered in the next five years, that will be fifteen
billion cubic feet, and the geology says there is, conservatively speaking, sixty*

one billion. At fifteen dollars per thousand cubic feet, we are talking seventy five billion dollars."

"Miss Warrick, are you listening?"

"Just don't milk the cow too hard, Mereth, and milk her intelligently."

She looked back at the group of expectant faces. Massie was here, and would be an invaluable and trusted advisor.

Something hidden. Go and find it.

Why not?

She drew a deep breath. And felt new life. Ty was gone but she was here, and the land was here and the challenge. Nothing could remain the same. It would be the greatest of all transitions, and she'd always loved transitions. As the world and life were wont to do, it was beginning all over again.

"Miss Warrick, did you hear me?"

Red Pierson approached her directly. "You can't handle it. You know that. There is nothing in your background or training to prepare you for this kind of enormous responsibility. You haven't the slightest idea what to do, even where to begin. You can't do it."

She caught Chris's eye and returned his smile, a slow smile that began gently and became a grin.

Armed with nothing more than a new and intractable conviction of who she was and an eloquent belief in herself, Mereth walked past Red Pierson. When she reached the library door, she turned back with two words.

"Watch me."